Daring men and women of courage and vision—the proud sons and daughters of a savage frontier

BOOTHE CARLYLE

Plagued by the memory of a tragic fool's mission, he sets out to tame the wilderness that once defeated him . . . and to conquer the ghosts of his haunted past.

KITTY KINCAID

Driven by devotion and love, she finds her destiny and her heart on the perilous trail west . . . and leaves tender girlhood behind.

BEN ADAMSON

On his wedding day, a madman drowned his dreams in blood. Now he looks to a remarkable child-woman to heal his ravaged soul.

OLIVER SHERROD

His youthful heart hardened by bitterness, he seeks vengeance on the hero he once worshiped—the man he holds responsible for the death of his sister.

LUCY SYMS

The shamelessly seductive minister's daughter, her sheltered life is devastated by the violence of nature . . . and the brutality of man.

THE KINCAIDS

BOOK TWO

PRAIRIE THUNDER

TAYLOR BRADY

AVON BOOKS  NEW YORK

THE KINCAIDS: PRAIRIE THUNDER is an original publication of Avon Books. This work has never before appeared in book form. This work is a novel. Any similarity to actual persons or events is purely coincidental.

AVON BOOKS
A division of
The Hearst Corporation
1350 Avenue of the Americas
New York, New York 10019

Copyright © 1993 by Donna Ball, Inc. and Shannon Harper
Mountain Fury excerpt copyright © 1993 by Donna Ball, Inc. and Shannon Harper
Published by arrangement with the authors
Library of Congress Catalog Card Number: 92-90434
ISBN: 0-380-76333-8

First Avon Books Printing: January 1993

AVON TRADEMARK REG. U.S. PAT. OFF. AND IN OTHER COUNTRIES, MARCA REGISTRADA, HECHO EN U.S.A.

Printed in the U.S.A.

RA   10 9 8 7 6 5 4 3 2 1

The Kincaids

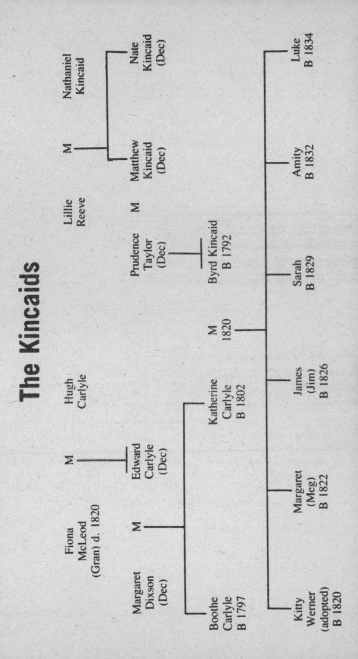

Chapter One

1837

Blue skies in April were a rarity in Cairo, Illinois. In the flat, fertile peninsula at the junction of the Mississippi and Ohio rivers, rain was the norm both spring and fall; farmers plowed and planted between showers, and, like the ancient inhabitants of the Egyptian city which was its namesake, the people of Cairo had learned to plan their lives around the flooding of the river.

But on the day Benjamin Adamson came to take Rose Shipton as his wife, the day was cloudless and warm, the breeze off the river was sweet-smelling, and the profusion of wildflowers and willows that grew along the banks were at the height of their springtime glory. Later, looking back on the day, many would remark that the biggest obscenity of all was how blue the skies were, how beautifully the day began.

The wedding was to be held after services on Sunday in the church that, having been destroyed by fire a month before and recently rebuilt, still smelled of fresh-cut pine. Reverend Morrison, whose four other churches along the river circuit allowed him to devote only every third Sunday to Cairo, preached a two-hour sermon extolling the virtues of the two young people who had vowed to devote their lives to the service of God.

After the sermon and before the wedding, grateful parishioners were given a much-needed opportunity to stretch their legs and partake of a midday meal. Baskets were unpacked and tablecloths unfurled on the banks of the river. Children, ever mindful of their Sunday clothes, played roll-the-hoop and blind man's bluff and tried to stay out of sight of their mothers; the women set out the food and gossiped about Benjamin Adamson and the shy young bride he had brought back from the East; men gathered in separate knots to talk about matters of more consequence. Not surprisingly, it was not the wedding that dominated their conversation but what was to come afterwards; more specifically, the journey west on which Ben and Rose, along with the other missionaries, were trusting Boothe Carlyle to guide them.

There were some who said Carlyle was only doing it for the money. The more astute among them guffawed at that and speculated that Carlyle had been approached in the first place because nobody else would take the job for the pay they were offering. Others argued it had to be because of Ben Adamson, for everybody knew that there wasn't much in this world Boothe Carlyle wouldn't do for Ben's mother, Caroline Adamson, or any of her brood. But it remained an unspoken consensus among them that this time Boothe Carlyle wasn't doing Ben or his mother any favor.

Caroline Adamson, the local schoolteacher, was liked and respected by every member of the community. Her girls had made good matches with local boys and were raising respectable families of their own. Now Ben was back from the seminary in Tennessee with a calling to bring salvation to the savages in the West. Nobody could fault the widow Adamson or the way she had raised her family, and in fact the only taint on her name over all these years had been her continued close association with Boothe Carlyle. For one thing, it had kept her a widow longer than was decent, when there were plenty of men who needed a good wife. For another . . . it was Boothe Carlyle.

It was not that they could ever—until recently, that was—pin a specific complaint against Carlyle. In the first place, he was Katherine Carlyle Kincaid's brother and Byrd Kincaid's brother-in-law, and no one in his right mind wanted to get on the Kincaids' bad side. Secondly, over the past fifteen years or so, Boothe Carlyle had been their own private link to the rest of the world, their source of news and their liaison in trade. He traveled west along the trail to Santa Fe and south to Texas and New Orleans, north to the Erie Canal and across to Oregon. He brought back exotic delicacies and even more exotic tales. Each time he returned, his arrival was greeted with a mixture of eagerness and well-concealed resentment. Each time he departed, he was watched with envy and carefully qualified resignation by those who did not have the freedom, or the courage, to go themselves. Boothe Carlyle was by way of being a local legend, and legends by their very nature were not permitted foibles or mistakes.

In 1835, Boothe Carlyle had made a mistake, and it had affected them all. He had led a caravan west, but it had never reached the Promised Land. Carlyle had brought over a dozen people into untold suffering and death, and though there were many versions of the story, only one thing counted: Boothe Carlyle had failed. For that and other sins, he had been tried and found guilty in the minds of every man in the community. For they and only they, claiming him as they did, had a right to do so.

Some folks said he'd been paid off to see that the expedition failed; others that he'd simply been drunk and careless. Whatever the reason, folks they knew had died on the trail because of Boothe's failure. Women and men, who'd trusted him with their lives.

Only the staunch support of Katherine and Byrd Kincaid and their respect for Caroline Adamson had kept the condemnation a silent one for this long. Now history was starting to repeat itself, with Benjamin Adamson and his missionaries the innocent victims, and there had been talk over the past few weeks, plenty of it. In honor of the Lord's day, however, and with no desire to account to their wives should the upcoming wedding be spoiled or in any way shadowed, today the men of Cairo kept their well-formed opinions to themselves. But they took their own satisfaction in watching Boothe Carlyle and remembering; in sharing grave, private glances; in sadly and silently predicting doom for poor Ben Adamson and all who followed him westward toward Kansas.

This was not, however, the time for bringing up past grievances, and today the most scandalous thing Boothe Carlyle did was to sit down to eat with Caroline Adamson and her family when, it was commonly held by some of the more vocal women, he should have sat with his sister and left Caroline to enjoy the last few hours with her only son before he went off into the wilderness.

It was not only the eagle eyes of the matrons and the stern, speculative gazes of the men which were focused on Boothe Carlyle. Kitty Werner Kincaid, Katherine and Byrd's seventeen-year-old adopted daughter, was filled with impatience as she sat on a blanket by the river between her younger sister Margaret and her brother James. She watched Boothe with an ache in her chest and frustration in her stomach.

Margaret, called Meg, who was fifteen years old and already putting on airs, followed Kitty's gaze and commented with a toss of her head, "Well, I don't care if Rose Shipton *did* go to school back east, I still say she's got about as much gumption as a field mouse and she's not all that much prettier, either. Ben could've done a lot better."

Kitty ignored her. It was typical of Meg's fifteen-year-old self-centeredness to think the only important thing going on today was the introduction of a new bride into the Adamson household. Didn't she realize that at this very moment Kitty's entire world was being pulled up by the roots? Who cared whom Ben married or whether he married at all, when tomorrow her entire life would be broken apart?

Her Uncle Boothe was going away, just as he always did. And he was going without her . . . just as he always did.

Things were different now. She was no longer a little girl, a child; she was a young woman, and she knew what she wanted. What she wanted was her chance—her only chance—to be with Boothe. All her life he'd whetted her dreams with stories of his adventures, and now it was time for her to claim those dreams for her own. It wasn't as if she couldn't take care of herself. She could ride and shoot as well as any man in town. A lot better than Ben Adamson, she thought, with a touch of resentment as she looked at him. And certainly a lot better than Rose Shipton.

There were eight sharing a picnic dinner at the Kincaid blanket, with children ranging from Kitty's seventeen to Luke's age three, and almost as many voices were talking at once. It was difficult to single out a voice, much less levy a reprimand, but Katherine Kincaid's sharp ears missed nothing. She directed a stern scowl at her daughter Meg.

"You watch your tongue, miss. It won't be so long till some fine young man takes you to the altar, and how would you like it if folks were talking behind your back on your wedding day? I'll not have loose gossip at my dinner table."

"Blanket," pointed out eight-year-old Sarah sagely. "It's a blanket."

James thought that was the funniest thing he'd ever heard and burst into squeals of laughter, tossing a bread crust across the blanket at his sister. Kitty could have screamed. She was straining to make out what was being said at the Adamson blanket across the way, but so far hadn't been able to hear a word. They were finishing early, probably so the bride could change into her fancy dress, and pretty soon they would leave. She had to talk to Boothe now. She just *had* to.

The food fight was cut off before it had a chance to begin, and Meg gave an impertinent toss of her head. "I don't care," she declared. "I'm never going to marry anybody anyway. Besides, she *is* a mouse. I heard Pa saying just the other day what does she think she's going to do out there with those Indians . . ."

Katherine gave her husband a sharp look, and Byrd shrugged his shoulders. "A man's got a right to his opinion," he said with a hint of a twinkle in his eyes.

"A man," Katherine pointed out coolly, "also has a right to remember little pitchers have big ears."

Across the churchyard, Ben and Rose got up, holding hands as they walked toward the river, their heads close together. Boothe was helping Caroline fold up the blanket. Surely, Kitty thought, he would come over now. How much longer could Miss Caroline keep him dawdling there? Kitty had counted on Boothe's eating with them today; without his support, she didn't stand a chance of convincing her parents to let her go with him. What was he doing, wasting time with Ben and Caroline Adamson when he knew her whole future was at stake?

James, who had gotten rowdy again, jostled Kitty's arm and spilled her untouched plate of food all over her clean apron. She pinched him hard and he squealed, and Katherine gave her one of those looks that each of the Kincaid children had spent a lifetime learning to avoid. Without being told, Kitty got James to stop squealing and cleaned up the mess, and by the time she looked around again, Boothe and Caroline were gone.

Meg, who did not like to have attention diverted from her for any reason, declared, "Well, I mean it! What is she going to do out there with those Indians and snakes and deserts and things? Uncle Boothe says—"

Kitty took a deep breath and knew she was on her own. She looked her mother in the eye and said clearly, "*I*'d know what to do."

It was as though everyone had suddenly been stricken dumb. Even Luke stopped squirming in his mother's lap for the cup of milk she held just out of reach and sucked contentedly on a chicken bone. Meg edged a little bit away from her sister, as though to be safely out of range of her mother's wrath, and every eye was trained on Kitty.

The only sign of emotion on Katherine's face was a slight tightening of her jaw. "We've had this conversation before, Kitty."

"No, we haven't!" Kitty cried. "*You've* had it! You haven't ever listened to me. All you did was say no—"

"That will do, Kitty." Katherine's voice remained quiet and firm, but her eyes met those of the willful younger woman with chilling force. "You're far too young to be going halfway across the country by yourself, and that's all there is to it. The whole notion is ridiculous."

"I wouldn't be alone," Kitty insisted. "I'd be with Boothe, and . . . and Ben. Besides, Rose Shipton is younger than I am and she's going!"

Young Luke squirmed in his mother's lap, waving the chicken bone, and Katherine shifted her head to avoid a greasy fist. "Rose Shipton will be a married woman," Katherine replied. "And besides, she has the call of the church."

"Lots of unmarried women go west," Kitty insisted. "I was reading in the St. Louis newspaper only the other day—"

"Is that what you want?" Katherine's carefully maintained control snapped, and two spots of color appeared in her cheeks. "To marry some filthy trapper and live like a squaw for the rest of your life? To be raped by some Indian or mauled to death by a wild animal or go mad from loneliness? To die in a place so barren they have to cover your body with rocks because there isn't even enough earth to dig a grave?"

Her voice was rising, and her arms had tightened around Luke until he began to whimper. She moved him off her lap and faced Kitty with a set jaw and a voice low enough to send chills down the spine of every listener. "I'm telling you right now, Kitty Werner Kincaid, no daughter of mine will ever waste her life that way, not as long as I have a breath in my body. Do you understand that? No daughter of mine!"

Kitty stood up, her stained apron clutched in her fists, her eyes blazing. "I'm not your daughter!" she cried, and tossed the apron on the ground. "I—"

Hot tears flashed in her eyes, and she couldn't finish. She whirled and stalked away.

Stunned silence echoed in her wake for perhaps thirty seconds. Then Katherine swallowed hard and lowered her eyes. She started to stand up.

Byrd laid a hand lightly on her arm. "Stay," he said quietly.

He rose and followed Kitty.

*　　*　　*

Ben lifted a low willow branch and held it as Rose ducked beneath it. He smiled at the picture she made in her delicate cotton dress, with her smooth brown hair brushed back from her face and her wide gray eyes alight with soft pleasure, the whole framed by a cascade of willow branches and bright sky overhead. She was even more beautiful than she had been the day he first set eyes on her. For Ben, it had been love at first sight.

In the year of their courtship, Ben had learned that Rose was as good as she was beautiful. Her father, the Reverend Shipton, was head of the Presbyterian teachers' college where Ben had gone to obtain his training two years ago. Rose was studying to be a teacher just as he was, but whereas Ben had planned only to return to Cairo and help his mother, Rose had higher ambitions. She was determined to minister to the Indians across the Mississippi, and when she and Ben had read the inspirational writings in the *Christian Advocate* citing the desperate need for a ministry among the savages, Ben, too, had discovered his calling. It had been like a miracle.

Through Rose's father, Ben had met the Reverend Syms and Martin and Effie Creller, who were planning an expedition to Kansas Territory, where they would join the beleaguered missionaries at the Pawnee mission. Ben couldn't ignore their enthusiasm and the nobility of their purpose. He knew at once that this was his destiny; with Rose at his side and the hand of God guiding his steps, he too would go west.

It had all happened so fast that Ben sometimes thought it had been a dream. Yet it was real, and he was glad. Had it been only three days ago that Rose had arrived on the steamboat from Louisville? And now the day after their wedding they'd be leaving with Boothe Carlyle to head west and meet the rest of their wagon train. It was only fitting that Boothe would be their guide, yet another sign of the divine hand of destiny at work. For two years, ever since the tragedy in the mountains, Boothe had refused to undertake another plains crossing. But now, when Ben needed him most, Boothe would be at his side. It was right; it was perfect.

Rose, stepping from beneath the willow, turned her face toward the sky. "Look," she said softly, "how beautiful everything is. What a perfect day for a wedding!"

Ben smiled indulgently. How like Rose to see the beauty in everything. He had been worried that she'd be disappointed when she first saw Cairo. It was far different from her home in Tennessee with its neat clapboard houses and the sturdy brick buildings of the college. In the seventeen years that Ben had lived in Cairo, things had not changed much, and it was still an ugly, decrepit-looking little town. Of course, more people had moved in; there were more farms in the surrounding areas and more wharves and warehouses down by the river. Now Cairo even boasted its own bank, and five saloons, huddled along the Mississippi, catered to the river men who plied the two rivers, loading and unloading produce and passengers for the transfer from one river to the other. But the streets were still unpaved and turned into seas of mud in the rainy season. The Mississippi flooded annually, and those who didn't build far enough away from it or didn't put their building on stilts suffered the consequences. There were flies and mosquitoes in the summer, icy winds in the winter, but still the settlers came.

Cairo had neither a hotel nor an inn, though a couple of the saloons rented rooms and served meals to the passengers waiting for the next boat. One saloon keeper's wife was famous for her pies and had made a name for herself up and down the river from St. Louis to Memphis. Most of the activity in the city took place along the docks, where the town's two stores were located—a seed and feed, and a mercantile. They were not much as stores went, each one room with crudely made shelves, but the townspeople were grateful that they could buy sugar, coffee and tea, a yard or two of calico now and then, and blades for their plows and scythes. The shopkeepers had great hopes of growing their businesses as the town grew; there was no doubt in anyone's mind that Cairo would prosper.

Most of the town's citizens were self-sufficient farmers, like the Kincaids, raising and growing all the food they needed. The land was fertile, livestock thrived, and the locals were enterprising. Near the wharves a few of them had set up makeshift stalls consisting of a board laid across two barrels with a piece of canvas strung up as a tent like shelter from the sun or rain. There they sold the extra produce from their farms. Hungry boat captains and crews, making a stop at Cairo, were quick to buy up home-baked breads and pies, apples and grapes, cheese and buttermilk. Settlers heading into Missouri, who'd chosen not to bring their livestock down the Ohio, eagerly sought the locals' chickens, pigs, milk cows, and mules to take with them across the Big Muddy.

There was a vitality in Cairo and a sense of the future that lay across the Mississippi toward the Rockies. It was a lure that few could resist. America was moving westward. Missouri had been a state since 1821 and was already civilized, settled by both established Americans and immigrants from Germany and Ireland. Missouri was now the jumping-off place for the unknown, for the Great Plains and the Rocky Mountains, for Oregon Country and California.

Andrew Jackson had been the country's president for eight years, from 1829 to 1837—years when the United States stretched its boundaries and spread ever westward. American traders and trappers roamed the mountains and valleys of the Rockies; missionaries pushed across Kansas; American colonies were established in Oregon; great trade ships sailed the seas from Boston and New York to the ports of Mexican California. Enterprising Americans fought for a foothold in California, acting as agents for the shipping lines that traded cotton and calico, tea and coffee, sugar and silk for cow leather for the shoe shops and tallow for the candle factories of the East Coast. The battle of the Alamo had been lost, but the Texan war for independence had been won. Under Sam Houston, the territory had become a republic in 1836, and some people were saying it would soon be a state. Two new states, Arkansas and Michigan, had been added at the end of Jackson's term. The country was growing fast.

Martin Van Buren, another Democrat, had succeeded Old Hickory in the White House, and there seemed to be no slowing the steady push westward, the relentless hacking away at the edges of civilization by land-hungry settlers. The government subdued the Indians and sent them to reservations. There were no obstacles Americans couldn't surmount. Ben sometimes felt as if the country was like an eager horse straining at the bit, begging to be given free rein.

"I wonder what it will be like," Ben mused, conscious of a rising excitement as he imagined the future. "Kansas and the mission."

The mission was something shadowy and mysterious to Ben. His only contact with the Indians had been as a child with the Shawnee, and he recalled the experience with the dim terror of a long-ago nightmare.

Rose, who knew even less of Indians, was full of confidence. "Just before I left home we received a long letter from one the teachers at the mission. Of course, it was written almost a year ago," she confessed. "He didn't say much about Kansas—except that he misses the trees back east. The work with the Indians is still slow, but sometimes God puts obstacles in our way to make our success sweeter."

Ben looked at Rose in amazement. How differently she saw things. Would he ever understand her?

"What is it, Ben?" The touch of her hand on his was like the wings of a butterfly brushing his skin.

"I was thinking about what it was like when we came to Cairo seventeen years ago. Mama and Miss Katherine say I can't really remember; they say I've just heard stories . . . but they seem so real."

"You were only five, Ben."

"But I still remember," he said stubbornly.

Rose didn't argue. "Now that I've met your mother and Miss Katherine, I can see what special women they are. I hope I can be that strong for you, Ben."

"You can, Rose. I know you can. Mama said she and Miss Katherine weren't special. They just did what they had to. They wanted to survive and keep us children alive."

And they did, Ben thought, through water and fire. They delivered us from Indians and pirates; they kept us from starving and freezing . . .

"They brought us through the wilderness," he said to Rose. "A bunch of women and children who by all rights should have died."

"But you didn't, by the grace of God."

By the grace of God and the strength of those women, Ben said to himself. Ben, his sisters, his mother and father, had been on a flatboat traveling down the Ohio. The Adamson family's future had been uncertain; his father had never made much of a living and hoped to do better in the West. But Ben's father never had a chance to prove what he could do. The flatboat was wrecked in a terrible storm and Ben's father died, along with many others.

The survivors had huddled on the shore, hoping for a rescue that never came. Finally, Katherine Carlyle had determined that help wasn't going to come while the river was in flood. She'd decided in that single-minded way of hers to walk to Cairo and the Mississippi River. Caroline Adamson, now a widow with three small children, had thrown in her lot with Katherine, as had most of the other women and their children. Maude Sherrod had two little girls and a half-grown boy named Oliver, who'd been the man of their party until they'd met Byrd Kincaid along the way. Byrd had been a trapper then, and a wanderer, and even a thief. Ben had always excused him for that because the goods he'd stolen had belonged to river pirates. Byrd had protected them as best he could, not only from the pirates but also from the crazed Calhoun brothers who were after Katherine. Ben was glad he'd been too young to realize how dangerous it had been for all of them.

One of the women had been pregnant. Ben didn't remember that part, but he'd heard the story a hundred times. Hilda Werner, a young German girl, had lost her husband in the wreck of the flatboat. She gave birth on the trail to a little girl. To Kitty. And then Hilda died and the other women buried her in the wilderness of an Illinois forest. The Shawnee attacked and took Kitty, and no one knew if they'd ever see her again. Months later, Boothe Carlyle, Katherine's brother, had found her and brought her back to them after they'd reached Cairo.

People had thought it was a miracle that they reached Cairo at all. They'd all been heroines for a while, the women who'd survived that trek through the wilds. Caroline and Katherine had decided to stay in Cairo; they'd had enough of travel. Two of the other women, Priscilla Wiltshire and her mother-in-law, Esther, had been worn down by the wilderness and hadn't stayed.

The land hadn't beaten Maude Sherrod, how-ever. She'd headed west to open a dry goods store, and come hell or high water, floods, fires, pirates,

Indians, or the loss of her husband and all the stock for her store, she was still determined. She'd sold homemade breads and pies down by the river for a while and then begun to barter with the riverboat captains for small items that seemed inconsequential to men but were much sought after by women. She'd traded with the ships' captains for needles, pins, thread, thimbles, coffeepots, and frying pans. She'd garnered a small nest egg and taken her family across the river to Cape Girardeau, where she opened a store that had become very successful, just as Maude predicted. Ben didn't know what had happened to the Wiltshires; he barely remembered anything about them except how pretty Miss Priscilla's blond curls were, but he did know about the Sherrods, and that made him think of Boothe Carlyle.

"Boothe says—" Ben stopped as he saw the faintest of frowns mar Rose's smooth forehead.

"I've heard stories, Ben," she began hesitantly. "Since I got here. I wonder if we did the proper thing telling Reverend Syms that Boothe was the right man to lead us through Kansas."

Ben tensed defensively. "You mean you wonder if *I* did the right thing, Rose. I was the one who suggested Boothe to your father, and he, in turn, recommended him to Reverend Syms and Martin—all on my confidence." He took a breath. "Well, I still believe Boothe is the only man for the job. What happened on that other expedition wasn't Boothe's fault; in fact, without him the consequences might have been even more tragic. He's a hero, not a villain, despite what certain low-minded people say. All my life, ever since we came to Cairo with Miss Katherine, Boothe and Byrd have been the two most important men in my life."

"It must be hard to grow up without a father."

"But I had Boothe; that's what I'm trying to explain," Ben said impatiently, and then immediately regretted his sharp words.

"Boothe went off west every year to trap or lead settlers or work for the army, but he always came back. That was the best day of the year, when we'd see him coming down the road toward the house, the sun shining on his red hair. The Indians called him Firebird because of that red hair of his. Anyhow, he'd be leading a pack mule all loaded with trade goods, some for Miss Katherine's children and lots for our family."

Ben smiled in remembrance.

"He'd stay around all winter and help with things that needed to be done, like laying in a supply of wood or repairing the roof. He taught me about hunting and fishing; he taught me all I know about being a man."

His voice softened with tenderness as he looked down at Rose. "Would I trust the life of the one I hold most dear in the world to anyone in whom I did not have perfect confidence?"

Rose touched his arm, her expression sweet and soothing. "Oh, Ben, you know I trust your judgment. And I know Boothe Carlyle has been like a father to you. I don't doubt for a minute that we've made the right decision in asking him to be our guide. He must be a good man, if you're so devoted to him."

Some of the tension left Ben's shoulders as he covered her hand with his. "He is, Rose," Ben assured her. "And if you love me, you'll trust Boothe."

"I do love you, Ben," she replied, her eyes glowing. "And I will never question you. Nothing will spoil this, the happiest day of my life."

Kitty did not go far; there wasn't far to go in a town like Cairo. There was a spreading oak set back from the riverbank; for most of her childhood she'd climbed over its exposed roots or hung from its lower branches. She stood there now and leaned her head against the cool, rough bark, absently rubbing the scar on her shoulder and trying not to cry.

She had been raised on the story of how she had gotten that scar from a Shawnee arrow before she even left her mother's womb. Katherine said it was a mark of greatness, a reminder that God, having spared her, would expect big things from her. But how was she supposed to do big things, or even find out what greatness meant, if she was never allowed to leave this riverbank?

She did not hear Byrd come up behind her, but knew when he sat down on one of the big roots a few feet away from her. He sat there silently, as was his way, waiting until she was ready to speak. Her Pa was the most patient man Kitty had ever known.

"It's not fair, Pa," she said at last, without turning around. Her voice sounded choked, and her fist tightened on her shoulder. "She won't even listen to me. She won't even *try*. It's just not fair."

"No," Byrd agreed slowly. "I reckon it's not. And I guess it don't help much that she's got her reasons."

"What reasons?" Kitty demanded bitterly to the tree trunk. "I'm seventeen years old. I'm not a little girl anymore. She treats me like a baby!"

There was a thoughtful silence. "I reckon to her, you always will be."

Kitty whirled on him. "But it's not fair!"

Byrd took up a twig and spun it absently between his fingers. His expression was calm and his tone mild, as they always were. "When your ma weren't much older than you, she lit out on her own for the trail west. Before she'd been gone a week, she saw half a dozen men die in a bad way. She was left to do a man's job in the wilderness, and I reckon she saw the devil's red eyes looking over her shoulder more than once . . . and it wasn't just herself she had to be afraid for, but the folks she had to take care of. She lost some of them."

He fixed his quiet blue gaze on her. "She lost your ma, Miss Hilda. She lost you, and I ain't never seen a woman so tore up as she was when them Indians took you away. It took near about all the strength I had to hold her back, and I'm here to tell you it ripped a piece out of me big enough to choke on, to stand back and watch it happen. You don't get over a thing like that. I reckon sometimes when your ma looks at you, she still sees a babe in arms and that big Shawnee carrying you into the woods. She promised Miss Hilda on her deathbed, you see, that she'd take care of you. And she's still keeping that promise, the best way she knows how."

Kitty turned back to the tree, her throat thick. "Stop it, Pa. You're making me cry. I hate to cry."

Byrd smiled a little. "I know you do, little girl. You're that much like my Katie."

Kitty squeezed her eyes tightly shut, and the tears hurt. Her voice was barely audible, no matter how she struggled to make it strong. "I didn't mean what I said."

"I reckon she knows that. But I want you to understand something. In a lot of ways, you're always going to be more of a daughter to your ma than the ones she gave birth to. She chose you, and she made promises to you even before you were born. You've been through life and death together, and that's a special thing. There ain't nothing you can ever do to change that."

Kitty took a cautious, somewhat stifled breath and lifted her head, staring up into the lacy network of leaves. She said steadily, "I know that, Pa. But . . . all my life I've known what it means to be a Kincaid. And I'm not one. I'm different, Pa, and nothing can ever change *that*. I need different things. I need . . . to find my own place."

Byrd was silent for a moment. Then he said, "Turn around, little girl, and look at me."

Reluctantly, she complied.

"Now I want you to look me in the eye," he said quietly, "and tell me that your place is out on the Solomon River, preaching the gospel to the Pawnee."

Kitty tried, but she couldn't hold his gaze. He knew she wouldn't be able to, and that shamed her. She turned away from him with a quick, frustrated gesture toward the riverbank. "Oh, Pa, don't you know how much of the world there is out there? Don't you ever look at the river and wonder where it's going or what's on the other side?"

Byrd smiled. "Yeah, girlie, I do. And every time your Uncle Boothe starts down that trail, it's near 'bout all I can do to keep from slinging on my pack and walking beside him."

She looked at him in surprise. "But—you never said . . ."

He tossed the twig aside. "There's a time for wandering and a time for staying. I got all my wandering done when I was a younger man. But your Uncle Boothe now, he's a different breed."

Kitty said swiftly, lowly, "He's not my uncle."

A new alertness came into Byrd's eyes, and Kitty felt her cheeks grow warm. She had to look quickly away.

"No, I reckon he's not," Byrd said slowly. "Not by blood." He stood up. "But I wouldn't be surprised if you didn't have more of the Carlyles and Kincaids in you than you think, little girl. It's not always something that's passed down through blood. Now, come on. We're gonna miss the wedding, and your ma won't take kindly to that."

Kitty hesitated. "In a minute, Pa. There's something I have to do first."

He looked at her for another minute, then nodded and walked away.

Chapter Two

Zeke Calhoun had ridden hard, stopping only to water and rest his exhausted horse before pushing on. He was a whipcord-tough, trail-dirty man with a seventeen-year-old thirst for vengeance in his heart. At last satisfaction was within sight. He had finally found the bitch who'd killed his brothers. The time of judgment was at hand.

For years he had thought she was dead. She *should* have been dead. But all this time she'd been hiding out on some farm outside Cairo, married and with a new name. And now she was his.

He'd been drinking with a keelboater in a saloon in Mud Flats, Kentucky, who'd told him about a red-haired trapper he'd had a run-in with. A man by the name of Boothe Carlyle. *Carlyle.* He had to be related to the lying, cheating bitch who'd killed Abel and Early. The Calhouns had had more than one run-in with that witch-woman, tracking her all the way from Mud Flats down the Ohio where, in the end, she and her band of ragged refugees had just about done them all in. Only Zeke had escaped, and it was up to him to take revenge in his brothers' names.

Well, he'd finish it now. He touched the Patterson Colt in his belt; the newest model and worth a dozen of any rifle. He could get off five shots without reloading, but one was all he needed.

A cold, thin smile tightened his lips when he remembered the face of that red-haired witch-woman. It wouldn't be long now.

Boothe helped Caroline pack away the remnants of dinner in the wagon. It had been a good, easy meal together, not unlike others he had shared at her table over the years. A lot of the talk had centered around the bridal couple, and Caroline didn't flinch anymore when Ben talked about the journey west. She had never once looked at Boothe with accusation in her eyes. All in all, the day was turning out better than he had a right to expect, but still there was an uneasiness in him, like the shadow of a thundercloud gathering in the back of his mind.

It could be because of Caroline, and what he was leaving behind. It could be because of young Ben, and what lay ahead. It could be because he knew how folks were thinking and talking, and none of it was good. Or it could be something else.

His grandmother had been what some folks called a seer, and she wasn't the first in her family. The gift was passed down through the generations, and though most times it landed with the women, occasionally it was picked up by a man. Sometimes Boothe knew things, in dreams or waking visions, or by just knowing. Not all the time, just sometimes. More than once his grandmother's gift had saved his life, and more than once it had failed him when he needed it most. But he couldn't argue with it or ignore it any more than he could stop the heat of the sun by closing his eyes to the brightness. He didn't understand it and didn't particularly want to; it just was.

Sometimes it felt like a shadowy thundercloud in the back of his mind, something he should know but didn't, something he should see but couldn't. Sometimes it meant nothing at all.

He stood by the side of the wagon while Caroline fussed with the blankets and the leftovers, looking across the way at the church. He had helped build that church and the one before it. A lot of his life had been put into this town, and now, getting ready to leave it once again, he couldn't quite remember why he had never been able to stay.

He looked back at Caroline. Her face was shaded by a sprigged sunbonnet with a circle cut out of the back to show off her hair. There wasn't a streak of gray in that hair, and though he knew she had changed over the years, just as he had, when he looked at her now she was just as young and pretty and gentle-faced as the day he had first laid eyes on her.

He had a lot to say to her, so much he didn't know where to begin. The trouble was, he should have started saying it ten years ago.

"I don't know if I ever told you," he said, "but you raised a fine boy. You don't have to worry about Ben."

Caroline glanced at him. "You did a lot of that raising, Boothe. Whatever man there is in him is due to you and Byrd Kincaid."

"A lot of folks're saying you've got no cause to be grateful to me now. That I put notions in the boy's head, when he would've been better off at home."

"They're a bunch of fools." Caroline's voice was stern, but he saw the hurt come into her eyes before she could hide it, the look a mother gets when she knows she's losing her son. She softened the look with a smile. "It was never my wish for Ben to go west, but a mother doesn't have much of a say in what a man does. Ben has to listen to a higher calling. I guess all men do," she added softly.

She looked Boothe straight in the eye. "If he has to go, you know there's not a man on earth I'd rather trust him with than you."

Boothe shifted his gaze away. "Maybe you're wrong in that," he said quietly.

"Boothe Carlyle, you hush that kind of talk! It's bad enough that you sit back and let everybody else go on with their wrongheaded notions without your starting to believe it yourself. Well, I don't have to listen to it, I'll tell you that much!"

Caroline Adamson was slow to anger, but she could be as fierce as a lioness in defense of her own. Boothe saw that anger blaze in her eyes for his sake, and he loved her. He wanted to tell her that. He wanted to tell her that hers was the face that stayed with him when he was cold and wet and aching from sleeping outdoors. Hers was the laughter he heard in the high mountain passes. Hers was the shadow that walked beside him on the trails. When he thought of home, he thought of her. When he measured goodness, he thought of her. He supposed she might have known all those things, in the way women have of knowing, but still he wanted to say them. He had just never felt he had the right to, not in all this time. And he certainly had no right now.

"A lot of years between us, Miss Caroline," he said quietly. "And I wasted most of them."

She held her head high and met his eyes without condemnation. "Yes," she said. "You have."

"And now I reckon it's too late."

"Is it?"

She had a way of looking at him that was half joy, half sorrow. It reminded him, all too poignantly, of all those lost years.

"I've waited for you before," she said. "I waited while you went down the river to sell a load of furs. I waited while you went over the mountains just to see what was on the other side. I waited while you wintered with the Kansa and summered with the elk, and I waited while you ran off with Sam Houston to fight his stupid war. I've spent half my life waiting for you, Boothe Carlyle," she said softly, and into her eyes came a smile that was so sad and so beautiful and so full of things Boothe did not deserve that it hurt him, deep in his chest. "You'll be coming back, and I reckon I can wait a little while longer."

The thundercloud in the back of Boothe's mind grew darker.

"I wish I was a different kind of man," he said gruffly.

She laid her hand, very lightly, very briefly, on his arm. "If you were, I wouldn't wait."

For a moment they stood there, just looking at each other, and then Caroline stepped away. People were starting to drift toward the church. "I'd better go see what I can do to help Rose," she said.

Boothe watched her go with the darkness nagging at him in the bright sunshine, and then he felt a touch on his sleeve.

"Boothe?" Kitty was flushed, and seemed a little breathless. "Can I talk to you?"

Boothe turned around, and Kitty saw the troubled, unhappy look on his face vanish into a smile. He always smiled when he saw her, and not the distant, patronizing smile most people gave their youngers when they were too tired or too busy to be bothered. Boothe was always glad to see her. Boothe had always, even when she was a child, made her feel important. He talked to her as if she was an adult, and as smart as he was. Even before she knew that she loved him, and that her destiny was to be always at his side, he had been her hero.

When people said awful things about him, she got mad enough to fight, and she had fought, too, sometimes with boys twice her size. Over the past year she had grown too big to fight with her fists; Caroline Adamson said it wasn't ladylike and, next to her mother, Miss Caroline was the finest lady Kitty had ever known. So these days her fights were on the inside. Now she was in the middle of the biggest battle of her life, a battle for her future, and for Boothe's. Boothe would not fail her now. They would win together.

"Well now, Miss Kitten," he said. "What can I do for you this fine spring day?"

He was the only person in the world who called her Kitten, and for that reason she loved the name. He extended his arm to her, just like a gentleman would to a lady, and she slipped her hand around it. She tried to calm the excited pace of her breathing as they walked toward the church. She tried to find just the right words, just the right tone of voice. She wasn't worried about Boothe not taking her seriously; he always took her seriously. But this was so important . . .

It was so important that she couldn't wait for the right words and she blurted out, "Let me go with you. Talk to my mother."

Boothe slowed his pace a little, and though he didn't answer right away, he was already shaking his head. He was a tall man, with thick red hair now slightly dulled by gray, and a ginger-colored beard. When the sun struck his hair, as it did now, flames seemed to dance around his head. The Shawnee used to call him the Firebird.

"Now, Kitten," he said. "You know I can't do that. I'm not about to get between you and your ma."

She stepped in front of him. Her heart was beating so hard it hurt, and the words she spoke had an airy, breathless quality. "But you want me to, don't you? You want me to go with you."

Boothe regarded her gravely, for a long time. Kitty saw the answer in his eyes, and it made her so happy she thought her chest would explode.

He cupped her cheek in a gentle, stroking gesture he was fond of using. "Sweet girl, it don't matter much what I want. What's meant to be, is. That's all."

"But I'm meant to go with you." She could barely whisper it. "Isn't that right?"

He didn't shift his eyes away, but it was as though he were looking at something else. It seemed it took an effort to bring his attention back to her, and he smiled. "Can I tell you a secret?"

She nodded, desperately holding back her impatience.

"Some time ago—I reckon it must be nigh on three, four years now—I had this dream. Had it a couple of times since. You were in it, looking just as fine and strong as you are today, racing bareback on a white pony down a buffalo trail on the plains, your hair flying out behind you and your body bent low against the wind, that pony kicking up dust . . . I can see it as clear as yesterday. I couldn't make much sense of it. You'd never been in plains country, and I didn't have any reason to think you ever would. Not then."

The pace of Kitty's pulse was so quick, so hard, that she could barely breathe. "Your dreams always come true, don't they?"

"Not always, but most times."

"Then I *am* meant to go with you! But how can I, if you won't talk to Mama?"

"It's not what your ma wants," he said. "Maybe not what I want for you, either. But if there's one thing I've learned in this life, it's not to fight what is." Then he tweaked one of her curls in a playful way. "Don't you fight it either, Kitten. You'll wear yourself out."

That was not the answer she wanted, not the answer she knew he wanted to give. But the church bells started ringing, and there was Katherine, waving to them from the steps. Boothe started to hurry Kitty along, but she caught his arm again. "We'll talk more about this?"

"Sure we will," he said, and that had to be good enough.

Nobody wanted to miss a wedding, and each one of the hard-slatted pews was filled to capacity. Some of the men lined up along the side to allow the elderly and gravid women to sit. The young children, even those who considered themselves far too old to be held, resigned themselves to finding places on their mothers' laps. Within moments the scent of fresh pine mingled with the odors of perspiration and wilting broadcloth, and the sunlight, slanting through motes of dust from the high windows, heated up the little building like an oven.

The bride wore a long lace veil, yellowed with age, over her Sunday dress and carried a bouquet of pink peonies picked from Katherine Kincaid's flower garden. Ben Adamson, blond and handsome and bursting with pride, couldn't stop smiling at her. Caroline Adamson sat in the front pew with her two daughters and their husbands, her eyes bright with tears and her face glowing. The Reverend Morrison, his collar starched and his shiny face cherubic, opened his prayer book and smiled benignly.

"Friends and neighbors, we are gathered here on this most happy of the Lord's days to unite these two fine young people in the holy bonds of matrimony . . ."

Kitty had arrived too late to sit up front with her family, but that was all right, because Boothe had, too. She squeezed into the back pew, and Booth stood against the wall beside her, and it was almost as though the two of them were together, a couple. Just having him near her made her ache with despair and strain with hope. She listened to the words of the ceremony and watched the bride turn shyly toward her groom, and she tried very hard not to hate Rose Shipton for what she had and Kitty did not.

But it wasn't going to happen. Boothe was not going to leave her behind. Somehow, some way, something she could do would change her mother's mind. If only Boothe would speak for her. Katherine had never refused to listen to her brother. If only he would go to her, and . . .

If only he knew how I felt. Kitty's eyes widened in surprise and a flush warmed her skin. That was it. Boothe didn't know that she loved him, not as a child but as a woman. He didn't know that her destiny lay with him. She had to tell him, and then he would understand, then her *mother* would understand. Then Boothe could not refuse to take her with him. Katherine could not refuse to let her go.

I have to tell him, Kitty thought, and her heart was beating so crazily with excitement she could hardly swallow. *As soon as the ceremony is over, I—*

There was a commotion behind her as the door opened and a bright square of sunlight was cast across her face. Several people stirred to look around. Then someone shouted, "Hey, what—"

Thunder exploded.

It was fast, as fast as it takes a man to fire three shots from a Patterson Colt revolver, but each action stood out in such separate, brightly colored detail that it seemed to take forever. A blossom of bright red burst upon the bride's white dress as she pitched forward into Ben's arms. The roar of horror from the congregation was like a single, distant scream, and they lunged to their feet, not all at once but in spurts and starts, like a wave trying to gather force. Children scattered. Mothers clutched their babies. Men lurched forward to push their womenfolk down. Not one of them had a gun. No one carried a gun to church anymore.

Kitty watched as Caroline rushed toward Ben and was thrown forward beneath the impact of another ear-splitting thunderbolt. There was a roaring in her ears, like the scream of a mad animal, and Boothe was turning, moving, pushing past her toward the door.

It took seconds. Only seconds.

Katherine Kincaid struggled to break the grip of her husband's arms, screaming Caroline's name. Byrd pushed in front of her, trying to force her to the floor, and the bullet that was meant for Katherine struck him in the throat. Kitty was screaming; she was on her feet and she did not know how long she had been there, her hands pressed against her ears, screaming.

She felt Boothe's hand against her shoulder, shoving her down hard, and instinctively, hysterically, she fought back, spinning around, tripping . . .

And he was there, the mad man with the lean stubbled face and the dirty hair and the flaming eyes, inches before her, his gun raised and his lips parted in a wild, triumphant grin. She couldn't stop her forward momentum and she didn't want to; she lunged toward him, fists upraised, clawing at him, and he never once looked at her.

Boothe slammed against him and the gun discharged once more into the air as the three of them crashed on the floor. Kitty smelled the smoke and felt the heat; the odor of him, madness and filth, seemed to penetrate her very pores. There was iron between her fingers and Boothe's hands were grappling with hers, then thunder and fury and blood splashing in her face, and the man beneath them jerked and lay still.

She never knew who pulled the trigger.

She never knew.

The silence was unnatural. Broken only by the occasional hiccoughing sob of a child, the stillness pressed down as thick and as acrid as the gun smoke that still tainted the air. No one moved; no one spoke.

Somehow Kitty was on her knees beside the body of the gunman. There was blood all over her hands and on her best Sunday dress. She could feel the wetness on her face and in her hair. But she couldn't feel anything else.

Boothe grasped the dead man by the hair and turned his face upward. The eyes were still open, the lips still split in that ghoulish grin.

"Zeke Calhoun." The soft voice belonged to Katherine Kincaid. Her skirts brushed against Kitty's face as she slowly dropped to her knees beside her. Her voice held no remorse, no anger; her eyes seemed to see far away. "It's only fitting," she said. "The past comes full circle."

And that was all.

Boothe got up and walked to the front of the church. His face was hard and his mouth tight. He knelt beside Caroline's body and lifted her into his arms. The congregation parted to let him pass, and he looked neither right nor left as he carried her from the church and into the sun-shine.

Katherine's arms came around Kitty. Kitty turned her face to her mother's bloodstained bosom and wept.

Chapter Three

Ben's life had always been simple. By the age of ten he had known what his future was to be: to go to school, to marry a woman of fine character and gentle spirit, to raise a family. Perhaps because he had never had a doubt that it would, the future unfolded easily and just as he had planned. He was accepted to Tennessee Bible College on a scholarship; he met Rose Shipton, the daughter of one of his professors, and knew immediately that she was the woman he was going to marry. The two of them had read William Walker's passionate letter to the *Christian Advocate* on the crying need for Christian missionaries in the far West, and even that decision had been simple. Almost like destiny.

He wasn't sure he believed in destiny anymore. He wasn't sure he believed in anything. He walked away from the small churchyard where his wife and his mother were buried, and the pain inside him was so big it seemed to have gnawed a black hole through his soul. He couldn't even feel the pain anymore. All he felt was emptiness.

Boothe walked beside him, grim-faced and silent. He had aged over the past twenty-four hours. So had they all.

Boothe reached his horse and laid his hand on the pommel. Without looking at Ben he said, "I'll be moving out tomorrow."

For a moment Ben did not know what he was talking about. All the plans, all the brave visions of the future . . . they seemed so distant now, like the memories of another man.

Ben said, "What about your sister?"

"Kate's a strong woman, and I've got folks waiting on me across the river. I gave my word," he said simply, "and I reckon my word's about all I've got left." His voice strengthened as he added, "Kate's got a good crop in, and a boy big enough to help. I'll be back to set the fields for next year."

"It was always Rose's dream," Ben said slowly. "I guess I never realized that before."

The streets were quiet, the windows shuttered. The schoolhouse stood silent and empty. Even the river moved sluggishly, restless and dark, and the sky had started to cloud. It would rain before morning.

Ben hadn't planned on saying it. His eyes were fixed on the river, and the words just came out. Afterward, he wasn't sorry he'd said them, but he wasn't glad either. It just didn't matter. "I guess I'll be going with you."

Boothe nodded and swung up onto his horse.

Ben caught the bridle lightly and looked up at the older man. "You loved her, didn't you?" he asked quietly. "All these years . . . you loved her."

Boothe met his eyes, but did not reply. Then he kneed his horse and rode away.

Ben stood there and watched the river, feeling as small and as alone as he ever had in his life.

I will raise up your sons and defend your daughters and love you, as best a man ever loved a woman, for the rest of my life.

Katherine knelt beside the grave and rested her hand on the wooden cross that marked it, just as she had once been accustomed to resting it upon her husband's shoulder. "You kept your promise, Byrd Kincaid," she said softly. "I guess that's all a woman's got a right to ask."

She rose slowly to her feet and turned around. The children were behind her, standing a few feet away, brave and strong like Byrd had raised them to be. Kitty, with baby Luke on her hip; Meg, standing close with one arm around James and the other around Sarah; Amity, holding on to Kitty's skirts, chewing on her thumbnail. Their heads, in varying shades of red, were like a colorful autumn forest— except for Kitty, with her Viking blond curls escaping her sunbonnet, the strongest and the bravest of them all. It was a family to be proud of.

Katherine walked over to them, touching each one of their solemn, upturned faces in turn. When she reached Kitty she took the baby from her and held him against her shoulder, her face buried in his silky soft hair.

Then she said, "Meg, why don't you take the children to—" She stopped, her throat closing suddenly because she had almost said, "To Miss Caroline." Caroline, who had helped bring each of Katherine's children into the world, who had

welcomed them into her kitchen and into her arms
as though they were her own. So much of the past
was gone now. So much of the future.

"To Miz Polks for an hour or two," Katherine
finished. "But I want you all back for supper. And
don't be walking home after dark."

"Yes, ma'am." Meg took Luke, who whimpered
a little when he was pulled from his mother's arms,
but Kitty produced a sugar treat from her pocket
and he quieted down.

Katherine watched them until they were out of
sight, then slipped her arm through Kitty's and
walked back to the wagon. Kitty took the reins,
as she always did, and handled them like a man,
better than most. Byrd had taught her that.

Kitty felt Katherine's eyes on her. "We're going
to be all right, Mama."

Katherine smiled and laid her hand lightly atop
Kitty's. "I know we are."

The house was cool and quiet when they arrived
home. Earlier, the womenfolk had been over with
covered dishes, had cleaned the house top to
bottom, had dressed the children, and then, at
Katherine's request, had quietly departed to leave
them to deal with their grief in their own way.

Katherine went up the steps, trailing her hand
along the weathered oak rail. Byrd had put up the
rail when Kitty started to walk and, as exploratory
as she was, kept tumbling off the steps. Each board
and plank had been hewn from river oaks and
hand-rubbed, notched into place without so much
as a sliver of a gap. It was a good house, a solid
house. A house built to last a hundred years.

Katherine remembered the day it had been finished, the friends and neighbors who had helped

build it, and the party they'd had after the last logs had been laid. And she remembered Byrd. "No point in doing it piecemeal," he'd said. "Make it big enough now and you don't have to add on later . . ." And they'd built it big enough to encompass the family they had both wanted.

That was the same day he'd made her the promise about the feather bed. She could hear his voice as though it were yesterday, not seventeen years ago. "By the time you get ready to bring forth my firstborn, wife, you'll have that feather mattress if I have to carry it on my back from Pittsburgh every step of the way."

She'd gotten her mattress, even before Meg had been born; it had been brought down the Ohio River on a flatboat from Louisville, Kentucky, and then Byrd had proudly driven it from the wharf in the big farm wagon, a huge grin cutting across his face. They'd never spent a night apart, not since they'd wed. The mattress had been re-covered and more feathers added, but there were still lumps and bumps and indentations from the pressure of their bodies over years of use. Katherine found comfort in that—comfort in the familiarity of the bed that she and Byrd had shared.

She wanted to keep things the way they'd been for as long as she could, not only for the children's sake but also for herself. With so much changing around her, she needed to keep a center to hold on to, and that center was her home. The Kincaid farm was no different from the others that circled north and eastward from Cairo, but to her it was the most special place on earth.

When they'd first married, Katherine had known more about farming than Byrd had. He'd been on the trail hunting and trapping since he was fifteen; Katherine had lived on the hard-scrabble farm in Kentucky with Gran until she was eighteen and had struggled to make a living from the land. Byrd, like many men who'd been wanderers, didn't easily settle in one place. While he and Katherine cleared the fields of trees and stumps, Byrd had hunted the local game, rabbit, squirrel, and deer, and traded the meat and fur for the staples that the family needed. Then gradually they'd tamed the land, plowed the fields, planted crops, and built the outbuildings that protectively circled their log house.

The barn was large enough to house the live-stock in bad weather, with room for storage of fodder and farm implements. The smokehouse was filled with hams and pork shoulders from the cold-weather killing of the hogs, while the root cellar was almost empty of peas and beans and potatoes that had been eaten over the winter months. The outhouse was well away from the spring, which provided clear, cold water for the farm. Nearby was Katherine's beloved apple orchard, just showing the first blush of bloom. How many pies she'd made from those apples over the years, she thought. She and Byrd had planted those trees fifteen years ago, the summer that Meg was born.

Even though Byrd settled slowly to farming, he became successful at it. Their corn crop was always abundant, with enough to sell or barter to those who hadn't been so fortunate. Katherine had a kitchen garden behind the house where she raised sweet potatoes, turnips, cabbage, peas, and beans. Caroline had started a small herb garden and insisted Katherine do the same. The tangy smell of mint or the heady scent of wild thyme would forever remind Katherine of her friend. Katherine had planted flowers, just as she'd promised Kitty's mother and her friend, Hilda, before her death. Yellow daisies and purple asters, deep blue morning glories and delicate white lilies of the valley bloomed in beds in front of the house.

The Kincaids were successful with their livestock, too. Their hogs seemed the fattest; their cows gave the richest milk; their sheep's wool was the thickest; and their horses were the strongest and most spirited. Byrd had teased Katherine, telling her it was because she fed the animals better than she fed the family. Katherine paid no attention and scattered dried corn and pumpkin seeds to the chickens that followed her around the barnyard like pets. The Kincaids did well in selling their livestock to new settlers in the area and to folks who were pushing on westward into Missouri and Arkansas. She and Byrd had shared equally in making decisions about the farm, as they did about the children. How hard it would be to make those decisions without him.

Everyone had been asking her what she was going to do now that Byrd was gone. She considered the question foolish. There was only one thing she could do, and that was live in the house that she and Byrd had built, rear their children, and take care of their farm. Ben had asked her to find a tenant for Caroline's house and suggested that she find someone to help her with the crops and livestock. Until then, the community would pitch in with what she couldn't do on her own. No matter how hard, no matter what the obstacles, she would never leave this house. She would never leave her home.

* * *

When Kitty came up from putting away the team, Katherine was sitting in the porch rocking chair, rocking slowly back and forth, a soft, faraway look in her eyes.

"Mama?" Kitty said uncertainly. "Can I fix you a plate of something?"

Katherine shook her head, extending her hand. "Let's just sit awhile. It's so quiet today. Feels nice, before the rain."

Kitty sat on the floor of the porch beside her mother, resting her cheek against Katherine's knee.

"I remember when your pa brought me this rocking chair," Katherine said. "Him and Oliver Sherrod—you remember Oliver, don't you?"

Kitty nodded.

Katherine pushed Kitty's sunbonnet down on her neck, baring her curls to the stroke of her fingers. "I was sitting here with Ben Adamson and his little sister in my lap, just rocking like I am today, and I looked up and there came Boothe down the road, with you in his arms. He'd brought you back from the Shawnee, and it was like a miracle. I've had a lot of happy days in my life, Kitty, more than my share, I warrant. But that was the happiest."

Kitty pressed her face against Katherine's skirts, closing her eyes. "Mama, I've got to tell you—"

Katherine's fingers never stopped their slow, gentle strokes across Kitty's hair. "No, you don't."

"Please." Kitty swallowed hard, tensing against the pain. "I said some awful things, Mama. Hateful things. I didn't mean them. Pa . . . Pa said you knew that. I hope he was right because I can't take them back, even though I want to and—I just want you to know that I'm sorry. Everything's all right now. We're going to take care of each other, just like we always have, and I'm never going to leave you. Not ever."

Kitty heard the smile in Katherine's voice. "What a foolish little girl you are. Of course you'll leave me, just like one day I'll leave you. It's the way of life, always has been and always will be."

Before Katherine finished speaking, Kitty was already shaking her head. All the pain and the horror she had struggled so desperately to bury came flooding to the surface, and it was all she could do to keep from sobbing. "Oh, Mama, who was that man? Why did he—" But she couldn't finish, because suddenly her mind was filled with the memory of the dead man's eyes and the feel of iron in her hand and the blood splattering on her face. She saw it all and felt it all again, and she couldn't speak; she could barely breathe.

Katherine's eyes grew opaque with a long and unimaginable journey into the past. "He held me to blame for killing his brothers."

Kitty's breath stopped. Again she felt the cold iron in her hand. Like mother, like daughter . . . "Did you?" It was barely a whisper.

Katherine met her daughter's eyes and replied simply, "Yes."

The questions bubbled up, and Katherine must have seen them in Kitty's eyes because she cut them off by saying quietly, "It's a long story. But Zeke Calhoun was a bad man. And badness has its own reasons."

And that was it. The world was full of badness, of spilled blood and raging eyes and death that came in the space between one heartbeat and another. Kitty had always known that, but . . . she had never *known* it. She had been a foolish little girl before, but no longer.

"Boothe will be leaving tomorrow, sunup," Katherine said. "I can't say, but I would guess young Ben will be going with him. And so will you."

Shocked, Kitty lifted her face to look at her mother. "No." At first the word was barely a whisper, for the mere prospect made her recoil. Only a day ago, leaving this place had been more important to her than life itself, but since then she had learned that nothing was more important in life than safety, than home. She no longer cared about what was on the other side of the river; she no longer wanted to know. All she wanted was to stay like this, safe in her mother's arms, forever.

"No, Mama, I can't," she said hoarsely. "I don't want to. I—I lied to you about wanting to be a missionary. I just wanted to go with them because . . ." But she couldn't tell her mother that, and she couldn't even look into her eyes while she thought it. She couldn't tell her that all she had wanted was to be with Boothe, and that she was plotting for Boothe's sake in church when suddenly God had flung down His punishment in the form of a madman with a gun. She couldn't say that. She couldn't even think it. So she finished, "Because I just wanted to go."

Katherine smiled. "I don't think anybody who's ever set on the trail west has had a better reason. The Carlyles have always had wandering feet, Kitty. Just like the Kincaids. We were driven out of Scotland into Ireland, then out of Ireland to Virginia, then to the Carolinas. And we couldn't stop there, but had to go on across the blue mountains, finally to Kentucky. Then Boothe, when he was just a boy, set off up the river and across the mountains, and when there was nothing left of the family but me, I followed him. When my feet first touched these banks, I swore I would go no further. But I always knew my sons and daughters would be moving and following trails I couldn't see."

Kitty looked up at her. "I'm not a Carlyle," she said simply, softly. "Or a Kincaid."

Katherine's hand tangled briefly, lightly, in Kitty's curls. "Being a part of this family has to do with more than having red hair and blue eyes," she said. "And you're as much a part of us, maybe more, than if you had my blood. Maybe that's why I've held on to you so hard, Kitty. Because I always knew you'd be the first to leave. It was wrong of me. You can't hang on to something that was never meant to stay."

Kitty pressed her face against Katherine's knee. "I don't want to leave you," she said thickly.

Katherine reached down and took Kitty's chin, raising her face and making her look at her. "There are a lot of reasons for staying at home," she said sternly. "Being afraid is not one of them."

"I don't care," Kitty answered. "I am afraid." And then she shook her head. "Oh, Mama," she said tiredly, "don't you see? I was just a little girl when I begged you to let me go. It was a silly, little-girl dream. I've got no business with those missionary people, and Boothe doesn't want me along. I'd just get in the way. So please, let's not talk about it anymore."

Katherine smiled. "Since when have you ever gotten in anybody's way? You're a strong, smart girl, Kitty. Ben and Boothe, they're good men but—well, they're just men. And they're both hurting now. They need you with them, more than they know. *I* need you to be with them, to rest easy in my mind. My brother's got a lot of hurt inside him, and hurt sometimes makes a man do foolish things. With you along . . . maybe I can be sure he'll come back to me."

And then Kitty was silent. Boothe, and his dream about the white pony. Boothe, who might need her. She had loved him for so long, she owed him so much . . . but how could he need her?

She lowered her eyes. "I'm not like you, Mama. I don't have what makes the Carlyle women special. I don't have anything that anyone would need."

Katherine stopped stroking her hair and got to her feet. She went into the house, and when she returned a moment later she was holding a small leather pouch in her hand. Kitty stood up.

"Before my gran died," Katherine said, looking down at the pouch, "I was afraid, too, because I didn't have the gift, like she did. But she told me I had gifts I didn't even know about yet, and she gave me this."

She reached into the pouch and took something out. It was a gold coin, dull with age and carved with strange writing. She held it in her hand for a moment, letting it catch the fading light. "The rest of these are for my other children. But maybe this one will help you find your own gifts." She pressed the coin into Kitty's hand.

Kitty closed her fingers around the heavy metal, feeling her mother's warmth and her mother's strength. Her throat was thick as she said, "I don't want to do the wrong thing."

Katherine smiled and, lifting her hand, touched Kitty's cheek. " 'Your seed,' " she said, " 'will spread throughout the land, to the shining mountains and the thundering waters and beyond. Your daughters will give birth to a new breed of man, and your name will not be forgotten.' Those are the words my gran said to me, Kitty," Katherine said softly, "and they are my gift to you. Go now, and don't disappoint me."

Kitty went into her mother's arms, holding her tightly. Tears wet her face. "I'll go, Mama," she whispered, "if you say it's right. But the same river that takes me away will bring me back again. We'll be together, and take care of each other, just like I said. So don't worry. I'll come back."

Katherine closed her eyes and drew a deep, slow breath through parted lips. She held Kitty more tightly, and didn't answer.

St. Louis, Missouri

The riverfront was rough and ready. Trappers, traders, drifters, and river pirates met at the taverns and grogshops that lined the Mississippi. But St. Louis itself, up above the levees, considered itself the queen of the river, a sophisticated city true to its French heritage. Wealthy merchants built their mansions along the newly paved streets. Glittering chandeliers hung in their huge reception rooms, the candlelight reflecting on gleaming walnut floors. The furniture was imported from England and the carpets from Turkey. Fine Irish linen adorned the tables, and elegant guests sipped the best French wines from Austrian crystal. The merchants of St. Louis, their fortunes made in the fur trade, lived like the millionaires they were. All except one.

His name was Sheldon Gerrard, and he sat behind a big desk in the dimly lit drawing room of what had once been one of the finest homes in St. Louis. Much of the furniture had been sold off, and there were blank spots of unfaded wallpaper where fine paintings had once hung. He used to be a wealthy man, a powerful man. He used to have two legs and a heart as strong as an ox.

He had been born a common man of common circumstances in Pennsylvania in 1800. Being born at the dawn of a new century, he had always known he was meant for greater things. He had escaped his beginnings as soon as he could, and set his sights westward.

Eventually he had ended up, as many ambitious men did, in St. Louis. He quickly grasped the notion, just as John Jacob Astor and Manuel Lisa had, of the profits to be made in the fur trade. But he didn't trade with the Indians—that was for men with no imagination. Sheldon Gerrard was made for grander things. He made enough money from his own furs to start a small company, hiring white trappers to go out into the wilds and bring back their furs exclusively to him. He could buy furs for two dollars a pound and sell them in St. Louis for four. By the mid-1830s, when the demand for beaver was waning, Sheldon Gerrard had made his fortune and turned his interests to even greater endeavors.

He had been to the Rockies, to the trapper rendezvous on the banks of the Bighorn and Yellowstone rivers. He had seen the wonders that westward land had to offer, and he was shrewd enough to know that the frontier would continue to push unerringly toward the setting sun. The men who got there first would make the most money.

Through the trapper rendezvous he had met up with Boothe Carlyle, reputed to be one of the best guides in the West. There Gerrard hatched his grand scheme and asked Carlyle to be part of it. If the stories coming back east about the riches of Oregon were only half true, it was still a veritable Eden. To populate this paradise, Gerrard and Carlyle put together a band of settlers willing to go to Oregon and found a new colony. Or perhaps a new nation.

Gerrard wanted no failures or misfits in his colony. He and Carlyle chose shopkeepers, teachers, a banker, farmers, a blacksmith—men and women who knew how to raise cattle and horses, how to grow fruit and produce, how to build boats and houses. Gerrard had heard that the soil of Oregon was fertile, the climate temperate; and trade routes to Mexican California and the riches of the Orient were there for the taking by anyone who could establish a foothold. Gerrard wanted more than a foothold. A man of vision could build an empire, and he intended to do just that.

Gerrard paid for the whole expedition and joined Carlyle in leading it. He wanted it to be his expedition and for the colony to bear his name. In return, the settlers would pay him a percentage of their income from crops, trade, or profits on their own endeavors. He encouraged entrepreneurs because he planned to take part of their earnings. It was a costly venture: fifteen wagons completely outfitted, a string of horses and mules, teams of oxen, other livestock, and enough supplies and arms to last the journey.

Had he succeeded, he would have been a king. Everything would have been worth the investment. But he had trusted Boothe Carlyle, and that had been his mistake. A fatal one in many ways.

Two years after the failure of the expedition, Gerrard was still paying the price. His capital was depleted. The financial panic of 1837 had left business stagnant, and a number of banks had failed. The worth of the investments Gerrard had held on to had plummeted. The times were not easy, and his income was only a small percent of what it had once been. Through his banker, a very discreet man, Gerrard had begun to sell off some of his personal valuables—paintings, a set of French china, a silver service. There were still plenty of *noveaux riche* in St. Louis who were eager to buy treasures from a gentleman in financial distress.

Gerrard kept up appearances as best he could. His frock coat hung from his shoulders without a wrinkle, his cravat was perfectly tied, his fingernails were clipped and buffed. His trousers were of a fine light wool material, one of the pants legs neatly pinned just below his left knee.

The man who sat across the desk from him was somewhat younger and a great deal less well-kempt; he had the toughness of hard living etched in lines on his face and the dust of the plains under his fingernails. He was exactly the kind of man Gerrard needed.

Gerrard took up a long thin cigar, measuring it between his fingers. "So," he said mildly. "He's going to try again."

The other man balanced his hat casually atop one knee. "So I hear tell."

Gerrard shook his head sadly, stroking the cigar between his fingers. "There's always some fool wanting to go west, isn't there? Looking for that pot of gold . . ."

"What did you want to see me about?" the other man said impatiently. "You could've got the news on Carlyle from anybody. And if you're looking to hire a killer, I gotta tell you—"

Gerrard smiled the small, narrow-eyed smile that never failed to make an onlooker's throat dry up. He said softly, "But I don't want him dead, my dear fellow, don't you understand that? Not right away. Not easily. I want him to suffer first, just like so many others suffered at his hands. I want him to feel half a man, like me; and I want him to watch everything he loves as it's destroyed. I want him humiliated, broken, ruined. I want him stripped of every shred of hope, every reason for living, and then, perhaps, I'll let him die."

The other man stared at him, silent and impassive, for a long time.

Gerrard's smile widened into something more genuine. He struck a match and placed it against the tip of the cigar, watching his companion in growing mirth as he puffed until the cigar caught. "You and I think alike in a lot of ways, my friend. That's why I trust you with the, er, delicate nature of the job I have in mind. But I worry sometimes that you miss the finer points of strategy. Revenge is not a thing to be gulped down like a cheap brew. One should linger over it, savor it, enjoy every nuance. That, you see, is the difference between a civilized man and a barbarian."

The other man's voice was flat. "What do you want me to do?"

"I want you," said Sheldon Gerrard, examining the tip of his cigar, "to make sure that Boothe Carlyle and his merry little band of missionaries fail to reach their destination as planned. I want Carlyle to fail again—horribly, painfully, and publicly. I want him to live with that failure for the rest of his life. I want to watch it destroy him."

The other man replied briefly, "It ain't just him going on this trip, and I'm no woman-killer."

"I don't care who lives or who dies; I leave the details to you. I don't really even care if that ragtag band manages to overcome the odds and get where they're going despite Carlyle. What matters is that *Boothe Carlyle fails*." After a moment he added softly, almost to himself, "I know his type. Always so sure they'll never make the same mistake twice. Something like this, it'll tear him apart inch by inch. It'll break him. And being broken . . ." His eyes lost their focus. His voice dropped a fraction as he stared into the distance. "That's worse than being dead."

"What's in it for me?"

Slowly Gerrard's eyes came back to him. His shoulders lost their tension as he sank against the leather chair, a man at ease in doing business. "Aside from a little revenge of your own?" he suggested.

A muscle in the other man's jaw flexed.

Gerrard pushed a sack across the desk. It clinked and showed the shape of coins. "Half now," he said. "Half when it's done. Two hundred in gold, my friend. Can you afford to turn it down?"

Though it was clear he could not, the other man

hesitated. "I don't know. This doesn't sound like something I'd be interested in."

Gerrard chuckled. "I don't see that you have many options. Who else would be as perfect for the job as you? You're a man with a past and not much of a future. By your own admission, you're walking on the other side of the law. Remember, *you* looked me up in '36 after you found out about your sister and her husband. *You've* stayed in touch with me. It's as if we've both been waiting."

The other man looked at the sack of coins, but did not reach to take it.

"It's more than the money, you know," Gerrard went on casually. "It's the future—yours and mine. The land along the Kaw won't belong to the Indians for long. There are rumblings in Congress about making it a territory. There'll be money to be made for a man who knows the country—who's been through it before, and survived."

For the first time, the other man smiled. "Still at it, are you, Gerrard? Still picturing yourself as king of everything west of the Mississippi." He shrugged. "Well, I reckon if you're offering me a piece of the fortune you're going to make out there, I ain't too proud to take it." He picked up the sack of coins, weighed it in his hand, then stuffed it in his pocket.

Gerrard's eyes were hard. "Nor too proud to seek your own kind of justice on Boothe Carlyle."

"If that was all I wanted, I would've taken care of Carlyle with a shotgun a long time ago."

Gerrard seemed to find that amusing, and his eyes twinkled as he stretched back to enjoy his cigar. "Subtlety," he replied, taking a great deal of pleasure in letting the word roll off his tongue, "is the mark of a civilized man. Remember that, my friend, and appreciate what you learn from me."

Ben asked Boothe in a low voice, "Maybe it's not my place, but do you think the grief has gone to Miz Kincaid's mind?"

The two men sat on Katherine Kincaid's porch after supper; Ben quiet and worried, Boothe cleaning a long rifle in the light that spilled through the open door. From inside came the usual sounds of home, though they were more subdued than usual: Katherine putting away the supper dishes, Meg singing in that soft, high voice of hers as she tucked the children into bed.

Boothe answered briefly, "N'sir, I don't."

"Then why is she sending a girl along with us?"

Boothe chuckled. "Kitty's not an ordinary girl and you know it, Ben Adamson. She always could ride you into the river, and she's got a better eye than any man I've ever known. She took her first rabbit when she was seven, and I'd trust her with my life if I had to. She had good teachers, her pa and me."

Ben looked uncomfortable. "Still, she's a girl, and it doesn't make sense, her ma letting her go. She's got no business out there on the plains."

"That worries you, does it?"

"Doesn't it you?"

Boothe took a moment to draw a soft cloth along the barrel, bringing the rifle to his shoulder and checking the sights. "I'm worried about all of us. This is no Sunday buggy ride we're starting on, and if I had my way, nobody'd be going. As for Miss Kate . . ." He lowered the rifle and made another adjustment to the sights. "She never does anything without a reason. She knows that when a man's got a woman to take care of, he's going to spend more time thinking and less time doing. I guess she figured I needed to be reminded of what was waiting back home."

"That doesn't make sense," Ben said uneasily. "There are going to be other women on the trip. And you're the best guide east of the Rockies. You've made this same passage a dozen times before. She's got no reason to think . . ."

Boothe let the rifle rest across his knees, looking off into the darkness. "This time's different," he said quietly. "I reckon we always knew that. Now . . . more than ever."

Meg's voice drifted through the door, the next verse of "Amazing Grace." *Through many dangers, toils and snares/I have already come* . . . Ben felt his throat tighten, and then his fists. *'Tis grace that brought me safe thus far/And grace will lead me home.* He wanted her to stop. He wanted everything to stop, the pictures inside his head, the aching inside his belly, the sudden surprise he felt when he tried to look to the future and saw only emptiness. But even after the last sweet notes of her voice died away, the song echoed in his head, buzzing around like an insect that you ducked to avoid, words without meaning, notes without melody. *Through many dangers, toils and snares* . . .

"The others won't like it," he said tightly. "She's not part of the mission. They're going to want to know why she's going."

Behind him, Kitty said, "Why are you going, Ben?"

He didn't turn around, because he didn't want to meet her eyes, and he didn't want to answer. Why was he going? Because they were expecting him, the Crellers and Reverend Syms. Because he had promised Rose. Because once, in another lifetime long ago, it had seemed the right thing to do. Why was he going? The question joined the words of the song in the back of his head, broken syllables, all mixed up and meaning nothing. He didn't know. He didn't even care to know.

Boothe set his rifle aside. "Come on out here, Kitten."

Kitty moved from the lighted doorway into the shadows on Ben's left. The two men were sitting on the steps; she sat on the rail, half turned to face the night-speckled path in front of the house, and let her feet swing free. The dark was filled with so many things. The coolness and the moisture that predicted rain. The lingering smells of supper drifting through the air. The soft sounds of the children turning in their beds. Her mother's low voice, speaking with Meg. The smell of gun oil, the horses snuffling in the barn, the sudden scuffle of movement as a rabbit bolted through the bean patch at the side of the house. These things she was hearing and smelling and seeing for the last time, but it didn't seem like the last. It seemed like the first.

I don't have to go, she thought. *No one will make me. I can stay here and watch the children grow and bring in the crops and tend the animals and be quiet and safe for the rest of my life, and nobody would think bad of me. Nobody would even think it was strange.*

But then she looked at Boothe, and at Ben, and she caught the scent of the river on the night air. And she knew that if she didn't go, there would be a part of her that was always missing, always aching.

None of them had to go. None of them really had a good reason to go, and maybe, as her mother had said, no man or woman who had ever turned their eyes west had known why. But they went anyway.

Boothe spoke to both of them. "We'll leave as soon as it's light enough to see, and we'll have to do some hard riding to make the rendezvous in Westport. Kitten, you take that big-chested dray. He's not fast, but he's got stamina and that's what we need. Roll up a change of clothes and your rations in a blanket; no need to load down your mount, and everything else we need we'll be getting in Westport. Make sure your boots are greased down good. And here." He picked up the rifle and handed it to her. "I got your pa's gun cleaned and ready for you. There's fancier pieces, I know, and lots of folks'd say better ones, but I'd sooner trust my life to a good Kentucky rifle any day."

There was a thickness in Kitty's chest as she took the heavy weapon in her hands. It was a good, sturdy rifle, far more accurate than modern imitators because of its smaller bore and long barrel, despite the fact that it had to be loaded with powder and shot, which some marksmen considered a cumbersome process. Her pa had taught her how to shoot as soon as she was strong enough to hold a rifle; her mother had insisted on it. Her mother had insisted on a lot of things, like teaching her girls how to smoke strips of game over a slow fire until it was hard and dried and would last for months; and how to bake a mixture of cornbread and water into flat little cakes that wouldn't spoil, and how to pick leaves from the woods that were edible even though they had their own vegetable garden; and how to build a snare for a rabbit and traps for fish.

Had she somehow known that one day Kitty would need those skills?

"How long will it take?" Ben asked.

"We ought to be leaving Westport by the middle of May. That'll give us plenty of time to reach the mission on the Solomon before . . ." He hesitated, and both Kitty and Ben knew he was thinking about another journey, and snow that had come too soon. "Before cold weather starts," he finished.

His voice was gruff and his eyes focused straight ahead into the night as he added, "Now get your gear together and get some sleep, both of you. There'll be no time for napping on the trail."

Ben stood up to go inside. He had already packed for the journey, days ago; tonight he would make his pallet on the floor of the Kincaid kitchen as he had done so many other, happier times.

Kitty hesitated for a moment, wanting to talk privately with Boothe, wanting to hear from his own lips that her presence on the trip was welcome . . . needing to hear that everything was going to be all right. That things were as they should be. But something about the set of his shoulders and the hardness of his jaw discouraged conversation, and after a moment she stood up and followed Ben.

At the door she turned back, and what she saw made her heart stop beating and her blood chill. Boothe was slumped forward, his face buried in his hands. The oaklike strength that had always been a part of him was gone; the invincibility that had enlarged him for so many years in Kitty's eyes had disappeared. She couldn't be certain, and she didn't want to know, but she thought he was weeping.

Perhaps she should have gone to him and offered comfort; perhaps she should have spoken and offered her strength. But she couldn't move.

She slipped her hand into her pocket and felt the smooth gold coin. It was cold and lifeless now and provided no reassurance. She remembered her mother's eyes when she had placed the coin in her hand. She thought of her father sitting beneath the big oak tree, looking out toward the river. She wondered about what lay beyond the river, and she felt cold.

She turned back into the house, confused and uncertain, and more unhappy than she had ever known it was possible to be.

Katherine was up at four A.M., making breakfast, packing provisions that would last the travelers until St. Louis. The children were still sleeping; the good-byes had been said last night. The day was gray and misty, the roads muddy. Katherine watched through the window as Kitty climbed up on the big dray, and she could not help thinking about another wet, muddy day, another leave-taking. She turned quickly back to her work.

Boothe came inside. "We're about ready to hit the trail."

She handed him an oilcloth packet. "I wrapped up some apple pie. It'll go good with a cold supper. Mind you eat it before it goes bad."

Boothe smiled. "I'm gonna miss your apple pie."

Katherine went to a small wooden chest in the corner and lifted the lid. She returned to him with a leather cord threaded through her fingers, on the end of which was an iron pendant in the shape of a Celtic cross surrounded by a circle.

Boothe said, "I near about forgot."

Katherine's face was grave with concern as she slipped the cord over his head. "You never forgot before."

Boothe fingered the pendant. "No. I reckon I didn't."

Katherine rested her hands on his chest. "Do you remember what Gran said when she gave it to you?"

"I remember."

" 'Have a care, Boothe Carlyle,' " she said softly, repeating their grandmother's words, " 'Remember that in the land of milk and honey there were also giants.' "

Their arms came around each other in a quiet embrace, and in an instant as clear and as certain as anything in his life, Boothe knew he would not see his sister again. Katherine knew it too. He heard her small, stifled intake of breath, and felt her arms tighten around him as though with her small strength she could keep him from the destiny that was his own.

But it was only for an instant, and then she moved a little away from him. He saw the sorrow and the dread in her eyes, and how badly she wanted to beg him to stay. And he felt a yearning deep inside himself that did not want to let go.

But all she said was, "You keep those young ones dry."

And all he said was, quietly, "Good-bye, Kate."

He turned and left the house.

Katherine stood at the door and watched them start on their way. Ben, his face tired and dull. Kitty, smiling with false courage as she lifted her hand to her mother. And Boothe, mounting up to ride away for the last time.

"Good-bye," she whispered.

But she couldn't stay to watch them disappear into the mist. As the small caravan started moving down the road, she turned back into the house and closed the door on the rain.

Chapter Four

Westport, Missouri

Oliver Sherrod sat outside Duke's Tavern, balancing the split-rail chair on its back two legs with his shoulders propped against the wall, and watched the girl move down the street. He wasn't the only man who was watching.

It wasn't that she was above the ordinary pretty, but in a town like Westport any white female with all her teeth was worth watching, this one more than others. She had brown hair that was tied back at the nape with a red ribbon and fanned over her shoulders; she swung her sunbonnet by its strings so as to show it off. She wore a serviceable brown skirt and a butternut-colored blouse, the garb of most westward-bound women, but she stepped high whenever she could so that the flash of white petticoat caught the sun. She was a young girl, sixteen or seventeen, with a narrow face and bold brown eyes, but there was nothing about the way she looked to get a man worked up. It was the way she moved, shoulders back, head cocked, swinging her hips just so, flashing a smile or a jaunty wave at the men who ogled her from doorways and street corners. She was plainly asking for trouble, and Oliver watched her idly, wondering how long it would take before she got some.

Duke's wasn't much of a tavern; the whiskey was barely fit for Indians, and the sour barnyard smell tainted the air even outside. But then, Westport wasn't much of a town. Set on the swampy plains where the Missouri and Kaw rivers joined, Westport was little more than a trading post that had grown too big for its britches. When it rained, the streets were lanes of slow-flowing sludge; when it was dry, as it had been for a week now, the dust was thick enough to choke on, and the gnats and mosquitoes swarmed in droves.

In the winter the population consisted mostly of trappers, traders, and Indians. But springtime brought pilgrims bound for the Santa Fe trail; in rickety wagons and cumbersome Conestogas, on foot and on horseback they straggled in, camping in the deep grass of the rolling plains that surrounded the town or on the wooded banks of the river, bracing themselves for the last leg of the journey. Rows of wooden shacks supplied the travelers with everything from wagon wheels to chewing tobacco, and corrals stood full of oxen to be traded for the horses that only a fool would try to hitch to a wagon for the trudge across the plains. Westport wasn't as big as St. Joe or Independence, but it was coming into its own, and there were fortunes to be made in the spring.

For those who meant to cross the Rockies, the

time for leaving had already passed. Every day though, a few more wandered in, outfitting their wagons for shorter journeys. Some traveled alone, some in groups of one or two families. And then there was the missionary bunch. The Carlyle party.

Unlikely as it seemed, Oliver had already figured the girl with the red ribbon was part of the missionaries. For one thing, he had sat outside the tavern and watched enough people come and go in the last few days to know who belonged to whom. For another . . . he just had a hunch.

As he watched, he knew he was about to have a chance to see if his hunch played out.

She sauntered along with her shoulders swaying and her head tossed back, pausing every once in a while to examine a bolt of dry goods displayed on a rack outside a store, or pretending to be interested in the contents of a harness shop when all she really wanted was to catch the eye of the wheelwright who was working next door. When she went past the door of the tavern across the street, she made a point of walking right into a man who was coming out.

He was a trapper, from the looks of him, squat-legged and squint-eyed, with a tobacco-stained beard and two missing front teeth. Apparently the young lady wasn't particular, however, because when he grinned an apology at her and ran his eyes up and down her figure, she tossed him that same bright catch-me-if-you-can smile and gave an extra little hitch to her step as she walked off.

The trapper watched her for a minute, grinning, then wiped his mouth on the back of his hand and started after her. Oliver got up and followed, though he took his time crossing the street.

By the time he reached her, the trapper had her by the arm, and the struggle she was putting up wasn't pretense. The trapper grabbed her hair, grunting, "Just a little kiss, that's all," and the girl shrieked. That's when Oliver stepped in.

He laid a hand on the trapper's arm. "I don't think the lady's interested, mister."

The trapper jerked his head around, but it wasn't Oliver's quiet voice or restraining hand that stopped him. It was the sight of the five-shot that Oliver was holding, plainly visible, in his other hand.

The trapper let go of her hair, spat deliberately on the ground as close as he could to her skirts without hitting them, and walked away.

"Well, I never!" the girl exclaimed breathlessly. "Can't a woman even walk down the streets?" Then she turned her eyes on Oliver, made them even bigger than they were, and said, "Thank you for your assistance. That was very gallant of you. Mr. . . ?"

Oliver held back a smile and touched his hat brim. "Sherrod, ma'am. Oliver Sherrod."

"I'm Lucy Syms," she replied. "And I must say, it's good to meet a *gentleman* in this forsaken backwater."

As Lucy looked up at him, a dimple appeared in her cheek, calculated and practiced. She liked what she saw. Her newfound escort was over six feet tall with soft brown hair worn long beneath the brim of a well-used leather hat. His eyes were gray and sharp, not soft, and his face beneath its stubble of light whiskers had that same sharpness. He was handsome, yes, but he was something better. He was dangerous.

Oliver's smile crept closer to the surface, bringing a pretty blush to the girl's cheeks. "I'm not sure I'd go so far as to call myself a gentleman," he replied, "but thank you kindly anyway. And if you don't mind a piece of advice, I'd be more careful if I was you. This side of the Mississippi, life is lean and a man mostly takes what he needs. It might be right smart of you not to go around reminding 'em of what they need, if you know what I mean."

She tilted her head back, her big eyes bright, and took his measure. "And what do you need, Mr. Sherrod?"

He grinned back at her. "Why, right now," he drawled, "not much of anything at all."

She giggled.

"Where're you headed? I'd be pleased to walk with you a spell," he said.

"Oh, nowheres in particular." She gave a studied shrug of her shoulders and tossed back her head again. "Just looking around. My folks are camped just outside of town."

"Maybe I'd better walk you back, then. It wouldn't do for a pretty little thing like you to go wandering around this rough place by yourself."

She liked that, and gave him a sparkling smile as she started walking, swinging her sunbonnet behind her.

"Santa Fe bound, are you?" he said.

Her brow wrinkled with a pouting frown, and for the first time she looked her age. Sixteen, Oliver guessed.

"Indian Territory, is all I know. My folks made me come. The whole thing is stupid."

"Rough country," Oliver agreed gravely. "I know it some, myself. Who's your guide?"

"Boothe Carlyle, and he's late. We've been waiting for him two days now."

Oliver kept his expression bland. "Fine man. One of the best in the business."

She cast him a quick, shrewd glance. "Do you think so? My pa doesn't. I hear he got a bunch of folks killed last time he went out."

"Well, a person hears a lot of things."

"I bet my pa would like to talk to you," she said suddenly, eagerly. "Maybe you could stop by the camp."

He smiled down at her. "Why, that's right kind of you, Miss Lucy. Maybe I will. Sometime."

They arrived at the junction of the Missouri and Kaw near midday, after seven hours of hard riding that began that day as soon as the horses could pick their way through the dim light of daybreak. It had been that way all across Missouri, and Kitty was tired. They all were tired, but the closer they got to their destination, the higher her spirits rose, and new energy began to seep into her limbs.

Even the horses, inspired perhaps by the fields of tall, waving grass through which they traveled, began to move a little faster, stride a little stronger. Kitty had never seen anything like the plains that stretched from the banks of the river to the horizon; it was like an ocean of undulating green, flat, unbroken, stretching out in all directions as far as the eye could see. Boothe warned her that she would grow mighty tired of that view before another week of traveling was done, but for Kitty it was a whole new world, and she couldn't get enough of it.

As they approached the town, they encountered

several groups of travelers in temporary camps drawn up in rough, wide semicircles along the plain. Boothe made inquiries and was directed to the Syms party.

The first thing Kitty noticed was that the campsite seemed awfully small for the sixteen people they were supposed to meet. She counted only three wagons. The second thing she noticed was that the contents of those wagons, now unloaded and neatly arranged to give the appearance more of a parlor than of a camp, were far more elaborate than she would have expected. There was a big leafed table covered with a white cloth and sturdy oak chairs drawn up around it. Smaller, pie-shaped tables held oil lamps with painted globes. There was even a pump organ with a brocaded bench. Kitty could not help wondering what they expected to do with that organ when it rained.

Two women were working over the cookfire. One was middle-aged and thin, her hair shot through with gray and her face lined in the way of women who work hard and suffer silently. The other was younger, with a pretty face and a shy glance, her breasts full with mother's milk. A baby slept in a wooden cradle nearby.

Two men came forward to meet them. One, who couldn't have been much older than Ben, was eager of step and quick to smile. The older man was tall and grave, with piercing dark eyes and a dark beard that elongated his face, narrow slumped shoulders, and bony hands.

"Ben!" the younger man exclaimed as Ben slid off his horse. "How good to see you! We were starting to worry—we expected you two days ago!" He clasped Ben's hand enthusiastically, but the smile on his face faded into uncertainty as he looked from Kitty to Boothe. "Where is Rose?"

"Rose is dead," Ben said briefly.

There were sounds of shock and horror from the women, and Kitty admired the way Ben withstood it.

"Dear Lord, Ben—"

"What—?"

But Ben shook his head, forestalling their questions.

The older man came forward. "We share your grief, Benjamin." He had a deep, powerful voice that seemed to boom even when he spoke at a normal level. "God has taken His most faithful servant to His bosom and spared her the suffering of this life. She would have wanted you to complete your mission. Praise be unto Him."

Ben looked momentarily uncomfortable, and Kitty felt distinctly awkward as she dismounted. One by one the eyes had moved from Ben to her, and she was acutely aware of how she must look in her rumpled brown merino and calico shirt, her sweat-crumpled hair stuffed underneath the wide-brimmed leather hat Boothe had insisted she wear to keep the sun off her back.

"And who is this?" the tall man demanded.

Before Ben could explain, Boothe replied, "This is my niece, Kitty Kincaid. She'll be riding with us."

The tall man stiffened his shoulders. "We made no provisions with you for family members, sir. This is a private mission . . ."

Boothe cut him off short, his eyes sweeping the camp. "Where's the rest of your party?"

There was a brief hesitation, and into it Ben spoke up. "Boothe, this is the Reverend John Syms. He organized the mission. His wife, Rachel . . ." The middle-aged woman nodded to him uncertainly. "And Martin and Effie Creller." The young woman managed a tentative smile, but her husband glanced at John Syms and said nothing.

"And this . . ." Benjamin looked relieved, then confused to see another man appear from behind the wagon. He was lanky and awkward-looking, with a pale face and straight brown hair that kept falling into his eyes. He clutched a book in his hands. "Beg pardon, sir, but I don't know you."

"Richard Singleton," Martin Creller supplied quietly at Ben's elbow. "He's a divinity student from Massachusetts. He joined us in St. Louis."

Richard mumbled something that could have been "How-do" but didn't meet anyone's eyes for more than a moment.

Boothe's gaze swept the gathering. "I count three men. I was told there would be eight."

"The others were unable to follow their calling," the Reverend Syms replied. "Like Joshua's troops we have been winnowed down to the strongest and most devout. We alone will make the journey into the wilderness."

Boothe's expression did not change, and no one but Kitty—and perhaps Ben—could have sensed his rising anger. "Come on, Kitten," he said. He swung on his heel and started toward his horse.

"Wait!" Martin Creller cried. "What are you doing?"

Ben said, "Boothe—"

Boothe did not look back. "Not even Joshua would be fool enough to take a party of three men through Indian country. Get yourself another guide."

John Syms made himself even taller. "We are God's army, sir!" This time his voice did boom. "We may be small in numbers, but our strength is without measure. We have nothing to fear."

Boothe put his foot into the stirrup and Kitty caught his arm. She didn't know why she stopped him. Throughout the journey she had not given a single thought to the people they would meet, or what it would be like to traverse the country with them. After less than five minutes in their company she was angry and at odds, and her sentiments were completely with Boothe. It would be easier, so much easier, to just mount up and ride back the way they had come.

But she said, "Boothe, you're not really going to leave them, are you?"

"That's exactly what I'm doing."

"But what will they do?"

"Find another guide."

"You know they can't find anybody else this late! Isn't that what you were telling Pa before . . ."

His muscles stiffened. "Then they'll go back east where they belong."

Kitty cast a quick glance toward the group. Reverend Syms looking like a drawing out of a book meant to scare little children. Martin Creller, conveying outraged stubbornness. Richard Singleton, hanging back in the shadows. And Ben, torn and uncertain. The women. The little baby.

"Do you really think they'll do that?" she said.

After a moment Boothe looked back over his shoulder. His voice sounded tired as he said, "No. I don't reckon they will."

He took his foot out of the stirrup and turned back to the group. "Are you folks set on doing this?"

John Syms answered for all of them, as he was apparently accustomed to doing. "We are servants of God. We go where He sends us."

Boothe looked at Ben. "What about you?"

Kitty wouldn't have been surprised if Ben had answered in the negative and gone for his horse. But neither was she surprised when, after a moment, he nodded and said, "I'm going on." She had never been able to figure him out.

Effie Creller stepped forward shyly. "Please—I'm afraid we've gotten off to a poor start. You must be hungry after your long ride. Come sit down and let me fix you a plate."

Boothe's voice softened. "Thank you kindly, ma'am. I reckon the young folks could do with a bite to eat, and I'd appreciate some of that fine-smelling coffee you've got brewing."

The women started dishing up plates of stew, and everyone gathered around the big table. Kitty was amazed at how white the cloth was. They must take it down to the river and wash it every day. She wondered how they expected to keep it clean when they had to carry their water in barrels across the plains.

Kitty *was* hungry. She had been hungry almost all the time since the day they left, for the bacon and cornmeal, while filling, left a big emptiness in a pallet that was used to the full table of a rich riverbank farm. The stew smelled so good it was almost intoxicating, and she had picked up her spoon to dig in before she caught Ben's eye. Embarrassed and impatient, she put the spoon down again while he murmured a brief grace. She still felt as though everyone was staring at her with disapproving eyes. Ben had never bothered to say grace on the trail, she recalled.

Everyone was seated around the table, but only she and Ben were eating. When Boothe was served a tin mug of coffee, the Reverend Syms said sternly, "Before we go any further, there are some things we should discuss."

"There are at that," Boothe said. He rested his forearms on the table, his hands cradling the mug as he swept his eyes over the camp. "First off, about half this stuff you got spread out here is going to have to go. You'd best get busy selling it in town tomorrow, because we don't have any time to waste. You get a good price for it, or you leave it sitting on the prairie, don't make no difference to me."

John Syms drew himself up, and outrage tightened Martin Creller's voice. "What are you talking about—sell it? These are our supplies, our furnishings for the mission—"

"We brought them all the way from Tennessee!" Effie Creller exclaimed.

Boothe nodded. "I appreciate that. But this table . . ." He thumped the solid oak. "It's too heavy, and too big. I'm surprised you got this far with it. Same with the chairs; trade 'em in for a couple of stools of split pine, if you've got to have chairs. Not much time for sitting out on the trail, though. And that organ . . ." He jerked his head toward the offending object. "It'll kill the oxen. Leave it here."

"But that was my mother's!" Effie Creller exclaimed.

And Martin demanded, "What oxen?"

Boothe answered Martin. "First thing tomorrow, you trade in your horses for oxen. Keep a couple for riding, if you want, but no more than can feed themselves off the prairie grass that grows mighty scant after we've been moving a month or so."

"That's absurd! We spent good money on those horses!"

Boothe met his eyes levelly. "And you're going to lose more than money when you try to ford a river with a team, or watch your animals drop in their traces from heat and exhaustion."

His gaze moved around the table. "You got three wagons. Each wagon will be outfitted with two extra wheels, two water barrels, a bushel of beans, a keg of salt, ten pounds of coffee, a barrel of dried meat and one of salted fish, a side of bacon. An extra canvas, a keg of gunpowder. Each man among you will carry two repeating rifles and fifty rounds of ammunition."

John Syms brought his hands down flat upon the table. His voice thundered. "That, sir, is enough! It was a mistake from the beginning to engage a heathen for God's work, and now our error has been brought home to us! We will not go armed into Judea!"

Boothe's small smile was lost in his beard. "So I'm a heathen, am I? Reverend, you don't know heathen until you've started across Indian Territory."

John Syms's eyes glowed, and Martin Creller's voice conveyed his indignation. "We will not take up arms against the brethren we were sent to save."

"And just who are your brethren, Mr. Creller? The naked Apache, the murdering Comanche?

They'd as soon slice your throat open as spit on you, and they'd never be proud to call *you* brother. I think you'll find it a lot harder to bring Jesus to the likes of them than it was to civilize the poor beat-up Shawnee, who got all the spirit whipped out of them twenty-five years ago back east."

A fine line of color crept up John Syms's jaw. "You blaspheme our work, sir!"

"No," Boothe replied mildly. "I'm just pointing out a few facts."

"The Shawnee mission has been a model of success," Ben said quietly. "You can't criticize the efforts there."

The tightening of Boothe's lips might have been a smile, but there was no amusement in his eyes. "Oh, yes. Mr. Isaac McCoy had himself an idea, all right, when he moved the Shawnee across the river and turned them into Christian farmers. Put 'em in houses, taught 'em English, even built 'em a printing press so they can read their Scriptures in Shawnee. But they're not Shawnee anymore. They're not much of anything."

"They have salvation," Syms said sternly, "and are better off for it, as any Christian man can plainly see."

"Too bad the plains Indians aren't Christian men," Boothe replied, meeting him straight in the eye. "Because it's them you need to save your convincing for, not me."

Martin Creller said, "We don't expect to have any dealings with the Comanche or the Apache. It's the Pawnee we were sent to minister to, and they're just as capable of understanding God's word as the Shawnee were."

John Syms added, "The Reverends Dunbar and

Allis have already established a mission, and they report great inroads with the Pawnee in the area. So if it is your intention to discourage our work—"

"How long since you heard from the good reverends?" Boothe interrupted.

There was the briefest hesitation. "It's been some time, but word travels slowly from the West."

Boothe nodded. "Could be because word travels slow. Could be because they're not there anymore."

One of the women made a soft sound of distress, and Martin glanced at Ben uneasily. Reverend Syms glared at Boothe. "The Pawnee are a peaceable people, it's well-known. They've never taken up arms against the white man."

"That's true," Boothe agreed. "But that don't mean they're not a warring tribe. In fact, you'd be hard put to catch them between wars. If they're not fighting the Kansa or the Omaha or the Sioux, it's somebody else; if they can't find a fight they make one."

Effie Creller looked at her husband anxiously. "That's not what we heard. Martin . . ."

But John Syms overrode her loudly. "We didn't hear it because it's either a falsehood or an unconscionable exaggeration. Of course the Indians have savage ways. That is why we were sent to reform them. There is goodness in all men, red and white, and all can be saved through God's grace."

Boothe looked into his coffee cup, then back down the table. He spoke quietly, matter-of-factly, and with no expression. "It seems a year or so back, some trapper friends of mine who were passing through Pawnee country came upon a camp where the Pawnee were keeping a Sioux squaw prisoner.

Well, she was a right comely thing, and my friends, they offered to buy her, but the chief wouldn't have none of it. The Pawnee were treating her real nice, honored in the tribe; she was well-fed, taken real good care of, and the trappers got the feeling she didn't much want to leave, either. Why should she?

"Then one day two big braves went and got the little squaw and took her over to a fire that was burning pretty good. They tied her up on a big spit and propped it over the fire and put burning slivers of bark under her armpits. And while she was screaming, the braves made a circle around her and shot arrows into her until God had mercy and she died. Then they cut down her body and cut the warm flesh into pieces, took those pieces out into the cornfield, and squeezed her blood over the newly planted corn."

There was a clatter at the other end of the table as Effie Creller pushed up and stumbled behind the wagon. In a moment they heard the sounds of soft retching.

No one spoke, and horror was as thick as smoke. Boothe looked at John Syms. "These are the people you want to make Christian farmers. To them corn is sacred, a gift from their eternal mother, and they've been living that way and believing that way for hundreds of years before the white man ever brought his brand of civilization to this country. Just how do you think you're going to change that?"

"You were not hired to frighten our women and cast shadows on our work," John Syms said coldly.

Boothe smiled a little and finished off his coffee.

"N'sir, that was for free. But mind, it's the last favor I'm doing you."

He started to stand up.

Syms continued in that same cold voice. "As a matter of fact, you haven't been hired yet at all. There are a few questions we would like to ask *you*, if you don't mind."

Boothe settled back, a bland, easy expression on his face. But his eyes were not warm. "I'll be glad to answer what I can. I reckon I owe you that much for your kind invitation, at any rate."

Kitty saw tension stiffen Ben's jaw, and he dropped his eyes. Dread felt cold in the pit of her stomach.

"Then tell us," Syms demanded, "why, the last time you undertook to guide such a party west, twelve people were left to die horribly in the mountains? Women and children and sick men, forced, some say, to consume the flesh of their dead in a faint, false hope of survival because *you* abandoned them?"

His voice didn't just thunder, it rang; it pierced like bullets shot from a rifle; it echoed. And when the last syllable died away and everyone at the table sat paralyzed in silence, a mild voice spoke up from behind Kitty.

"I'd be kinda interested in the answer to that myself."

Kitty twisted around. The man who spoke was not a member of the original party. He had a dark-haired girl with him, but she didn't look like she belonged to him. He was wearing the loose-fitting cotton pants and calico shirt of a native to these parts, his lower legs protected by buckskin leggings, a pistol stuck into his belt. His face was shadowed by a flat-crowned, wide-brimmed leather hat much like the one Kitty wore, and she couldn't see his eyes. But his voice was easy, and his face looked almost familiar.

"You see," he added, and stepped a little closer to the table, "my sister was one of them that died up there in the mountains."

And then Kitty knew who the man was. It was Oliver Sherrod.

Chapter Five

Kitty vaguely remembered Oliver from her childhood; she had been five when his family had moved across the Mississippi to Cape Girardeau. The Sherrods had been one of the families who crossed the wilderness with Katherine Carlyle all those years ago, and Kitty remembered the stories of how Oliver, only fifteen at the time, had been the only man on the trek until Byrd came along, of how they had fought off the Shawnee on the day Kitty was born, and how Oliver had saved them from river pirates while Katherine stole the boat that would take them all to safety. Katherine had never been very fond of Maude Sherrod—at least she never acted as though she was—but Kitty remembered she had cried on the day the Sherrods moved across the river to open a new trading post. And she never spoke of Oliver without a soft smile in her voice.

Maude Sherrod had died of fever five years ago, and her youngest daughter, Amy, remained behind with her husband to operate the trading post which was now a prosperous general store. When Kitty was growing up, she was sometimes allowed to go across the river with her pa to trade or shop at the store, and Oliver always used to tease her and slip her stick candy. Of course, that was a long, long time ago.

There had been another daughter, Judith, and she had died. Kitty knew the circumstances of that death all too well, and she couldn't help wondering whether Oliver, too, was remembering as he stood before Boothe.

Oliver had struck out on his own, and since then when her parents talked about him it had been in hushed, disappointed tones. Kitty got the impression he had done something bad, or a lot of bad things, or maybe he just hadn't lived up to the hopes her mother had for him. Nothing she saw now did anything to dispel that impression.

He had changed. He used to have quiet, friendly eyes; now they were hard and quick. He had always had a ready smile for a little girl, but now that smile seemed too ready, too easy, and there was no warmth behind it. All of Kitty's defensive instincts bristled, and she glanced quickly at Boothe.

Boothe's expression remained unchanged. He seemed neither surprised nor troubled by Oliver's appearance. He said simply, "Hello, Oliver."

Oliver took off his hat and nodded around the group, that same easy smile still in place. "Ladies," he said. "Gents. The name's Sherrod. Hope you don't mind me breaking in like this, but Miss Syms here was good enough to ask me to stop by."

John Syms glared and looked as though he didn't know whether to reprimand his daughter for consorting with strangers or to demand an explanation from the newcomer. All eyes were on Oliver, however, and eventually curiosity overcame his sense of discipline. Lucy looked peeved to have the attention so easily diverted from herself as John Syms turned back to Boothe.

"I asked a question, sir," he said sternly.

"And I'll be pleased to answer it."

Kitty wished at that moment to be anywhere else. She had never heard the story, not in its entirety, from Boothe's own lips. She hated these people for making him tell it. She hated herself for listening. But there was a part of her, a part she hated more even than John Syms's blunt, prying questions, that wouldn't have turned away even if she had been able to.

Boothe's eyes were steady, his expression unaffected. He said, "Two years ago a fella by the name of Sheldon Gerrard from St. Louis had himself a bright idea about bringing settlers into the Northwest Territory, staking himself out a big piece of land, and setting up a colony—farmers, miners, lumberjacks—taking what he could and shipping it back around the horn to the East. He'd heard the land was rich, and he wasn't far wrong at that. He had it figured so's to make himself a fortune.

"The only trouble was, he wasn't the only man with that idea, and it was his plan to get there before anybody else could stake the claim he had in mind. We left from St. Louis with fifteen families, all of them thinking about nothing but the piece of the dream that had been promised them. Sherrod's sister Judith and her husband, Michael, were two of those dreamers." He didn't look at Oliver. He just kept looking at John Syms.

"Like I said," he went on, "we left from St. Louis, and that was the first thing I was against. It was rough, crossing the Missouri with all those goods, and we lost some supplies. Put us almost a week behind by the time we restocked. We lost three men and a team on the plains. Still, coming into the mountains we should have had plenty of time before the first snow . . . but we didn't. An early blizzard penned us down. We were low on supplies. We tried to wait it out, but pretty soon I knew we weren't going to make it. The only chance we had was if somebody went back for supplies. So I started out of the mountains. Broke my leg, which put me behind some, and by the time I got back to them with men and supplies from the fort, there were only eight survivors. Gerrard was one, but even he came out of it minus a leg; gangrene. Oliver's sister Judith—she didn't come out at all. Neither did her husband."

All very simply spoken, very matter-of-fact. It had happened, it was over, it was done. Yet the silence that settled over the table was heavy with horror and cold with dread, as though an icy wind from the future had suddenly drifted downward to chill them all.

Boothe's gaze moved slowly around the table. "If you want me to tell you it couldn't happen again, I won't, because it could. This here is a dangerous trip you're set on, and there's no pretending it's not. You've got warring Mexicans to the south of you and Comanche to the west and Pawnee right where you're fixing to settle. It's coming on summer and there'll be storms the like of which you've never seen, lightning and thunder and water up over the wagons. We've got rivers to ford and creeks that run as strong as a river, and then out on the prairie there's the wind that never lets up, whining and blowing dust in your face—I've seen men go crazy from that wind. And if the wind don't get you, the emptiness will—nothing as far as the eye can see but grass and sky, a space so big you feel like you could fall right into it and be swallowed up. There's nobody to call for help out there if you get sick or hurt, no towns if you run out of flour, and no folks if you ladies get a hankering for somebody to talk to. It's a big land out there, big and beautiful, and a lot of folks've tried to claim a little piece of it for their own. But not many have made it."

The faces around the table were subdued and worried. Effie had returned, looking pale and strained, and she was kneeling by the cradle, stroking her sleeping infant's hair. Kitty knew what she was thinking. Kitty would never have tried to take a baby across the plains. Whatever had persuaded this woman to do so?

At last Martin Creller said quietly, "Are you suggesting we turn back?"

"I'm telling you that if you're bound to do it, you do it my way. And that means you fill your wagons with what supplies I tell you, you move when I tell you and where I tell you. And you carry guns. All of you."

His eyes went around the table one more time, but everyone else was looking at John Syms. Boothe stood up. "I reckon you could use a little time to talk about it. Let me know what you decide."

He walked over to his horse and Kitty rose immediately to join him. Ben stayed behind.

They took their horses and led them away from the camp to graze. Kitty's tone sounded a little muffled as she said, "Is it really going to be that bad?"

"Worse."

And then she saw on his face what he had kept so carefully concealed from the others throughout the calm recitation of his past. The pain of memory, dark and sharp-edged, clouded his eyes and tightened his mouth. Kitty hoped suddenly and intensely that the missionaries would decide not to go on. That they could all go home, safe where they belonged.

A voice spoke behind her. "I can't believe it, but it must be little Kitty, all grown up and pretty as a picture."

Kitty turned sharply to look at Oliver. He was grinning at her, his hat held loosely against his thigh, looking as though he expected her to be glad to see him. Maybe she would have been, despite the things she had heard about him—or, rather, *not* heard about him—if it hadn't been for what he'd said to Boothe. If she hadn't been so worried about what he was going to say or do now, and how much he held Boothe responsible for what had happened to his sister Judith in the mountains.

Boothe removed his horse's bridle, ignoring Oliver. Kitty demanded bluntly, "What are you doing here?"

Oliver nodded back toward the table. "Seemed like that was a private conversation."

"You know what I mean."

He looked over at Boothe, who was removing hobble strings from his pack. "I'm on my way to Utah Territory. Heard about your setting up this trip, and thought I'd ride along a spell."

Nothing in his manner or in the way he looked at Boothe did anything to dispel Kitty's suspicion. "What for?"

Oliver turned back to her. "How's your ma and pa?"

"Pa's dead," Kitty said tightly. Then she had to look away.

The silence was brief and shocked. "I'm sorry. I didn't know. Your ma?"

A lump was rising in Kitty's throat that felt like hot lead, but there was such genuine concern in Oliver's voice that she couldn't refuse to answer. "About like you'd expect. She's strong."

Oliver nodded soberly. "She always was."

Boothe finished hobbling his horse to graze and straightened up. He tossed a couple of the leather thongs to Kitty and she caught them, grateful for the chance to look busy.

Oliver spoke quietly to Boothe. "What happened to Kincaid?"

Boothe barely glanced up. "Zeke Calhoun. He showed up at Ben's wedding a few days back, guns blazing. We figure it was Katherine he was after, but three died. Four, counting him, in the end."

For a moment Oliver's heart tightened and he thought, *Katherine. Thank God, at least, it wasn't her.* Out loud he said, "Zeke Calhoun. That son of a bitch."

It had been seventeen years, but he remembered every second of his last encounter with the Calhouns as though it had been yesterday. Zeke Calhoun, his brothers and a band of thieving river pirates they'd hooked up with on the Ohio had tried to stop five women and a passel of kids from making their way out of the wilderness. Oliver had killed his first man in that battle for survival, and he hadn't regretted it a moment since. In fact, the only thing he regretted now was that they hadn't killed the last of the Calhouns that day, before Zeke had a chance to get away and bring grief to Katherine all these years later.

He spoke his thoughts out loud. "We should've killed the bastard when we had the chance."

Kitty's voice sounded strange and choked. "If you had, then it all would have been different . . ."

"We can't go back and change the past, Oliver," Boothe said curtly, looking at the other man. "You know that as well as I do."

Oliver said nothing. They all knew Boothe wasn't talking about an incident seventeen years ago, but one much more recent. The time when Oliver had lost his sister, and Boothe had lost everything.

"Somehow I get the feeling you just didn't happen by on your way west," Boothe went on quietly.

Oliver walked over to Boothe, painting that easy smile across his face again. "Lots of folks happen by here on the way west. This little mud hole is getting to be a right popular place. Never know who you'll run across."

Tiredly, Boothe said, "You got something to say to me, boy, you say it and be done. I'm not much of a man for playing games."

"No," Oliver murmured. "You're not."

Kitty took a stake from her bedroll and found a flat rock with which to pound it into the ground. She looped one end of the hobble string around her mount's back leg, and the other around the stake, then she slipped off the bridle, stroking the horse's forelock and murmuring to it all the time.

But she never took her eyes off Boothe and Oliver.

The two men faced each other, each of them easy in his stance and mild in his face. But their gazes were alert and their muscles tense. Kitty could see that from where she stood.

Oliver squinted into the sun as he looked over Boothe's shoulder. "If I told you I didn't hold you to blame for losing Judith, I reckon you'd know I was lying. But what's done is done, and no amount of blame casting is going to bring my sister, or any of them others, back out of their graves. No matter what I think of you, you know the trail west, and if you need an extra gun, you've got one."

Boothe looked at him for a long time. "How do I know that gun won't be pointed at me?"

Oliver just smiled. "Looks to me like you've got bigger things to worry about than that." He nodded toward the table. "With that bunch under your feet, you're gonna need all the help you can get."

Only later did Kitty realize he hadn't answered Boothe's question. But she supposed Boothe knew it all along.

At the table Effie touched her husband's arm anxiously. "Maybe he's right, Martin." She glanced uneasily toward the cradle, where the baby still slept in the shade of the wagon. "Maybe we should turn back."

"Effie Creller," Rachel put in sharply, "we knew this wasn't going to be a Sunday social when we started out."

Her husband responded firmly, "We didn't come all this way to turn back now." He spared his wife a sympathetic glance. "Men like that," he said more gently, "they enjoy scaring folks. Makes them feel bigger somehow. I wouldn't worry about it."

Richard spoke up shyly from the end of the table. "Maybe—maybe we could find someone else to guide us."

Everyone else ignored him; Richard was the kind of man folks naturally ignored without meaning to or even thinking about it. But Lucy spoke up eagerly. "What about Mr. Sherrod? He said he knew the country."

Her father glared at her. "This is no business for you, Lucy. Get to the wagon and tie up your hair. You look like a hussy, strutting around here like that."

Sulking, Lucy went to the wagon and made as much noise as possible, clattering around inside. But John Syms had more important things on his mind, and he turned to Ben. "What about this Sherrod fellow? Do you know anything about him?"

"He might know the country," Ben answered carefully, "but he doesn't know a thing about where we're headed. Not many men do, other than what they've heard from folks like Boothe Carlyle."

"He's a danger and an abomination," mumbled Syms.

"He's all we've got," Martin pointed out.

"He wants us to carry guns," Rachel said nervously. "John, we never counted on—"

He silenced her with a look. "We don't take orders from the likes of him."

"Yes, sir," Ben said quietly. "If you want Boothe Carlyle to guide you, I'm afraid you do."

Nobody answered that.

After a long time Martin said, "We've got to do something. If we wait much longer, we'll be stuck here until next spring."

Ben got up from the table and went over to his horse, where he removed a rifle from the scabbard. He turned to face them, the rifle cradled beneath his arm. "You know my vote. I'm going on. And I go armed."

He walked over to where Boothe, Kitty, and Oliver stood. At Boothe's mildly questioning look, he just shook his head.

Boothe reached down and plucked a stem of tall grass. "Reckon we can camp here tonight. Mosquitoes shouldn't be too bad, this far back from the river." He glanced at Oliver. "Old Rocky still frying up them biscuits of his in town?"

Oliver nodded, grinning. "Only place for twenty miles you can get a decent meal—if you don't mind picking the soot out of your side meat, that is. Ought to take the young folks in tonight; bet they've got a hankering for home cooking after a spell of trail chow."

Kitty couldn't believe it. They were talking like old friends. They were talking about biscuits and side meat while their fates were held in the hands of strangers. Stupid, sallow-faced strangers who had no more business setting off into the wilderness than . . . than she did. *Let them say no,* she prayed silently. *Let them pack up their organ and their crazy, self-righteous notions and go back home. Let* me *go home.*

John Syms got up and came over to them, walking as straight as an arrow and looking as black as Satan. He stood before Boothe, stared him straight in the eye, and said, "We have decided to engage your services, on the terms and pay Ben has already discussed with you. Tomorrow morning we'll purchase rifles along with the other supplies

you suggested." He looked as though he could have
choked on the words. "But," he added sternly, "we
will not use those rifles against our fellow man, and
you should understand that from the outset."

"You'd be surprised what you'll do when your
fellow man's got you pinned against a rock with an
arrow pointed at your throat," Boothe said mildly.
"Meantime, I'll be careful not to waste my ammunition defending you."

John Syms swallowed hard, contracting his enormous Adam's apple. He jerked his head toward
Kitty. "I suggest you make some arrangements to
send the girl home. Our contract with the church
specifically excluded unmarried women."

Kitty felt her cheeks flame and she wanted to
ask about the dark-haired girl she'd first seen with
Oliver, but Boothe didn't give her a chance. "The
girl stays with me," he said. He started to walk away,
as though the discussion was ended.

"This is not your expedition, sir," John Syms
said loudly. "It's mine! I say who will and will
not go—"

"And while we're on the subject . . ." Boothe
jerked his head toward Oliver, not breaking his
stride on his way to unsaddle his horse. "Sherrod'll
be coming along too."

A dark, ugly color began to creep up John Syms's
face. "This is outrageous! I refuse to authorize—"

Boothe looked at him. "And if you was a smart
man, you'd keep your mouth shut and be grateful
to have both of them along."

He didn't raise his voice; he didn't have to.
He just held Syms's eyes and spoke to him as he
would to someone with good sense. "There's safety
in numbers, Reverend, and neither one of these

two is afraid to load a rifle and point it at a target. But then, it comes to me that maybe you're not a very smart man because you seem to be having a little trouble understanding one thing. On this trip, I'm in charge. It's my job to get you from here to Pawnee country alive and in one piece, and I'll do whatever I have to to get that job done. So for the next three months the chain of command goes like this: There's me, and then there's God. And until I hear the voice coming from the burning bush with my own ears, there's just me."

The Reverend Syms looked as if he didn't know whether to choke or spit. Then he turned abruptly on his heel and walked away. Ben watched him go, looking unhappy, but said nothing.

Boothe turned back to his horse. "Come on, Kitten, let's get these animals taken care of. Sunup comes early, and the day's not half done yet."

After a moment, Kitty went to unsaddle her own horse, and to help Ben with his. She knew she should have been glad the matter had been resolved so easily and proud that Boothe had fought to have her stay, but she wasn't. The wide fields of waving grass didn't look nearly as appealing as they had an hour ago, and home seemed very far away.

Kitty built her own cookfire that night, away from the others, despite the fact that the nice Mrs. Creller made an effort to walk over and tell Kitty she was welcome to add her provisions to theirs and join them at the table. Kitty thanked her kindly but tended her own fire—and her own men. Mrs. Creller was pleasant enough, but Kitty knew she couldn't swallow another bite at Reverend Syms's table. Besides, tending camp made Kitty feel useful, with a reason for being there.

She didn't expect Oliver to join them; he was too busy being charming to the other side of the camp—to the dark-haired girl named Lucy in particular. Kitty was surprised, though, that Ben stayed to eat with her and Boothe. She would have expected him to cast his allegiance with those he had come to serve.

The dying day left a purplish, star-studded twilight behind. Ben and Boothe sat by the fire to oil their saddles and talk about the route, and after a while Oliver stopped by. Kitty went to check on the horses. It wasn't the first time she had felt more comfortable with animals than with people. In fact, with very few exceptions, animals had always been better company than most people Kitty knew.

The horses snorted and shuffled forward when they heard her coming, and Kitty paused beside each one, greeting it with her hands and her voice. But her eyes were on the campfire and those who were gathered around it in some kind of peculiar male communion that was incomprehensible to anyone but the participants. Ben, who had stuck by Boothe's side when everyone else turned against him, even though Kitty knew in her heart that he didn't want to go on; he hadn't even wanted to come this far. Oliver, whose perfectly timed appearance seemed a little more than coincidence to Kitty and whom Boothe knew shouldn't be trusted . . . but he was trusting him anyway. And Boothe . . . Boothe. She didn't know what to think about him anymore, and that hurt her, disturbed her, more than anything.

"He's good-looking, isn't he?"

Kitty turned to see the dark-haired girl—Lucy—standing beside her. Her hands were clasped behind her back, her head tilted at a jaunty angle, and she was watching the campfire. Because Kitty didn't know which one of the three men she was referring to, she didn't answer. She couldn't imagine why the girl would say such a thing anyway, or what difference it made.

Then Lucy's eyes narrowed. "I found him first," she said sharply. "So you just keep your distance."

Oliver, Kitty thought, with a mixture of surprise and resignation. The girl was even stranger than she had thought at first. She shrugged. "Don't worry."

Lucy seemed to relax a little, and she circled Kitty once, looking her over with a speculative, slightly impish look in her eyes. Kitty ignored her, turning back to the horses.

Then Lucy demanded abruptly, "Are you a'scert of Indians?"

Kitty swallowed hard and soothed Ben's gelding with firm strokes across its withers. The horse was becoming nervous at the sound of the other girl's voice. "We won't be seeing Indians for a long time yet."

"Oh, yes, we will," Lucy replied smugly. "Shawnee. The mission's not more than a day's travel from here, and we're riding up to them. Making camp right in the midst of 'em. That's what Pa said. His friend Reverend Lykes is in charge there. You know what else Pa says? He says that civilized or no, an Indian is still an Indian and all the women have to stay in the wagons. What do you think they'd do to us if they caught us away from our menfolk?"

She sounded more excited than worried, but the last part of Lucy's speech all but washed over Kitty. The cold lump that had formed beneath her breastbone when Lucy first said the word "Shawnee" was spreading now, and had already reached her fingertips. She turned slowly.

"The Shawnee?" She tried to keep her voice steady. "We're going there?"

Lucy's nod seemed to hold equal parts enthusiasm and malice. "They smell, you know," she informed Kitty. "Pa says it comes from eating raw flesh. Even *human* flesh."

Kitty turned abruptly and walked away.

She moved into the shadows, away from the campfire, away from the sounds the others made. The baby was crying, and dishes were clattering as someone did the washing-up in a gallon bucket they had filled from the river. The voices of the men were low and sporadic. The prairie was dotted with other campfires, some distant, some close, and the spots of light looked like fireflies caught in a big black bowl. Fragile, vulnerable, lost.

Kitty's fingers absently worried the scar on her shoulder. She wasn't afraid. She knew Indians didn't eat human flesh . . . at least, not the Indians in this part of the country. But they had killed her birth mother. They had almost killed Kitty. And then they had stolen her away when she was just a little baby and couldn't defend herself. They had stolen her like a pack of wolves might steal a haunch of meat, and if it hadn't been for Uncle Boothe . . .

She started as she heard a step behind her. Boothe stood beside her and for a moment didn't say anything.

She blurted out, "That girl—Lucy—says we're going to the Shawnee."

He nodded. "That's right. Them missionaries, they think they ought to have a good look at how this civilizing is done." There was a slight note of bitterness to his voice as he added, "Might not hurt them much at that, to see the difference between talking and doing."

Involuntarily, Kitty shivered.

A new alertness came into Boothe's voice. "Bothers you some, does it, girl?"

There was no point in lying to him. "I can't help it," she replied in a low, muffled voice. "All my life I've heard about the Shawnee and what they did, and sometimes I have bad dreams . . . I know it's silly, but sometimes it's almost like I can remember them."

Boothe was thoughtful, taking her seriously as he always did. "Maybe you can," he said after a moment. "But I wouldn't wonder at what your remembering has been shaded some by the stories we've all told you. Sometimes it's a smart thing to be a little bit scared of what you don't know, but the only way to get shed of that fear is to see the fearsome thing up close. And I reckon that's another good reason to make camp with the Shawnee."

Kitty supposed he was right; no one knew more about Indians than Boothe did, except perhaps her pa. Now there was just Boothe. She wanted to feel more confident, but she didn't.

Someone started playing the organ. "Amazing Grace." The notes were eerie as they drifted across the prairie, haunting and out of place.

After a time Boothe said, "Something else is eating at you, Kitten. More than just the Shawnee."

Kitty cast around in her mind for a single answer. So many things were wrong, so many things frightened her, how could she pick just one? She spotted Oliver, leaning back on one elbow in the flickering light of the fire, grinning at someone across the way. She didn't have to guess who it was. Lucy.

"I wish I knew more about Oliver," she said. "Ma and Pa used to worry about him and now . . . well, he worries me too."

"A man's past is his own business," Boothe replied.

She wanted to argue with that, but it didn't seem right. Boothe knew what was best, he always had, and she was used to trusting him. The fact that she would even consider questioning him now was perhaps what bothered her most of all.

And he knew it. He must have, or else he would not have prompted, gently, "What else? Something's on your mind; let's have it all."

She wanted to stay silent; she wanted to respond that it was nothing. But she thought about this afternoon, when he had almost left all those missionaries behind to fend for themselves across the plains. She thought about the night before they left Cairo, when she had seen him so broken and alone . . . and she didn't want to, but she couldn't help it, she thought about the twelve people who had died in the mountains without him.

She couldn't look at him, and her voice was very low and strained as she said, "Sometimes . . . I think I don't know you at all."

Boothe was silent for a long time. When he spoke, it was almost like not saying anything at all. "We've got a full day ahead tomorrow. Best turn in."

Kitty was left standing alone in the dark, and the prairie seemed bigger and emptier than anything she had ever known.

Oliver stood well away from even the flickering campfires of the others, smoking his pipe and looking out over the prairie. He too was thinking about the Shawnee, letting his mind roll back seventeen years to the fierce band of painted Indians who had attacked the small group of women and children in the wilderness. He had sighted the murderous savages with his rifle, he'd heard the screams of the women begging him to shoot, he'd seen Byrd Kincaid fall beneath their arrows . . . and he had been unable to shoot. That had been his first test of manhood; his first failure. Even after all these years, the shame burned within him.

He'd been twenty when he and his mother and two sisters left Cairo for Cape Girardeau across the river. He'd had mixed feelings about leaving Cairo. He had wanted to stay near Katherine, but seeing her married to Byrd Kincaid was torment. Oliver had loved her since he was fifteen, though he had always known he never had a chance with her. Byrd was the better man, and always had been. Byrd Kincaid, along with Boothe Carlyle, had been the epitome of all Oliver was not: heroes of their time, strong, steadfast, unerring. Byrd deserved to win the hand of Katherine Carlyle; Oliver did not.

Yet leaving Cairo was a fresh start for Oliver, a second chance to be the kind of man who counted for something in this country. It had been his idea to take the first load of trade goods from the family mercantile store down the Santa Fe trail, and it had been a good plan. He'd loaded the wagons with those rare materials pioneers never had enough of: windowpanes, glass bottles, mirrors, tacks, nails, butcher knives, axes, thread, calico, and needles.

The Santa Fe trail was safe—most of the time. The traders from Missouri, who opened it up, had learned there was safety in numbers, and since 1824 two hundred or so men with at least a hundred wagons had undertaken the trek each year. The eight-hundred-mile-long trail began in Independence, Missouri, and cut southwest, through a corner of the Flint Hills. The trail meandered farther south and hugged the bends of the Arkansas River for a while, then turned abruptly toward New Mexico across a bad patch known as the Cimarron Desert. That fifty miles was the roughest part, Oliver thought. He wasn't used to such heat, or to the dust and the dryness that made it hard to catch a breath. He'd grown up where it was green and moist, and after the first twenty miles of travel with the slow-moving ox-drawn wagon train, Oliver was praying aloud for rain. That was when an oldtimer told him what it was like when the rains came and flash floods washed away wagons and men, and turned the desert to a knee-deep mire of mud.

The sun, the winds, the heat, and the rains were more of an enemy than the Indians, Oliver learned. The Kiowa had made an agreement with the soldiers not to attack the train, and the Osage and the Kansa had been paid off, too. Now and then the train was accompanied by a guard of soldiers from Fort Leavenworth, but that was merely a show of force. The only Indians the travelers really had to fear were the Comanche, and they were usually busy harassing the settlers moving into Texas.

Oliver arrived in Santa Fe, his hands callused and hardened from handling the ox team and his face sunburned despite his broad-brimmed hat. He was bone-weary, but feeling very much a man among men.

At the end of the trail he'd sold the wagon and oxen and traded for New Mexican blankets, turquoise jewelry, silver, and even some gold dust, then returned to Cape Girardeau with a team of the famous Mexican mules known in the States as "Missouri mules." He'd made a handsome profit.

Even his mother had praised him for his success; his simple idea had turned out to be better than anyone could have imagined. He returned home with pockets bulging and a head full of adventures of his own, feeling every bit as heroic as Boothe Carlyle had ever been. He'd made the trip for five years and it had been more successful each time. He was no longer just a merchant; he was a trailblazer.

But perhaps that new image of himself had been more dangerous than being jealous of Boothe and Byrd. Maybe it made him cocky, because when trouble came he wasn't prepared for it. In fact, looking back, he could see he had brought it on himself.

There had been a woman and a fight. Oliver liked to think it had been a fair fight, but he knew it wasn't. The other man had ended up dead and Oliver had ended up on the run. Another mistake, another failure, and nothing had been the same since then.

When a man was on the run, the only ones he felt safe with were his own kind. Thieves, murderers, schemers, liars, and cheaters . . . Oliver had known them all, learned their tricks, played their games. He had learned a lot he wished he had never needed to know, done things—more than a few— he wished he hadn't had to do. He had regrets, but he had survived.

He hadn't even been able to get back to Cape Girardeau for his mother's funeral five years ago. Years later, when he'd finally learned of her death, he'd returned home to find only his sister Amy and her husband. He had visited his mother's grave, but there had been no grave for his other sister, Judith. Judith and her husband, Michael, lay in an unmarked grave on the trail to Oregon.

He heard the story of what had happened from Amy. Boothe Carlyle had come to Cape Girardeau with grand plans for an expedition to Oregon and news of the big financier named Sheldon Gerrard who was sponsoring it. Judith and Michael had immediately caught the flame of excitement, and who wouldn't have? If Oliver had been there, he, too, might have signed on with Boothe. And that was what angered him the most. He might have done the same thing.

Amy had tried to talk Judith out of the trip, but neither Judith nor Michael was to be dissuaded. "But it's Boothe," Judith kept saying over and over again. "Boothe wouldn't take us if there was any danger. If we can't trust Boothe . . . "

They had trusted him. And he had killed them.

For a long time Oliver had blamed himself for not being there to stop Judith. But now, as he stood smoking in the dark, alone with the prairie and his own black thoughts, he realized he blamed himself for more than that. If he had been there, he would have advised Judith to do just what she had done, to follow her dream, to trust Boothe . . . Because in Oliver's eyes, Boothe had always been infallible. Because of Boothe, and men like him, Oliver had spent a lifetime trying to be what he was not: a hero.

Now Oliver knew Boothe Carlyle was not a hero, and he never had been. It was too bad Oliver hadn't realized that until it was too late.

Chapter Six

Two days later, the small calvacade rolled out of Westport, Missouri, crossing into Indian Territory and an uncertain future. The draft horses had been traded for teams of sturdy, plodding oxen and each wagon had two more rifles in its store of supplies. But neither the organ nor the table was left behind. Boothe frowned darkly but did not waste time repeating what would clearly go unheard. Ben ended up driving a fourth wagon, into which many of the mission's supplies had been transferred in order to lighten the load on the oxen. By that time the missionaries' funds were almost depleted, but it was the only compromise they were willing to make.

The pace was slow, barely ten miles a day, and Boothe promised it would get even slower once they reached the heart of the sun-drenched plains where the grass was sparser and dehydration was a constant concern. For a while, they could follow the Santa Fe trail laid out earlier in the century by caravans of traders, but soon it would dip south along the Arkansas River toward New Mexico, far away from their destination. Their wagon train would proceed west, following another old trail for a while, one laid out by Zebulon Pike in 1806 when he explored the West. He'd crossed the Kaw River into northern Kansas, but few followed that route now. For years, trappers and traders had gone north, up the Missouri River toward Canada, like Lewis and Clark in 1804. The few settlers who braved the trip to Oregon Territory started that way, too, and then turned west along the Platte toward the mountains. The middle course, through the heart of Kansas Territory, was rarely used except by buffalo hunters and a few foolish bands of missionaries—like themselves.

They had had a dawn start and only a brief midday rest to water the oxen, but even then, the sun was setting when the Baptist Shawnee mission finally came into view. Kitty barely knew when they arrived. It looked like any number of other small towns they had passed on their way to Westport: small wooden houses, rows of tilled fields, washtubs simmering over outdoor fires, neatly planted orchards, and livestock grazing in corrals.

Gone were the visions of fierce red-skinned warriors in colorful turbans and painted faces. The men and women she saw wore calico and homespun, just as she did; they stared at her with the same curiosity with which she regarded them, and though some of them still wore faded turbans around their heads, for the most part their straw hats and leather boots were just like those of any other farmer up and down the river. The knot of fear that had been eating away at Kitty's stomach since she had first learned of their destination slowly resolved itself into something like disappointment.

After the War of 1812, as settlers moved west, there was the inevitable clash with the Indians as the white man took, by force if necessary, more and more land which the red men had always considered theirs. Some tribes, like the Sac and Fox of Illinois, were decimated, their numbers destroyed by the onward movement of the settlers. Only a few members of those tribes managed to flee west and hide across the Mississippi.

The politicians in Washington decided that other tribes would be moved across the Mississippi and given land of their own. Hardly had the war ended when the government hatched its plan to move the Five Civilized Tribes—the Cherokee, Creek, Chickasaw, Choctaw, and Seminole—to Indian Territory in the West. Some went more willingly than others; the Cherokee refused to move at all and quickly declared themselves a republic, saying that their removal from their territorial lands was unlawful. Vainly they fought in court—and lost. Under armed guard, caravans of Cherokee Indians set out westward from their homes in North Carolina and Georgia on the Trail of Tears, so called because so many died of maltreatment and illness along the way. The Seminoles stayed in Florida, resisting and fighting their removal until their numbers, too, were decimated by their battles with the soliders.

The Shawnee were herded west, also. Some bolted and fled to Texas, but most of them ended up on the edge of Kansas Territory, in the newly established missions, where their white

friends were determined to turn them into gentlemen farmers.

The travelers pulled their wagons into a wide
field beside a whitewashed house with a railed
fence. Next to the house was a church with a
wooden steeple, and some other, smaller buildings
scattered about that might have been stores or even
a schoolhouse.

The door of the little white house opened and
a plump woman with a careworn face came out,
followed closely by an equally plump man in a
frayed and none-too-clean frock coat. The woman wiped her hands on her apron and squinted
into the setting sun, then raised her hand in a
greeting and rushed forward to meet the newcomers.

Kitty hung back as embraces were exchanged
among the women and much fuss was made over
the baby. Invitations were offered and accepted
for them all to take supper inside the house. It
looked as though the women were not going to
have to be sequestered inside the wagons after
all, and Kitty couldn't help wondering whether
the missionaries were as surprised as she was at
what an Indian settlement really looked like.

All of her fears had come to nothing. She would
make camp for Boothe, just as she always did.
The others would eat inside and talk about printing presses and sermons, and tomorrow morning
they would be on their way. There were no savages here.

Then she felt Boothe's hand on her arm, and
he led her forward. "Reverend Lykes," he said.

A certain wariness came into the plump man's
eyes as he regarded Boothe. "Mr. Carlyle. I'd heard

you'd undertaken to guide these good people on their way."

"This is my niece, Kitty Kincaid," Boothe said. "We've got some old friends to pay our respects to while we're here."

Kitty was aware of the questioning glances that were directed at her, and she shrank from them. She had no friends here. She didn't want to pay her respects to anyone.

"I was hoping you might have heard something from White Feather," Boothe went on.

Reverend Lykes managed to look both sour and sorrowful. "Then your hopes are in vain, sir." He directed the rest of his comments to Reverend Syms. "Our efforts here have not been one hundred percent successful. Some of the Shawnee, as you'll see as you walk through the village, still refuse to sleep under a roof. Others refuse to be rehabilitated at all. White Feather is one of those. He left the reservation five years ago and has gone completely renegade. I understand he has a band of followers with him now, and they spend their sorry lives bringing death to any white man who happens to wander into their territory. I should be careful, if I were you."

He turned back to Boothe. "It only goes to show that no matter how well you think you know an Indian, you never know his mind."

Boothe did not respond to that.

After a moment Mrs. Lykes spoke up, a little hesitantly. "Won't you and your niece join us for supper, Mr. Carlyle?"

Boothe tipped his hat to her. "Thank you, ma'am, but, like I said, we've got folks we need to see."

"But surely the child is tired—"

Boothe must have sensed that Kitty was about to speak up for herself and gratefully agree to share supper at the missionaries' table—a prospect that, under other circumstances, would have been her last choice—because he touched her arm again and repeated firmly, "Thank you, ma'am. Another time." And he guided Kitty away.

Had she had her preference, Kitty would have stayed with the wagon, made camp, and minded her own business. The dusty little village disturbed her. The sight of once-proud Indian braves with their backs bent to the plow made her sad, and the women . . . they all looked old. None of it was the way it was supposed to be.

After a moment Boothe inquired conversationally, "What do you think, Kitten, about a man needing rehabilitatin' just because he won't sleep under a roof?"

A group of boys were playing with a rag ball in front of a cabin. They scurried inside when she looked at them. "I think it's wrong," she replied unhappily. "It all seems—so wrong."

"I guess you won't be having any more bad dreams," Boothe replied.

Kitty suspected he was right. But there was a part of her that was going to miss those dreams.

The farther they walked from the main village, the more sterile and desolate the community became. All the houses were the same, small whitewashed cabins separated from their neighbors by a series of split-log fences. Once, a dog barked halfheartedly from the shade of a spindly cottonwood tree, but it soon stopped, as if exhausted by the effort. Chickens scratched behind one of the houses, but there was no other sign of life. Everything was neat and orderly and unnaturally still. Kitty felt an involuntary prickle down her spine at the oppressive atmosphere, as if all the lifeblood had been drained away.

"Not so many years ago," Boothe said, "the Shawnee were a rich tribe. They dyed their cloth and mixed their paints with ground-up stones—stones you and I would pay a pretty penny for today. The squaws would spend all winter tanning a hide and working it with beads, or weaving a blanket to tell a story, and when it was done it was a thing of magic, like nothing you ever did see. That's how you tell a rich tribe, you know, Kitten, because they have time to spend on fancy work like carving stones and weaving cloth. They don't have to worry about hunting or planting because they've got plenty laid by. The braves decorated themselves with colored feathers and wore necklaces made of amethysts and onyx and beaten copper. But they didn't value them like we do, because they're fine to look at and hard to come by, but because they were a gift from mother earth, and they meant strength, and purity, and good hunting. They were rich because they knew the language of the land.

"They learned the lessons of the fox and the weasel, and they hunted by imitating the animals that were born to the woods. They watched the fish and the birds, and knew when a bad winter was coming or an early spring. They made their homes in the hills and the hollows, and ate what grew on the trees. They were bred to the woods, and they were kings in their own land."

He made a gesture around him. "Look at this. There aren't any trees. There isn't any game to be hunted. There aren't any hills for shelter. What are they supposed to do here? They aren't kings anymore. There's nothing to be king *of*."

Kitty tried to understand what Boothe was saying. "But they have a place to sleep and crops to eat—" she began.

Boothe shook his head in disgust. "Fields and orchards and fences. Fences," he repeated. "Don't these blamed fool do-gooders know fences started the Shawnee fighting the white man to begin with? The Shawnee are wanderers. Wandered all the way from the Carolinas 'cross the Tennessee to Ohio. And then the settlers started putting up their fences and cutting off their trails, and the Shawnee fought for their right to wander. And now look—" He waved an arm angrily. "All fenced in."

Kitty was confused. What seemed good wasn't; what appeared to be right was all wrong. She wanted to talk to Boothe, to ask him more, but he took her arm and led her up a path to a cabin at the edge of the road.

Boothe lifted the moth-eaten blanket that served as a door. The blanket was heavy with dirt, and when he moved it a cloud of dust tickled Kitty's nose. "Mirawah," he called softly.

Kitty smelled something cooking inside, and when she looked in, a broad woman was bending over an iron pot set on a stick fire in the middle of the room. Without looking around, she said, "Firebird."

And then she turned, and her dark, wrinkled face was wreathed with a smile. "You've come."

Boothe touched Kitty's arm, urging her to step forward. When they were inside and the blanket had fallen again, the room was completely dark except for the orange light of the fire. The air was smokey and hard to breathe, and it was very hot inside.

"I've brought her back to you," Boothe said quietly, "just like I promised."

The woman's smile faded as she looked from Boothe to Kitty. Kitty's heart started beating with an uncomfortable rhythm under the stranger's scrutiny, for in the dim light she couldn't tell whether those dark eyes were angry, curious, despising, or sad. She couldn't, in fact, tell very much at all about the other woman except that her face was broad and square, like the rest of her body, her skin sun-dark and leathery. Her black hair was severely parted in the middle and plaited into two long strands down her back, and she was wearing a cotton skirt and a faded red shirt.

And then the woman walked forward and lifted her hand. Before Kitty knew what was happening, she had grabbed Kitty's shirt at the shoulder and pulled it down. The top two buttons popped, and Kitty gave a smothered cry of indignation and alarm. But when she twisted around for Boothe, he was no longer there.

Kitty backed away, fumbling with her disarranged shirt, truly frightened now. But there was a strange softness on the woman's face, and she was looking at the scar on Kitty's exposed shoulder. "My spirit child," she said. "You have come back."

Kitty pulled her blouse together and took another backward step toward the door. The woman smiled. "You don't know me, but your heart remembers. They would call you my milk child. But to me you will always be my spirit child."

And suddenly Kitty understood. She stopped backing away. "You—you're the one who took care of me, when . . ."

"You were starving," she replied simply, "and my breasts were filled with milk. The Great Mother had taken my own suckling son only two suns before they brought you to me. But what She gives, She also returns. I gave you life, and you—gave me life."

The faraway expression on her face faded. "They call me Mary now. It is my Christian name. What are you called?"

"Kitty," she managed after a moment.

The woman frowned. "And what means Kitty?"

Kitty hesitated. "Little cat."

"Ah." Her expression cleared into a smile. "It is good. Little cat. You were too small for naming when I knew you, but in my heart you were known as Warrior Woman."

Warrior Woman. Kitty repeated the words to herself, testing the syllables. Warrior Woman.

The woman turned back to the fire. "Come. Sit. I have a good rabbit in this pot, make a fine stew."

Kitty slipped her hand into her pocket and felt the reassuring weight of Katherine's coin. She moved into the room.

She sat on a hard, backless bench with one crooked leg and ate rabbit stew from a wooden bowl. The rabbit was stringy and the broth tasteless, but she didn't mind. After a time she said, "Why Warrior Woman?"

"You were wounded in battle before you were born," replied Mary around a mouthful of stew. Her back teeth were rotten or missing, Kitty had noticed, and it was difficult for her to chew. "What else should you be called?"

She tore off a piece of hard bread from the round near the fire and soaked it in broth. "Every name has its own power, its own spirit. Just as each rock and tree, and fish that swims and bird that flies, has its spirit."

Kitty understood that. She wasn't sure how she knew, but it seemed natural to her. Perhaps because so much of her heritage had been passed down from Gran Fiona, who had taught her grandchildren, Boothe and Katherine, to treasure the worth of all things. And those grandchildren had taught Kitty.

"The spirit that comes to you with your naming stays for all your life," Mary went on. "You were lucky. Your spirit came before you were born." Her eyes twinkled. "The cat is a great warrior, you know. Even little cats. So you have two spirits, and they are the same."

Kitty tried to smile, but shook her head. "I don't think I'll ever be a warrior."

"Not every warrior fights with spears and arrows," Mary replied gently. "And you, Little Cat, have weapons of your own."

Mary touched a finger to her head. "Here . . ." She touched her breast, over her heart. "And here."

She opened her hand to Kitty, and after a moment, Kitty extended her own hand to her. Mary took her palm in her plump, work-roughened fingers, and turned it upward. "Strong hands," she said. "Healing hands. With these hands you can speak to the creatures of the forest, and take the pain from those who are hurting." She raised her eyes to Kitty. "You will give life to those you love, just as I once gave life to you. There is no other way."

A little self-consciously, Kitty withdrew her hand. "I—I was afraid to come here," she confessed.

"Why did you come?"

"I don't know," Kitty admitted. "I don't know why I ever left my home, or what I'm doing on this trip, or what will happen to me when we get where we're going. Nobody wants me here. There's no reason for me to be here. I don't know why I came at all."

Mary smiled and moved close to Kitty, laying her hand lightly upon Kitty's cheek. "Soon," she said, "you will know."

And looking into the other woman's gentle dark eyes, Kitty thought that perhaps she already did.

Effie Creller didn't know what to make of any of it. It was hard to love a man with a dream, and from the beginning, this trip west had frightened her, though she tried hard not to let Martin know. She had grown up the daughter of a farmer in a comfortable white house, with four brothers and sisters; she had expected to be the wife of a farmer and spend her life in the fertile Tennessee Valley raising children and crops. But then there was Martin, with his passionate dark eyes and a calling that was grander than any of her small needs, and there had never been a question about following him into the wilderness.

She believed that every human being had the right to know the word of God. She believed that every man, woman, and child had the right to clothing and shelter and all the food they could take from the ground. She believed that all had the right to read the Bible and enjoy the enlightened freedom of American justice, and she believed her husband's calling to civilize the savages was right and noble.

But these Indians did not seem civilized to her. They seemed broken.

After a supper of fried pork, cornbread, and new peas and potatoes, they all sat in front of the fire while Rebecca, Mrs. Lykes's Indian girl, cleaned the table. Effie had started to help, but a frown and a small shake of the head from Mrs. Lykes had stopped her, so she had taken the baby into the small back room to nurse. When she returned, Rachel and Mrs. Lykes had taken out sewing, and the men sat on the other side of the room, drinking coffee from chipped porcelain cups and talking.

"The trouble with the Indians here," Reverend Lykes was explaining earnestly, "is that they don't appreciate what we're trying to do for them. They just won't give up their old ways."

Effie laid the baby on a pallet she had made for him before the fire, glancing uncomfortably at the Indian girl Rebecca. But if the girl had heard what Reverend Lykes said, she gave no indication. Her face was stoic and impassive as she carried the big washpan of dishwater toward the door.

"Don't pour that on the walk, Rebecca," Mrs. Lykes called. "Go around back." She gave a small shake of her head as she returned to her sewing. "She's been working here for two years and I have to remind her every night. Indians can be very stubborn."

Effie sat beside Mrs. Lykes on the wooden settee and wished she had brought some sewing of her own. Lacking that, she picked up a torn shirt from Mrs. Lykes's basket and found a needle and thread in the pin holder. The other woman smiled at her.

"Stubborn," repeated Reverend Lykes. "And sometimes lazy. We have to stay after them every minute just to make sure they get their own crops in on time. Time, it means nothing to an Indian. They just can't connect starving in the winter with planting in the spring. Back east in the forests they planted in the summer and hunted in the winter, but it's not the same here. They've got to understand that."

The girl Rebecca came back in, and Effie couldn't stay silent any longer. "I don't understand how they can be lazy and have fought the kind of wars they did back east." Everyone stared at her, and she blundered on. "After all, they survived all these hundreds of years before we came to help them, so they must have known something about preparing for the winter."

"I don't think you understand, Effie," Martin said stiffly.

Reverend Lykes only smiled benignly. "They were defeated in those wars, Mrs. Creller. That's why the United States government sent them packing across the Mississippi to Indian Territory."

Effie had embarrassed Martin, and she was sorry. She hadn't meant to cause a scene, but hadn't he always told her that the truth must be told? She was from Tennessee, and she'd grown up with tales of Tecumseh, the great Shawnee chief, and his heroic efforts—which had almost succeeded—to stem the tide of advancing settlers across the land. Effie's grandfather had told her how Tecumseh had fought to establish an Indian state. He urged tribes from the Gulf of Mexico to the Great Lakes to band together and fight the white man as one people, to resist the settlers overrunning Indian land. But Tecumseh's grand design was badly defeated at the battle of Tippecanoe at the hands of General William Henry Harrison, who won a decisive victory over the Indians and blunted their hopes for a nation of their own. The next year Tecumseh was killed in the War of 1812 fighting with the British against the Americans. With his death, the hopes of the Shawnee to remain in their ancestral lands along the Ohio River were lost forever.

"My grandfather fought in battles against the Shawnee," Effie said. She could feel the heat from the flush on her cheeks, but she didn't stop. "He said they were the best fighters he'd ever seen— and the bravest and the smartest!" Then, surprised at her outburst, she quickly looked down at the sewing in her lap, avoiding Martin's gaze.

Mrs. Lykes did her best to fill in the awkward silence that followed. "Well, it's different here for the Indians, that's for sure. No chance for fighting, very little for hunting." Her voice was patient, her words automatic, as though she was repeating a litany she'd memorized. "But they didn't ask to come, and it's not easy, trying to change a whole way of life in a few years. With God's help alone, we will succeed and they will all be better for it." She forced a smile.

John Syms nodded in agreement. "We know we have our work cut out for us with the Pawnee, but seeing the success you've had here is all the encouragement we need. Tomorrow morning we hope to look at your printing press and your school. Education is the first step, I believe, in driving out the heathen devils that have corrupted the red man's mind."

Reverend Lykes was quick to agree. "We can publish the Scriptures in the Shawnee language now; we even have our own newspaper, the first in the territory. You're right, sir; education is the way. We're making great strides here winning the minds and the hearts of the pagans to the light of Jesus Christ. Rebecca," he commanded, almost imperially. "Say one of your Bible verses for our guests."

The Indian girl stood up straight, folded her hands in front of her, and recited in perfectly accented English, " 'And Moses stretched out his hand over the sea; and the Lord caused the sea to go back by a strong east wind all that night, and made the sea dry land, and the waters were divided. And the Children of Israel went into the midst of the sea upon the dry ground: and the waters were a wall unto them on their right hand, and on their left.' "

"Remarkable—" Reverend Syms began, only to catch a look at his host's annoyed face and break off in mid-sentence.

"She will say that verse no matter—haven't you spoken to her?" Reverend Lykes addressed his wife.

Mrs. Lykes pursed her mouth in reprimand. "Next time the New Testament, Rebecca," she said sternly.

"I don't understand," Effie protested. "Surely the Holy Word is the Holy Word, and I think her recitation was quite impressive."

Reverend Lykes seemed embarrassed. "Rebecca has a particular fondness for that passage," he

explained, "and it's become something of a trial
for us. You see, we don't like to encourage these
people to hold on to their past—it can only impede
their progress in the end, you understand—and it
seems the Shawnee have some pagan myth about
their creation on an island in the middle of the sea.
It seems their Master of Life—that's what they call
him—caused the waters to part so that the Shawnee
could leave, much like the children of Israel. Not,
of course, that there's any comparison. As we keep
trying to explain to them, theirs is just a myth, while
the miracle God performed for Moses is—well, the
word of God. I'm afraid the Indian mind isn't quite
refined enough to understand the difference."

Rebecca's face was bland, but Effie thought for
just a moment she caught a glint of amusement in
the dark eyes. Then Mrs. Lykes was ordering another recitation. "From the Sermon on the Mount,
perhaps, Rebecca." But before the girl could begin,
the baby began to whimper.

Effie put her sewing aside and started to rise, but
Rebecca was standing right in front of the pallet,
and she turned and bent as though to pick up
the child. Effie lunged for her baby and struck
the other girl's hand away, snatching up the child
protectively.

The baby, sensing his mother's distress, began to
cry louder, and Rebecca lowered her eyes. "Among
my people," she explained softly, "the children
belong to all. No child ever cries for want of a
mother's touch." She started to rise.

Effie was ashamed. "Wait," she said.

Rebecca turned.

Carefully, Effie released the tightness of her grip,
shifting the baby in her arms. She tried to smile at

Rebecca. "His name is Adam," she said. "Would you like to hold him?"

"Effie!" Rachel exclaimed. "Have you lost your mind? That girl is an Indian. There's no telling what she had her hands in last!"

Mrs. Lykes puffed up as though she had just been accused of being a poor housekeeper, or as though her taste in furnishings had been questioned. She said stiffly, "Rebecca is very good with children."

Effie ignored both of them. Her eyes held Rebecca's, and she cautiously held the baby away from her body, offering him to her. She saw the softening in the other girl's liquid dark eyes, and after a moment, Rebecca opened her arms to receive the baby.

Effie watched carefully, holding her breath, as Rebecca stood cradling little Adam, rocking him back and forth and humming a soft, tuneless song under her breath. After a time Adam's wails were reduced to fretful, halfhearted whimpers, then to gurgles. Effie released her breath and went back to her seat.

Martin was scowling, and Rachel's lips were tightly compressed as she drove her darning needle back and forth into a frayed sock. Mrs. Lykes looked proud and self-satisfied. Effie didn't notice much about any of them. She shared a smile with Rebecca and went back to her sewing.

Boothe approached the circle of light cast by the fire. In its flickering shadows sat an old man, his shoulders wrapped in a tattered blanket, his feet bare beneath broadcloth trousers. Behind him was an unwalled hut woven of tree limbs and blankets, and inside were his only possessions—his medicine bag, his pipe, an elk antler, and another blanket.

Boothe waited, saying nothing, until he was recognized. Without looking up, the old man leaned forward and drew a circle in the dirt. Booth knelt and filled the circle with a cross.

The old man looked at him. "He-Who-Remembers-Tomorrow," he said, "is welcome in my camp."

Boothe sat cross-legged by the fire. "Gray Cloud," he replied. "You have been much with my spirit since I crossed the river."

"You take more of the white men where they do not belong."

The words made Boothe feel ashamed, but he held the old medicine man's eyes. "Yes."

"Why do you do this?"

"They will come," Boothe replied simply. "To try to stop them is like holding back the moon."

"They will come," agreed Gray Cloud sadly. "We are aging, you and I. And too tired to hold back the moon."

"I'm sad to hear of White Feather's going," Boothe said. "He is my brother."

Gray Cloud smiled. "He is a younger man. Still he tries to hold back the moon."

"If the soldiers find him, they will kill him."

"Then he will die as he has lived. Free."

"It is a noble thing," Boothe agreed.

"The mountains will welcome you, my friend," Gray Cloud went on. "You have been away too long."

"No," Boothe said sharply. "I do not go to the mountains. I take these people to the land of the Pawnee, where the Great Mountains shine in the distance and the river flows slow. But I go no further."

Gray Cloud looked at him for a long time. Then he said, "Tell me your dream of the wolf."

Boothe felt no surprise at Gray Cloud's knowing the secret dream that had risen to haunt him three times as the moon grew full. Nor was there any questioning the fact that Gray Cloud knew this was why he had come to him tonight.

"In my dream," he said, "I walk alone in the mountains, high above where the snakes sleep. It's a place I've never walked before, where the blue spruce grows tall and the water runs clear. On the trail I meet a wolf with a black coat, a wolf as big as a man. The wolf charges at me. I have my rifle, but I do not fire." There was no point in concluding the dream, in describing the feel of sharp teeth sinking into his throat, the dizzying sensation of lifeblood seeping out of him, the waking, cold with sweat and sick with wonder. "The dream puzzles me," he finished simply.

"You wonder why you do not fire your rifle," said Gray Cloud.

Boothe nodded.

"Tell me."

The telling sounded foolish, but he spoke aloud anyway. "I have never seen anything like this wolf. Proud, beautiful. To take its life would not be right."

"But it would take yours."

"Yes."

"We have always known that the difference between living and dying is not so great a thing as the white man believes. Perhaps you have come to learn this as well."

But Boothe was still disturbed. The dream could not be of the future, for it made no sense. And no man should dream of his own death.

He said, "Have you ever known of a black wolf?"

Gray Cloud smiled. "Many things I have seen, and many things I have not. Come, let's smoke the pipe together. You have brought tobacco?"

Boothe had, and he unrolled the pouch as Gray Cloud went into the shelter with slow steps to retrieve his pipe. He lit the pipe with a twig set over the fire—the fire he had brought to this place from the great woods and which had burned without dying all these years. In this way past and present were united, and the future was given hope.

Gray Cloud offered Boothe the first draw on the pipe, as a gesture of respect. When Boothe returned the pipe to him, Gray Cloud looked deeply and steadily into his eyes.

"Your medicine is strong, my friend," he said, "but you have never met the black wolf." He drew on the pipe and was silent for a long time, staring into the fire.

"You dream tomorrow," he said at last. "And I think I shall not see you again."

Boothe did not answer, and that night, not surprisingly, he dreamed again of the wolf in the mountains.

Chapter Seven

There was an air of subdued expectation as the party prepared to leave the next morning. Once they crossed the Kaw River, they would leave behind all semblance of civilization and enter the beginning of untamed wilderness. After that, they would be completely on their own, traveling for almost three months across some of the most inhospitable country ever imagined by man.

The Reverend and Mrs. Lykes came out to say good-bye, bringing gifts of crockery and textbooks to be used in the mission—*More useless junk to tire out the oxen,* Kitty thought. Reverend Syms was having trouble getting his team hitched up, so, after making sure Ben's team was securely in its traces, Kitty went over to help him.

It was almost comical, watching the tall, skinny man wrestle with an animal four times his size and at least twice as stubborn. But Kitty held back her smiles as she advised, "It won't do any good to pull at his harness like that. That only makes him mad."

Perspiration slickened Syms's face and his scowl was formidable. "I don't need any help from impertinent young girls, thank you, miss."

As far as Kitty was concerned, he could struggle with the beast until he wore himself out, but the sun had already burned away the dew and Boothe was impatient to leave. "I guess not," she agreed, running a soothing hand between the ox's eyes, "if you want to stay here and build a house. But if you ever want to make it across the river, you're going to have to get this team hitched up."

She heard a giggle behind her and saw Lucy Syms disappearing quickly around the corner of the wagon. Kitty walked over to the other ox, leading it by the harness. "You're trying to hitch them in the wrong order," she said. "This one's the leader. The other one won't go anywhere unless this one goes first."

"That's nonsense," replied Syms, huffing as he pulled again, cruelly, on the harness. "They're just dumb animals."

"That dumb animal is going to take a chunk out of you if you don't stop torturing him," Kitty said sharply, and snatched the lead out of his hand.

She led both animals to the wagon, and within three minutes, had them in their traces. Lucy peeked out from the seat atop the wagon. "How do you tell them apart?" she taunted. "By the smell?"

Kitty ran her hand again along the sensitive area of the first ox's brow, between the stubby horns and down its nose. "This one," she replied, "has sweeter eyes. Thoughtful-like, and patient. He's kinda slow in the head, but he'll tolerate all kinds of abuse"—she couldn't help slanting a dark glance at the reverend—"before he loses his temper. This one here, though . . ." She turned her attention to the dominant animal. "He's got a little of the devil in him. He'll work all day for you if you treat him right, but when he's had enough he'll let you know. He's used to being in charge."

"Only a pagan would treat animals like they were human beings," the reverend said shortly. "They're beasts of burden, and they have no intellect at all."

Kitty looked at him coolly. "Some beasts of burden," she said, "are a lot smarter than people. At least they know when to follow a good leader."

She turned on her heel and stalked away, but she hadn't gone two steps before she stopped. Coming across the field toward her was a woman, and she was leading a white horse.

The hustle and bustle of the breaking camp slowed and then died away. The women straightened up from dousing their fires; the men turned from checking the wagons. Everyone stared in silence as Kitty went slowly forward to meet the Shawnee woman.

For a long moment the two women simply looked at each other. Then Mary transferred the rope by which she led the white pony into Kitty's hand. "May the feet of this pony carry you safely to what you seek," she said formally, "and may the wisdom of the Great Spirit guide your steps."

Kitty's fingers closed around the rough hemp, and her throat was so full she couldn't speak. She threaded her fingers through the pony's coarse mane and pressed her cheek against its neck. Then she turned to Mary. "It's too valuable," she began. "I can't—"

But Mary's eyes remained impassive, and Kitty knew that was exactly the wrong thing to say. She stepped forward and embraced the other woman, and for a moment her eyes burned and her throat hurt and she was afraid she was going to cry.

"Mother," she whispered. She closed her eyes and said the word again. "Mother."

She stepped back and touched the other woman's cheek, just as Mary had done to her the night before, when they had talked until dawn. "I shall miss you," she said.

"Go in peace, Little Cat," she replied. "You will always be with me . . ." She touched her heart. "Here."

Kitty watched as she walked away, watched until she disappeared behind a dip in the road. She heard John Syms mutter, "Pagan," but she ignored him. She turned and hoisted herself atop the pony, and for the first time since the journey began she wasn't afraid.

They followed the course of the Kaw River along its forested southern bank, and the traveling was pleasant. Hickory, elm, and cottonwood trees provided shelter from the heat of the day, and Oliver proved his worth to the expedition by riding ahead each day to hunt, and returning to camp with strings of quail, rabbit, and squirrel, enough for all. In the cool of the evening the men walked to the river and set out fishing lines, returning the next morning to gather their breakfast. Kitty recognized many herbs, mosses, and edible roots and berries, and with Katherine's frugality ingrained in her, made a point of laying by a supply. One day she filled half a bushel basket with sweet potatoes she found growing wild, and everyone feasted that night.

The tall bluestem grass was plentiful, and the livestock, too, were well-fed. The river breeze was always cool, and there was plenty of water for washing, so that the women did not have to dip into the precious supply secured to the wagons in water barrels. Often they passed other travelers— traders, mostly, moving by canoe or barge down the Kaw toward the Missouri, and they never felt as though they were completely alone. The first leg of their journey was, in fact, so deceptively easy that it was only natural to begin to doubt Boothe's warnings of the dangers that lay ahead.

They reached the river crossing late in the afternoon. Boothe rode to the lead wagon and held up his hand. John Syms pulled reluctantly on the reins and brought his team to a halt. "Why are we stopping so early?" he demanded. "We've got a good four hours of daylight left."

Booth raised his voice to be heard as far back as the fourth wagon. "We camp here tonight," he called. "Tomorrow morning we cross the river. We don't know how bad the river is up ahead, and this might be the last good chance we get. You men . . ." He returned his eyes to John Syms. "Start unloading the wagons."

"Unload the wagons?" John Syms was scornful. "We'll drive them across. Surely you don't mean for us to carry our supplies across the river on our backs?"

"Like I explained to you before," Boothe replied patiently, "your wagons are overloaded. That river-bed is nothing but silt, and the water's going to be over the wheels if not higher. You'll get bogged down before you're halfway across."

"My table!" Rachel exclaimed. "We can't let it get wet."

"That's right, ma'am. So you'd best make plans to leave it on the bank." Boothe rode back to the next wagon to give the same instructions to the Crellers.

Effie Creller flatly refused to leave her organ behind, just as Rachel had refused to part with her oak table. While John Syms still insisted they would have no trouble driving the wagons across, Martin finally persuaded him that if they made two trips with half a load each time, they should be able to safely transport all their goods. Boothe shook his head in disgust and left them to it.

By the time they had taken care of the teams and made their camps, almost an hour had passed. Oliver immediately announced his intention to go down to the river and see what he could catch for supper, garnering the dark scowls of Martin Creller and John Syms, who needed all the help they could get unloading the heavy furniture from the wagons. Boothe made no pretense, but deliberately lounged in the shade and began whittling on a hickory branch.

Ben's wagon was lightly loaded with only the provisions for him, Kitty, and Boothe, and a few of the extra supplies the missionaries had not had room for in their own wagons. There was no need for him to unload, so he went to lend a hand with the Crellers' wagon. And though Kitty was loath to help anyone who didn't have the good sense to listen when somebody told them how to help themselves, it shamed her to see Effie

Creller, Rachel Syms, and even the sullen Lucy carrying boxes and tugging at heavy barrels. So she followed Ben.

The baby was whining fretfully in his cradle, which was only natural after a long day of being jostled around in the wagon. For the most part he had been remarkably even-tempered throughout the journey. Because she wasn't particularly anxious to start unloading crates of dishes and flour sacks, Kitty let Ben go ahead and turned toward the cradle at the side of the wagon.

Effie had placed the cradle beneath the shade of a low-branched elm tree just a few feet away from the wagon. Though Kitty had kept her distance from all of them, Effie Creller always seemed friendly enough, and she didn't think the other woman would mind if she rocked the baby for a while and tried to calm him.

She was only a few feet away when she noticed something odd about the shadows of the branches overhanging the cradle. A second later she knew what it was. She had barely broken into a run before the long, thick-bodied snake dropped from the lowest branch into the cradle.

Kitty snatched up the baby in a single swoop. The baby began to wail furiously; Effie Creller's head snapped around. "What are you doing with my baby?" she demanded in shrill alarm.

"A snake—" Kitty started to explain, but Effie, reaching her, had already seen it.

She screamed. Everyone started running toward them. Effie grabbed the baby from Kitty and held him close to her breast, still screaming for her husband. Ben was the first to understand what had happened, and he tipped the cradle over. A big black snake, five feet or more long, spilled out and lay writhing and coiling on the ground.

Boothe was on his feet and had almost reached them, but when he saw the nature of the disturbance he turned around again. Still, Rachel screamed, and Lucy began a cacophony of high, shrieking yelps, and even the men jumped back when they saw the size of the snake. "Kill it!" Rachel shrilled. "Kill it, someone, kill it!"

Martin ran to the wagon for his gun.

"It's just a black snake!" Kitty cried. "It won't hurt anybody!"

"Oh, Effie. Oh, the poor baby! Is he bitten? Did it—"

The snake slithered a few feet forward and Lucy screamed and clutched her father. "Kill it, Daddy!"

Kitty looked at them all in disgust. "If you'd just step back and stop your yelping, it'd probably crawl away by itself."

Effie, gulping for breath, looked up from her examination of little Adam and answered Rachel's question. "No, he's all right. Kitty—" She looked at Kitty, her eyes wide with wonder and gratitude. "Kitty saved him."

Martin returned with his rifle, and Kitty was glad to be distracted from her embarrassment. As Martin started to raise the rifle to his shoulder, she lunged forward and grabbed the barrel. "Don't do that!" she exclaimed. "I keep telling you that snake is harmless!"

Rachel turned eyes on her that were filled with contempt and horror. "It's a snake!"

"That doesn't mean you have to kill it. It was here before you were!"

Ben stepped forward and gently took the rifle from Martin. "Better let me have that. You're liable to shoot somebody in the foot."

"Shoot the filthy serpent Ben," Reverend Syms commanded shortly, "and be done with it."

It had become a battle of wills. Kitty looked Ben in the eyes and said, "Ben, don't."

"What kind of woman," Reverend Syms demanded coldly, "would plead for the life of a snake?"

"The kind of woman," Kitty returned, "who has respect for *all* of God's creatures."

Effie looked quickly from Kitty to the reverend. "She's right."

An astonished silence fell, and all eyes turned toward her. Even Kitty was surprised to find Effie taking her side, and it seemed to require a lot of courage for Effie to meet John Syms's eyes and go on. "I was raised on a farm. Black snakes are harmless. They keep the rats out of the corncrib. There's no need to shoot it."

And then Lucy screamed again.

While they had all been discussing the fate of the snake, Richard Singleton had stepped forward and with a long branch, gently prodded it away. In an instant the snake slithered toward the river and was soon lost in the grass.

Ben grinned. "Well, I guess we could track it down, but it might take a while to shoot every snake in these woods." He returned the rifle to Martin.

Kitty was the only one who shared his grin. The whole incident *had* been ridiculous, and if John Syms hadn't made her so mad—if everyone hadn't made such a fuss—it all would have passed unnoticed in a matter of minutes. Martin, looking awkward and a little embarrassed, turned back to the wagon, and Reverend Syms, followed by his wife, turned sharply back to his own work.

Lucy stood close to Ben, her eyes big as she looked up at him. "I hate snakes, don't you?"

Ben shrugged. "I can think of things I like better."

She touched his arm lightly. "You really would have shot it, wouldn't you?"

"Probably not. Waste of ammunition."

He turned to follow Martin, and Lucy watched him, a frustrated, thoughtful frown puckering her brow until her mother called her to get back to work.

Richard Singleton was already fading into the background again, and Kitty stopped him as he started after Lucy. "Thank you," she said. "That was real brave of you."

He looked startled at first, as though he couldn't believe she was talking to him, and then a faint flush of color stained his pale cheeks. "I don't reckon anybody's ever called me brave before," he muttered shyly. "Anyway, snakes don't bother me."

"Me, either," Kitty said, "but that wasn't the brave thing. Going against Reverend Syms was."

He obviously didn't know what to say to that, and the blotchy color in his cheeks grew darker. Kitty could see she was making him miserable, just by trying to be friendly, and she wondered what it must be like to be so painfully shy. He ducked his head and mumbled, "Excuse me, ma'am. Got work to do." He was gone before Kitty could say another word.

Effie Creller stood close to Kitty. The baby had almost stopped whimpering, and when she held him against her shoulder, he lifted his head and looked around curiously. "You saved my baby," Effie said simply. "Thank you."

Now it was Kitty's turn to flush. "I didn't save him from much. You know that."

Effie smiled, her eyes warm. "Just the same, I thank you."

Kitty cast around for something constructive to say. "If you've got a piece of cheesecloth," she suggested, "we might could fix up some kind of cover for the cradle, so you won't have to worry about him again."

"I think I do," Effie said, and passed the baby to Kitty. "Let me check the wagon."

Kitty held the baby up before her, smiling as he reached one chubby fist forward to grab her hair. "Well, little man," she said, "if this is the worst that happens to us before we get to the Solomon, I guess we're going to be all right after all."

Oliver Sherrod had killed his first man, and loved his first woman, when he was fifteen years old. He had crossed a wilderness and awakened every morning to stare death in the eye at a time when most young men his age were putting on school uniforms and daydreaming about pretty girls in pink hair ribbons. His growing up had been far, far different from what he had imagined.

Byrd Kincaid had taught him what he needed to know about manhood and survival. Boothe Carlyle had fired his secret dreams for adventure and exploration. Both men had been heroes to him in a way, and by the time he had discovered how unusual such men were, it was too late for him.

There were two types of men who left the security of their lives back east for the uncertainty of the edges of the world: the good and the strong. The good men brought their families and their tools and their livestock, and worked themselves into an early grave trying to build nothing less than what they had left behind. The strong took care of themselves and did what they had to in order to survive.

Oliver learned early on that he was not a particularly good man.

He could never be the man Byrd Kincaid was, and Boothe Carlyle wasn't such a hero after all. Oliver did what he had to, and the doing became easier with every year that passed.

Still, it was a strange feeling, seeing them all again. Kitty, the infant who never should have survived the womb, all grown up and as feisty as Katherine Kincaid had ever been. Sometimes just glancing at her would catch him unawares with a pain in his chest, plunging him briefly into the past. With her blond hair and round face, she bore a striking resemblance to the shy, long-suffering woman who had borne her, but when her eyes flashed and her fists curled and she stared down Reverend Syms, she was Katherine all over again, and no one else. She was following in her mother's footsteps, figuratively and literally, doomed to repeat the journey of the past. Just as they all were.

And Ben, whom Oliver had known since he was a baby. Strange to think of him as a man now. Stranger still that he had cast his lot with these missionaries, whom he surely knew were God's biggest fools. Oliver and Ben had made that first journey for survival together, yet how differently they had turned out now.

And Boothe, Katherine's brother. The reason Katherine had left her home and crossed the Ohio in the first place. Boothe Carlyle, the fallen legend, sallying forth again to lead a band of pilgrims to their deaths.

Once, these three had been family to him. Now he didn't know them. Still, it was strange, being with them again, and more often than not he felt as though he had lost something. It was something he would never be able to get back.

It was twilight when he drew in his fishing line and started back to camp with a string of a dozen catfish slung over his shoulder. He could smell the cookfires burning and knew the hard work was done; if he lingered too much longer he might miss supper altogether.

He had just crested the riverbank when he heard a sound to the left of him. An instinct born of having met too much danger in too many unexpected places caused him to slip his pistol from his belt as he followed the sound to its source.

A man was crouched on the ground, half hidden among the bushes, swinging his arms high over his head and then down again as he plunged a knife into the ground. The sounds Oliver had heard were gasps and grunts of exertion. Oliver moved quickly forward, and then stopped as he recognized the man, and saw what he was doing.

It was Richard Singleton, and he had killed a snake. He had not only killed it, but stabbed it, sliced it into a multitude of pieces. The pieces had stopped wriggling, so there was no telling how long he'd been at it. His face was red and glistening wet, his expression fierce, and so intent was he on his task that he didn't even notice Oliver.

Something about the scene faintly disgusted Oliver, even alarmed him, and he started to call out, then changed his mind. There was, after all, no law against a man killing a snake, no matter how viciously he chose to do it.

Oliver slipped away quietly and continued back to camp. But the incident disturbed him for a long time.

Boothe couldn't help noticing the way Kitty glared across the fire at Lucy Syms, who had cornered Ben in a conversation near her wagon. To Boothe's way of thinking, it was a look of pure jealousy, and he couldn't resist teasing her a little.

"You beat that biscuit dough any harder and we're going to be having rocks for supper," he commented, glancing up from the careful stitches he was making in his saddle blanket. "What's got under your hide?"

Kitty began to pinch off rounds of dough and fling them into a pan with unnecessary force. "That Lucy Syms," she said tightly. "She's shameless. Look at her flirting with everything in pants, and poor Ben not even a month a widower."

"Bothers you, does it?"

"Of course it does. A girl ought to have some pride."

"Doesn't look like she's doing Ben an awful lot of harm. Of course, I reckon he's a bit too smart to take a gal like that seriously, but you know, Kitten, the worst thing that can happen to a man is for him to live out his life alone. I reckon Ben's smart enough to know that too."

"You live alone," Kitty pointed out, "and you do just fine."

There was a very long, very heavy silence, and it was poignant enough to make Kitty turn and look at Boothe. The expression on his face was tight with pain, and he was looking down at the half-mended blanket in his hands without seeing it. "Boothe?" Kitty prompted softly.

He didn't look up right away, and his voice was low. "No," he said, "I don't do fine. And the biggest mistake I ever made in my life was not realizing that until it was too late."

Kitty's throat felt tight. "I—don't understand."

"Miss Caroline," he said simply, and he looked at her. The bleakness in his eyes was like a great dark shadow that spread across the distance between them. "All those years we wasted—I'll never get that time back. I'll never get her back. She's gone, and I guess I'll spend the rest of my life wondering if she ever knew how much I loved her."

Kitty's head reeled. Miss Caroline? But she was so old. She was just the schoolteacher, and nobody ever paid any attention to her . . . Nobody except Boothe.

He had loved her. Of course he had loved her, and Kitty felt like a fool for not having realized it before. All that time Kitty had spent pining her childish heart out for love of Boothe, he had held affection for another woman, a real woman . . . a woman, Kitty understood now as she looked back, who had loved him in return with all the quiet devotion he deserved. So much of Kitty's romantic fantasies about Boothe had revolved around the lone wolf image he had presented, but he had never really been alone at all. What a child she had been.

Not a day had passed since the shooting that she had not learned something new about Boothe. He had changed in her eyes. But this . . . this realization brought the biggest change of all. The biggest truth. And suddenly everything was clear for her.

She had not loved Boothe at all. Not in the way a woman loves a man. Not in the way he had loved Caroline. She had loved the life he led, the stories he told, the oaklike strength he presented, and the magic he brought into her life whenever he appeared. But now . . . maybe she had changed, too. Because now she saw Boothe as he was, as he had always been: just a man. A great man perhaps, certainly a brave and adventurous man, but just as vulnerable to hurt and failure and mistakes as all men were. And she felt selfish and ashamed for having nursed her own silly hurts and imagined passions all this time without ever guessing at his suffering.

She came over to him and sat beside him on the log. "I'm sorry," she said gently. "I didn't know."

"No reason for you to," he said gruffly, and took up his mending again.

"I think—she must have loved you a great deal."

Boothe looked at her. "You're a fine girl, Kitty," he said. "It's good to have you here."

Kitty smiled and pressed her cheek against his shoulder, offering comfort to her Uncle Boothe.

After supper, Reverend Syms called a prayer meeting, and Ben was obliged to go. Since the organ was unloaded, it seemed a good idea to take advantage of the chance to hold a service with real music, and the night before the river crossing that would take them on the second major leg of their journey was certainly an appropriate time to ask for the Lord's guidance and protection.

Ben asked Kitty and Boothe to go with him, but Boothe replied that he preferred to do his praying on his own. Kitty was even less subtle. She gave him a withering look that spoke eloquently of what she thought of any service conducted by Reverend Syms, and turned back to sweeping the camp. Ben understood. He wasn't in much of a mood for praying tonight, either. He hadn't been in the mood for a long time.

He supposed that was the first of his sins. By far the most damning was the anger that nestled so securely and so completely inside him that he could no longer remember when it had not been there. At first he thought he was angry because of his loss, because of the two women he had loved who had been taken so swiftly and so unjustly from him. But slowly he came to realize that the anger was because of Zeke Calhoun, because he had died before Ben had had a chance to kill him. That was a terrible truth to know about himself.

He couldn't talk himself out of it, he couldn't think his way around it, he couldn't pray it away. And the worst was, he didn't care.

He stood in the circle around the organ and mouthed the hymns, and when Reverend Syms read his text, Ben could not have said, three minutes later, what it was about. When everyone else bowed his head in prayer, his eyes remained open, looking around.

Once he had felt a close kinship with these people, a sense of rightness and purpose. But that had been when Rose was with him. Rose, the keeper of the dream . . . Perhaps the dream had died with her. Or perhaps it had never belonged to him at all.

Now he felt like an impostor, and these men and women were strangers to him. He did not understand how they thought or why they behaved the way they did, or what was important to them and why it was so. Once, he had understood. Once, he had cared. But now, where there had been answers there were only dull, lifeless questions. Where once there had been passion there was now emptiness. And that was his greatest loss. A madman had taken his mother and his wife in a brutal shower of blood and violence, but only Ben could deprive himself of that sense of purpose, the reason for being. It was gone, and he did not know how to get it back, or even if he wanted to.

That was his biggest sin.

The prayer meeting lasted just long enough for his feet to start to tingle and his back to ache from standing in one position for so long. It was the persistent crying of the baby that finally—and mercifully, Ben thought—brought the meeting to a close. He lingered no longer than was polite, to say good night to the Symses and Martin Creller, and to say a few words to Richard Singleton, who never made much of a response.

As Ben walked back toward his own camp, Lucy fell into step beside him. He noticed—he couldn't help but notice—the movement she made to unfasten the top two buttons of her blouse, fanning herself with her hand. "My, it's warm out tonight, isn't it?" she commented.

Ben agreed that it was, though the temperature was in fact moderate.

"I was thinking about taking a walk down by the river," she said. "Bet it's cooler down there."

"You ought not to go wandering off by yourself."

She slanted a glance at him. "Maybe you'd like to go with me."

They were less than ten yards from the campfire, where Kitty sat with her knees drawn up and her chin propped on her fists, watching them and pretending not to. Ben was annoyed.

"Not tonight," he said. "We've got a hard day ahead, and I'm going to turn in. You should, too."

Lucy stepped in front of him, gazing up at him with eyes that seemed twice as big as they normally were. "Don't you think I'm pretty?"

He could have been nicer to her, Ben supposed, but his refusal to do so was only another one of his failings. He looked down at her and without a shred of courtesy in his voice said, "I thought you'd set your sights on Oliver."

She made a face. "Him? He's old. Rude, too. Sweet as he could be until we got on our way, and now he won't give a body the time of day. But you . . ." She reached up a hand and toyed playfully with a button on his shirt, sliding him a catlike smile. "You're a lot nicer. I've always thought so."

Ben deliberately took her hand and moved it away from his shirt. "Good night, Miss Lucy," he said, and walked away. After a moment he heard the sharp crunch of leaves underfoot as she flounced back to her own camp.

Ben walked past Kitty without greeting her and shook out his bedroll a few feet from the fire. Boothe was already asleep directly across from them, or at least he was lying down with his hat covering his eyes. Ben could feel Kitty watching him as he sat down to take off his boots.

"I want to ask you something," she said.

"I don't want to hear a word about that girl. You ought to have better manners anyway, spying on folks."

"Her?" Kitty's voice was scornful. "There's nothing wrong with her that a good hiding wouldn't fix, and I'm surprised her pa hasn't already figured that out. I don't want to talk about her."

She scooted around, her arms still encircling her legs, so that she was more fully facing him. "What I want to know," she said earnestly, "is what those people are doing this for. If they just wanted to help folks, they could've done that back east. And it's not like they care about the Indians, or know anything about them. They don't even want to learn anything about them. What do they think they're going to do when they get to the Solomon? Why go all that way when they don't know what they're going to find when they get there or what they're going to do or how to go about doing it . . . or anything at all, except that they won't be welcome?"

Ben frowned, tugging at his boot. "Why are you asking me?"

"You ought to know. It was part your idea, wasn't it?"

"No," he replied shortly. He would have left it at that, but she was still looking at him, so he shrugged. "Who knows why people do what they do? Everybody's looking for something different, I guess. Just like you. You're the one who was whining and pestering your folks to let you come for three weeks before we left, and for what? You've got no more business out here than any of the rest of us."

Kitty's voice sounded muffled as she answered, "Not at the end. At the end I didn't want to come."

Ben was surprised. He hadn't known that. He started to ask her about it, then let it drop. He lay back and flipped the blanket over his shoulder. "Don't sit up all night staring at the fire."

"I won't."

He closed his eyes.

"Ben? What about you? What are you looking for?"

Ben opened his eyes, looking up at the stars through the lacy breaks in the leaves. "I don't know, Kitty," he said tiredly. "Maybe we all just came out here to die."

It wasn't until after he had closed his eyes again that he realized that, for him at least, it was the truth.

Chapter Eight

The missionaries had crossed the Mississippi by ferry and had traveled up the Missouri by barge. To this point rivers had been squiggles on the map, an efficient means of transport, a place to wash and water the livestock and fish for supper. Rivers meant cool breezes and easy hunting, an artery of the network that connected them, however distantly, with civilization. But they had never had to cross on foot before, and after that day they would never think about rivers in the same way again.

When Boothe rode across the river, the water rose to his knees before he reached the other side. John Syms did not say anything else about how much simpler it would have been to drive the wagons across fully loaded. Boothe secured a rope to a tree on the opposite bank while Ben tied off the end on the near bank, and between them they rigged up a pulley by which they could transport some of the lighter crates. Holding on to the rope for guidance over the slippery, miry river bottom, the women walked across. Effie was clearly terrified as the water crept upward, over her waist and toward her armpits, and she held the baby as high as she could. Eventually she had to let go of the rope to hold Adam high on her shoulder, and she refused to go another step. Kitty called encouragement to her from the opposite bank, and Martin started sloshing toward her from the wagon, but it was Rachel, who had started across right before Effie, who turned back and reached her first. Between the two of them they got the baby across with nothing more than a wet bottom to show for his adventure.

Benjamin drove his wagon across with little trouble, though the oxen had to struggle to pull the wheels out of the mire and onto the safety of the bank. Richard drove the smaller, lighter wagon that contained mostly cooking supplies and food-stuffs; and with John Syms's stronger oxen pulling his wagon, he made it across in one trip.

By the time Martin Creller was making his second trip across, the river bottom was so trampled and disarranged that even the oxen had trouble gaining footing. Midway across, the wagon became stuck in the mud. Martin shouted and slapped the reins. He used the prodding stick. He even got out of the wagon and waded waist high in the water to the head of the team and pulled on the harness.

"He'll never get them across like that," Kitty muttered. The oxen were tired and were having enough trouble keeping their heads above water; they clearly weren't inclined to pull the heavy wagon out of the mud as well. Had it been Kitty's choice, she would have unhooked the wagon and let it sit there.

That was not a very practical solution, however, and the choice, fortunately, was not Kitty's to make. Boothe, whose clothes had not even dried out from helping Syms across, waded back in to help Martin with the team, while Oliver and Ben went to the back of the wagon to try to free the wheels.

Ben's boots sank calf-high into mud as he reached the back of the wagon, and he barely restrained an oath. Oliver had no such inhibitions, and swore loudly as he reached down into the water to feel for the bottom of the wheel rim. "It's got a foot of mud covering it," he said. "we're going to have to cut pry boards."

But no one wanted to spend the rest of the afternoon doing that, so when Boothe called from the front of the wagon, "Ready!" both Ben and Oliver grasped the lowest spoke beneath the water and leaned their weight into the wheel.

At first Ben thought their effort was useless. He lifted and pushed until his back muscles burned and spots danced before his eyes; Boothe and Martin shouted and whistled, and the oxen thrashed their heads, but nothing happened. And then, abruptly, the wheel moved. Not much, just an inch or two, but the sudden lurch of forward motion was enough to cast Ben off balance and send him down on one knee with a splash. And then, just as unexpectedly, the wagon rolled backward again.

Ben struggled to regain his feet, but the mud sucked at him, and too late he released his hold on the spoke. The wheel rolled backward as he tried to scramble out of its way; he felt its heavy weight thump against his shoulder, pushing him down, but even then he thought it would be all right. Then he realized he couldn't move, and before he could take another breath, water rushed into his mouth and nose.

Oliver did not know how long it was before he glanced in Ben's direction; maybe only seconds. But no more time was lost in wondering what had happened: He saw the empty space where Ben once had been, he saw the faint shadow of movement just beneath the muddy surface, and a stab of cold fear went through him that had the sharp, acrid, and all-too-familiar taste of death to it. He let out a hoarse shout; he splashed across the few feet of water that separated them and fell against the wagon wheel. He shouted again, *"Boothe!"* as he saw Ben in the water below, drowning.

He grabbed hold of Ben and pulled, but could lift him only a few inches. Those few inches weren't enough, and Ben's face didn't clear the water. His eyes bulging, he flailed his free arm and grasped Oliver's shoulder with enough strength to drag him under, too, but he could not free himself.

Boothe's face drained of color as he splashed around the side of the wagon. He dropped to his knees on the other side of Oliver and got his hands beneath Ben's shoulders, but could lift him no further than Oliver had been able to. He turned frantically to the wagon wheel, floundering under water until he found the place where Ben's shoulder was pinned. He tried to dig away the mud, but it fell back into place like quicksand.

"Hurry!" Oliver gasped. "For God's sake, do something. He's drowning!"

Martin appeared just then, grasping the side of the wagon as he stared in horror and disbelief. "Oh, my dear Lord," he whispered.

"Get back up there!" Boothe shouted at him. "Get that team moving!"

Boothe stumbled to his feet and got his shoulder against the wheel, shouting to Martin, "Pull!"

The wagon wheel shifted a fraction, sending a flood of fresh mud through the water. Oliver felt Ben slipping from his arms and desperately he shifted his position, trying to pull him up. It was no use. Ben couldn't hold his breath any longer, and bubbles of water gurgled to the surface. Oliver knew Ben's next instinct would be to try to draw in air, as any drowning man would. He shouted, "No!" and clapped his hand firmly over Ben's mouth and nose. And then, drawing a deep breath into his own lungs, he ducked under the water. Pinching Ben's nostrils shut as he had seen the Indians do, he breathed his own breath into Ben's lungs.

Ben's fingers were still strong on Oliver's arm. His chest rose with the breath. Oliver emerged from the water, shaking his head, drew another breath, and did it again.

Kitty had seen Ben fall and hadn't thought much of it. She saw the wagon slide backward, and Ben slip beneath the water, but it took a moment for her to believe it. Yet, even before Oliver reached Ben, she was sliding down the riverbank, splashing into the water.

It seemed to take forever. The water dragged at her skirts. The current pushed and tugged at her. The mud filled her boots and sucked her down. People were shouting at her on the bank, but the voices were like the bothersome hum of insects; all she could hear was Boothe's voice, raw with terror and desperation; all she could see was Martin's face as he stumbled back toward the oxen, and she knew Ben was dying.

Knee-deep, and she was moving by inches. Hip-deep, and she was sobbing, slapping at the water with her hands as though she could push it out of her way. Waist-deep, and her foot caught on a root; she fell and went under. She came up swimming, kicking at the heavy skirts that twisted around her ankles. When she was a few strokes from the oxen, she planted her feet on the river bottom and lunged forward.

Martin's face was white and filled with terror. He was flailing at the oxen with his stick, and the animals, sensing his panic, were thrashing their heads and trying to back up.

Kitty screamed, *"No!"* and lurched for the harness.

The wagon wheel rolled backward against all of Boothe's efforts to the contrary, silt drifted up like blood in the water, and Ben's hand lost its grip on Oliver's arm. Oliver tightened his lips against the scream of protest that wanted to tear itself out and hyperventilated to get more air in his lungs. He said, "Hold on, son." He knew Ben couldn't hear him beneath the water, but he repeated anyway, "Just hold on, we ain't licked yet. I can keep doing this all day, just as long as you keep holding on. We're gonna do this thing. We are."

He drew in another deep breath and ducked under the water again.

Kitty shouted to Martin, "Get away!"

"No! I—"

"You're scaring them! *Get away!*" And without waiting for him to respond, she brought up her hands and pushed him flat against the chest, knocking him down. She swung herself toward the lead oxen, wrapping her arms around its neck for balance and crooning, "It's okay boy, come on, fellow, you can do this, please . . ."

Desperately, she tried to make her voice calm, her heartbeat slow. She had learned long ago that animals could sense such things. They knew when you were scared or mad, even when you tried to pretend you weren't, and they reacted to it. So she tried not to think about Ben. She tried not to think about hurrying. She tried not to think about dying. She just pressed her cheek to the oxen's face and murmured over and over again, "Please, please, come on, you can do it, you can, it's all right, just please . . ."

Nonsense words, soothing words, meaningless syllables that pushed the panic out of her head. She worked her way around to the front of the team, holding on to the harness and keeping her gaze steadily locked with that of the lead beast, applying a steady, encouraging, forward pressure on the harness. "Come on now, that's good, you're going to make it this time . . ."

The oxen gave a great lunge forward and the wagon moved—not just an inch, but a foot or more. Boothe shouted, and it had the sound of victory. Kitty continued pulling and Martin scrambled to his feet, grabbing the other side of the harness. Slowly the wagon began to lift itself from the mud and roll forward.

Oliver pulled Ben up and out of the water, and his first instinct was to clutch the boy to him in a fierce, possessive embrace. But Ben needed air. He was coughing and gasping and spitting up foul river water, and Oliver supported him with one arm and used the other to pound him on the back.

Boothe turned from the wagon wheel and stumbled back to them, falling on his knees beside them. In a moment Kitty appeared, wet to the bone and looking almost too scared to take another step. Fluid rattled in and out of Ben's lungs and then was expelled in gushes. He was too weak to stand up and it took both men to hold him above the surface of the water. But after a time, an endless time, his face lost some of its bluish color, and he opened his eyes.

Boothe laid his hand on Ben's back. "God must be smiling on you, son," he said, his voice strained. "It don't even look like anything's broken."

Then he glanced at Kitty and Oliver. "Good job," he said. "Both of you."

Ben's coughs were slowing down. He seemed to be taking easier breaths. His eyes began to focus, and he looked at Oliver. "Thank you," he said hoarsely.

Oliver replied gruffly, "Hell, I reckon I spent too much time keeping you alive when you was a kid to let you go toes-up on me now." But he couldn't meet Ben's gaze for long, and abruptly he got to his feet.

Kitty knelt down, slipping her arm around Ben's waist. "Come on," she said shakily, "you need to get into some dry clothes and let me have a look at that shoulder. Boothe, help me get him up."

Ben made a face as Kitty laid the warm poultice across his shoulder. "What is that?"

"Comfrey. It'll draw out the bruising. I made you some tea from it, too. It's good for the inside. Here, drink this."

Kitty had made a pallet for Ben in the back of the wagon, where she usually slept, and at first he had been glad to rest there. But as the afternoon wore on and he slowly regained his strength, he was proving to be a difficult patient.

Ben turned his head and pushed the cup away. "Stop fussing. Where's my shirt?"

Kitty sat back on her heels. "Since when did you get so bashful?"

"I'm not bashful. I just don't like being fussed over." He reached too suddenly for his shirt, and a spasm of painful coughing seized him. Kitty moved quickly to help him lie back against the sacks of flour and meal she had arranged as pillows.

There were minor scrapes and scratches across his chest, and a long dark bruise that was angriest at the hollow of his shoulder, spreading down across his ribs. Kitty had treated the scrapes with ointment and the bruises would heal with time, but it would take more than time to erase the real scars of this day.

For the first time Kitty realized that any one of them—or all of them—might truly die without ever seeing home again.

There was still a slight rattle to Ben's breathing even after the coughing passed. She could see the discomfort with which he took each breath, and as she leaned over him to rearrange the poultice on his shoulder, she found herself feeling just a little bashful. She hadn't seen Ben without his shirt on since he was a skinny boy and they used to go swimming together. How much had changed since then. His chest was broad and strong, and she noticed the long smooth muscles of his arms, the warmth of his skin. He was no longer a boy but a man, and the realization made her feel strange.

She handed him the tin mug of tea, and this time he took it without protest. She sat on the floor of the wagon, close to him, watching as he drank. After a moment he said, "Where did you learn all this—about herbs and mosses and such?"

She shrugged. "From Mama mostly. I think she learned a lot of it from Gran Fiona, and what Pa and Uncle Boothe picked up from the Indians."

He sipped the hot brew in silence, then smiled. "I think Martin is half convinced you're a witch, the way you handled those animals."

"Let him think what he wants. I can do the driving for you for the next couple of days."

For a brief moment Ben looked as though he would have liked to object. "Yeah," he agreed. "I guess you'll have to."

He stared into the mug, his expression sober. Then he said abruptly, "Can I tell you something, Kitty? I don't want to preach the gospel to the Indians. I don't think I ever did."

Kitty said nothing. She did not feel it was her place to comment.

"I know that sounds bad. God could've let me die today, but He didn't. But somehow . . . I don't think it was God's doing so much as it was yours, and Oliver's, and Boothe's. And when I came up out of that water, everything was different."

After a moment Kitty asked quietly, "Do you want to turn back?"

He lifted his eyes, looking toward the opening of the canvas at the dying day beyond. The river sounded close, whispering and gurgling, and the tree frogs were humming an erratic chorus. "No," he said slowly, as though he were just discovering that fact for himself. "I want to see what's out there."

Kitty knew then how disappointed she would have been in him had he said yes, and that surprised her. She reached into her pocket and drew out the coin, looking at it before handing it to him.

He took it curiously. "What is it?"

"Mama gave it to me before I left. It's from the Old Country, the old times. For good luck, I think."

Ben turned the coin over in his hand. "It feels like gold. What's that writing on it?"

"I don't know."

"It's not Latin or Greek. Maybe . . . something even older."

"Maybe it's a language nobody uses anymore, and everybody's forgotten. I think that's why she gave it to me . . . to remind me about all those people who have gone before me that nobody even remembers anymore . . ." She struggled to put her thoughts into words. "But I wouldn't be here if it weren't for them. They didn't just cross prairies, they crossed oceans. And they didn't know what they were going to find on the other side, either. Maybe they didn't even know why they were going. They just wanted to see what was out there."

Ben returned the coin to her, and as he placed it in her hand their fingers touched and entwined briefly in an instinctive gesture of understanding.

Kitty looked at the coin for another moment,

then returned it to her pocket. "I begged my folks to let me come because I thought I wanted to marry Boothe," she said.

She watched Ben's face carefully for a reaction, but he gave none. "And do you still?"

She dropped her eyes. "Now he's just Uncle Boothe. But that was never the real reason. Ever since I was a little girl, I've known I had to cross the river . . . just to see what was on the other side."

Ben smiled at her, and they didn't need to say anything else.

"I'm glad you're alive, Ben."

"Yes," he agreed softly, and leaned back, closing his eyes. "So am I."

Lucy wondered if the two people inside the wagon had any idea that the sun setting behind the canvas cast their shadows in perfect relief, as though it were a gauze curtain instead of a heavy piece of cotton separating them from the outside world. Lucy could see with perfect clarity the way Kitty bent over Ben and put her hands on his unclothed chest and how she sat close to him, their heads almost touching. The girl was a hussy, Lucy thought spitefully. She had no business tending a sick man all by herself. Both Lucy's mother and Mrs. Creller had volunteered their services, but Kitty had sent them away. She was a hussy.

Lucy had even begged her mother for a little of the soup stock from last night's supper, which she had thinned down and seasoned herself with spices brought all the way from St. Louis, to speed the invalid's recovery. Angrily she tipped the bowl over and poured its contents on the ground. He didn't deserve it. He seemed to be recovering just fine.

She didn't like Ben, anyway. Not any more than she liked Oliver. Neither one of them had what it took to appreciate her. None of the men on this dreadful trip were worth the bother it took to get them interested. And what was she going to find when she finally reached that godforsaken place on the banks of the Solomon River? Indians. More animal than man, completely uncivilized, utterly hopeless. What kind of future was there in that for a girl her age?

Things had been different back home. Back home every boy in the county had been panting after her, without her having to do more than bat her eyelashes. Lucy had learned early on that the world was run by men, and that a woman could have anything she wanted as long as she made sure the man who had it wanted *her*. A pretty smile, a toss of the head, that simple art of making a man feel full of himself—that was all it took. Unspoken promises were a powerful tool, but without a man to dangle them in front of, a woman was impoverished and alone.

It was too bad, she thought sourly as she turned back toward her own wagon, that her charm didn't work as well on women as it did on men. It was beginning to look as though the only person on this trip who ever got her way about anything was Kitty Kincaid.

Lucy was scuffing her steps, scowling at the ground, and she almost bumped into Richard Singleton before she noticed him. Of course, Richard was easy not to notice; she didn't guess he had said more than a dozen words in a row to anybody since they had left St. Louis. But she smiled at him anyway, just as she smiled at every man, and held her shoulders a little straighter and her head a little higher.

Something about the way he swallowed convulsively when he saw her, the way he jerked off his hat, and the way she felt his gaze on her even after she had passed made her stop and turn around. She strolled back over to him, her smile deepening.

"Mr. Singleton," she said sweetly, "I've just done the silliest thing. I was bringing this bowl of soup for Mr. Adamson when I dropped it on the ground." She slipped her arm through his, looking up at him and dimpling her cheeks. "I wonder if you'd carry it for me while we walk back to camp?"

Sheldon Gerrard maneuvered his rolling chair across the room to the big window. Then, balancing himself carefully and bracing his hands on the sill, he lifted himself upward. The stump of his left leg banged against the chair and threatened to overbalance him, but he held on to the window frame and stood tall. Sometimes he could still feel pain in the phantom limb. Sometimes he could still smell the gangrene that had rotted away his flesh, a little more each day, and sometimes he could still see Boothe Carlyle's face as he swung the hatchet that severed his leg from the rest of his body. And he could hear his own screams for mercy, pleading with the other man to let him die . . .

He had brought himself to the window tonight to watch the shimmer of the sun setting on the river, to let the never-ending movement of the bold, brassy city take over his mind and soothe him. There were people everywhere he looked. Women in fancy dress goods imported from Europe

and brought down river from Pennsylvania and
Charleston, South Carolina. Trappers in coon caps
and leather leggings. Bankers and metalsmiths in
the silk top hats that were fast replacing beaver
hats and making those trappers an extinct species.
Traders, unloading canoes and barges at the wharf,
or setting off empty to bring back more of the
riches of the. West. Everyone moving, everyone
with someplace to go, some dream to fulfill.

St. Louis was a town built on dreams. Dreams of
people who didn't know any better, people who
couldn't stay still, people who just had to keep
pushing for that pot of gold at the end of the rain-
bow. For some, the dream came true, but whether
it did wasn't important. What mattered was that
they dreamed, and the dream kept them alive.

For Sheldon Gerrard, the dream came once in a
lifetime, and when it was gone there was no getting
it back. When it was stolen, it was worse than losing
a leg, worse even than losing your life. No price,
none at all, was too great to exact in return.

Gerrard thought of Oliver Sherrod's message,
sent from Westport; he'd made contact with
Carlyle. Retribution had been set in motion.
Gerrard wasn't sure how much he trusted Sherrod, but Sherrod wanted Boothe Carlyle brought
down as much as he did.

Gerrard reached into his pocket and idly fingered a coin. He drew it out and held it up to
catch the glint of the dying sun.

It was very old, very rare, and worth far more
than he had paid for it in the goldsmith's shop in
Pennsylvania. The smithy hadn't known anything
about it and in fact was getting ready to melt it
down for ore, fool that he was. Gerrard suspected

that the coin, like so many similar treasures, had been salvaged off a dead man's body, which only made it all the more precious.

Once, he had collected such things: the rare, the beautiful, the unobtainable. He had parted with many of them to finance the expedition to Oregon. But the coin he had kept, to remind him of what once had been, of what he might have become.

He often spent hours looking at it, trying to imagine what the symbols on it depicted, trying to picture the nature of the people who had once lived and were now forgotten, who had crafted such a coin. Civilizations rose and fell, men wove their way across the earth without leaving so much as a track in time, but the things they created—the things they *dreamed*—survived the centuries. Just holding the coin made him feel connected to something grand and noble, something bigger than himself, just like his own dream had been. The dream that, except for one man, would have been fulfilled.

Slowly, Gerrard's fingers closed around the coin, blotting out the sunlight that danced on its edge. His face grew hard; his eyes, lost at first in the vision of the past, slowly darkened.

"You should have let me die, you son of a bitch," he said softly. It was spoken like a vow, and his fist tightened on the coin. "You should have let me die."

Chapter Nine

The traveling gradually grew harder over the next few days. The trees, even along the creek banks and streambeds, were fewer and farther between, and the soft, leaf-covered ground gave way to tall, coarse grass that waved like a billowing sea in the ever-present breeze. In the distance the rugged shape of the Flint Hills beckoned, promising relief from the tedium of the flat prairie lands, but they inched toward them at a dismayingly slow pace.

The sun was hot and dry, and insects crackled in the air. Sometimes, just to ease the monotony of the never-changing landscape, the women would climb off the wagon seats and walk alongside, looking for wildflowers or weaving the tough grass into decorative braids. All except Rachel, who was terrified of the snakes she was sure were hiding in the grass, and remained grimly mounted on the wagon box with her husband.

Kitty's pony, Snow, was tied to the back of Ben's

wagon and trotted along behind with an air of resignation. Kitty tried not to look at him too longingly or too often, for until Ben recovered the use of his arm, she was condemned to the hard plank seat and limited view from the top of the wagon. She was a strong girl and accustomed to hard work, but the reins had already bitten blisters into her hands, the constant sawing motion of trying to keep the oxen in line had turned her shoulder muscles into burning, aching knots, and every time the wagon hit a rut it felt as though a new nail was being driven into her tailbone.

She glanced at Ben as he climbed back onto the seat beside her from the back of the wagon, where he had gone to secure a canvas flap that was scattering dust over the foodstuffs. "How're you feeling?" she asked.

"Like a danged fool." With a sour look he indicated the arm that was strapped to his chest with several strips of torn sheeting. "I hate letting you do all the work while I sit up here like some kind of rich city boy in knickers."

"You're lucky I'm here to do it."

"I reckon so," he admitted grudgingly.

Then Ben glanced at her. She sat with her legs apart and her elbows resting on her knees to ease the strain on her back; the floppy-brimmed leather hat was pulled down low on her head, but the wind had already unwound her braid into a tangled mass of wayward curls across her neck and shoulders. Her face was bronzed by sun and dust, the sleeves of her shirt rolled up above her elbows. He grinned. "You look like one of those mule skinners that used to come through Cairo and tear the place up with their drinking and swearing."

She scowled. "You don't exactly look like you stepped out of a five-cent magazine yourself."

He laughed, but Kitty felt uncomfortable. She supposed she had always known Ben was good-looking—before he went away to school all the girls in Cairo were forever chasing after him—but it had never meant much to her before. Even now, with his hair tousled like wheat in the wind and his face brown and his blue eyes crinkled in the sun, there was something about him that made a girl want to fuss with her hair and put on her best apron and pinch her cheeks to make them glow. And that irritated Kitty.

She said abruptly, "You should be able to take the reins tomorrow."

"I could take them today."

"And break open your shoulder again so you'd never be any good to anybody."

Ben was silent for a moment. There was more than a note of testiness in Kitty's tone, and he knew he'd made her mad, though he didn't know how. He didn't want to argue with her, partly because she was right—she usually was—but mostly because, since the accident, Kitty had seemed to be his only friend.

Long hours in the sun had gradually cleared out the congestion in his lungs, and his shoulder, though still stiff and aching, was not the fiery mass of pain it had once been. But sometimes he awoke at night coughing up phlegm and reliving the nightmare under water, shaking, drenched with sweat, terrified. Boothe was not the kind of man who would understand fear, and Oliver, though he had saved Ben's life, was once again distant and cavalier. As for John Syms and Martin Creller— Ben was gradually beginning to realize he did not know them, or even like them very much, and if it had not been for Rose, he would never have chosen them as friends.

With Kitty he did not have to pretend, or be careful, or act as though nothing had changed when everything had. She knew without his having to say it, how in one brief moment that he hadn't asked for or expected or even deserved, the insides of his world had been ripped out and scattered to the wind. His shoulder would heal, and eventually the nightmares would stop. In a few days, or weeks, the coughing would go away, and he would be able to take a deep breath again, though the remnants of that time under water might linger for years in the form of chest colds and unexpected weakness. Still, he was alive, and he would get over it. But at the age of twenty-two, he had never expected to look death in the face and walk away. That was something no man could experience and remain unchanged. That was something he would never get over.

Looking straight ahead, he said, "You know, it's funny. All those years, watching you grow up, I never thought much about you except that you were a sassy thing, and your folks spoiled you something terrible. But it don't seem to've hurt you none." He glanced at her quickly, then away. "I shouldn't have said what I did before, about you having no business here. I'm glad you came along."

At his words, pleasure unfurled inside Kitty like a flower stretching for the sun. But she wouldn't let him see it. "I reckon you've got cause to be," she replied grumpily, "seeing as how I'm the one that's been cooking your meals and cleaning your wounds and driving your wagon for the past two days. It's about time somebody started appreciating me."

"I appreciate you," he insisted, confused. "I just said it, didn't I? What do you want me to do?"

She shot him a dark look. "Stop saying I look like a mule skinner."

He broke into an incredulous grin before he could stop himself. "Is that what's got your back up? I thought your mama raised you better than to be vain."

"My mama didn't raise a mule skinner, either."

He settled back, his eyes twinkling. "Pretty girls ought not to frown like that. It makes them look like mule skinners."

"And stop flirting with me. You sound silly."

"What do you know about flirting?"

She gave a toss of her head that was purely instinctive. "Maybe more than you think, Ben Adamson."

He looked at her for a moment longer, then uncomfortably away. He thought about what John Syms had said about the sins of the flesh and the dangers of having too many single men—and women—on a trip like this. He thought about the little girl who used to follow him around, pestering him with questions and dogging his shadow. He thought about Kitty straightening up from the body of Zeke Calhoun with blood on her hands and in her hair, and he thought about her falling beside him on her knees in the water and putting her arms around him.

He thought about Rose, but their time together

seemed so long ago . . . almost as though it had never happened. His days with Rose were like a faraway dream, something to be deeply cherished and looked upon fondly, but they no longer had anything to do with his life.

Then, though he knew he probably shouldn't have, he said without looking at Kitty, "You are a pretty girl, Kitty. Real pretty."

He saw her smile beneath the shadows of her hat, and he was glad he had said it.

"Look!" Effie said, stretching up her arm and opening her hand to Martin. It was filled with rich, black soil. "I've never seen such black dirt. Just think what a body could grow here!"

Martin grinned down at his wife, who was walking beside the wagon, keeping up with the pace of the oxen easily, often moving off ahead to pick a flower or exclaim over some oddly shaped stone— or to scoop up a handful of dirt. "A farm girl to the bone," he teased her. "You just can't get it out of your blood, can you?"

"There are worse things to be," she replied saucily, and Martin felt a surge of affection for her as she flung out her hand and let the wind scatter the soil.

These moments of communion, of smiling at each other and talking like they used to, had grown rarer as the journey grew longer, and Martin couldn't understand why. Too often their conversation turned to arguments that ended in stiff-lipped silences, which lingered even after evening prayers, and they went to bed—Effie inside the wagon with Adam and Martin beneath it—feeling the hurt and the pressure of all they had left unsaid.

Their life in Tennessee had been simple and pre-dictable, and they had known from the beginning what their marriage would be like. She cooked his meals and kept his house and welcomed him to her bed at night; he clerked at his father's feed and seed, and on Sunday, if he was lucky, they traveled to a church in a nearby village or cross-roads that was in need of a preacher. From the moment Martin asked her to marry him and Effie said yes, they had both known that this place of western skies and painted Indians would be their eventual destiny. In that they had been united.

When little Adam was born, Martin had worried some about making the trip, but Effie never hesi-tated, never asked him to reconsider. She was his wife; where he went she would follow, and where he was called she would answer. Even throughout the hardships of travel thus far, of sleeping under a canvas roof and cooking over a temperamental outdoor fire and cleaning dishes with damp rags instead of soap and water, she had not complained. He had not expected her to; she was his wife.

She hadn't complained, but she had changed, and she was changing more every day in subtle ways that were hard to define but nonetheless difficult to adjust to. It had begun that night at the Shawnee mission, when she had spoken up in defense of the Indian girl without anyone inviting her opinion. He had never known Effie to be outspoken about anything before, especially at the risk of embar-rassing him—as she had most certainly done that night. And then there was the business with the snake. Back in Tennessee, if something like that had happened, she would have gone into hysterics and he would have had to ride for her mother to come put cold compresses on her head while she took to her bed. That's what he would have expected her to do, just as he had always expected himself to protect her, to lead the way while she followed. But it wasn't like that anymore. Maybe it never had been, really, and he had just failed to notice.

Sometimes Martin felt as though he didn't know the woman he had married.

The baby cooed, and he glanced down at his wife, striding beside the wagon with his son strapped to her back like a trapper's pack, and the brief contentment he had felt a moment ago vanished again into the more familiar unease and irritation. Their latest argument had occurred when she had spent the evening at Kitty Kincaid's fire and had come back with that heathen-looking contraption for carrying their baby.

She had said something about having admired the way the Shawnee women carried their young around on cradle boards strapped to their backs while they kept their hands free for work, and she had gotten Kitty and Boothe Carlyle to help her rig up something similar with part of a rush basket and some scraps of cloth. Martin told her he didn't want his wife acting like a squaw, that they had come out here to civilize the Indians, not to become like them. Effie retorted that she didn't see anything uncivilized about a woman making life a little easier on herself, and maybe there were some things about the Indians that didn't need changing. She never used to sass him like that. And this morning, as bold as you please, she had brought out that contraption and strapped little Adam into it, knowing full well how it would irritate him.

The worst part was, his son had never looked happier, bouncing up and down on his mother's back, waving his fists and twisting his head beneath the shade of his bonnet, trying to take in everything at once. No, what upset Martin most, if he were completely honest with himself, was that Effie had done this thing without even consulting him. She had taken a notion in her head and gone straight to Kitty Kincaid, and when Martin had disapproved, she had ignored him. That wasn't like Effie. That wasn't the girl he had married.

Was it?

And now, because he was feeling disgruntled again, he couldn't resist saying, "You better watch the sun on that baby's face. He's going to get burned."

She didn't even hesitate in her jaunty step or glance up at him. "A little sunshine never hurt anybody. It builds good bones."

"Did you learn that from the Indians, too?" he muttered.

Then she did look up at him, calmly and without malice. Her own face, always ruddy from the outdoor life she loved so much, would soon be nut-brown from the sun's glow. "No," she replied. "I learned it from my mother. And yours."

Martin fixed his gaze on the oxen's backs and said nothing.

When she spoke again, something had changed in her voice. He should have been prepared, but he wasn't.

"Martin," she said slowly, carefully, "I want you to teach me how to drive the team."

He stared down at her, astonished. "What for?"

But he already knew why—because Kitty Kincaid

did it. Kitty Kincaid, who talked to animals and rode bareback and didn't have the modesty of an alley cat. Kitty Kincaid, who had been welcomed into the Shawnee camp like a lost child, which, considering who her relatives were, might not be so far from the truth. John Syms said she was a witch, and maybe he was right. She had certainly caused enough trouble on the journey so far to be the devil's handmaiden.

Effie replied, with a troubled frown creasing her forehead beneath her wind-crumpled bonnet. "I've just been thinking. We've got a long way to go yet and . . . what if something happens to you, like it did to Ben Adamson? I need to know how to drive."

For a moment Martin didn't know what to say. Since Ben's accident, the thought that it could have been any one of them had not been far from anyone's mind, and hand in hand with that thought was the realization that there might be worse to come. But Effie shouldn't be thinking about it. And even if she worried, in the way women do, the last thing Martin would have expected of her was that she would be planning on how to get along without him.

And yet . . . there was a disturbing thread of logic behind her reasoning. If he were laid up, who would take care of her? All of the men, except Oliver Sherrod and Boothe, had their own wagons to tend. Boothe would as soon unhitch the team and put Effie and little Adam in Ben's wagon as not, and Oliver was too rough-and-ready to be trusted with a woman and baby.

Still Martin said sharply, "Nothing's going to happen to me."

Her reply was even. "Maybe not. I hope not. But just in case . . ."

"You're not strong enough to handle this team. They'd wear your arms out."

She looked up at him, squinting in the sun. "I'm stronger than I look, Martin."

And in that moment, Martin knew that was what really bothered him. Maybe she was stronger than he'd guessed. Maybe she could make decisions and speak out about things and get along without him if she had to. Maybe she wasn't the docile Christian girl he had always thought, true to the teachings of St. Paul and content to walk forever in her husband's shadow. Why had he never realized that before?

"I'll get someone else to teach me," she said.

He could forbid her, and he should, but he didn't. Maybe because he suspected it wouldn't do any good, and he didn't want to find out.

A long time passed with nothing but the creak of the yoke and the rattle of the wheels for company. Then Martin said quietly, "Effie . . . if something happened . . . if I were killed . . . what would you do?"

She was silent for a long time. They had never talked about such things before; he didn't like to talk about them now.

Then she said, "I'd go on." She looked up at him. "I'd have to, wouldn't I?"

Martin turned his attention back to the team and tried not to think about all the new things he was learning about his wife. But he couldn't help thinking about them, and worrying, a lot. All he could do was refuse to offer to teach her to drive the wagon. It wasn't much, in the big scheme of things, but for a while it made him feel better.

They reached the Flint Hills just before sundown after days of hard traveling over open plains. After the long stretch of flatlands, the rugged, gently rolling hill country was like passing into another world, but Boothe warned them to enjoy the change of scenery while they could: Once they left the Flint Hills, nothing remained but miles of monotonous prairie.

The first thing Kitty did was to mount her pony and, with the excuse of gathering firewood, trot off through the hills. Another person might have seen little appeal in the stony, wind-swept countryside, but Kitty was enchanted. The soil was rocky; grassy knolls bisected by slabs of exposed stone that made riding treacherous in places. But her pony was surefooted and strong-hearted, and he seemed to catch Kitty's enthusiasm as he gamely negotiated steep climbs and slippery descents.

She paused at the top of a rugged outcropping, with the wind sweeping through her hair and the last faint rays of the sun tingling her cheeks, and looked out over the landscape. Groves of cottonwood and elm trees, rocky knolls scarred with barren slabs of flint, dips and swells of tall, blue-stem grass—It wasn't lush or restful; it was a rough, hard land meant to mock the lazy or the inept; farming would be a constant battle against rocks and roots, and living in a place like this would be a daily challenge. Yet there was something wild about this place that struck a chord in Kitty, set off a tingling in her blood, and made her feel that the long weeks of travel had all been worth it, just to see this country.

It came to her, sitting astride her pony and tasting the wind in her face, that, although there were surely more beautiful places on earth, with quiet streams and lazy rivers, shady oaks and lush wildflowers, if she had the whole world to pick from, she would choose to build her home in a place like this. It was worth the journey, just to know that.

Twilight descended abruptly, and reluctantly she made her way back to camp, stopping at the last minute to hurriedly fill her arms with dried wood. Boothe already had a fire going when she arrived, and she expected a scolding for being gone so long. But he merely shot a teasing glance at her and said, "Have a nice ride, did you?"

Kitty slid off her pony and let the armful of dried sticks clatter into a loose pile beside the fire. Her face was still flushed with exertion, and her eyes glowed with excitement. "It's so different," she said. "This country—everything we've passed through—it's like nothing I've ever seen before, or even known was *there*. And it's good land, too." She waved her arm to indicate their surroundings. "Sure, it's rocky, but you could build a strong, sturdy house out of those rocks. And if it were me, I wouldn't try to farm it. I'd raise sheep, or cows, or even horses. There's plenty of grass, and natural shelter from the weather—you wouldn't even have to raise a barn. Why hasn't anybody thought of that? Why hasn't anybody tried to settle here?"

Ben came up with a pot of water and beans to cook. Kitty did not point out that he should have waited for the water to boil before adding the beans; it wouldn't hurt them to eat mushy beans for one night and it was her fault, anyway, for not being there to start supper.

"You forget this is Indian country," Ben said. "I'd say, to their way of thinking, it's already settled."

Kitty *had* forgotten that, and she was ashamed. But she felt compelled to defend herself. "I haven't seen any Indians. And it seems to me, as big as this country is, there should be room for people who want to make a home without interfering with the Indians."

"There should be," Boothe said, "but it don't work that way. Indians are a far-roaming people, and while it might take only a few acres to feed a farmer in this country, it takes hundreds of miles to feed an Indian tribe. But it's more than that." He took the pot from Ben and set it over the fire. "You should've waited for the water to boil to add the beans."

Kitty went to the wagon and unwrapped the salted cloth from a slab of bacon, then cut off a good-sized slice. "What?" she said over her shoulder. "What more?"

"The idea of owning a piece of land, of marking out a stake and staying there, is something the Indian doesn't understand," Boothe explained. "To their way of thinking, we're just caretakers here, and nobody owns anything. That gives them the right to move wherever they please and take whatever they choose, and that's why there's never going to be room for white settlers and Indians to live side by side."

Because the contour of the land did not permit the wagons to spread out, the camps formed tight circles tonight, and the cookfires were nearly adjacent. Martin, who was building up his fire next to

Boothe's, had been listening intently. "That's all going to change once they're educated," he said. "When we teach them proper farming methods, and how to build strong houses and obey God's laws, they'll be content to settle in one place and raise their families."

Boothe met his eyes for a long, thoughtful moment. Then he said, "Mr. Creller—and begging pardon of the ladies—that's like trying to teach a bear to use a privy. How can you make somebody understand what they can't even imagine, and wouldn't see the sense in if they could?"

Kitty dropped the bacon into the pot of beans and water, and sat back on her heels before the fire. "Still," she said hesitantly, "everything was Indian country before we started settling it, wasn't it?"

"That it was," Boothe agreed. "We couldn't change them then and we won't now. All we could do is push them further west. Pretty soon there won't be any place left to push."

"Just as well," commented John Syms. "This is wild country, unfit for anything but the beasts of the field. No decent man would ever try to raise his family here, away from God's grace and God's people."

"I know a good many Indians that'll be glad to hear you say that, Reverend," commented Boothe dryly. "But I think you're wrong. Where there's land, there's always going to be somebody wanting to claim it. We all came from stock that was itching to get out of the Old Country, where there were too many cities and too many people. Now the cities back east are starting to get crowded, and that same stock will be moving on, looking for more land. Not many have traveled this trail yet, but them that have—like you folks, and the brethren that went before—will be sending back tales about how tall the grass is and how rich the dirt and"— he shot a glance at Kitty—"how strong the hills are, and pretty soon they'll come, with their wagons and their axes and their plows, marking off their land and raising their crops. Maybe just a handful at first, then a few more, but that's all it takes."

"It *is* good farmland," Martin murmured.

"It's beautiful, too," Kitty added. "Maybe it is wild, but people have lived in wild places before."

Boothe nodded. "I don't know, but I've been told these hills look a lot like Scotland. I reckon that's why I like them so much."

Scotland, Kitty thought, and a little thrill went through her. It was a place she had no connection to and no claim on, but it had the familiar ring of home. Though her blood was not Carlyle, she had instinctively felt the pull of these hills, and that made it her home, didn't it?

Effie looked up from the pot of stew she was stirring. "That's where your folks are from, aren't they, Mr. Carlyle?"

He nodded. "Partly. A long time ago."

"Is that where your cross came from?" Ben asked. "The Old Country?"

Boothe fingered the leather thong around his neck and drew the pendant that was suspended from it out of his shirt. "I reckon so. It's been in the family a long time."

Effie took a step closer to Boothe's fire. "What an unusual piece!" she exclaimed softly. "Is it iron?"

Oliver, just returning from watering the horses, noticed the direction of Effie's gaze. "I'll be damned," he said.

He received frosty stares from Reverend Syms and Martin, and Effie retreated in embarrassment, but all had learned the futility of trying to reprimand Oliver for his bad language. He ignored them and squatted down next to the fire, gazing across the flames at the pendant suspended around Boothe's neck. Oliver gave a small shake of his head. "All those years of knowing you, and I never saw it in the flesh. Fact is, I reckon I'd forgot about it, and I never thought I would." He glanced at Kitty. "That thing"—he nodded at the cross Boothe was now tucking back into his shirt—"saved our lives. Your mama ever tell you that story?"

Kitty hesitated, knowing that if they were to have a corn pone for supper she needed to start mixing the batter right then. The other women would have their men fed and bedded down before she even got started, and she had wasted too much time today. But so far from home, in the midst of these people who were not strangers but were far from being family, all the willpower in the world could not have persuaded her to refuse a story of the old days—even if it was one she had already heard.

So she said, "Mama told me a lot of stories. So did Pa."

Oliver needed no more encouragement. His thoughts were already traveling back seventeen years. "It was the day the Shawnee came and took you. I reckon Ben's too young to remember."

"I remember," Ben said. His face was grim in the firelight, his eyes lowered. All around the campsite, activity slowed or ceased as, one by one, the members of the party strained to catch Oliver's words, even those who pretended not to listen.

"We'd already had one skirmish with the Shawnee," Oliver said. "Byrd was bad hurt and one man was dead and"—his voice was bitter—"God knows I wasn't no help when it came to fighting. We were outnumbered anyway, we knew that. Our only chance was to bargain our way out, and when the Shawnee came back, your ma marched right up to them with her head held high and that's just what she tried to do."

The campsite was silent now. Even Lucy, who only a moment ago had been rattling dishes and slamming down the lid on the water barrel to proclaim her displeasure with her evening chores, drew closer to her mother and listened. Rachel absently stirred her pot with a long-handled spoon, but her face was turned toward Oliver. Even the shadows seemed suspended, waiting to unfold the dangers of the past . . . or the present.

"But them Indians was a tricky bunch," Oliver went on. "They took what we offered, all right, and then went to take our women, too. And then your ma, she reared herself up and she said, 'Take me. Take me and let the others go.' "

There was wonder in his eyes and reverence in his voice when he spoke of Katherine. Kitty felt herself swell up with pride, and choke up with longing.

"Then she flung off her bonnet. I never did understand why she did that, but she must've known what she was about, because them Indians was purely fascinated by all that red hair of hers. They started jabbering away in Shawnee, and Byrd—he knew a little of it—he told your ma they were talking about the Firebird." He looked across the fire at Boothe. "That's when Miss Katherine got this real strange look on her face, and she knelt down on the ground and drew that cross with the circle around it. They acted like it was a sign from God. They took what we'd offered them, but let us be."

He did not add what Kitty already knew—that they had taken her as well, though they had done it as a gesture of respect to Katherine, and to save the life of a starving infant.

Oliver looked across at Boothe, a faint line of puzzlement between his eyes. "I always figured it was because of you. Because they knew you. But it was more than that, wasn't it?"

Everyone was looking at Boothe with new respect now, even as they were eyeing the shadows that danced at the edge of their campfires with new uneasiness. It was a tale from nearly twenty years ago, but it was told firsthand, and three of their members had been witnesses to it. The Shawnee were a tame tribe now, Christianized as the travelers had seen with their own eyes. Yet they had been capable of treachery and murder; what more might the group expect from the Indians of this untouched, unprotected place?

They were in Indian country. They had known that for days now. But knowing it in the mind and feeling it in the bones were two very different things.

Boothe nodded in answer to Oliver's question. "A blood oath is a powerful thing to the Shawnee, and they counted me brother. But the reason they did was mostly this." He drew out the cross again. "All the tribes know this sign. It's a sacred thing to them."

Ben frowned. "Why?"

"I don't know," Boothe admitted. "There's things about the Indian language, and spirit world, I don't reckon we'll ever understand—any more than they'll understand ours."

"It's not such a mystery," John Syms said. "The cross is a symbol of our Lord, and the Indians aren't as ignorant as we'd assumed. Even the heathen recognize the wonder of God's power."

Boothe smiled faintly. "Reverend, the Indians were here thousands of years before any white man ever came to spread the Word, and they knew the sign of the cross long before our Savior ever died on it. For that matter . . ." He ran his fingers along the circular outline of roughly hammered metal. "I can't prove it, but I've got a notion this thing here is older than Calvary."

"Impossible," Syms said dismissively.

"That's blasphemy," Martin added darkly.

But both men were staring intently at the cross around Boothe's neck.

Boothe just shrugged. "Maybe. I just know that folks have a way of thinking the world is a lot younger than it is . . . Here in America, especially. We call it the New World, but it's not. The Indians talk about a people that were here before they were, and the Indians have been here longer than we can imagine. We're the newcomers here, some might even say intruders. Compared to what's gone before us, we haven't even been here long enough to leave a smudge on the history books. So maybe we shouldn't be so all-fired quick to come in and try to change what we don't understand."

There was a long, long silence. Kitty looked around her and saw the hills that were older than time, and wondered what peoples they had sheltered before her. She thought how small they were, this little band of travelers, how insignificant beneath the great bowl of the sky and the vastness of the prairie and the fullness of time itself. The others must have felt it, too, for there was an uneasiness in their faces as they turned awkwardly back to their pots, their water barrels, and their wagons.

Even John Syms's voice held a little less authority than usual as he said quietly, "Sometimes, sir, I think you are an emissary of the devil himself."

Boothe smiled. "No, sir, I was raised a Christian man. It's just that I've lived long enough to know there's more than one way of praying, more than one way of believing. And out here, all alone, a man needs all the faith he can get."

John Syms went back to his own fire and opened up his Bible. After a while he began to read out loud. Rachel sent Lucy to the wagon for a pinch of flour to thicken the stew, but there was a preoccupied frown on the older woman's face as she picked up her spoon again.

John was right, of course, she thought. This was a heathen land, and Boothe Carlyle was a wicked man with dangerous notions, and none of it—not this place, not the savage Indians, not the likes of Boothe Carlyle and his lot—were fit concerns for God-fearing folk. From the moment John had made the decision to go forth into the wilderness, Rachel had known that God might demand a blood sacrifice from His children. They might die out here, all of them. John said there was no greater glory than to give one's life in the service of the Lord, and John was always right. But Rachel had not wanted to come. That was her secret. John would forever put the salvation of the world before the welfare of his family; that was the source of his greatness and her own regret.

But now she worried that Boothe Carlyle might be right; that the Indians could not be educated or changed, that they might all be brutally killed or worse, and their sacrifice would have been for nothing. She knew what the Indians did to women, and there was her Lucy, young and pretty and far too incautious for her own good . . .

Lucy came strolling back just then, and Rachel frowned at her. "What took you so long?" she whispered over the sound of John's voice. "This stew's fixing to burn on the bottom and you don't even have the plates out yet."

Lucy sprinkled a handful of flour over the pot and Rachel caught her smiling back over her shoulder. She looked around and caught a glimpse of Richard Singleton ducking behind the wagon.

Rachel brought the spoon up with a sharp rap across Lucy's wrist. "What are you doing?" she hissed angrily. "Smiling at that boy like that! What've you two been up to back there? Have you lost your senses?"

Lucy rubbed the back of her arm and scowled at her mother defiantly. "You never want me to have any friends! All I was doing was—"

Rachel gripped her daughter's arm hard, but not nearly as hard as the anxiety that was gripping her own belly. "You listen to me, miss—"

"Woman!" John bellowed, looking up sharply. "Is there something more important than the reading of God's word?"

Lucy looked smug as Rachel released her arm and murmured, "No, John."

John resumed his reading, and Rachel kept her counsel. If they had had a son, it might have been different, but Lucy was Rachel's responsibility. She could not involve John in her worries.

After a while she filled a bowl with stew and brought it to her husband. They bowed their heads while John prayed for guidance through these troubled times and deliverance from the unbelievers among them. Rachel prayed her own silent prayer that, while her husband saved the world, God would give her the strength to save her family.

At Kitty's fire, supper was late, the beans were mushy, and there was no corn pone. The men ate without complaint, even Oliver, who, having grown weary of trying to mind his manners at other camps, had lately taken to adding his provisions to theirs. While Kitty, scowling over the inadequacy of the meal, wiped the dishes and muttered about somebody needing to bring in fresh game before they all forgot what it tasted like, Oliver filled a pipe with raw-smelling tobacco and wandered off to smoke it. After a time, Ben followed him.

The memories of the past weighed heavily on both men, each in his own way, and they stood silently for a time, lost in their own thoughts. Then Ben said, "You're right, I was too young to remember a lot of it. But I remember being hungry and scared and cold at night. And I remember the Indians, and people dying. It must have been bad. A lot worse than I ever knew."

Something rustled in the dark bushes beyond them; a stone grated as it was kicked aside by small, scurrying claws. Oliver drew on the pipe, creating a faint orange glow from the bowl. He said, "Not nearly as bad as what's ahead of us now."

Ben thought he was probably right, but it didn't frighten him as much as it once might have. When he had begun this trip he had felt nothing: not fear, eagerness, remorse, or zeal. In those few brief moments when death had closed its hand around his throat, he had felt everything more intensely than he ever had in his life, and fear no longer held the power over him that it once had.

"What happened to you, Oliver?" he said quietly.

Oliver did not look at him. "What do you mean?"

"We've heard things about you. Not all of them good."

A glint of amusement played in Oliver's eyes as he glanced at Ben. "Trying to save my soul, boy?"

"Why not? You saved my life. Seems the least I can do."

Oliver drew again on his pipe. "My soul's not worth saving. Don't waste your time."

"Miss Katherine used to speak highly of you. She was mighty proud of you when I was growing up."

Ben thought he saw Oliver flinch in the dark at the mention of Katherine's name. When he spoke his voice was low and rough. "I don't reckon she's too proud of me these days."

Ben said nothing.

Abruptly, Oliver knocked his pipe against a tree, emptying it onto the stony ground with a shower of sparks. "You want to know what happened to me? Crossing a goddamn river happened to me. Looking into a western sun happened to me. Looking and thinking and wanting more than I had.

This land happened to me. It changes men, that's all, and anybody that takes it on deserves what he gets."

He turned on his heel and started back to camp, and then he looked back. He studied Ben, standing there alone in the darkness. "You should've stayed home, Ben," he said quietly. "You and that little gal Kitty . . . You should've stayed home."

Chapter Ten

They left the Flint Hills behind and moved out into the vast, endless prairie. Many times over the next weeks Kitty would think back with longing on the rugged shapes of those hills, the shady crags and bold vistas, for that place in her memory was the only relief from the monotonous sameness of the journey.

The land was flat, unbelievably flat. Though they could sometimes feel the tension in their calf muscles that signaled an uphill slope, the flatness didn't change, the land showed no contour. They moved their feet, the wagon wheels turned, but they never seemed to be going anywhere, and the horizon never drew closer.

Sometimes they passed through sunflower fields that went on for miles, even days. At first these vistas delighted the women. They plucked armloads of flowers and brought them back to the wagons, only to discover they were full of bugs and had to be cast away before they infected the flour and the meal. Occasionally they came upon patches of little purple flowers with prickly leaves that pulled at their skirts, but mostly it was grass—yellow-green, waist-high, crackling grass that rippled with the movement of unseen creatures and billowed in the wind. Moving through that grass was like dragging oneself through water, and every step stirred up a cloud of insects that buzzed and swarmed and tried to dart into the mouth and nose.

Sometimes they saw a fox, dashing through the grass, but mostly it was prairie dogs, poking their heads up out of their holes and sniffing the wind, then dropping under cover again. Once Lucy almost got sprayed by a skunk, and after that she was a lot more careful about wandering off on her own. That night, Oliver brought to the stew pot a stripped carcass that he claimed was prairie dog. Kitty could taste the difference, but she ate it anyway. The strong, gamy taste of skunk made a nice change in the diet when fresh meat was getting harder and harder to find.

The sun was merciless, but so was the wind. It was a dry, steady wind that soaked up perspiration before it had a chance to cool, that tugged at clothing with hot bony fingers, that settled into the ears with a low, constant moan that made the travelers shout to make themselves heard and then forget why they were shouting, for the wind by then had become as common as the sound of their own blood, pulsing through their veins.

They forgot what it was to be clean. Dust, too fine to see in the air, was driven by the wind into the pores of their skin and the fibers of their clothes; it sifted through their shoes and darkened their feet; it caught in their hair despite the hats. They breathed it, they ate it with their food, they scraped films of it off the tops of the water barrels, they slept wrapped in it at night.

At first they joked, saying now they understood why no one but Indians would live here and how it made sense that there wasn't any trail through this wilderness. But as day after endless day wore on they didn't joke anymore. It was all they could do to keep moving.

Boothe always rode ahead, sometimes by as much as a mile, to scout for water and the next campsite, and to warn against hidden gullies, which were always a danger because even a man on horseback couldn't always see them until he had stumbled right into one. Sometimes those gullies were less than a wagon's length across and easy to avoid. Sometimes they broke the ground for a half a mile or more, causing a detour that could easily lose them half a day.

That was the case as Boothe rode back to the caravan in the midafternoon and drew up beside Ben, who was driving the lead wagon. "We're going to have to cut to the north," he said, pushing back his hat and wiping his brow. His sleeve left a clean patch across his dusty forehead. "There's a creek bank about two miles up where we can camp for the night. It's not much, but it'll give the stock some water."

Ben nodded and pulled on the reins, slowly turning the wagon. He glanced at the sky. "Looks like we might get some rain, too."

Boothe's expression was a little worried as he looked toward the low bank of clouds that was building on the horizon. "Maybe," he agreed noncommittally. "Maybe it'll pass us by."

But it didn't. The clouds bred like rabbits, first a few, then a few more, then double that amount and double again. The sun scuttled in and out of cover, flinging down black shadows and bright patches. The wind turned faintly cooler and the travelers lifted their faces toward it, drinking in the taste of moisture in the air.

"Rain!" exclaimed Effie, pushing back her bonnet and tilting her face up to let the wind ruffle her hair. "I'd almost forgotten what it felt like! Oh, I hope it's a long one. I'm going to stand out in it with a bar of soap and wash my hair!"

Kitty laughed. "If you do that, everybody'll think you're as crazy as I am."

Effie's eyes twinkled back at her. "Maybe I am."

Though she usually rode Snow, Kitty was walking in the grass beside Effie so that she could hold little Adam. She had raised five brothers and sisters, and if there was one thing she missed about home more than any other, it was the weight of a baby in her arms. The chubby boy bounced on her hip, kicking his feet and pushing fistfuls of Kitty's hair into his mouth as he concentrated myopically on the view over Kitty's shoulder. Patiently, Kitty unwound another strand of hair from his fist as she said, "It will be good to fill the water barrels, though. And let the rain beat the dust off the dishes."

But a sudden, fierce gust of wind made her swallow a startled cry as it caught the hem of her skirt and flung it upward, plastering her petticoat to her legs. It was so strong that she actually staggered backward, and she heard Snow, who was tethered to the side of Martin's wagon, whinny in alarm.

Adam squealed with excitement and Kitty struggled to hold him with one hand while slapping down her skirt with the other. Effie was fighting to get her bonnet back on as another gust of wind swept by.

"Effie!" Martin clapped his hat to his head with one hand as he shouted down at her. "Get in the wagon!"

The wind fell back to little more than its usual level, and a bright patch of sun made both women squint. Effie started to protest, then Martin gestured with one arm toward the forward horizon.

They could see the slanting fog of silver rain moving toward them, a clean diagonal line that swept across the prairie as far as the eye could see. Behind the glinting mask was a bank of dark clouds that rose up from the ground and stretched their fingers to the sky. Jagged lightning streaked upward, followed by a clap of thunder so loud that Kitty's teeth ground together. Adam started to wail.

"Maybe you'd better take him inside," Kitty said, raising her voice a little as the wind rose again. Effie was already reaching for the baby, and the wind snatched at Adam's bonnet and blew it off his head. A shaft of alarm went through Kitty and she cried, "Tie the cradle down!"

Fighting the wind every step of the way, Kitty went back to untie Snow. The usually placid pony was snorting and tossing his head as the wind slapped at his mane, and Kitty did not want to add her weight to his struggle against his instincts for flight. Thunder exploded with a force that made the ground shake, and Snow reared up and pawed the air, stretching the rope taut in Kitty's hand. When his forehooves struck the ground again he twisted and started to bolt, but Kitty lifted her voice to him, pulling on the rope to guide him forward, toward Ben's wagon.

The ferocity of a storm was nothing new to Kitty, nor to any of them. They had all seen houses incinerated by lightning and crops beaten into the ground in a matter of moments by hail; they had all, at one time or another, lain huddled in their beds while thunder blasted and lightning popped and rain pounded like a thousand furious hammers on the roof. But here on the open prairie they were small and vulnerable, and nature's fury was immense. It was as though none of them had ever known a storm before.

The animals felt it most deeply, as naturally they would. They smelled the electricity in the air, they saw the long lines of grass go flat before the approaching band of rain like a tide racing toward them, and they heard the high-pitched squeal of the wind in their ears. Their senses fired off conflicting signals, their human owners shouted at them and whipped the reins, and they rolled back their eyes and tried to run; changed their minds and balked; bellowed and fought in their traces.

Boothe's horse reared and danced, and he fought for balance as he shouted to Ben, "Stay away from the creek bed! With this much rain it's bound to flood!"

"Kitty!" Ben yelled. His hat flew off his head and tumbled across the prairie. "Get in the wagon!"

Kitty tied Snow to the wagon, fumbling with the ends of the rope the wind kept whipping back and forth. She got the knot secured and grasped the back of the wagon to climb inside when the wagon lurched to a stop, swaying back and forth as the oxen fought in their yoke. She started to turn, and suddenly a flap of the canvas ripped loose and struck her across the face, hard enough to knock her to the ground.

Kitty got to her feet with her face stinging and her vision blurred, the involuntary tears that streamed down her cheeks blown away by the wind before they even had a chance to leave tracks in the dust. Ducking her head and fighting the tangle of her skirts, she clung to the wagon with one hand to pull herself along as she made her way toward the team.

Ben was climbing down from the wagon box when she reached him. "No!" she shouted, lifting her arm to him. "Take the reins! I'll do it!"

The first hard, slashing needles of rain hit her as she reached the oxen's heads and grabbed the yoke.

All the teams were balking, some trying to turn and gallop away from the storm, others lashing out at their yokes, still others standing dumbly with their heads lowered, refusing to budge an inch. Martin saw Boothe dismount and go to the head of John's team, and Oliver do the same for Richard, and he knew he had no choice. "Effie!" he called, twisting to shout over his shoulder into the back of the wagon.

Effie checked the straps that secured the cradle on either side to heavy crates of tools and laid a quick, comforting hand on Adam's stomach. "Hush," she said. "Mama's going to be right back. Everything's all right." The baby screamed and thrashed his hands and feet, and with one last anxious look at him Effie clambered toward the front of the wagon.

A wave of rain hit her in the face as soon as she poked her head through the opening in the canvas, but that was only the forerunner of the real storm. The band of rain was like a battalion of dark giants marching steadily forward, now only a few hundred yards from the lead wagon, and where it began the world ended.

"Take the reins!" Though his mouth was only inches from her ear, Martin had to shout to be heard over the roar of the wind and another, earth-shattering roll of thunder. "I have to go to the team's head!"

Effie stared at him for a moment, then climbed hurriedly over the seat.

His eyes were narrowed against the rain and dark with anxiety as he passed the leather straps to her. "Just hold on tight! Brace your feet, don't let them pull you off. When I signal, give them a slap!"

"I can do it!" she shouted back, and wound the straps around her hands. "Go on!"

He hesitated for a moment longer, doubt and worry scarring his face, then he kissed her quickly and sprang to the ground.

The first leaping step the oxen took almost propelled Effie over their heads. She braced her feet against the front board of the wagon box and wound the straps another turn around her hands, so tightly that blood throbbed and her fingers turned white. She could hear Adam screaming in the back and rain was whipping through the opening of the canvas, no doubt soaking him. Her bonnet dripped and molded itself to her head and she could barely see Martin's figure, less than eight feet in front of her.

He waved his arm at her and Effie slapped the reins. The oxen lurched forward, the jolt of movement tearing at her shoulder muscles. She gritted her teeth and slapped the reins again. The rain made its own roar over the rumble of the wind, pounding on the canvas, driving into Effie's mouth and nose and eyes. Martin was a blur at the head of the team, dragging the oxen into motion, then running beside them as they picked up the pace . . . and then suddenly he wasn't there anymore.

Effie's heart stopped. The oxen kept moving, but Martin had fallen. She couldn't see him, he was going to be trampled beneath wheels and hooves . . . She screamed and lurched to her feet, and the unsteady rocking of the wagon almost flung her to the ground. She pulled on the reins, but the team ignored her, and she screamed Martin's name again.

And then she saw him. Stumbling to his feet, grasping for the yoke, and waving her onward. Effie sank back into the seat and tried to concentrate on holding the reins steady, but sobs of relief and fear were shuddering in her throat.

Soon not one wagon was visible to another. Lightning sparked and cracked with hardly a breath between one jagged spear and the next, and the rain was no longer coming down in sheets—it was a tidal wave, surging and receding and gathering force to slam against them again with twice the power. Boothe struggled from one wagon to the next, shouting orders no one could hear, mostly trying to get a head count.

Kitty struggled to free the oxen from the yoke, blinded and choking on mouthfuls of rainwater.

The wind battered her and she had to hold on to the yoke to keep from being swept off her feet. Ben grabbed her arm. "Get under the wagon!" he shouted. "I'll do that!"

His face was a blur beneath the whipping drapery of rain; his wet clothes pressed against his body and billowed backward where their fullness allowed them to do so. He staggered a little against the force of the wind, and both of them almost lost their balance.

"Snow!" Kitty cried, turning the oxen over to him. "My pony!"

"Leave him!"

But she tore away from Ben's grip and pulled herself along the wagon bed toward the pony, who was frantically trying to free himself from the restraint of the rope. She knew she couldn't get him to shelter; she didn't even know where shelter was. All she could do was try to free him and give him a chance to save himself. Her breaths were like sobs as she struggled with the knot in the wet rope, and suddenly there was a great shrieking, flapping noise overhead. Snow lunged wildly and the rope broke. Kitty whirled around to see a huge piece of canvas soaring through the air. She thought she heard a woman's scream, and she knew it was the Crellers' wagon that had been hit.

She lunged toward the sound and straight into Ben's arms. "It's Effie!" she cried. "The baby!"

She didn't know if he heard her or not. She caught one glimpse of his face, hard and wild and raw with urgency, and then he dragged her down, pulling her beneath the wagon, pushing her face down with his weight half on her and half off, and she knew then the meaning of real terror. He had abandoned the oxen, Snow was gone; he had turned his back on the Crellers and their baby because there was nothing they could do. All they could do now was try to save themselves. From an afternoon rainstorm to a matter of survival in less than an hour; that was desperation, that was hopelessness, that was terror.

As soon as Martin brought the wagon to a halt Effie scrambled to the back to snatch up Adam. She was trembling with exertion and fear, and she couldn't even catch her breath to murmur to him. Wind slammed against the wagon, causing it to rock precariously, and Effie held the baby tighter to her breast. Adam had already gone purple with screaming; his cries were now little more than scratchy choked wails. Effie squeezed her eyes shut tightly as thunder crashed around them and tried to pray, but all that came out were inarticulate sounds that were half gasps, half sobs. Then there was a great ripping sound; wind and water slammed against her and Effie screamed as the canvas tore off the wagon and was borne away.

Martin's heart stopped as he felt the wagon lurch beneath the impact of the wind and watched in horror as the entire canvas covering was snatched away. More than his heart, his whole world stopped when he heard Effie's scream and saw his wife and child huddled and helpless beneath the raw power of the elements. He had gotten the team unhooked and was struggling to hold them down, knowing that the minute he released them they would bolt, when his family's very survival depended on the safety of that balky team of oxen. But survival was a matter of the here and now. Never had a truth been more intensely, terrifyingly clear to him than it was at that moment.

He dropped the reins and ran toward Effie, slipping and sliding into the water that was already rushing over the tops of his shoes. He got his arms around her, crushing their son between them, and he didn't think he could ever let go. The wind drove knife points of rain into his back. Effie was screaming something into his ear, then somehow she broke away, thrusting the baby into his arms as she climbed out of the wagon. Clinging to each other, they fell to the ground and crawled beneath the wagon, sheltering the baby between them as the wind roared and the wagon swayed.

Rachel sent Lucy to tie down the canvas at the back of the wagon while she and John tried to unhook the team. Lucy couldn't believe that her mother would send her out alone. The rain roared against the canvas roof, but sheets of water were already whipping in through the open flaps, and there was no way to tie them down without going outside. When Lucy peeked out, her face and hair were immediately soaked, and she could see nothing, nothing at all except gray water and flashes of blue-white light that shook the earth. She couldn't move. She clung to the inside board of the wagon and ducked her head against the slapping waves of rain, and she had never been so scared in all her life.

Then someone grabbed her shoulders, shaking her. "Can't stay here!" The words came in snatches, and thin, bony hands were trying to drag her over the side, out into the storm. "Lightning—dangerous!"

It was Richard, looking like a drowned mouse with small darting eyes. She fought against him as he pulled at her, but her struggles only overbalanced her, and she fell out of the wagon against Richard and they both tumbled into the mud. She was raging at him, spitting water and slapping at him, but he got here in a sharp-fingered grip and dragged her up and away.

Seconds later the earth exploded in a flash of blue and white, and a dark steaming circle appeared on the grass only a few inches from where they had been standing. Richard pushed her under the wagon and when, a few moments later, Lucy's parents joined them, no one noticed that Richard had his arms around her and was holding her tight—no one except Lucy. Her father began to pray, but his loud, strong voice was drowned out by the rain, the words snatched up and cast aside by the wind. Her mother's mouth was open, but no sounds came out. Lucy wanted to pray, too, but she couldn't remember any prayers, so she clung to Richard, holding him tight, and thought that would make her feel better. It didn't.

Kitty thought that this, then, must be what it felt like to die. Not a quick, sudden blast of pain, a merciful darkness, and the soft sweet bliss of the ever after—but pain and fear that went on and on, the roar of the wind that wouldn't stop, fire that stabbed at the earth and thunder that deafened, and just when you thought it couldn't get any worse, it did; it just kept getting worse and worse, and it wouldn't stop.

Her fingers were wound together with Ben's in a grip that had long since turned her hand numb, and his other hand was pressed against her head, fingers digging into her skull as he held her face close to his shoulder. Shudders of fear rocked her body and seemed to spread to his; she clung to him with the same desperate ferocity with which she clung to life as the wagon creaked and swayed over their head and rivulets of water raced across the ground beneath them, crawling between her breasts and her knees and inching into her shoes.

She thought about Effie and the defenseless baby. She thought about Boothe and Snow, lost in the storm. And she thought they must all be dead, washed away in the flood or battered by the wind or crushed beneath the fiery fingers of lightning. Only she and Ben remained, they and the rain and the wind that wouldn't stop, that only grew louder and fiercer and would surely topple the wagon with the next blast, pinning them and crushing them into a slow, agonizing death. She wanted to scream, she wanted to pray, she wanted to beg for deliverance, but all she could do was cling to Ben and think, *Stop it, stop it, please stop . . .* over and over again until the words lost their meaning.

And then, as quickly and as surely as it had come upon them, the storm moved away. The thunder dwindled from claps to roars and then to booming rolls that came less frequently. The rain pattered, then dripped. The wind began to whisper, stirring standing puddles of water. And when Kitty dared to open her eyes, she saw misty shafts of sunlight twinkling on the grass beyond the wagon.

Slowly she felt Ben's muscles unclench, then her own. Their stiff fingers untangled from each other's. Kitty pulled herself from beneath the wagon and stood up on legs that were shaky and aching, bracing herself against the wagon. Ben stood beside her.

Already sunlight was beginning to dapple the rain-soaked meadow; puffy white clouds scuttled away to reveal a canopy of blue. The wagons stood where they had been abandoned, only the Crellers' showing signs of damage. In the distance an ox lowed, and two of the animals stood not twenty feet away, contentedly munching on the wet grass.

Kitty heard the fretful squall of a baby, and relief went through her like a wave of dizziness. As she turned she felt a nudge on her shoulder, and Snow pressed his wet nose into her neck. A gurgle of disbelieving laughter caught in Kitty's throat as she wrapped her arms around the pony's neck.

One by one they emerged, wet, battered, and dazed. Effie, passing the baby to her husband as she turned with the stunned expression of a sleepwalker to examine the wreckage of her belongings. Lucy, falling to one knee as she tried to stand up, and being gently helped to her feet by Richard. The Symses, covered with mud and grass, looking slowly around, not touching. And then Oliver struggling up the slight slope that led to the creek bed, dragging the torn canvas that had been blown from the Crellers' wagon.

It took them several moments to realize that it was over, that they were alive. Kitty looked from face to face and saw the same emotions that were building in her . . . wonder, disbelief, amazement. And the sheer, incredulous joy.

Someone whispered, "Blessed be."

Another murmured, "Hallowed be Thy name."

Kitty felt the touch of Ben's hand on her shoulder, a quiet, soul-stirring affirmation of what they had survived. And she lifted her hand to squeeze his fingers. The joy inside her was so intense it had no words.

John Syms stepped forward, his palms turned upward and his face raised to the sky, and began to sing in a deep, rolling bass. "'Praise God from whom all blessings flow . . .'"

His wife joined in with a reedy soprano that nonetheless sounded beautiful in the clear, calm air. " 'Praise Him all creatures here below . . .'"

Effie's voice joined the chorus, her arm around her husband's waist and her face pressed against Adam's cheek. Kitty drew a breath, wanting to sing, wanting to shout, wanting to laugh out loud . . . and then she stopped.

Where was Boothe?

She looked around frantically, her heart pounding. She twisted to look up at Ben, but his brow was furrowed with concern, his eyes searching. The voices swelled, raised in reverence and joy, and then a rich, rolling baritone joined in. " 'Praise Father, Son, and Holy Ghost . . .'"

Kitty whirled, and there was Boothe coming toward them, his shirt torn and his face muddy, his wet hat slapping against his thigh. With a strangled cry of joy, she moved toward him, stopping to touch Effie's hand, and Oliver's sleeve, and joining her own voice to the chorus. When the last joyous strains of the song died away, she was hugging Boothe and he was hugging her. Ben joined them, and when Kitty looked up again everyone was reaching out to someone else, laughing, touching, embracing.

Boothe met Syms's eyes across the melee and

grinned. "Well, Reverend, I reckon God must have His heart set on you folks bringing salvation to the Pawnee after all. I got the rest of the stock tied up downstream, and there don't seem to be much harm done."

His smile faded as his eyes went to the Crellers' wagon. "Looks like most of your supplies made it through," he said, by way of comfort, "but I don't reckon that organ'll be going much further. I know it meant a lot to you, ma'am."

But Effie just flashed him a big smile and declared, "It was too heavy anyway. It was wearing out the oxen."

Martin tightened his arm around her waist, and Boothe grinned. "Well, I tell you what. Before those pipes dry out and swell up, let's get her off the wagon and see if she's got any music left in her. Be a shame to let a fine instrument like that die out here on the prairie with nary a song to mark her passing."

The atmosphere was festive as the men lent their backs to sliding the organ onto the ground. There were more important things to do, of course—mending canvas, drying clothing, checking supplies. But those were easy to ignore. They were alive, they were triumphant; they had passed through their baptism of fire and they could endure any trial, conquer any adversity. Tonight, they celebrated.

Rachel Syms brought out half a smoked ham she had been saving since Westport for their first supper at the Pawnee mission. Kitty uncovered the last of the sweet potatoes, and Effie found a half-dozen apples that had not gone soft. Ben discovered a handful of hard candy wrapped up in his dry shirt, and Kitty laughed when she remembered his secret fondness for the stuff. Even Oliver dug into his saddlebags and produced a pouch of relatively dry tobacco for the men.

Effie sat down at the organ with a flourish worthy of a concert pianist, and everyone laughed when the first chord that came forth was a clash of nonmusical notes. But after a few more pumps a discernible melody came through, and Effie launched into a hearty, full-bodied rendering of "Rock of Ages." They all sang along, with enthusiasm if not harmony, moving back and forth before the fire, smiling at one another, laying out dishes and wringing out clothes. As the sun went down they feasted, and Effie struck up the notes of a lively tune from the Tennessee hills. Over the shocked stares of Reverend and Mrs. Syms, Kitty swept a curtsy to Boothe and, linking arms, they swung into a high-stepping reel.

Oliver gave a shout and clapped his hands in time to the music; Ben threw back his head and laughed. When Kitty swung toward him, Ben caught her arm and picked up the steps of the dance. Oliver bowed deeply to Lucy Syms, and she ignored her father's stern frown as she twitched her skirts and sashayed toward him.

"Now see here!" Reverend Syms demanded. "Stop this nonsense! Lucy—" Effie played louder, and even Martin kept time to the music with a dinner fork and the back of a plate. John Syms turned to his wife. "Mrs. Syms!" he barked. "See to your daughter!"

But just then the partners changed again; shy Richard Singleton had somehow gotten the courage to step in for Lucy, and before any of them knew what he was about, Oliver Sherrod had grabbed Rachel Syms's hands.

She went scarlet and tried to pull away; the reverend was so shocked it was a moment before he could even get the words out. "Young man, have you lost your senses? Take your hands off my wife!"

But Oliver just laughed and swept Rachel, blushing furiously and stammering protests, into the midst of the circle of dancers. John Syms watched the breakdown of godliness with dismay, but how could he uphold his authority when his own wife and daughter were participants in the mutiny? And then he saw Boothe Carlyle draw out a small jug of something that did not contain spring water, and he knew the end was near. Boothe drank from the jug and passed it to Ben, who hesitated and caught the reverend's eye. For a moment there was hope, then Ben tilted the jug in a small salute and drank with relish. The reverend turned his back on them all and sought solace in the rear of his wagon, where he spent the rest of the evening praying for strength . . . and listening to the music and the laughter outside.

The liquid spirits Boothe added to the occasion were hardly necessary, for the night itself, the victorious atmosphere, the laughter and camaraderie were intoxicating enough. Whether Kitty was whirling in Ben's arms to the steps of a reel or kicking up her heels with Boothe in the Highland fling, she could close her eyes, and briefly, gloriously, she was home. The house was filled with children, Pa was sawing on the fiddle, friends and neighbors were dancing, her mother's face was flushed and her curls were flying as she whirled around the room . . . But when Kitty opened her eyes, there was no sense of disappointment, or loss. Because Boothe was stamping his foot and clapping his hands and calling cadence, and Ben's eyes were twinkling down at her, and she thought that maybe this was what home really meant: not a place, but a state of mind.

Richard had never imagined that the time might come when he would be dancing with a girl like Lucy, touching a girl like Lucy, looking into the fiery, star-speckled eyes of a girl like Lucy. He didn't know how he'd ever had the courage to walk right up to her and ask her to dance, but he'd done it. He had thought she would be mad at him for pushing her down in the mud like that this afternoon, but she wasn't mad at all. In the end he hadn't had to ask her anything at all, he'd just held out his hand and she'd taken it. Even though he couldn't dance she pretended not to notice; she was smiling at him, tossing back her head and laughing for him. She *liked* him. Never had a day been as glorious as this. The night was magic, and his blood was on fire.

He remembered how they had lain together in the rain and how she'd clung to him, so scared and trembling, and even though he'd thought they were both going to die, she had made him feel strong; he'd lived so that he could protect her. He felt alive and full of bold, raw courage. His skin was so hot he thought it would singe his clothing, and he had never loved anything as intensely as he loved Lucy Syms. When the music stopped so that Mrs. Creller could change places with Rachel Syms at the organ, Lucy leaned back against the wagon frame, all breathless and flushed and fanning herself with her hand, and Richard seized his opportunity.

He clasped her hands in a hot, bone-breaking grip and filled up his eyes with her until he thought he would burst with loving her. "Miss Lucy, I think—I think you're beautiful!" he whispered breathlessly.

She tossed back her head and laughed in that light, trilling way she had, then she tapped him on the shoulder with her index finger and declared, "You've got two left feet, Mr. Singleton, but you *do* say the prettiest things! And anyhow, I don't care. I want to dance and dance all night!"

She lifted her arms to him, and he felt as light on his feet as a feather buffeted by the breeze as he led her back into the steps of the dance.

Rachel Syms did not know any songs except hymns, but no one minded. They danced until the organ gave out, and then they sang. Boothe put the cork back in the jug to save it for another day, and he led them all with his warm, vibrant baritone. He had always loved to sing.

When little Adam was asleep in his cradle beneath the stars and everyone was settled down around the single big fire, Kitty reluctantly left the festivities to check on the stock. Ben went with her.

The grass was dry, but the ground was still mushy in places under their feet. The air had a clean, fresh-washed scent to it, like springtime born again. The brilliant, star-studded sky was bigger than the world, bigger than the universe, yet so sparkling clear the little orbs of silver seemed at times to be suspended from the sky, and it took their breath away just to look at it.

Kitty said amiably, "I don't need you watching out for me, you know, Ben Adamson."

"I know. But do you mind the company?"

"No, I reckon not." She took a deep breath and tilted her head back to the sky. "My, isn't it fine out tonight?"

"That it is," Ben agreed, but he thought the finest thing was the way Kitty looked with her bonnet loose around her shoulders and her hair a tangled mass of curls. He walked close to her and didn't step away when the contour of the land caused their arms to brush together, or her skirt to flutter against his legs. Neither did she.

The chorus from the campfire followed them, sweet and clear on the night air. "Amazing Grace." The familiar tune caused a prickle to go through him, a tug on the invisible silver cord that stretched across the miles and bound him to home. He remembered sitting on Katherine Kincaid's front porch, numb and empty, talking about why they should leave Kitty behind. The rain had been coming, the air had smelled like green hay, and Meg's voice had been honey-smooth, heartbreakingly sweet.

He didn't miss Rose anymore. The door on that part of his life was closed, quietly and finally, as it was meant to be. He didn't feel empty anymore, and he was glad Kitty had not stayed behind.

The low of an ox greeted them, followed by the snuffle of several horses in succession. Kitty began to sing along softly as she checked their tethers. Her voice wasn't as pretty as her sister's, but in the starlit prairie it caressed the night like a breeze through the grass. Soft and girlish, a gentle lullaby.

Kitty straightened up and gave her pony a last affectionate stroke along the flank, but she did not start back toward camp immediately. She stood bathed in the silver-gray starlight, looking out over the endless stretch of prairie with an air of contentment, humming softly under her breath along with the distant voices. *Through many dangers, toils and snares/I have already come . . .*

"Long way from home, Kitty," Ben said quietly.

She nodded and turned her eyes to him. "A long way to go."

'Twas grace that brought me safe thus far/And grace will lead me home.

Kitty smiled and again leaned her head back toward the sky. "But oh, Ben, just look at those stars. Makes you want to reach out and grab yourself a handful, doesn't it?"

Ben did not look at the stars. He looked at Kitty, and before he knew it, or even knew that he wanted to, he reached forward and took her face in his hands and kissed her lips, long and soft and tender.

He was still holding her face in his hands when she opened her eyes. She looked at him thoughtfully, with a hint of a question.

Ben did not know what to say. His breath was lodged like a lump of clay in the center of his chest, and his stomach was twisted in knots. Finally he managed hoarsely, "I'm sorry."

"What for?"

He dropped his hands quickly, and then his gaze. "I don't know." All he did know was that he shouldn't have kissed her, and all he wanted was to kiss her again.

"Look at me, Ben Adamson," she said.

He did. Her eyes were quick and bright, and the breeze ruffled her hair, showing off glints of muted gold. Her head was cocked a little to the side, her voice thoughtful.

"Was it just a sky full of stars and being a long way from home that made you do it?" she asked.

Ben smiled. He couldn't help smiling when he looked at her, not any more than he could help lifting his hand and twining one of her curls around his finger. "I don't know that, either," he admitted.

Her eyes were luminous, dark, soul-catching. She reached up, calmly unwound her hair from his finger, and said matter-of-factly, "I reckon you'd better think about that, then, before you go trying to kiss me again."

"I reckon I'd better."

She nodded, though it seemed to Ben a little color came into her cheeks, and stepped away. They started back to camp, neither of them hurrying.

The singing had stopped by the time they arrived, and everyone was getting ready for bed. No one paid much attention to them when they walked up; Rachel was looking around the camp with an irritated, half-worried expression on her face.

"It must've been an hour ago that I saw her," Effie said. "She was with Mr. Singleton."

Rachel's face tightened and she called sharply, "Lucy! Lucy, get back here this minute!"

Kitty felt a sinking in her stomach. She had known Lucy's propensity for wandering off alone would get her in trouble someday. Even Kitty, whose sense of direction was excellent and who knew how to take care of herself in almost any situation, wouldn't have gone farther than shouting distance from the camp at night. No one with good sense would.

Then Rachel noticed Ben and Kitty, and a frantic note entered her voice as she demanded, "Did you see her? Did you see Lucy?"

Ben shook his head. "But we just walked down the creek bank a few yards to check the stock. She might have gone the other way."

"She couldn't have gone far," Kitty added. "She'll be back soon." But she was thinking how easy it would be to get turned around on this vast, unmarked prairie where even the stars looked all alike. If Lucy had left the creek bank . . .

Rachel turned impatiently and walked to the edge of the camp. "Lucy!" she shouted. "Lucy!"

Reverend Syms came out of the wagon in his shirtsleeves. "What's all this racket? What has that girl done now?"

"Lucy!" Rachel shouted again. "Where are you?"

She turned back to the camp, her hands twisted tightly together, and demanded of no one in particular, "Where can she *be*?"

Oliver's gaze moved slowly over the camp, and he said quietly, "For that matter, where's Singleton?"

Boothe had sat down to take off his boots. Now he was pulling them on again, his face grim. After a moment, Oliver put his hat on and reached down to pick up his saddle. "I'll take the west bank," Ben said.

And then there was a movement, a crashing, scuffling sound in the grass. Everyone tensed, and out of the corner of her eye, Kitty saw Oliver's hand move toward the gun in his belt.

Lucy stumbled into camp. The fire had died

down to an orangish glow, and in the uncertain light it was difficult to trust one's eyes. Lucy's hair was tangled and disarranged, and there seemed to be something wrong with her face—it was smeared with a dark substance and looked swollen on one side. Her dress was torn, exposing one small breast and a white shoulder to the firelight. There were dark smudges on her chest and throat. But most startling of all were her eyes, glassy and unblinking, staring straight ahead. She just stood there with her arms dangling at her sides and her neck stiff, not seeing, not moving, not making a sound.

The shock was a palpable, riveting silence that was broken after an endless moment by Rachel Syms's choked gasp. But Kitty was the first to move. All she could think about was how she would feel if it were she standing there with her breast exposed for all the world to see, and she went quickly to Lucy and tried to draw the torn pieces of her dress across the girl's naked chest. In a moment Effie was beside her, wrapping a shawl around Lucy's shoulders. Lucy didn't move. She hardly seemed to notice them. She was like a dead person . . . only she wasn't.

"My baby," Rachel whispered brokenly. "What happened to my baby?" She took a step toward Lucy but didn't quite make it. She fell to her knees with both trembling hands slowly going to her mouth as though to hold back a scream or fight off sickness.

Kitty felt herself go weak with a heavy wave of nausea and revulsion, for up close the shadows couldn't conceal what they all knew to be true. It was clear what had happened to Lucy. Her mouth was swollen and crusted with blood; a dark bruise was forming on the side of her face. The marks on her chest and shoulder were fingerprints, and her breast showed a clear impression of teeth marks. A man's teeth, a man's bruising fingers. The hem of her petticoat was torn and trailed around her feet, and it was splotched with blood.

Effie swayed a little, her face chalk-white and her eyes horrified smears of dark horror as they met Kitty's. Rachel, on her knees behind them, began a high, thin keening. Kitty tried to get her throat to work and couldn't; she tried again and managed, hoarsely, "We'd better get her in the wagon."

After a moment Effie gathered herself and took Lucy's other arm. They began to lead her on halting, sagging legs toward shelter.

Rachel staggered to her feet, stifling sobs with her fist, and reached out for her daughter. Lucy didn't turn her head, or blink, or say a word.

John Syms never moved.

A long, hard look passed between Boothe, and Ben, and Oliver. Their jaws were like iron, their eyes like ice. Boothe picked up his rifle and checked the load. Oliver took his pistol out of his belt. Ben lifted a coil of rope off the nearest wagon and settled it on his shoulder.

Without saying a word, the three men left the camp, fanning out in separate directions.

Kitty sat up long after the muted sounds of Rachel's sobs and John Syms's low, strained voice had stopped. Long after the lanterns were out and the moon had set. She sat with her back propped up against the wagon wheel and her hands hugging her elbows and waited until she heard the sound of footsteps returning.

Three men had left the camp; three men came back.

Ben sat down beside her. He smelled of moldy creek water and perspiration and exhaustion. Without speaking, he sought her hand and his fingers closed around it.

She didn't ask, and he didn't say.

After a moment, Kitty lifted her arm and drew his head down to her shoulder. They stayed like that, resting against each other, until the first pink rays of dawn touched the distant horizon. Maybe Ben slept. But Kitty's eyes wouldn't close, and she sat wakeful and pained, standing watch against the shadows of the night.

Chapter Eleven

Lucy slept. In her sleep her brow furrowed and her hands clenched and unclenched, and she made choked, mewling sounds, battling demons of the night. Rachel sat beside her, soothing her brow with damp cloths, and when John couldn't stand the sight or the sounds anymore, he went outside and stood alone in the night. He didn't know what to do. He didn't even know what to feel. There was shock, and there was rage, but mostly there was the question, numb and agonizing: Why had God chosen to visit this unspeakable horror on him?

And there was shame. Shame because his own daughter had stood there naked and violated for the eyes of heathens to mock. Shame because he, the spiritual arbiter of right and wrong and Christ's representative on earth, had been singled out for this humiliation; shame because the devil had crept into this camp and he had not recognized him. Shame because he, the strongest of them all, was helpless.

He had stared at his daughter's bruised and bleeding body, and he had not known what to do. He had watched three men take up weapons and go off into the night, and he had not known how to act. He looked into his wife's shocked, agony-filled eyes and listened to his daughter's whimpers in the night, and he was lost in the wilderness of violence and evil, defenseless and confused.

"My God, my God," he whispered, "why hast Thou forsaken me?"

No answer came but the whispering of the wind through the tall grass.

When dawn turned the sky to gray, Rachel came out of the wagon. Her eyes were red-rimmed and swollen, her lips thin, and her shoulders slumped with fatigue. She looked at John, and he thought he saw a brief pleading in her eyes. She wanted him to comfort her, but he didn't know how.

"She hasn't said a word. Her eyes are open— but she doesn't see me. And she doesn't speak."

"The Lord cares for His own," John said.

"The Lord didn't do much for her last night, did he?" Rachel snapped back.

"Woman, you blaspheme!"

Rachel's lips went tight, then she turned to the wagon and took the water bucket off its hook. "Why did you bring him here?" she demanded lowly. "He was a stranger. We could have left him in St. Louis, but you insisted on taking him in!"

"He was Pastor Sheppard's nephew," John asserted. His voice didn't carry nearly the conviction it should have. "A man of God—"

The bucket clattered noisily against the wagon wheel as Rachel whirled. Her eyes were narrow slits of dark fire. "That *man of God*," she spat in a low, violent voice, "raped my daughter!"

John Syms drew back his shoulders, tightened his fists. "Where were you when she ran off into the dark with that man?" he demanded. "The girl is your responsibility. You should have—"

Rachel stepped forward in two strides, drew back her arm, and slapped her husband across the face. Then she turned on her heel and walked away.

John Syms went slowly back to the wagon, the stinging imprint of her hand on his face and impotence burning in his belly. He thought then of many things he should have said, could have done. But it was too late.

Rachel walked blindly along the creek bank, concentrating only on trying not to stumble until she got out of sight of the others. She thought over and over again, Why didn't He just let her die? Why didn't He let them all die? Why didn't He strike them down with one merciful blow from heaven? Why put them through this torment, through this life that was only a step above hell, when all they had wanted to do was serve Him?

The thoughts were blasphemous, she knew that. She *wanted* to blaspheme. She wanted to shake her fists to the sky and call down God's wrath, and maybe while He was busy punishing her He would leave her baby alone.

Rachel Syms had buried three children already, all sons. She had known agony then. She had felt her heart wither up into a hard little ball and rest there, cringing from another blow. Yet she had suffered God's judgment. She had accepted His right to call His own home. She had even, in time, managed to praise Him for sparing her

little ones the pain of this life. But Lucy . . . She had
gloried in her, perhaps too much. She had taken
pride in her bright spirit, her pretty features, her
quick laughter. That was her sin; this was her punishment. Because Lucy wasn't laughing anymore,
and maybe she never would again, and the God
she served was a God of wrath, not justice.

She knelt beneath the shade of a cottonwood
tree and dipped her bucket into the creek
mechanically. Her legs strained as she stood
up, and some of the water sloshed over the
heavy bucket to dampen her skirts. Then the
shadow of a movement caught her eye. Slowly,
still carrying the bucket, she walked around the
cottonwood tree.

She saw the boots first, dangling about six feet
above the ground, swaying a little in the breeze,
rustling the leaves and making an odd creaking
sound. Her eyes moved upward, over a pair of
legs; a lean torso; limp, dangling fingers. Richard
Singleton's face was bloated and black, his neck
broken by the snap of the noose. A stream of
blood was etched between his puffy lips, and his
eyes were blank and staring. Just like Lucy's.

Rachel didn't scream. She didn't drop the bucket and cover her face, and she didn't recoil in horror or run sobbing back to the camp. She watched
while the green bottle flies began to gather and
buzz around the corpse. She stood and stared while
the sun rose higher and glinted off the dusty leaves
of the tree. And she felt something within her grow
cold, and die.

Out loud she said, "Good."

Her face was hard and her shoulders square as
she walked back to camp.

* * *

It could have been so many things. The wind that dogged them day and night, that dulled the eyes of the women and hardened the faces of the men, filling their food with grit and their lungs with dry, bitter dust. The monotony of flat, sparse buffalo grass and the brassy bowl of a sky and wide open land that went on and on without a break. It could have been disease or storm or prowling animals or bad water or a simple accident that left them at the mercy of the elements . . . There were a thousand things to break the spirit out on the prairie, a thousand ways to die.

But in the end, it had been none of those unforeseen disasters that sapped the lifeblood out of the travelers. It had been one of their own. Like a man who rolls up a rattlesnake with his bed, they had brought their own destruction with them and hadn't even known until it was too late.

Boothe thought about that a lot over the days that followed—about the things a man could be prepared for, and the things he couldn't. The things he could prevent, and the things he was better off not even trying to stop. He dreamed about the wolf again, and it made him angry. Why should he dream about a wolf he would never see when his dreams couldn't warn him about a storm that swept across the flatlands and left devastation in its wake, or about a snake in the guise of a man?

They all grew leaner as the weeks passed, browned by the sun and toughened by hard work. Water grew scarcer, as did firewood. For a while the women spent their days plucking dried grass and bundling it for the cookfires, but when even that grew too scarce and too green to make a good fire, Boothe sent them scouting for buffalo chips. Even Kitty was appalled at first, declaring angrily that she would not serve anything out of a pot that had been cooked with manure, but they all soon found they had no choice, and grew used to it.

The Crellers' baby was fretful and cried most of the time. There was no way to keep his linen clean on the trail, and he had a nasty diaper rash that grew worse as the days wore on. When Boothe told Effie that the Indians didn't put diapers on their little ones, and he had never seen an Indian with a rash, Effie Creller drew herself up and replied with cold dignity that although she would tolerate many things for the sake of this godless wilderness, she was not about to turn her baby into a naked savage. And then she burst into tears.

Kitty made an ointment of axle grease and powdered ashes, and it helped some, but not much. A few days later, when they stopped for nooning, Boothe noticed that Effie had placed the baby on a pallet in the sun, without his diaper.

And they moved on, day by day, inch by inch.

They traveled four abreast across the open prairie, with Oliver now driving Singleton's wagon. Fatigue wore heavily on them all, dulling their expressions and weighing down their steps. Nooning wasn't the social occasion it once had been, and with sundown came the chores of camp-making, a meal, and then bed. There wasn't much singing anymore. Or much praying, either.

Lucy Syms had not spoken a word since that

night. Her mother dressed her and brushed her hair, and sometimes made her walk alongside the wagon for exercise and air. Most of the time, though, she stayed huddled beneath the canvas cover with her eyes squeezed slightly shut, making little noises to herself. Boothe noticed that the atmosphere among the others was noticeably less tense when Lucy was out of sight.

No one ever spoke about Richard Singleton, or what had happened that night. No one liked to be reminded of it.

The mood of the travelers worried Boothe. Their tension and their sluggishness were an open invitation to carelessness, and an accident of any sort this far from civilization was one thing they could not afford. It was for that reason perhaps that Boothe's own senses were particularly sharp, acutely attuned for the slightest sign of danger. In the middle of a cloudless afternoon on the empty prairie, he found it.

He was riding about two hundred yards ahead of the wagons when he suddenly stopped, his eyes focused on the horizon, listening hard. He didn't move, waiting for the wagons to catch up to him.

Ben drew abreast of him first. "What is it?"

"Indians," Boothe said. "Riding hard."

Ben's muscles tensed and he squinted toward the horizon, but he saw nothing.

"Just wait," Boothe quietly answered his unspoken question.

Kitty drew up beside him on Snow. "Why're we stopping?"

"We got company," Boothe said. He sat easy in the saddle, gazing across the empty prairie, but there was a tight edge to his voice that sent sharp alarm through Kitty. "You'd better spread the word. And it might not be a bad idea for you females to stay out of sight."

Kitty didn't hesitate. She whirled the pony and rode to the Crellers' wagon.

"Get the baby inside," she commanded breathlessly to Effie as she dismounted. She lifted her voice. "Mrs. Syms—Lucy! Get in the back of the wagon and stay there! Indians are coming!"

Martin slowed the wagon. "I don't see anything."

When Effie hesitated, Kitty grabbed her arm. "Hurry!"

Just as Oliver pulled his wagon abreast of the Crellers', they saw a wavering line appear on the horizon. They were little more than specks, barely distinguishable as riders, but they were moving fast, and in the few moments that Kitty stood paralyzed by the sight, the figures grew close enough to identify as men . . . and not just men, but brown-skinned, gruesomely painted men with feathers in their hair.

Kitty's heart slammed against her rib cage as she jerked on Effie's arm and began to pull her toward the back of the wagon. Little Adam whimpered in his sleep, flailing one fist over the basket sling that was mounted on his mother's back. Reverend Syms murmured, "God save us," in a dull, awed voice, and Rachel was already pushing Lucy into the back of the wagon.

Martin stared, mesmerized, as the riders drew closer. They spread out across the prairie, two dozen abreast; savage, alien beings with skin the color of a new penny. Some carried spears, others bows, and still others rode with rifles held aloft. Martin's throat was dry and his stomach cold with panic; he let the reins drop and fumbled for the rifle in the bottom of the wagon box.

"Put that away, son," Boothe said calmly. "These here are the Pawnee brethren you came to save."

Boothe nudged his horse and rode out to meet them.

Martin saw Oliver draw on his jacket to hide the pistol in his belt, and his hands were slippery on the stock of the rifle as he slowly returned it to the floorboard—but close, angled across his feet so that he could get to it if he had to. Ben sat calmly in his own wagon, and even at this distance, Martin could see the sweat trickle down John Syms's face. The wagon rocked a little as Kitty moved forward to peek over Martin's shoulder, and he wanted to snap at her to be still, to be quiet. But he couldn't speak, and he dared not take his eyes off the approaching spectacle.

Boothe rode forward about a hundred feet, then stopped. The Indians kept coming; it seemed like a legion. The prairie was aswarm with Indians, the ground echoed the thunder of their hoofbeats, and Kitty, peeking out between the canvas flap at the front of the wagon, felt sick with fear. They could encircle the small band of wagons in an instant. They could ride right through Boothe. They could raise their rifles or throw their spears and their targets would be clear; those in the wagons wouldn't have a chance.

But they didn't raise their rifles; they didn't throw their spears. They drew up their horses in a straight line less than three feet from where Boothe sat waiting for them and there they stopped, one lone man and an army of Indians, regarding each other.

They had plucked their eyebrows and beards until their faces were hairless. Their heads were bald except for a single horn of hair, stiffened with animal grease, which some of them had decorated with feathers or beads. Their naked chests were hairless, too, and painted with bright streaks of red and blue. Dust clung to their buckskin leggings and moccasins, and they rode tall, unshod stallions without saddles.

Kitty sank away from the opening in the canvas as far as she could without losing sight of what was going on outside. It was hot beneath the canvas and the air was close; sweat trickled into Kitty's eyes and crawled from her armpits down her sides. Her stomach was wrapped into a cold, hard knot, and her heart was beating so hard she could barely draw a breath. Was this how Katherine had felt, meeting the Shawnee all those years ago? Had anyone ever been as frightened as she was at this moment?

Boothe lifted his hands in what Kitty thought, for one horrifying moment, was a sign of surrender. Then his hands began to move, weaving elaborate patterns in the air, and when he stopped, one of the Indians, the center one, made similar motions accompanied by the grunts of a guttural language Kitty couldn't understand. Sign language, she realized. Boothe was talking to the Indians.

Suddenly Adam began to whimper. Kitty whirled on Effie, her hand striking out in the same swift motion to clamp down hard on the other woman's arm. "Keep him quiet!" she whispered.

But the baby's whimper was fast growing into a wail, and Effie's eyes were stricken with terror in a white, dusty face as she bounced the baby on her shoulder and frantically tried to undo the buttons of her dress to offer the baby a breast.

Kitty's fingers dug into Effie's arm and she hissed again. "Hush! For God's sake, keep him quiet!"

But it was no use. Adam began to scream, and when Kitty looked out the opening again, it was to see one of the Indians break away from the line and lead his horse in a leisurely manner toward their wagon. She saw Martin's hand creep toward the rifle at his feet and close around the stock. Kitty sank back, dizzy with fear. They were coming for the baby. They were going to steal little Adam just like they had stolen her, and there was nothing, nothing she could do about it.

She knew then that Katherine had never been this afraid. Katherine had stood right up to the Shawnee and bargained for the freedom of those she protected. Katherine hadn't cowered in the back of a wagon in a pool of cold sweat and waited for disaster to overtake them. But Kitty was not Katherine Kincaid's daughter, and she never would be.

Effie offered the baby her breast, but he refused it, drawing up his arms and legs and screaming louder. His face was red, his voice loud enough to rattle the canvas.

Kitty gasped as the back flap of the canvas was abruptly drawn aside, and she turned, dry-mouthed, to face the hideously painted red-brown face that looked in. The Indian's eyes slowly swept the interior, inventorying the food and supplies, and when his eyes stopped on Effie and the baby, Kitty's heart froze in mid-beat. She thought of what she could do, what she should do. She thought of Martin's hand on the rifle and of Boothe only a few yards away. If she screamed, someone would come, surely someone would stop him—but there were too many of them. No one could stop them, and besides, she couldn't make a sound. She couldn't even draw a breath.

Then the Indian dropped the flap and moved away.

Kitty's and Effie's eyes met in dumb wonder and relief. Slowly Kitty's fingers unwound from Effie's arm. She felt like a rabbit trapped by the eyes of a snake, waiting, trembling, too paralyzed to run and knowing death is certain . . . and then the snake slithered away, the danger was gone. Another chance. She started to breathe again. It was over.

But it wasn't over. The following moments were among the most excruciating of Kitty's life as she crept again to the front flap to see what was going on. The Indians had dispersed and had begun to wind their way among the wagons, stopping to inspect, examine, sometimes dismounting and looking inside. Boothe continued to converse with them. Once, he said something with his hands that made the others laugh. Kitty thought that was a good sign, but it wasn't because then one of the Indians came forward leading her pony.

Snow! They were going to take Snow!

She lurched forward toward the wagon seat, but Effie's hand, hard on her shoulder, stopped her. Kitty felt a surge of shame then that the courage she was unable to muster for little Adam came now for the sake of a horse, and she sank back, closing her eyes and trying to breathe deeply. *Let them take him,* she thought. *Let them take the horse if only they'll go away and leave us alone.*

And then Martin said softly, "Look."

Kitty turned back to the wagon flap with Effie crowding close behind, little Adam screaming in her ear. Boothe was gesticulating to the Indian with the horse, making wide movements toward the sky and the ground. All the others were mounted, as though in preparation to go. The Indian with Snow conferred with his leader, and then, scowling darkly, dropped Snow's reins and swung astride his own horse. In another moment the entire assembly turned their horses and rode away.

Boothe started back toward the wagons, but no one else moved. It was as though they were all marionettes on broken strings; no one knew what to do or say or even think. After a moment Effie brushed passed Kitty as she climbed over the wagon seat to join her husband. Finally, Adam's wails died down to a whimper.

Martin passed a shaky hand over his face, staring at the rifle that still lay on the bottom of the seat. His voice was low and choked with strain as he said, "I would have done it." He looked at his wife, something akin to disbelief in his eyes. "I would have shot them, Effie, if I'd had to."

Effie put her arm around him and pressed her head to his shoulder. Martin took his son from her arms and held them both, silently.

Kitty climbed out of the wagon on unsteady legs just as Boothe rode up. He handed her Snow's reins, and she looked up at him. "How did you do it?" she asked hoarsely.

He smiled as he swung down. "I told them it was a witch's horse," he replied simply. "Bad medicine."

He looked off into the distance, where a cloud of dust obscured the riders' departure, and added seriously, "That wasn't what done it though. They were going into battle and couldn't afford to be tied down by an extra horse. That's the only reason we'll be moving on with our wagons as full as they were when we got here."

Kitty leaned against Snow, resting her cheek against his warm, bristly neck, and let the tension drain out of her in a single long breath.

The others were gathering around them: John Syms, climbing slowly from his wagon, looking haggard and sweat-drenched; Martin, with his arm around Effie; Ben and Oliver, coming from the sides. It was Oliver who picked up on Boothe's last words.

"A war party, huh?" He tried not to sound worried, but it showed in his face. "Who're they out for?"

"Shawnee," Boothe said briefly. His own jaw was tight. "White Feather's band."

Kitty looked up. "Isn't that—isn't White Feather your friend? The one you asked for at the mission?"

Boothe nodded. " 'Pears he's on the rampage, crossed the Pawnee path once too often. He's out to the north, somewhere—least he was the last they knew. If we're lucky we'll miss him; the last thing we need is to get tangled up in the middle of a tribal war."

But there was anxiety in his voice and sorrow in his eyes. Kitty wondered if he regretted that he would not be able to help his old friend fight, because she did not see how a small band of renegade Shawnee could ever be a match for the warrior braves they had just encountered.

Boothe turned to John Syms. "I asked about your missionaries, Reverend. Seems they're still out there, holding down the mission school. I told them you folks was heading out to join them, to teach their children. That's when they laughed."

John Syms flushed crimson, and Martin and Effie looked uneasy.

Oliver couldn't resist a taunt. "Looks like you just missed a fine chance, Preacher. You should've whipped out your Bible and started bringin' them in to Jesus. Could've saved a whole slew of 'em in one blow; maybe saved a few Shawnee, too."

Oliver's eyes were twinkling as Syms turned on his heel and stalked away. The others looked embarrassed, for no one had forgotten how John Syms had been first to crawl in the back of the wagon when the Pawnee appeared. Then Martin said quietly, "I guess we've all learned a few things about ourselves today."

Kitty watched him lead Effie back to the wagon, and she remembered her own distinct lack of courage when it counted. She guessed they *had* learned a few things, and none of them were particularly pleasant.

Shaken and unsure, they all returned to their wagons and prepared to go on. Ben's wagon creaked and lumbered behind Boothe's lead, and then came Oliver's. But there was a commotion at the Symses' wagon, and Effie had gotten down to help. Curiously, Kitty rode her pony over.

Lucy Syms was curled up in a ball beneath the wagon at the far forward end. Her arms were locked around her knees and her face was buried in her skirts, and the only sounds that came from her were smothered gasps for breath. Rachel was down on her knees, pleading with the girl; Effie had gone around to the forward wheel to try to coax her out. John Syms stood nearby, looking impatient and frustrated.

"I'll move the wagon forward," he insisted. "She'll move when she sees it start to go."

"No!" Effie cried. "She might get under the wheels—you'll crush her!"

Rachel looked near tears. "Lucy, you listen to your mother! Come out from there this minute!"

Lucy only hugged herself tighter.

Effie got a hand through the wheel and touched Lucy's shoulder. The girl fought wildly and wrenched away.

"I don't know what to do!" Rachel cried. "Every time I get near her she fights me—I can't drag her out!"

"It was the Indians," Effie said. "They must've scared her bad."

Kitty slid down from her pony and crawled under the wagon.

"What are you doing, girl?" Syms demanded. "My wife told you—you can't get near her. She'll claw your eyes out!"

"Get away from there!" Rachel said angrily. "You're going to scare her worse! Leave her alone!"

Kitty inched along the grass beneath the wagon. She started talking in a low, quiet voice long before she got near the girl. "Lucy, it's time to go now. The Indians are gone; it's time for us to go, too. Don't be scared. Nobody's going to hurt you." She spoke on and on, not saying much, not caring what she said, just talking soft and sweet as she would to a skittish horse or a storm-shy chicken. Eventually Rachel stopped yelling at her and John Syms climbed up on the wagon seat, and when she was about three feet from Lucy, Kitty stopped. She didn't reach out to her or make any sudden movement. She just kept talking.

"It's all right now, Lucy. Nobody's mad at you. You can come out. I'm going to help you out. Everything's going to be fine. We've got to go now. Don't be scared. Come on. Give me your hand."

Lucy didn't move, but she didn't seem to be breathing quite as raggedly, either. Kitty inched forward and very gently fastened her hands around Lucy's face, slowly raising the girl's head to look at her. She looked into her eyes and saw the madness there, and it made her feel weak and ill. But she kept talking. She kept looking at her, just as she would at a dog that had been beaten once too often and had been backed, snarling and shivering, up against a wall. She kept talking, and she reached down and took Lucy's hand. "Come on now, we're going out in the sun. We've got to go now. I'm right with you. Come on."

She started to move and met resistance. Then Lucy started to move, too. Together they crawled out from beneath the wagon.

Rachel reached too abruptly for her daughter, and Lucy shrank back, leaning against Kitty. Rachel's lips tightened with hurt and astonishment, and Kitty slowly disentangled Lucy's hand from hers. "It's all right," she said. "Your mother will take care of you now."

This time when Rachel reached for Lucy, the girl let her put an arm around her shoulders. But she was still looking at Kitty.

Rachel looked at Kitty, too, with uncertainty and something like grudging respect. Kitty could see how hard it was for the other woman to say simply, "Thank you."

Then she turned and led her daughter away.

Effie smiled at Kitty as she went back to her wagon, and Kitty mounted Snow. They moved off again into the sun, but none of them were quite the same as they had been only an hour ago.

Chapter Twelve

A herd of buffalo was not like a herd of cattle or sheep. Herd, when talking about most animals, might mean fifty or a hundred or even up to five or six hundred. When talking about buffalo it meant thousands upon thousands, more than a man could count; most times more than he could even see.

They were mammoth creatures. When they grazed they left the land barren. When they lay down they left craterlike depressions in the ground deep enough to form small lakes. When they moved the earth rumbled and the day turned to night.

Three men stood off on the prairie and gazed across at the herd. It was a big one; as far as they could see the prairie was shadowed with their dusty forms. The men licked their lips and grinned at one another, eager for the chase. This would be a good one.

Their names were Rufus, Cob, and Hammock.

Like others of their breed, they were ex-beaver trappers who had fallen victim to their own greed. Having glutted the market with beaver fur, they now turned to the mammoth buffalo, whose hides were just coming into vogue back east as carriage robes, shoes, and coats.

Sometimes they ate what they killed, sometimes they stripped off the hide to trade with the Indians or ship back east. But mostly they did it for the fun of killing, for the thrill of running down the beast, for the triumph of plunging themselves into the midst of the thundering roar of the primal beast and coming out alive.

Rufus Bradley lifted his rifle and gave a shout: *"Oooeee!"* And the three men plunged forward into the throng.

When they heard the thunder, all eyes automatically went to the sky, worried and uneasy. Afternoon storms were not unusual; though none so far had been as vicious as the first, they all lived in dread of the lightning and pounding hail. Even the livestock began to shy and toss their heads, but the sky was a clear, unrelenting blue.

The thunder had a different quality, too, Ben noticed as he glanced across at Oliver for enlightenment. Oliver looked as puzzled as he was. It wasn't the usual rise and fall or clapping boom of faraway thunder; it was more like a steady roar, a vibration that grew clearer and louder—and closer—with each passing minute.

Kitty drew up her pony beside the wagon. Her skin had turned a golden-brown color over the weeks, her hair an even lighter shade of blond. The floppy-brimmed hat shaded her face, but her eyes were dark with worry. Like everyone else, she had grown tense, alert to any nuance of possible disaster and too quick to pick up signals of trouble. Yet Ben hated to see that look in her eyes because he remembered when once it hadn't been there, and that time was so long ago and far away it was like another lifetime.

"What do you think?" she said.

He could only shake his head.

Then they saw Boothe riding toward them. He wasn't just riding, he was racing, bent low and beating his stallion with his hat, kicking up a cloud of dust in his wake. He was shouting before he reached them, but no one could hear the words.

They brought the wagons to a halt, and when his heaving, lathered horse grew close enough to choke them with its dust he shouted, "Stampede! Heading this way!" He didn't dismount, or even rein his horse. "Circle the wagons, lock the yokes— get the livestock in the center! I want every man who can ride to get his gun—we've got to try to turn them!"

It took them a moment to realize what he meant by "stampede," but while they were understanding, they were moving. They had seen small knots of buffalo over the past few days, always at a distance and even that was too close. They were huge, ugly-looking beasts, and even one of them, charging at a wagon, could do considerable damage. A stampede . . .

They turned the wagons into a rough circle, and when the teams were unhitched and turned out into the center of the circle, they had to push the wagons together to make a crude fortress. It was laborious, time-consuming work, and before they finished they could see the dark cloud on the horizon. They could feel the ground vibrating beneath their feet.

Martin, Ben, and Oliver were mounted in record time, but there was no horse for Reverend Syms. "Stay here!" Ben told him, and he had to shout now over the panicked lowing of the oxen and the ever-increasing roar of the approaching stampede. "Protect the women!"

But when Kitty jumped out of the wagon with her rifle in hand and started toward her pony, Ben swung his foot out of the saddle and grabbed her arm. "Are you crazy?"

"I can shoot! You'll need every hand—"

"You can't leave these people alone!" That was not what he wanted to say, but he knew instinctively that was the only argument Kitty would hear. "Stay *here*, for the love of God!"

She jerked her arm away, but Ben caught it again. "Kitty, please." His voice was low and intense. "We need you here."

And then she knew what he was saying. The men were riding off into an unknown danger and they might not come back. He didn't trust John Syms's survival skills, and neither did Kitty. So there was only she.

The implication left her numb.

She pulled her arm away, though more gently this time. "Don't you go getting yourself hurt out there, Ben Adamson," she said, and her voice was rough with the emotion that clenched at her throat. "I've got better things to do than to keep patching you together."

He smiled and swung astride his horse. In a single motion he kicked his mount into action and lunged after Martin and Oliver. Kitty stood there with a cold hand clenched around her heart and a terrible, selfish, and wholly pointless urge to call out to him, to make him come back. And she knew then just how much she did not want to lose Ben.

The oxen were restless, and even Snow was snorting the air uneasily. She got the pony to jump over the low barrier formed by the interconnecting wagon hitches and led him to the center of the small circle. Syms was trying to order his wife and daughter back into the wagon, out of the way of the clumsy hooves of the oxen, Adam was crying, and Kitty coughed against a sudden spate of windborn dust.

And then Effie said softly, "Dear God in heaven."

She was staring, chalk-faced and immobile, over Kitty's shoulder. Kitty turned and her head reeled with the impact of what she saw.

The horizon was black with the thundering swarm of mammoth beasts. They spread out over the prairie like ink tipped from a bowl, not just a few, not just a hundred, but thousands, in a thick, unbroken expanse. They were running, charging, dashing madly this way and that, and just when Kitty thought there surely were no more, the mass remained unbroken. More and even more flowed over the horizon.

They were headed straight for the wagons. And their men were riding right into them.

Martin saw the wall of living thunder rushing toward him and it was all he could do to keep his seat, to keep from reining his horse wildly and running the other way. His eyes couldn't comprehend what he saw; all his numbed mind could register was the single thought, *We can't do it. There's no way* . . . He saw the same stricken look on Ben's face, and Oliver shouted something to him, discharging his rifle into the air as he dashed by, but Martin didn't catch the words and within moments his companions were swallowed up by the cloud of dust that preceded the onrushing stampede.

The herd was as big as the state of Tennessee. A man could ride half a day and never get behind it, never even see its broadest end. Four men with rifles were like insects in the midst of them. They would be consumed in an instant, trampled to pulp. There was nothing they could do against a force so great, nothing at all . . .

The tidal wave was headed for his wife and child. It would wash over them and leave nothing but debris in its wake. The roar was deafening in his ears. He could see nothing but gray dust and moving shapes. He knew he was going to die.

He charged forward into the mass, shouting and firing his rifle blindly.

It happened in an instant, but it lasted forever. Rachel began to scream, "We're going to be killed! We're all going to be—"

"Under the wagons!" Kitty shouted.

"Dear Lord in heaven!" Syms cried. "Dear God preserve us, look at them!"

The oxen began trotting around in circles, looking for escape, and Snow reared up and pawed the air. Kitty released his rope and grabbed Effie's arm. "Get under the wagon!"

Effie tore her gaze away from impending disaster like a sleepwalker abruptly awakening, and ran for cover. Kitty turned to the Symses. Already the air was thick with dust, and the pounding of hooves sounded as though it would tear the earth apart. "Hurry! Get under cover!"

John Syms tugged on his wife's arm, but she held her ground, staring, screaming, "We're going to die! They'll trample us, we can't—"

Kitty grabbed her and shook her. "We *are* going to die if you don't get under the wagon! Now!"

One of the oxen bellowed and flung itself against a wagon. Too stupid to go over, it was trying to go through the barrier in a desperate effort to escape. Kitty turned to run toward the frightened beast, but something got tangled up in her skirts and she almost fell.

It was Lucy, her eyes mad with terror, clinging to her legs. Kitty turned to her, trying to shake her off. "Go to your mother!" she shouted. "Let go of me!"

Lucy opened her mouth in a soundless cry and clung harder. Rachel stumbled forward and tried to pull Lucy away, and when Kitty looked up the air was black with dust and she could see the eyes of the beasts.

"Hurry!" she screamed, and pushed them both hard. She dived under the nearest wagon just as a tremendous force slammed broadside against it.

Ben knew what it was like to ride into hell. Hell was hot and airless, filled with deafening bellows and the fiery eyes of mad, rampaging beasts. In hell you couldn't feel the ground beneath your feet or see your hand in front of your face or hear the sound of your own hoarse screams. You were all alone and defenseless.

He didn't know what they were supposed to be doing or how they were going to accomplish it. A hundred men couldn't have turned that herd. The best they could hope to do was scatter the leaders, break the herd apart, and in that way prevent the full force of the wave from crushing the wagons and those they'd left behind.

So he rode head on into the melee, fighting his frightened horse, shouting and waving and firing his gun into the air. Buffalo thundered past on either side of him, huge shoulders jostling against his legs, shoving his horse, tossing him back and forth. Once he went down, his horse's forelegs folding beneath him, and he thought surely that was it, he was breathing his last mouthful of dusty air and seeing his last blur of movement. But his horse scrambled to its feet again and he was still alive. He looked up and saw a huge beast, head down, charging toward him less than six feet away; he fired blindly and the creature dropped in its tracks so close his horse had to leap over the corpse.

He wondered about Boothe, and Martin, and Oliver. He wondered if he were the only one left alive. He wondered about Kitty, and he couldn't think about the wagons crushed to splinters beneath the rampage. He couldn't think about bodies torn and broken, half buried in the trampled earth. Sweat streamed down his face and caked his eyes with mud. Every breath was a cough that wracked his lungs, and his shoulder muscles were on fire from waving the rifle and struggling with his horse. He knew he wouldn't last much longer. No man could. But the buffalo kept coming.

He thought he saw a figure, a man on horse-back materializing through the dust. He turned his horse toward it.

Martin's horse danced and turned in circles as it found itself in the thick of the herd. He jerked on the reins, but he had never been an expert horseman; he didn't know what to do. He did know that his only chance for survival was to hold on to his rifle as hard as he could, even if it meant losing control over his horse.

Buffalo swarmed around him, rushed at him, tangled themselves together and fell in their desperate flight. Roars of pain and fear filled the air. His horse reared; Martin felt a crushing pain in his leg as a buffalo slammed up against him. Consciousness spun and wavered, and with his last ounce of strength Martin held his place in the saddle as the sea of buffalo surged around him.

The oxen were going crazy, dashing into the wagons, flinging themselves against one another, and Kitty knew the least of this day's work would be that their teams would escape and be lost in the stampede, or would kill themselves trying to get away. Snow's frantic screams and bucking only agitated them more, and when Kitty looked out from beneath the wagon she saw buffalo hooves tearing up the ground not three feet from her face.

The Reverend and Mrs. Syms had their arms around each other, their faces contorted with terror or silent prayer; Lucy's mouth was open in a soundless, endless scream, and her arms were wrapped around her head. Kitty couldn't see Effie or the baby, but it didn't matter. They were all dwarfed by the magnitude of the prairie's wrath. Insignificant and defenseless, they had no chance of survival.

Desperately she thought about Ben and Boothe, and with the desperation came anger, the helpless rage of one pushed to the brink of despair. Where were they? Why had they left her alone? Why had they thought for one minute that they could go up against this Goliath of merciless destruction and make a difference? Men were fools, all of them; why weren't they here defending the ones they loved, *why had they left her alone?*

She wanted to sob, but her throat was too dry. She wanted to cover her head and scream like Lucy; she wanted to give way to the madness and meet death with blank and staring eyes. But just then she saw one of the oxen fling itself against a wagon brace with enough force to knock itself off its feet; dazed, the creature scrambled upright, shook itself, and prepared to charge again. And there must have been some hope left in Kitty after all because she couldn't let the animal escape and be trampled. Without the livestock they would be stranded on the prairie and would have no chance for survival, none at all.

She pulled herself out from under the wagon and fought her way through the dust and thunder, tripping over her skirts and repeatedly wiping her streaming eyes as she called in a high, soothing voice to the animals. She got her arms around the neck of the most agitated ox, but it backed away from her, bellowing and kicking out its heels. It thrashed its head and flung her off; she landed in the dust with a breath-robbing force and when she tried to regain her feet, frantic hands were plucking at her.

Lucy was clinging to her, her eyes squeezed tightly shut and her arms clamped around Kitty's waist in a death-grip. Kitty couldn't push her off; her shouts went unheard. She grabbed the girl's shoulders and shook her, but to no avail. She dragged Lucy to her feet, and when she looked up it was to see a mammoth, shaggy creature leaping over the barrier of the wagon yokes.

The oxen roared; Snow screamed and reared. With one enormous surge of strength Kitty pulled Lucy out of the way and onto the ground, beneath the shelter of a wagon. The buffalo charged frantically around the enclosure, slamming against wagons and ripping canvas until, with a great splintering sound, it broke through two linked wagon yokes and charged across the prairie.

Then Kitty did cover her head, and close her eyes, and wait for the worst.

But it never came. Kitty did not know how long she stayed there, numb with fear and terrible resignation; hours or only a few minutes. But gradually she became aware of Lucy's hoarse sobs next to her and the sound of her own breathing. The earth-shaking thunder was growing more distant. The frantic bellows of the oxen had lessened, and Snow had stopped screaming.

She opened her eyes and saw the dust was clearing. The grass outside the barrier of the wagons was churned up in chunks, like a field plowed for planting, but no dark hooves raced past. Slowly she pulled herself out from under the wagon and stood up.

Nothing could have spoken more eloquently of the awesome power of nature than what Kitty saw as she looked around. As far as she could see in any direction the prairie grass had been flattened, the earth gouged and torn, scattered to the sun as though sifted from a giant's hand. Dust hung like a veil in the air, moving slowly across the prairie with the sluggish breeze.

The yoke of Oliver's wagon had been splintered and the wagon itself pushed a half turn out of line with the others. The canvas on Ben's wagon was torn half off and the Symses' wagon leaned drunkenly on a broken wheel. Only one of the oxen had escaped, and was wandering in dazed circles about fifty yards away.

Later, Kitty would realize that the full force of the herd had passed some distance north of them; less than a dozen stragglers had actually approached the wagons. But at that moment, as she stood there letting the full impact of the destruction sink in, all she could think of was how incredible it was that they should still be alive, and how much worse it could have been.

Behind her she heard a dry sob. Rachel Syms stood beside her wagon, her face haggard and dust-streaked, her hands held out in supplication. "Why?" she said. "Why does God keep sparing us only to bring down more torture on our heads?" She turned to her husband, her voice torn between despair and a plea. "Why? Can you tell me that?"

John Syms had no answer.

Effie spoke up in a small, quavering voice. "Where are they? Where are the men?"

They all turned their eyes back to the horizon, but saw nothing. And the long wait began.

*   *   *

Oliver came first, a small lone figure against the barren prairie, riding a slow-moving, almost staggering horse. Every heart clenched. There was no sign of Ben, or Boothe, or Martin. Kitty forced herself to turn away, hurriedly building up a fire and putting together a pot of coffee to keep her hands busy and her mind from thinking the worst.

Oliver had not seen any of the others, and he seemed almost too tired to answer the frantic questions that were thrown at him. He slid off his horse and let it stand, sitting down against the broken wagon wheel with his hands wrapped around the coffee cup Kitty placed in them, staring at it as though the effort to lift it to his lips was simply too much. Kitty kept moving, unsaddling Oliver's horse, rubbing it down, offering it water from a cooking pot.

Then Boothe came, leading a riderless horse behind him. His shoulders were slumped, and he moved toward them with excruciating slowness. Kitty's throat felt as though it were filled with lead as she watched him approach, focusing her eyes on the horse that trudged wearily behind. Ben? Was it Ben who would not be coming back?

She was unaware of Effie standing behind her, just as rigid with dread as she was. The baby had cried himself into an exhausted sleep and was tucked away in the wagon, and Effie stood with her hand shielding her eyes against the sun, desperately trying to make out the identity of the riderless horse.

Kitty heard Effie's strangled gasp at the same moment she recognized the horse, and she was ashamed of the relief that went through her, no matter how quickly it was followed by sharp sympathy and concern for her friend.

"Martin!" Effie cried, and she ran the last few steps to meet Boothe. "That's Martin's horse! Where is he? What happened?"

She touched the horse, examining it as though looking for a sign that she had made a mistake. Its left flank was bleeding, and she could not tell whether the splattered blood on the saddle had come from animal or man.

Boothe dismounted. "I don't know, ma'am. I spotted the horse about half a mile back, but no sign of your husband." He looked at Kitty. "Or Ben."

His eyes moved around the camp, taking in the damage and the number present with no change of expression. "If they're not back in an hour, we'll go looking."

Kitty swallowed hard and walked forward to touch Effie's arm. "Maybe they're together," she said. "They'll be all right."

Effie's face was white and as stiff as crepe paper, but she managed to nod and walked back to camp.

They waited. Kitty tended the wounded animals and the exhausted men. Effie and Rachel began to clean up some of the debris around the camp. John Syms brought out a hammer and saw, and demonstrated a hitherto unsuspected skill for carpentry as he began repairs on the damaged wagons. Not a single minute passed that someone's eyes didn't move toward the horizon.

And then Kitty spotted him, a single rider moving across the prairie. Even at that distance she could see the glint of sun on Ben's light hair; she recognized the distinctive way in which he sat a saddle. She felt dizzy with relief and gladness, and for a moment she couldn't speak.

By the time she found her voice, she had noticed something else. "Look," she said hoarsely.

Ben was dragging something behind him that looked like a travois made of a rolled saddle blanket. But whether the man inside that travois was alive or dead, none of them could tell.

They hadn't known other men were involved until they were in the thick of the hunt, and even then they'd been hard put to believe their eyes. Rufus, Hammock, and Cob had charged into the herd from separate directions, started them running, then fallen back to pick off the straglers at their leisure. They had brought down maybe fifty of them, shooting as fast as they could reload, and if they'd had better guns they could have tripled that number.

When they'd thinned out the flank runners and before their horses had tired out too much, they'd increased their speed to catch up with the center of the herd. What they shot there hadn't been of much use by the time the hides were torn and the meat trampled by the stampeding herd, but that hadn't mattered much; they had liked to see them fall.

It was about that time that Hammock could've sworn he saw another rider in the dust cloud, waving his hat and firing his rifle, and damned if it didn't look like he was trying to turn the herd back on itself. Hammock took aim and fired a shot, but the range was too far; he didn't have a chance of hitting him. Pretty soon the rider was swallowed up by shifting bodies and swirling dust, and there was no point in trying to track him down. But somebody had encroached on Hammock's territory, and he was mad.

When they rendezvoused later, Cob had a similar story, and they sat atop their lathered horses scratching their heads and trying to puzzle it out. The hunt had been all but ruined, with the buffalo charging this way and that and breaking up into groups and trampling all over themselves so a man couldn't get a decent shot if he'd had a chance, and somebody was going to have to pay. The thing was, they couldn't figure out who that somebody was. The prairie was for buffalo hunters and Indians; settlers would have taken the trail north up the Platte. There was no doubt the men they had seen had not been hunters. And they all agreed that they had not been Indians.

About that time they realized Rufus had not come back.

They set about stripping off some hides to tan, not very serious about it and not doing a very good job. They sliced off a couple of buffalo steaks and roasted them over a dung fire, and when Rufus still hadn't come back they went out to look for him.

They found him about an hour later, his chest caved in and both his legs ground into the dirt, lying dead from a bullet hole through his head.

Martin's right leg was broken, but it was a clean break and it would mend. He was covered with scrapes and bruises and had a nasty knot on his head, but he would live. Boothe poured whiskey down his throat before he set the leg, and Martin, in his pained and drunken delirium, kept bemoaning the fact that he'd lost his rifle. Effie smiled through her tears as she bathed his face and told him it was all right; they still had one gun left.

When Boothe snapped his leg back into place Martin passed out from the pain, and when he drifted into a more natural sleep, they left him where he lay, on a pallet beneath the shade of a wagon.

Kitty checked with Effie to make sure there was nothing Martin needed, and then went about trying to put together supper. Lucy had finally been persuaded to return to her mother, but with her eyes she followed every step Kitty took. Kitty knew she should try to spare a smile for her, but she couldn't. She knew she should be grateful that they had been spared as much as they were, but she couldn't. One of their water barrels had been smashed, and the other was thick with mud. There was grit in the flour, and molasses had spilled into the beans and the meal, drawing flies. Small losses, minor upsets, but they were enough. Her lips were grim and her movements abrupt as she tossed aside pots and emptied out sacks.

"At least you didn't have to patch me up," Ben ventured, standing beside her.

"You're in my way," Kitty said, and he stepped back to let her pass.

"What're you mad at?"

Kitty shook the dust out of a blanket with several vicious snaps, then turned on him. "You," she said, her eyes blazing. "You and Boothe and all you men and your blamed stupidity! You could've been killed, all of you, and then what would we have done?"

"I imagine you would've done just fine," Ben said mildly.

"And now look at us! Martin's hurt and the wagons are smashed and—"

"Kitty." Ben smiled and reached forward to touch her arm. "I think you were worried about me."

Kitty wanted to shout back that of course she was worried, she was worried about all of them, but something about the way he smiled made a lump form in her throat and she couldn't speak. All she wanted to do was lay her head on his shoulder and let him tell her everything was going to be all right.

"Men are supposed to protect women," she said thickly. "They're not supposed to go riding off to get themselves killed."

He touched her chin lightly. "Now who in the world told you that?"

In another moment or two she would have jerked her chin away, but right then it was good just to look into his eyes, to know he was alive and safe and that he had come back to her. The moment lasted perhaps a fraction longer than it should have, and at any rate Kitty never had a chance to break it because just then Boothe spoke up quietly.

"Riders coming." He reached for his rifle. "And they don't look friendly."

The two men were rough and unshaven; their tangled hair hung below their waists, and the reek of their buffalo-skin coats arrived long before they did. Each carried one rifle and had two others strapped to his saddle; their pouches bulged with ammunition, and long skinning knives hung in sheaths around their necks. They were met by Boothe, Oliver, and Ben, each holding a rifle but not yet aiming it.

The first rider carried a mangled corpse across the front of his saddle. He drew up before the three men and pushed the body off with the butt of his rifle. It hit the ground with a dull thud and rolled over as though it were made of straw, a gruesome remnant of what had once been a man, the round bullet hole in his head clearly visible.

"Name was Rufus," said Hammock in a low, flat drawl. "One of you folks mistooken him for a buffalo. We call that plain-out murder in this part of the country."

No one spoke for a long moment. Ben allowed his eyes to stray in ill-concealed horror to the corpse on the ground, and Oliver looked over the speaker's shoulder toward his companion, alert for an unexpected move. Boothe never took his gaze off Hammock.

"You started that stampede," Boothe said. "You nearly got us killed. If you lost a man in the middle of it, it ain't my fault."

Cob raised his rifle to his shoulder. "We come to shoot us a killer."

Before he got his eyes to the sights, three rifles were trained on him.

Hammock grinned. "Prairie dogs," he said contemptuously. "Goddamn greenhorns. You think we's scert of the likes of you? We can blow you out of your boots before you get your fingers on the trigger."

"Two of us, you can," Boothe agreed mildly. "What about the third?"

Hammock didn't look threatened, and Cob kept his rifle trained on Boothe. There was an eagerness in his stance, almost a madness, and Boothe knew if that madness let go one of them was going to die.

Hammock looked around the camp with the lazy, alert gaze of a man who might be talking about the weather one moment and flinging a knife through a man's throat before he finished his sentence. His eyes noted Martin, stretched out on the pallet, and Effie, who got slowly to her feet beside him, and Lucy, clinging to the side of the wagon and staring at them dully.

He said, "Got yourself some fine-looking females there. What you doin', bringing white women way out here?"

"Mister, I ain't a killing man," Boothe replied, "but if you don't turn and ride, it won't do my conscience no harm to see you splattered all over this prairie."

Hammock just grinned. "I don't figure you'd get off the first shot, but for old Rufus's sake it might jes' be worth takin' the chance."

His knife was halfway out of the scabbard when the sharp click of a rifle bolt behind him stopped him.

"Don't do it, mister," Kitty said.

She stepped out from behind the wagon, her rifle raised to her shoulder and the sights trained on Hammock. Effie sprang down from her wagon bed with her own rifle, imitating Kitty's stance. And then Rachel appeared, holding the rifle awkwardly, but looking cold-eyed and determined.

Hammock's grin widened as he took them all in. "I'll be dog-damned. You got them females trained, mister. I reckon they're worth a sight more'n I figured."

"I'd say you and your partner are outnumbered," Boothe said coldly. "Ride." He cocked his weapon.

Hammock's grin faded, dissolved into something cold and hard and evil as he fixed his gaze on Boothe again. "You got no business out here," he said. "You're gonna learn that, one way or another."

He turned his horse sharply. "Cob! Let's git!"

"A decent man buries his dead," Boothe said.

Hammock turned around and spat deliberately on the ground. "You kilt him. You bury him."

No one lowered his rifle until the dust clouds had disappeared. Boothe turned to the women and spoke mostly to keep their minds off the mangled corpse on the ground.

Rachel was leaning back against the wagon; Effie drew a shaking arm across her brow. Kitty looked as though she might be ill as her eyes fixed on the dead man.

"I don't reckon any of you ladies know how to use them things?" Boothe said.

No one answered.

"Well then, I'd say it was mighty brave, what you just did. But don't do it again. Men like that are wild dogs. You never can tell what they're going to do. Next time we have company, you stay in the wagons." He looked sternly at Kitty. "That means you, too."

Kitty dragged her eyes away from the corpse and drew herself up stiffly. "Fools," she said. "All men are fools."

And then she saw the smile in Boothe's eyes and knew that all he'd meant to do was get her mind off the dead man.

But Boothe's smile faded as he turned back to Ben and Oliver. "Starting tonight," he said, "we post guards. Now, let's get to burying."

Chapter Thirteen

It took a day to make repairs and get under way again. Because there was no wood with which to fashion a new yoke for the wagon Oliver had been driving, it had to be left behind. Most of the contents were distributed among the other wagons, but those things that were not considered necessary for survival—books, extra blankets, yard goods—remained scattered on the prairie for the Indians to scavenge. They kept telling themselves it could have been much worse, but that was a hollow comfort no one really believed.

Effie took over driving their wagon, making Martin as comfortable as she could on a pallet in the back. For the first few days he drifted in and out of delirium, but he was in enormous pain and everyone assured her that was normal. Rachel and Kitty took turns minding the baby and bringing food for the invalid and Effie. Kitty came every night to check Martin's wounds and to bring herbal teas or compresses. Effie had always known that without one another none of them could survive, but that truth had never been so clear to her as it was in those days after Martin's accident.

Martin's wounds gradually began to heal and his leg to mend. Consciousness was an agonizing condition, but the pain was as much mental as physical. He lay in the back of the dark, stuffy wagon with his leg throbbing and sweat dripping from his hairline to soak the blankets beneath, and he had too much time to think.

It had all seemed so clear when he started out, so imperative and grand. He had devoted his life to the service of God, and God had sent out a call he couldn't ignore. Not once had he questioned the rightness of his decision.

But he had seen the hand of God sweeping across the prairie in all its terrifying glory, and he had known his own smallness, his own insignificance in the great plan of nature. He had felt the weight of a rifle in his hand and known the urge to kill. Effie told them that a stranger had been shot to death in the stampede, and perhaps it was his bullet that had felled him; perhaps he was now a murderer, but he could not even summon the energy for remorse. He had watched his wife grow stronger while he grew weaker, and now he was helpless, struck down by forces which, before his journey began, he couldn't even begin to comprehend.

Father, he prayed silently, *all I've ever asked is the strength to do Your will, but I don't know what Your will is anymore. I know You have visited this misfortune on me for a reason, but help me to understand . . .*

He didn't know what he was doing here, why he had brought his wife and child on this senseless journey that could only end in death. What was there for him here, what was there for anyone?

He had believed, he had truly believed, that he had been called to bring salvation to the Indians. Indians who had roamed these plains for thousands of years, who had survived storm and stampede and blistering summers and deadly winters for untold centuries without him. What could he offer these people who made the earth their home and the sky their roof? Had not the hand of God already fallen over them in blessing? Hadn't His love already been made manifest in the game that fed them and the rain that fell to swell their streams? Would being able to read the word of God make His presence any more real to them?

He had barely survived a few months on these vast plains the Indians called home. He had nothing to teach them, nothing at all. He was the least of nature's miracles, for a God who could create the grandeur and the power he had seen had no use for his puny services.

He lay in the back of the wagon day after day as the miles crept by, fighting the pain that wracked his body and the doubt that wracked his soul. And gradually, his prayer was answered. He began to understand.

They were in the thick of Pawnee country now; the Solomon River and the mission that was their destination were less than a hundred miles away. Another man would have let his guard relax and would have begun to congratulate himself on a job well done. Ten days, a minuscule span in comparison to how long they had already traveled, a few grains of sand in the hourglass that marked their progress. Ten sunrises, ten sunsets. Ten blazing afternoons that sapped the strength and dulled the senses, ten nights in which danger could lurk behind any shadow. A man could die without water in ten days, or bleed to death without anybody knowing it, or be drowned in an unexpectedly swollen creek, or be taken by surprise by what hid in the grass or rose up out of the night. In the back of Boothe's head an indefinable thundercloud drifted, and he could not relax his guard.

He had seen no further sign of the buffalo hunters, but he knew they would not give up so easily. They were out there somewhere, waiting their chance, and Boothe almost wished they would make their move so he could be done with it. They were the least of his problems. He did see signs of Pawnee, but they had no quarrel with the white man and posed no threat to their ultimate safety. Another encounter with them might mean the loss of the horses, but as long as they had the oxen they could make it to the mission. Neither the Pawnee nor the buffalo hunters caused that thundercloud to swell and prey on his mind. It was the things Boothe did not know about that worried him.

Oliver rode with him when he went out to scout the trail. It had rained that morning and the grass was damp, the air not quite so hot. Both men's minds were preoccupied with thoughts of the journey's end, as were the minds of everyone on the train.

After a time Oliver said, "How does it feel to be a part of history?"

Boothe glanced at him.

Oliver made a sweeping gesture with his hand over the wide open prairie. "All this—it won't be

empty for long. You were right in what you said—
it's good farmland and folks are hungry for it.
Pretty soon the tracks them wagons are making'll
be a road, and you won't be able to ride down
it without seeing houses and plowed fields and
fences. Maybe you're one of the first to bring the
pilgrims out this far, but you won't be the last. Like
I said, history."

Boothe looked out over the land which now was
tracked with nothing more than buffalo wallows
and gopher holes, and he remembered a time
when no one had crossed it except strong men
with a yen to see its mysteries. Men who set out
on foot or mule back with nothing but a staff
and a pack and the knowledge that somewhere in
this vast, untouched land they would see the face
of God. The Hudson Bay Company had brought
industry to the wilderness, the beaver were gone or
going, and the time for those men was fast passing
away. It wasn't Boothe's fault, or the fault of any
one man. But trying to stop them was like pulling
back the tides.

He answered quietly, "Fact is, it feels kinda sorrowful. If it was up to me, I'd leave the country to
them that's been taking care of it all this time. But
it ain't up to me."

Oliver let his horse wander to a stop, resting
his hand on the pommel, and turned to look at
Boothe. "Why'd you do it then?" he asked seriously. "Why're you bringing these pilgrims out here
where they can't do nothing but harm?"

Boothe's own mount stopped next to Oliver's
and lowered its head to nibble at the grass. Boothe
was quiet for a long time, looking out over the
prairie. "I reckon I had a debt to pay."

"Or something to prove." Oliver's tone was easy and matter-of-fact, but he kept his eyes on Boothe, and after a moment Boothe met his gaze.

"Yeah," he admitted. "Maybe."

The two men on horseback sat silently for a time, mere specks against the expansive backdrop of earth and sky. The journey was almost ended. Soon Boothe Carlyle could count the safe delivery of two families and three wagons among his successes, and in that way, perhaps, the failure of the past would be wiped away. That they had made it this far was a miracle, and when Oliver looked back on what they had been through he couldn't help wonder what kind of man would have attempted it in the first place. A crazy man, he decided. A man driven by something no one but he could understand, to shake his fist in the face of God and try to steal back his own redemption.

"You think risking the lives of all these people was a fair price to pay for your soul?" Oliver asked.

An expression crossed Boothe's eyes that Oliver had never seen before, or expected to see. It was surprise, coupled with uneasiness. Boothe looked away. "I'll get them through," he said.

It was pride, Oliver realized. Pride that had persuaded Boothe to take on this fool's mission, pride that made him keep going when a sensible man would have turned back. Pride that had killed Oliver's sister in a mountain blizzard two years ago.

"You used to be my hero," Oliver said quietly. "I spent most of my life wishing I could do the things you did, go the places you went, see the things you'd seen. Wishing I could be like you."

Boothe nudged his horse into motion, his eyes squinted against the sun. "I reckon the hardest thing in the world to forgive is a fallen hero."

Oliver didn't answer, but let his horse fall into step again beside Boothe's.

After a time of silent riding Boothe said, "I reckon you're right about it though. The Indians, the wild elk, the mountain men I knew—their days are numbered. Pretty soon this country will be filled with farmers and schoolhouses and pretty little churches, and as big as it is, this land don't have room for the wanderers and the settlers both. Men like me, we're a dying breed, and there's nothing worse than having outlived your time."

The two men rode on across the prairie, growing smaller and smaller against the broad blue sky.

It was hot. As the afternoon wore on, the air retained the humidity of morning rains, and it was hard to breathe. Insects swarmed in abundance, and their clothing never seemed to dry completely. Kitty had transferred Adam's cradle board to her own back, but the baby was not her only concern. Lucy had taken to following Kitty around like a lost puppy, plucking at her skirts, watching her every move with big dark eyes, nudging up against her like a kitten seeking warmth. Kitty couldn't turn around without tripping over her, she couldn't raise her voice without bringing fear to the other girl's eyes, and the effort to be patient when what she really wanted to do was shake Lucy loose like she would a bothersome burr wore on her nerves more severely than the heat, the tedium, and the hardship combined.

She tied Snow to the back of the wagon and

walked so that she could give the baby some air. Lucy dogged her shadow. Adam was fretful, as he almost always was, and after a time Kitty stopped to remove the cradle board and carry him in her arms. Effie, who was separated from them by the Symses' wagon, watched until Adam stopped crying, then smiled at Kitty tiredly and pressed a hand against the small of her back, stretching out the kinks.

Kitty bounced the baby against her hip, patting his back. His diaper was wet, but that couldn't be helped.

"I wonder what will happen to him," she said.

Ben glanced down at her.

Kitty adjusted the baby's bonnet more securely on his head and paused to press her cheek briefly against his. "He's been through so much already, and he's not even a year old. It doesn't seem right. Babies should have quiet cradles and clean linen and a fire to sleep in front of. They shouldn't have to worry about Indians or buffaloes or being carried through cold streams or lying in the mud while lightning strikes three feet away. What's all of this going to do to him?"

"The same thing it does to all of us, I guess," Ben said. "You didn't have a cradle when you were born. I wasn't exactly grown when I was in my first Indian fight. Seems to me this country breeds its own kind of man. You either get strong or you die."

His matter-of-fact tone made Kitty shiver, and she held Adam a little closer. Her tone was muffled as she said, "You didn't used to talk like that. You used to be different."

He glanced down at her. "We all did."

Kitty didn't know if that was a good thing.

The sound of a woman's cry sent a shard of glass through her nerves. Kitty jerked her head around just in time to see John Syms slide from his seat and slump over the wagon box. Rachel screamed again, grabbing his shoulders to keep him from toppling over the side of the wagon as the reins slipped from his hands and dragged along the ground. The oxen, plodding at their own pace, began to swerve gradually toward the right, heading for Effie's wagon. Effie, startled by the commotion in the next wagon, forgot her own team. A collision was imminent.

Clutching the baby to her, Kitty ran toward the head of the team. Adam began to wail indignantly. At the last moment, Effie jerked the reins hard and brought her team to a stop. Kitty grabbed the harness of the lead oxen on the Symses' wagon with one hand, holding on to Adam with the other, and by the time she had slowed the team to a halt Effie had leaped from her wagon and was beside her, taking the baby from her arms.

Rachel sobbed, "John! Dear God, help me, something's wrong—someone help me! He's dead, I think he's dead!"

Kitty stepped on the wagon wheel to pull herself upward, but Lucy was clinging to her skirts, making frightened mewing sounds as she tried to drag her back. Kitty pushed her away impatiently, but at the girl's stricken look she paused and said as gently as she could, "It's all right. I'll be right back."

She pulled herself up onto the wagon box and stumbled over Rachel, who was trying to lift her husband's head and shoulders into an upright position. "Is he dead?" Rachel kept whispering frantically. "He can't be dead, dear God don't let him be dead!"

Kitty wedged herself against the seat and helped Rachel lift the reverend's head. He was unconscious, his face gray and his lips white, but his skin was hot to the touch and he was breathing.

"Kitty?"

Ben was standing beside the wagon, his eyes dark with worry. Rachel looked at her desperately, pressing her husband's head to her breast. And Kitty felt dread congeal in her stomach; helplessness weighed her down like an anvil.

"We'd better get him in the back of the wagon," she said.

Everyone looked at her as Kitty walked up to the fire. "Any change?" Boothe asked

Kitty shook her head. "Chills and fever. He can't keep anything down. It could be anything."

No one voiced the long list of deadly diseases that "anything" encompassed: cholera, typhoid, scarlet fever, even smallpox. The Symses' wagon had been isolated about ten feet from the others, but no one took the quarantine very seriously. They had probably all been exposed by now.

"How much farther to the mission?" Ben asked.

"Ten, twelve days, by wagon," Boothe answered. "A rider could make it in less."

"They might have medicines there."

"They might not."

Effie hugged little Adam to her. "We can't just stay here and wait. What if—what if someone else gets sick? The closer we are to the mission, the nearer help will be."

Then Martin spoke up. He was forcing his recovery, and insisted on leaving the wagon by means of a crutch fashioned of a wagon board every time they made camp. "We don't have a choice," he said flatly. "If what we're carrying is catching, we'd take it right to the mission with us."

Rachel had come out of the wagon to fetch more water from the barrel, and she heard the last part of the conversation. "What're you saying?" Her voice held a shrill note of panic. "Of course we have to go on! We have to get help for John. We can't just stay here!"

"There's no guarantee there'd be any help at the mission," Boothe said.

Martin twisted around painfully to face her. "It's not just the other missionaries we have to think about," he said, more forcefully than anyone had ever heard him speak before, "but all those children—Indian children. Do you think God sent us out here to kill them? We've got no more right to force our diseases on them than we have our way of thinking."

Effie looked at him with surprise and wonder in her eyes, and when Martin gazed back at the others they all were staring at him. He felt compelled to defend himself. "What I'm trying to say is, I read somewhere that the Indians aren't built like we are . . . maybe because they don't live like we do. Even if John recovers—and I pray God he does—and Indian might not. And I don't think we can take the chance until we're sure what kind of sickness it is we've got on our hands."

"You're right, of course," Effie said softly. "I was being selfish." And there was a new respect in her eyes as she looked at her husband.

"But that's crazy!" Rachel exclaimed. "We can't just stay here and—and wait for him to die! You're inhuman, all of you. How can you even consider such a thing!"

Kitty spoke up quickly. "Maybe it's nothing. Maybe it's just the heat, or—"

"One of us could ride ahead," Oliver suggested. "See if there's any help at the mission."

Boothe shook his head. "Martin's right. Who knows what kind of sickness we'd be carrying with us. It wouldn't be right."

"You're not leaving us behind!" Rachel insisted. Panic had crept into her face and voice. "You're not going to leave us alone out here!"

"Nobody said anything about doing that, ma'am." Boothe's voice was calm but strong, and it seemed to take the edge off her approaching hysteria. "Anyhow, we're not doing anything tonight. Let's just wait till morning and see how he is."

After a moment Rachel went back to the wagon, and Effie moved away to put Adam down for the night. The men silently dished up their supper from the pot, and Effie brought a plate of stew to Martin. She sat down beside him. "I never heard you talk like that before about the Indians. Like you understood them. I always knew you had compassion for them, but I never realized you . . . cared so deeply."

Martin hesitated, looking at his plate. "I guess I didn't, when I first started out. And I still don't understand them, or pretend to. But I know I want to."

He looked at her soberly. "I've spent a lot of time these past few days, Effie, thinking about

what we're doing and why we're doing it. I still
don't have the answers but—I don't know, maybe
knowing that I don't is all I needed. I was pretty
arrogant when I started out. We all were. I thought
I could save the world. I thought I could teach
the poor red man all he needed to know . . .
Now, I think maybe what I want to do is let him
teach me."

Effie slipped her arm through her husband's and
rested her head against his shoulder. "I love you,
Martin."

"I've always loved you, Effie," Martin said quietly.
"But I never knew how much I needed you until
lately. And I just wanted to tell you—I'm real proud
to have you for a wife."

She smiled at him. "I guess we can all learn a lot
from each other, can't we?"

"That we can," he agreed soberly. "That we surely can."

Kitty's stomach was in knots, and she couldn't
eat. She kept thinking about John Syms, and what
could be wrong with him, and wondering who
would be next to come down with what he had
and whether they would all die and lie where
they had fallen until the vultures ate away their
flesh and the sun bleached their bones. John Syms
had been a plague and a pestilence since they had
started, and now his very presence threatened to
bring death to them all.

To make matters worse, Lucy seemed to have
sensed the distress that permeated the camp and
was under Kitty's feet even more than usual. When
Kitty scraped off her plate and got up, Lucy was
immediately by her side, those big eyes fastened

on her, waiting for her to make her next move.

"Stay here," Kitty told her. "I'm going for a walk."

Lucy wound her fingers around Kitty's skirt.

Kitty jerked the material away. "I said stay here! Leave me alone, won't you?"

Ben took Lucy's arm gently, and though she cringed from his touch and the sound of his voice, he managed to turn her away. "Miz Creller," he said, "the girl probably ought not to go back to her folks' wagon tonight. You think it would be all right if she bedded down with you?"

"Of course." Effie slipped her arm around Lucy's waist and started leading her toward her wagon. Lucy twisted around and wouldn't take her eyes off Kitty, but at least she didn't scream or cry, as she often did.

Kitty kicked out at the ground as she walked away from the fire. "Why does she do that?" she demanded tightly. "She never liked me before—why can't she leave me alone now?"

Ben walked beside her. "She's hurt and broken inside. She's drawn to your strength."

Kitty snapped her head up with a sharp, derisive sound. "Me? I'm not strong."

"If you don't think so, you're the only one who doesn't." Ben's voice was quiet and matter-of-fact. "You've held us together, Kitty, don't you realize that? We've all turned to you for something at one time or another, and you've made a difference. Everybody else has met their breaking point, but not you."

As he spoke, Kitty was shaking her head, her steps slowing. "No," she said thickly. "No, I've been scared every minute since we started."

"We all have. I don't guess any of us knew what we'd bargained for when we signed up."

They had stopped walking. The glow of the fire and the reassuring murmur of voices were far behind them; ahead was nothing but a flat, monochromatic expanse: sky and earth, shades of gray and black. One could almost imagine walking on into that blackness a step or two and being swallowed up forever.

There were tears in her eyes and Kitty did not know why. Angrily, she tried to blink them back, squaring her shoulders. Looking straight ahead, she said, "We're never going home again, are we, Ben?"

"I don't think so."

She couldn't help it; the tears spilled over. "I'll never see Mama again. I promised her I'd come back. I promised her—but I won't."

Ben's hand fell lightly upon her shoulder. "I think your ma always knew that."

Kitty turned to him, and then her head was on his shoulder, his arms holding her, and she was weeping softly into the material of his shirt. "This isn't what I wanted. This isn't what I wanted at all . . ."

Ben's hand stroked her hair. "I know."

"I never should have left, nobody wanted me to come. If I hadn't pestered Mama so bad she never would have—"

"Your ma casts a long shadow," Ben said firmly. "The kind that's hard for anybody to grow in. She knew that. She wanted you to go, Kitty. She knew it was the only way you'd ever find your own place."

"But I haven't. I haven't found anything."

He put his hand under her chin and slowly tilted her face up to look at him. "Haven't you?"

She didn't answer. She just stood there with her face bloated from crying and her eyelashes wet and her vision blurred, and she let him do the talking.

He took a breath. "I've known you all my life, Kitty Kincaid. But I never knew it was you I wanted to spend my life with. The good Lord set it down that men and women were meant to be together, and to His mind it was a man's highest calling. I want you to be with me, Kitty. I want you to be my wife."

For the longest time she could only stare at him. "Me? You want me?"

"If you'll have me."

Kitty wondered if her mother had felt like this when Byrd Kincaid proposed to her. She wondered if any man had ever been as handsome as Ben was, standing there in the darkness of the prairie, holding her, or as kind and good and strong. She wondered, if she spent her whole life searching, whether she would ever find a man as close to the heart of what was right, and right for her, as he was. And she knew the answer was no.

She opened her mouth to speak, but her throat was so thick that for a moment no words would come out. Then she managed, gruffly, "This is foolishness, Ben Adamson. We—we don't even know if we'll be alive two days from now."

"Maybe," he agreed soberly. "And I guess that's why I figured I'd better go ahead and say this now. It's been rough, Kitty, rougher than I ever expected or guessed it could be. But . . ." He hesitated, as though unsure how to put the next thought into words. "I think we—all of us—have never been more alive. Do you know what I mean?"

"Yes," Kitty whispered. And maybe it had to do with nothing more than standing alone in the dark between earth and sky, being held by the man she loved.

He smiled at her. "Maybe that's all we came out here to find."

She rested her head against his shoulder again and thought that perhaps it was.

Chapter Fourteen

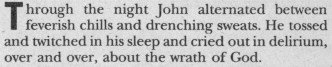

Through the night John alternated between feverish chills and drenching sweats. He tossed and twitched in his sleep and cried out in delirium, over and over, about the wrath of God.

Rachel tried to reassure him. "God tests the ones He loves," she told him, pressing another wet cloth to his forehead. "You've told me so over and over."

"No," he gasped, tossing his head away from her touch. "No, you don't understand. I've sinned . . . the sin of pride—He's taken my child, my only child . . ."

"No," Rachel said fiercely, "He hasn't taken her. Lucy is going to be all right."

"Oh Lord," he cried, "forgive me, for I was blind and did not see . . ."

And then, toward dawn, he gripped her arm, waking her out of a fitful, exhausted sleep. His eyes seemed clear and lucid, and he said lowly, "Wife. I should not have brought you here, or the child. I

271

was wrong, so wrong. Forgive me, if you can."

Rachel leaned forward to kiss his cheek, and it was cool and dry beneath her lips. Tears wet her lashes as she closed her eyes, and after a time, they slept.

It was the change in the weather that woke Boothe; a gust of warm, humid air that forecast a stormy morning. The wind died down before he threw back his blanket, but the sense of unease remained. The sky was heavy and overcast, and too warm for this time of the day. Dawn had barely broken, but there was a yellowish cast to the sky, and after that first gust of wind the air was heavy, too heavy.

Kitty was already up, and he saw her go to the Symses' wagon. Effie Creller came out of her wagon, looked worriedly at the sky, and went to stir up her fire. Ben, who had had the first watch last night, was just beginning to rouse beneath the wagon.

And then Boothe knew what was wrong. It was too quiet. Stillness lay over the breaking day like a shroud.

The oxen and the horses had been hobbled only a few yards from the camp. But the space where they had been was now empty.

Boothe picked up his rifle, which he always kept next to him while he slept, and called sharply, "Ben!" He could clearly see where the hobble stakes had been pulled out of the ground and discarded, the livestock driven off. "Get your gun and let's go!"

Ben looked startled as he sat up, and then he noticed the missing livestock. He reached quickly for his boots.

Kitty climbed out of the Symses' wagon, followed closely by Rachel. Both women looked puffy-eyed and exhausted, but on Kitty's face was a look of profound relief, and Rachel Syms was smiling.

"He's all right," Kitty said, coming toward Boothe.

"The fever broke at dawn," Rachel put in.

"It must have been the heat," Kitty added. "He's still weak, but we should be able to travel today if someone drives his wagon—" She broke off, noticing for the first time what she should have seen right away.

"The oxen!" she gasped. And then, looking around frantically, "Snow!"

Ben ran up, his lips grim and white around the corners. "They're gone—both rifles. They were in the wagon box . . ."

"Where's Oliver?" Boothe demanded.

A slow and horrible suspicion darkened Ben's eyes and caused shivers to grip the back of Kitty's neck as she looked around.

"He had the last watch," Ben said.

"Check the other wagons," Boothe commanded tightly.

Since the encounter with the buffalo hunters, everyone—even the Symses—had taken to traveling with both rifles loaded and within easy reach on the wagon seats. No one had thought to put the rifles out of sight during the night, and it had been an easy matter for someone to collect every weapon in the camp and leave them defenseless.

"It's my fault," Ben said angrily. His hands were clenched into tight fists and his cheeks blotched with color. "I should have kept my rifle close by. I should've known better."

"Why?" Kitty said. It was like a plea. "Why would he take our guns and our oxen?"

Boothe glanced at her, but didn't answer. Kitty remembered her mother's words, *Badness has its own reasons.* She had thought that only applied to men who would open fire in a crowded church and kill for the love of killing. But Oliver had his own kind of badness, and she should have known it from the first. She felt sick for having ignored that knowledge for so long.

John Syms had come shakily out of his wagon, and Martin propped himself up on the crutch. Lucy huddled close to Kitty, and baby Adam cried for his breakfast. Everyone was looking at Boothe, waiting for instructions or advice or a miracle.

"He's had at least four hours to drive off the horses," Boothe said. "We'll never catch them. But the oxen would've slowed him down; he probably drove them a couple of miles and let them go. We might be able to spot them on foot."

But his voice lacked its usual brusque confidence, and he looked older than Kitty had ever seen him. Everyone was thinking the same thing. Only two men were strong enough to search, and it might take them days to find even one ox— assuming Indians or buffalo hunters didn't find it first. Meanwhile the camp would be virtually unprotected, and anything could happen to two men on foot out there on the prairie.

"If we had sent someone ahead to the mission yesterday . . .." Kitty said quietly. She didn't finish the sentence, even though it was what everyone was thinking, because it was pointless to voice if-onlies out loud. If someone had started riding for the mission yesterday, help would be on the way. Oliver must have worried that they would send someone today, and that was why he had made his move last night.

But why? Why would he want to leave them all here to die?

"We did what we thought was best," Ben said. "If we'd sent somebody out, it probably would have been Oliver anyway."

Kitty felt ashamed. Ben was right, and her thoughtless comment had lowered everyone's spirits at a time when hope was hard enough to find. She raised her chin, pushing back a strand of hair the wind blew across her face. "If the three of us split up, we'll have a better chance of spotting something."

Boothe was already shaking his head, and to everyone's surprise, John Syms spoke up. "I can walk. We'll cover four directions—"

"No," Rachel said sharply.

"You're too weak," Kitty added. "It won't do anybody any good if you collapse on the prairie—"

And then Martin said, "Look."

Kitty's heart gave a foolish little leap as for one wild moment she thought he might have spotted Oliver. But something about Martin's expression—too intent, too stunned—told her that wasn't the case even before she turned to follow the direction of his gaze.

At first she saw nothing, and she thought that was because the sky had darkened to such an extent that it was difficult to see anything more than a few dozen yards away. The air had an ominous gray-green cast that tasted faintly electric, and the wind seemed to shift directions every few seconds. *Another storm*, she thought in dismay. *The animals will be wild with fear* . . . And then she remembered the animals were no longer her concern and she thought about Snow, all alone on the prairie in the middle of a storm, and she wanted to cry.

All that was in the few seconds she scanned the prairie, erroneously expecting to see a man on horseback approaching them, leading their lost livestock. And then, at the moment the phenomenon registered with everyone else, she saw it.

A part of the gray sheath of the sky had separated itself against the horizon line, forming a dark swirling tunnel of clouds that stretched upward and outward, gathering breadth and depth as it moved. And it was moving, with what looked like incredible speed, toward them.

"Cyclone," Boothe said.

His voice was short and clipped, and the sound of it tore all eyes away from the mesmerizing sight in the sky and galvanized them into action. Clutching Adam to her breast, Effie turned to run. Rachel grabbed Lucy and cried, "In the wagon! Quick!"

"No!" Hot fear gripped the back of Boothe's neck as he saw the elements of a nightmare begin to gather form and draw breath. "Stay away from the wagons!" He caught Effie's arm and pushed her in the other direction. "Get as far away as you can! Run! Now!"

Effie's face was torn as she looked back at her husband, but just then the first strong gust that presaged the storm tore at their clothing and caused them all to stagger and try to twist away from it. "Go on!" Martin shouted to her. "I'll keep up—do what he says, keep the baby safe!"

Lucy started to cry and struggled to twist away from her parents as they both tried to persuade

her to follow Effie. Boothe and Ben went to help
Martin. "There's a gully about a quarter of a mile
due west!" Boothe shouted against the ever-rising
force of the wind. "Try to make it there. If you
can't—just drop! Drop to the ground and stay
there!"

Kitty would be forever after amazed at how
quickly it happened, though she should have
long since grown accustomed to the suddenness
and ferocity of prairie dangers by then. Lucy was
sobbing, sinking to the ground in an immobile
mass with her arms covering her head. Her parents were trying desperately to drag her to her
feet. Ben was shouting at Kitty to go, to follow
Effie, to hurry. And when Kitty looked up again
she could see the twister, a huge, writhing mass
with its pointed finger dragging destruction across
the prairie and its seething top cup whipping out
winds that roared through her ears and stung her
face and took her breath away.

Kitty fought the wind to where Lucy lay, curled
up on the ground, and she remembered the last
storm and the aftermath that had left Lucy mute
and all but witless. Her heart surged out to the girl
even through her own fear, and she dropped to
her knees beside her. "Lucy!" she cried. "It's me,
it's Kitty! Lucy, you've got to get up now, we've
got to go—hold on to me, that's right. I'll take
care of you. It's going to be all right, just hold on
to me!"

She pulled Lucy to her feet, and both of them
almost fell again beneath the force of the wind.
Rachel reached for her daughter, sobbing, but
Lucy clung to Kitty, burying her face in her shoulder. "I'll take care of her!" Kitty cried, waving

her parents on. "Go on—run! We're right behind you!"

Kitty never saw the look on Rachel's face because the wind blinded her, and when she could see again, John Syms had his arms around his wife's waist and they were both just shadowy forms disappearing into the swirl of dust and darkness.

Ben and Boothe had Martin between them, carrying him at a stumbling, staggering run. Kitty struggled ahead, fighting the wind and Lucy's clinging weight every step of the way. She dared not look up or around, for she could feel the hot-cold breath of the storm clawing at her neck, and if she saw it, if she once even guessed how close it was, she would be paralyzed; she wouldn't move another step. Dust swirled and blinded, stones tumbled, clumps of grass actually plucked themselves from the ground, roots and all, and thudded against her legs. Once something more substantial flew by, barely missing her face— a wooden board or a tree branch. There were no trees for miles. *Is this it, then?* Kitty thought. *We're dead already, alone without our livestock on the prairie—is this God's mercy, to send a quick death to us all?*

But God was not so generous with His mercy, or else He had decided the time was not, after all, right. Stumbling along blindly, clinging to Lucy as much as Lucy clung to her, Kitty felt a pair of hands grab her, and another pair push her from behind. With Lucy still wrapped in her arms, she slid down a small decline and felt, rather than saw, the other figures close beside her. On their faces in the dirt, they waited and prayed for the storm to pass them by.

And so it did. They heard the roar and felt the earth tremble and gasped for air in its wake, but the full force of the twister swept by them to the east and lasted no more than half a minute. The wind died down; rain fell in torrents for perhaps five minutes, and then it too faded to a gray drizzle. It was over, and they were alive.

Muddy, drenched, and dazed, they got to their feet and climbed out of the gully. Adam was wailing; Lucy still clutched Kitty's hand with enough strength to crack the bones. It was the Symses who had pulled Kitty to safety, and Rachel came forward on shaky legs to draw her daughter into her arms. Martin, Ben, and Boothe had not made it to the gully, but had flattened themselves against the ground some fifty yards away. Effie gave a little cry and started running toward them as Ben and Boothe helped Martin to his feet.

No one was hurt. They looked at each other slowly, one pair of eyes meeting the other in a combination of dread, question, and disbelief. It was almost as though, having prepared themselves so well to die, they were suspicious—even disappointed—to find themselves still whole, still living.

Rachel came slowly forward, sheltering Lucy with one arm, and stood before Kitty. A little awkwardly, she lifted her hand and wiped a smear of mud from Kitty's cheek. "Thank you," she said huskily, "for my daughter."

Kitty made herself smile, though it stretched her tired, dry lips to do so. "I don't know why she likes me so much," she offered weakly.

Rachel held her eyes. "I do."

"Kitty!" It was Boothe's voice, reaching her across the distance. She turned toward him.

Effie had joined her husband, and the two were embracing. Ben was walking toward Kitty, but Boothe's arm was lifted in the opposite direction and Kitty turned to follow his gesture.

Walking slowly, with his head down and his steps plodding, the white pony moved across the prairie toward her. A cry of joy exploded from her throat, and she ran toward Snow.

He was uninjured, though dirty and exhausted. Whether he had been frightened by the storm and instinctively sought his way back to the place he had once felt safe, or whether he had been traveling all night to reach her—as Kitty preferred to think—he had arrived. One horse could mean the difference between life and death to them now. The mood was almost jubilant as Kitty climbed astride Snow, with Ben holding the rope that was still looped around the horse's neck, and the group started back toward the wagons.

Their steps slowed as the first vestiges of what the storm had left behind came into view.

Nothing remained of two of the wagons but splinters. Of the other one, a wheel could be seen there, an axle here. A sheet of canvas was spread like a tablecloth in the middle of the prairie.

They continued walking, like somnambulists hoping someone would wake them from the nightmare. But the vision didn't go away as they got closer; it only grew more vivid. They walked straight into the heart of the disaster and stopped. For a long time there was no sound, no movement, not even a breath. Then suddenly Effie began to laugh.

It was a high, thin, hysterical giggle that slowly gained momentum and swelled toward a shriek.

All eyes swiveled on her, and her laughter grew. Martin tried to reach for her, but she pushed him away. The baby started to slip from her arms, and tears rolled down her cheeks as her shoulders shook and she choked on laughter.

Kitty slid from the pony and went quickly to Effie, taking the baby from her. Rachel tried to take Effie's shoulders, but Effie flung her away violently. The laughter came to an abrupt, breath-robbing halt, and she looked around wildly. "Don't you see?" she cried. "Don't you see—we're never going to get out of this alive! It's God's joke, don't you see, God's cruel joke, and it's *funny!* It is!"

She started laughing again, but the laughter turned to sobs, and she sank slowly to her knees, her face buried in her hands.

Martin made it to his wife's side and leaned down to touch her shoulder, but once again she wrenched away. No one else approached her, as though the madness that had so briefly touched her was a contagious thing and they all stood too near the edge of control to risk catching it now. The sound of Effie's ragged, despairing sobs echoed like a penny dropped down a well, reflecting and magnifying their own hopelessness, until at last, mercifully, the sobs faded to silence.

She sat on the ground, her head sagging, plucking at the dirt with her fingers. Without looking up, she said shakily, "Give me my baby."

Kitty walked over and returned Adam to her. Effie held him, rocking him slightly, but she did not stand up.

Boothe walked away and stood with his back to them, the rifle held loosely at his side, looking at nothing in particular. Fatigue seemed to drag at his feet and legs, and his shoulders were slumped. Kitty went to him.

"Boothe," she said. Everything inside her felt shattered, held together by the thinnest of threads, and she wanted to ask him what would happen next, what she should tell the others . . . what they could *do*.

He turned to her. The Firebird had gray in his hair, and his eyes were bleak. He looked older than Kitty had ever imagined he would be, and there were no answers in his face. Kitty had never been as frightened as she was in that moment.

"I—I'm going to ride Snow out a little ways and see what I can find," she said hoarsely.

He nodded. He didn't tell her to be careful. He didn't advise her which way to search. He didn't offer to come with her. He just nodded. And she left.

Slowly, they sifted through the pieces. A coffee-pot, a sock without a mate, a Bible that wasn't even wet . . . each discovery was brought back to camp and laid out for all to see, like a sacrifice on an altar. As the sun grew higher, Ben and John scavenged enough pieces from the broken wagons to form a crude shelter of canvas and scrap lumber.

Boothe tried to assess their situation. There was a creek about two hundred yards west; it was muddy, but it wouldn't kill them. Effie had found a sauce-pan and a china teacup, but not one barrel of flour or slab of bacon had survived intact. The mission was a little over a week away. If Martin rode the pony and they started walking . . .

But Boothe couldn't finish the thought. His mind was fuzzy, and he was unable to concentrate. He kept thinking about Oliver, and the last conversation they had had. *You think risking the lives of all these people was a fair price to pay for your soul?*

The funny thing was, Oliver had thought he'd done them in. Whatever his reasons, and Boothe didn't condemn him for any of them, Oliver wasn't to blame. God would have struck them down anyway, would have struck *him* down for his arrogance. Because Oliver had been right. They'd all been right from the beginning. Any man who would take on this country, who would shake his fist in the face of the Almighty, deserved what he got.

Boothe just couldn't learn that. Twelve men and women dead in the mountains, and still he came back. The only woman he'd ever loved, her life wasted and ended too soon because this land kept calling him back. Because there was something inside him that was cussed enough, and stubborn enough, and sinfully proud enough to think that if he played the game long enough one day he'd win.

But this game of living and dying was not his to call, and it was happening all over again. A crippled man, a woman with a baby, a witless girl . . . his own niece, and Ben, the closest thing to a son he would ever know. Their graves were already being dug, and they had only him to thank.

John Syms stood beside him. "How strange are the ways of God," he said quietly. "He spares a teacup but leaves us no tea. A book of sermons survived, but not a scrap to eat."

Boothe glanced at him. "I reckon you was right, Reverend. You'd have been better off with somebody besides a heathen lightin' your way across the prairie."

There was a slight tightening of Syms's lips, as though he felt an inner pain quickly repressed. "Perhaps," he said carefully, "I chose my words too hastily. I recall another man who undertook to lead his people through the wilderness, and I can't think his trials were more than yours have been . . . mostly because the people he was trying to save were never willing to put their faith in him."

Boothe registered dim surprise. He said flatly, "That may be, Reverend, but unless God starts sending down some manna pretty soon, none of his children are going to make it to the Promised Land. And there's no point fooling yourself about that."

"Don't underestimate the workings of the Almighty," the reverend replied complacently. "You're no Moses, Boothe Carlyle, but so far you haven't proven to be the kind of man who sits back to wait for death. I don't think we're beaten yet."

Boothe thought about that, slowly and without much emotion, and decided that perhaps his worst failing was that he didn't know when to quit. Perhaps they would all be better off if he did, but a man could only be what he was born to be, and Boothe Carlyle had never expected to die in bed. After a time, he said thoughtfully, "I reckon I always knew I'd be walking up to meet my end with a sword in my hand. But I'd be mighty grateful for a taste of that manna 'long about now."

He noticed the activity at camp had come to a stop as the others turned their eyes toward the prairie. Boothe followed their gazes and saw Kitty approaching. She was alone, leading no horses and no oxen—not that any of them had really expected she would find anything, but their disappointment was acute anyway. Boothe walked forward to meet her.

Kitty slid off her horse, shaking her head to their unspoken questions. Her hair was tangled and her face drawn and haggard, streaked with white marks in the dust that could have been made by rain or tears.

"I found one of the oxen," she said with difficulty, "at the bottom of a ravine about a mile due south. It was that big fellow that belonged to Mr. Syms. His leg was broken and—he was suffering pretty bad." She swallowed hard. "No sign of the others."

Boothe looked at her for a moment in silent sympathy, then passed his rifle to Ben. Ben mounted Snow and rode south.

That night they feasted.

Kitty could not make herself eat any of the meat, though she knew she should keep her strength up. She had hardened herself to help with the stripping of the carcass, and she had shown the other women how to build low fires of green grass to smoke and preserve thin slices of beef. No one knew how long the one ox would have to last them. No one knew what the future held at all.

She walked down to the creek to wash the blood off her hands and try to rinse out her apron. When she climbed the bank again in the twilight, Ben was waiting, keeping watch for her.

"Why bother?" she said dully. "If the Indians come, we don't have to worry about the buffalo hunters. If the buffalo hunters come, we don't have to worry about the Indians."

Ben took her arm. "I'd rather not worry about either."

"Oh, Ben," she said tiredly. "Do you think there's ever going to be a time when we don't have to worry about anything again?"

"No," he replied soberly. "I don't think life works that way. But we are going to get out of this, Kitty."

"No," she answered emotionlessly. "We're not going to make it. I know that now. There's nothing left. We don't have a chance. And it doesn't matter."

She felt Ben's muscles tense. "As long as we're alive, there's a chance."

She shook her head. "The other night you said I was the only one who hadn't reached the breaking point. Well, now I have. I'm tired of being brave, tired of pretending, tired of waiting to die. I can't take any more. I'm not too proud to admit it. I just want it to be over."

Ben took both her arms in a rough grip, turning her to face him. He looked into her eyes for a long intense moment, and then he said, "I won't listen to you talk like that. Do you think I'm going to lose you, too? You're not going to die, Kitty, I won't let you. I asked you to marry me, and you're not getting out of giving me an answer that easily."

His words made Kitty feel small and ashamed. But she couldn't give him an answer. They walked back to camp together, silently.

They sat close to the fire, everyone waiting for someone to speak, for someone to tell them what to do, for someone to draw down a miracle—waiting for Boothe to produce that miracle, full-blown and ready to use. But he didn't. And the silence went on and on.

At last Boothe said, "We could start walking. If Martin rode the horse, we could make it to the mission in maybe two weeks. But that's a long stretch of open prairie, and I can't guarantee what's out there. One thing I do know. We don't have any water, or a way to carry it if we did. We have one gun between us, and the only ammunition is what I've got in my pouch. We could use that up killing rattlesnakes. Here we've got shelter and water, and if anything comes at us we can pretty much count on seeing it before it gets too close. We don't have much choice."

He looked around the circle, the flickering light of the fire shadowing and aging his face. No one understood why he hesitated—no one except Kitty, who knew what he was going to say only a moment before he spoke the words. "I'm going to have to leave you folks and ride ahead to the mission for help."

"No!"

Both Kitty and Ben spoke at once, but they did not need to share a glance to share the thought. Boothe could not repeat the past. If he rode away and left those in his charge behind, even though it seemed the only right thing to do at the time, if he returned too late, if he were absent when they needed him most—if it happened again, Boothe would be destroyed. And maybe it was superstition, but the mere act of his leaving seemed to set them all up to repeat a fate that had already been lived once.

"No," Ben repeated lowly, and his indrawn breath revealed his effort to discipline his emotions into logic. "No, I'll go. You're the only one who can take care of the ones left behind. If there's trouble, they'll need you. Among us all, you're the only one who can't be spared. I'll go."

"The boy makes sense," Reverend Syms murmured.

"He's right," Kitty echoed quickly, though a stab of dread pierced her at the thought of Ben going out there alone. But Martin couldn't ride, and John Syms would be helpless on the prairie, while she . . . "I'll go with him," she said.

Ben stared at her and she could feel his protest rising, so she hurried on. "It will be safer with two. Snow's a strong pony. The extra weight won't slow him down much. You always taught us to travel in pairs, Uncle Boothe, whenever we could. That way if—something happens, one of us will be bound to make it through."

Boothe looked at her for a long time, his eyes thoughtful, gentle, and far too knowing. Then he nodded. "All right," he said. "You both go. Let's see what we can do about rigging up some kind of canteen for you. You leave at first light."

The possibility, however dim, of receiving help brought hope they all thought they had lost, and with something positive to do, they all set about doing it. Martin suggested that a scrap of oilcloth, which once had wrapped a stack of books but had most recently been found tangled in the prairie grass, might serve to line a canteen made of wagon canvas. Rachel and Effie tore their petticoats into cloths with which to wrap pieces of smoked beef. Kitty checked Snow over from head to foot, taking no chances on a hidden stone in his hoof or a scrape on his hide that might become infected.

As soon as Ben was alone with Boothe, he said angrily, "Why did you do that? You're crazy if you think I'm going to let her go with me! She's staying here, where it's safe!"

Boothe smiled vaguely. "Safe? You sure you don't want to pick another word?"

"You know what I mean. She's staying with you!"

Boothe shook his head sadly. "That's just why she's got to go, son. She's got a better chance with you than with me. And I owe it to her mother—and to yours—to get the two of you out of this if I can. I might not be able to do much else, but I can do that."

Ben looked at Boothe and knew he was serious. He had never doubted Boothe's judgment before, and he couldn't do so now. But everything within him protested.

"She's going with you, Ben," Boothe said quietly. "You'll take care of each other. That's all I can do for either of you."

The morning dawned hazy and hot, and the sun had barely broken the sky before Ben and Kitty were ready to leave. Effie embraced Kitty and held her tightly. When she finally stepped away, she tried to smile, but her eyes were bright with tears.

"There's so much I want to—" Her voice caught, and it was a moment before she could finish. "Come back," she said simply.

Kitty nodded, for it was hard to make her throat work. She kept telling herself she would see Effie again. She kept repeating it to herself. "Be strong," she whispered, brushing her cheek against the other woman's.

"You, too," Effie said.

Kitty turned to Lucy. The girl was sobbing and clinging to her mother, though Kitty did not know how much of what was happening she really understood. Kitty went over to her and took her face in her hands. "I'll be back," she said firmly. "It won't be long. I promise."

Lucy's sobs faltered, and Kitty could have sworn the girl was making an effort to be brave. Rachel pressed her fingers to her lips and had to look away quickly to stop her own sobs.

Kitty started to turn away when she noticed Reverend Syms holding out his hand to her. She hesitated, then took his hand. He clasped her fingers in a firm salute, and said soberly, "Godspeed."

Embarrassed and uncertain, Kitty nodded and turned away.

Then there was only Boothe. They stood looking at each other for a long time before Boothe lifted his hand and removed the Celtic cross from around his neck. He draped the cord over Kitty's hair and hat, and the heavy weight of the pendant settled between her breasts. "God go with you, Kitten," he said.

Kitty fingered the cross within the circle, and she felt dwarfed by the weight of it, awed by the significance; she wanted to give it back, but she couldn't.

"I love you, Uncle Boothe," she said thickly.

She turned quickly to mount the pony in front of Ben.

Boothe watched them ride away, growing smaller and smaller across the prairie, with an ache in his chest and a heaviness in his bones. He knew he would see Kitty again, at least one more time. But his dreams had promised him nothing about Ben.

Chapter Fifteen

Cecil Hammock and Cob Bradley were good at two things: tracking and killing. They weren't great intellects—under most circumstances neither could hold a thought for more than two minutes at a time—but when it came to what they knew best, they were capable of surprising strategy and complex planning, and it helped if they had a grudge to gnaw on in the meantime.

They had followed the pilgrims for a few days, observing their habits, plotting their direction, and watching for a chance. Like coyotes stalking a group of elk, the more they watched the hungrier they got. But they did have one advantage over the coyotes: they knew when to back off before their instincts got the better of them.

They learned two things about the pilgrims while they watched—that their leader was no fool and that they were headed northwest, toward the Solomon. They already knew they were outgunned, and the two of them wouldn't have much of a chance at an ambush on the open prairie. What they had to do was swing around and get ahead of the travelers, to pick their spot and let the prey come to them.

They didn't talk much during the day, even less at night. When they did talk, it was on one subject.

"I got me an itch, Cob," Hammock commented, lazily skinning a rattlesnake they'd shot for supper. "That yeller-haired bitch—now you remember, she's mine first."

Cob scowled into a cup of tar-black coffee. "I'll git to 'er, don't you worry none about that. And I'm going down the line, from the idiot girl to the old prune, you just watch me go. But first I'm gonna get that redheaded son of a bitch. Gonna carve his balls up and throw 'em in this here stew pot; then I'm gonna scalp him naked. He's the one that shot Rufus, I bet it. Shot 'im down like a Injun. He thinks he's not gonna pay for that, he's got another think coming."

"Will you shet up about Rufus?" Hammock tossed the skinned snake into the boiling pot. "I woulda kilt him in another day or two anyhow. He was starting to get on my nerves."

In a movement so quick no eye could have followed it in the dark, Cob whipped out a skinning knife and held its blade up before Hammock's face. His eyes glittered. "You want I should kill you? Maybe you're starting to get on *my* nerves!"

"Shet!" Hammock's eyes narrowed off into the distance, and he got slowly to his feet. "Comp'ny's coming."

*　　*　　*

The major disadvantage to traveling alone, and traveling quick, was the lack of provisions. The cyclone that had devastated Boothe's party had brought nothing but rain to Oliver; his coffee was soaked, the beans were wormy, and he'd eaten the last of the corn pone for breakfast. He could have ridden on to the mission on an empty stomach, reprovisioned, and been on his way across the mountains long before any of those he'd left behind came by to identify him, but he didn't want to. That is, he didn't want to go on an empty stomach. He was wet, hungry, and bone-tired; he had time enough to tend to his own comfort before continuing.

He had been tracking Cob and Hammock much of the day, mostly in an effort to stay out of their way. But as the sun started to set and he got hungrier, he had another thought. He could see their fire clear across the prairie, which was as good a sign as any that they weren't laying in wait for anybody. He approached the camp boldly, and when he was close enough he stopped his horse and called, "Hello, the camp!"

He was rewarded by the click of a rifle bolt that carried clearly through the darkness and a voice that demanded, "Who's that?"

"A friend."

He walked his horse carefully forward, and by the time he reached the circle of the fire, he made sure his hands were high and visible.

"Hey, Hammock!" Excitedly, Cob threw the bolt on his rifle and took aim. "It's that egg-sucker from the wagons! I got 'im!"

Hammock threw out an arm to knock the rifle off center. "Hold on." He frowned suspiciously at

Oliver. "What you want? Come to meet your Maker, or jes' passing the time of day?"

"Just passing," Oliver answered easily. Very carefully he swung down from the saddle. "What you got cooking in that pot smells mighty good."

"I'm gonna kill you, mister," Cob insisted. That wild gleam was back in his eyes. "I said I would and I will."

"What for?" Oliver spread his arms but kept his hands near his belt, where the coat concealed his pistol. "I got no quarrel with you."

He wondered if he could even get the gun out of his belt before the crazy one blew him to kingdom come, and he was beginning to reconsider his decision to stop. Boothe never would have made such a mistake. Boothe—

He clamped down firmly on the thought. He wasn't so far from his horse that he couldn't still dodge a bullet if he had to, and Boothe had always said it was better to have one friend than two enemies. That was exactly the mistake Boothe had made when he had taken Oliver on.

Then Hammock said, "Hey, Cob. Look."

Oliver swore silently as Hammock lowered his rifle slightly and walked over to Oliver's horse. He should have hidden the rifles before he ever rode up; he could have sold them in the Northwest Territory for a pretty penny, for more than enough to pay his passage east. But if the rifles bought him his life tonight, or even a meal, he wouldn't complain.

Boothe never would have made that mistake, either.

Hammock flipped back the corner of the blanket that hid the six rifles strapped to the back of

Oliver's horse. "Oooeee!" he exclaimed, rubbing his jaw in appreciation. "Where'd you get all them firesticks, boy?"

Oliver shrugged. "Where do you think?"

Hammock turned shrewd, narrow eyes on him. "Them wagon's full of guns, is that it? Is that how come all them folks is way out here doing nothing—'cause they're taking guns to the Injuns?"

"Kill 'em!" shouted Cob. "Kill 'em ever' one!"

Hammock took a threatening step toward Oliver. "We got no use for Injun lovers out thisaway, mister."

Oliver was so startled he couldn't think of a good lie, and the only thing that would come out was the truth. "Hell, no! The wagons don't have anything in them but regular store goods. What you see right there are the only weapons they had."

"What're you doing with 'em?"

So far the truth had served him well, and it was becoming more obvious by the minute that anything he could do to put himself in a good light before these two would serve to his advantage. "I stole 'em," he replied casually.

"What fer? You was ready to stand up 'n' fight fer 'em last I saw."

"Things change. I didn't much like the way the boss was running things, so I lit out. Took their horses and oxen, too, but didn't have much use for them. The guns was all I kept."

Hammock looked like he didn't want to believe him, then mulled it over in his mind. "All them women. They wouldn't be filling their wagons with guns, I reckon. They'd have fancy dress goods and furbelows and pretty beads to dress theirselves up with. Maybe a ham or two, and some white flour. Been a long time since I tasted ham. Near 'bout as long as since I had me a white woman, right, Cob?"

Cob began to laugh excitedly, a nervous sound that resembled a mule's bray. Oliver kept his face impassive, but everything from his gut up was tightening into hard, cold knots.

Hammock jerked his head at Oliver. "He'p yerself to what's in the pot. You been riding all day?"

Oliver didn't have to answer that; it was readily visible from the state of his clothes. His mere presence had pinpointed the location of the wagons.

"Shit, Hammock!" Cob said angrily. "You gonna let him sit and eat when we ought to be killin' him right now?"

"We can kill him later if we have to," Hammock replied. He followed Oliver over to the fire. "Don't see much point, though, when we got all them pretty ladies waitin' fer us, and their menfolks without a gun between them, sittin' like ducks on the water ready to be knocked over and plucked."

Oliver squatted by the fire and picked up a wooden bowl he saw lying next to it. The sight of what was floating in the pot gave him momentary pause, but he scooped up some broth anyway. "I figured you fellas had give up on those wagonfolk."

"They kilt Rufus!" Cob cried.

Whirling on him, Hammock shouted, "Shet up about Rufus!"

"He's my brother, Ham," Cob replied, though in a slightly more subdued tone.

Hammock squatted down beside Oliver. "We ain't giving up, just playing it smart. Figured they'd walk right into our arms sooner or later. But now I'm thinking it might be right smart to turn around and catch 'em where they lay. I'm gettin' tired of waitin' anyhow. I got me a itch."

"I don't know," Oliver said, drinking from the bowl. "Two men against four. And they're Indian fighters, all of 'em. They know enough tricks, they don't *need* guns."

He paused just long enough to let that sink in. Hammock was beginning to look worried.

Oliver held his gaze. "Sounds to me like you could use an extra hand."

Ben would not take Boothe's rifle, and he had never known what it meant to be alone until he was out on the prairie with a woman to protect and not even a strip of leather with which to fashion a slingshot. Not that Kitty would thank him for wanting to protect her—and not that she needed it—but he worried anyway. It didn't comfort him to know that the people back at camp needed the gun more than he did, or that he had made the right choice in setting out for help. He could only pray that Boothe had been right when he'd said Kitty was safer with Ben than with him, but Ben didn't think so.

The first day, Snow attacked a snake and Ben was thrown; neither he nor the pony was injured, however. That night they made a cold camp and shared a piece of soft smoked meat; the beef had not been smoked long enough to last more than a few days, and Ben knew he would have to think of some way to trap some game if they were to make it to the mission. Neither one of them said it, but they knew their chances of completing the journey were slim. They kept their eyes sharpened for some sign of the stolen horses or oxen.

Early on the second day, Kitty picked up tracks, by the purest coincidence. If she hadn't let the pony have his head, swerving back to the south as he picked up the scent of a small stream, they never would have seen them. At first they both thought the tracks might be from their own stolen horses, but it soon became clear that the animals were not riderless. There were three men, and they appeared to be cutting across Ben's and Kitty's own trail.

"There were only two buffalo hunters," Kitty said, pushing her hair back beneath her hat.

"Two that we saw. There might've been more."

Her expression was thoughtful. "Maybe it's not them. Maybe it's somebody else. Trappers, maybe."

"Or Indians."

"Indians don't shoe their horses. I say we follow them for a spell."

Ben shook his head. "They're going the wrong way. It'd cost us too much time."

She looked at him steadily. "Ben," she said, "we've got half a canteen of water and enough meat to last us three more days if it doesn't poison us first. These men might be able to get help to the wagons where we can't. We can't afford *not* to follow them."

Ben knew she was wrong; in his heart he knew she was wrong. But he had no good answer for her, and if there was a chance, any chance at all, of getting those folks they'd left behind moving again . . . He had no choice but to agree.

They found the camp not long after sundown,

its fire burning as bold as a beacon in the night. At Ben's insistence, they tethered Snow to a stump out of sight and crossed the remaining two hundred yards on foot, staying as low and as quiet as they could.

The mumble of voices reached them before they could make out any shapes, and they strained to hear the words. Two dozen yards away, Ben forced Kitty down and they crawled closer on their bellies, trusting the dark and the grass to hide them.

Then they froze. A tall, lanky figure moved before the fire and for an instant was fully illuminated as he bent to refill his coffee cup. "Oliver," Kitty breathed.

Ben gripped her arm hard. They backed away as fast as they could.

Even when they were safely out of hearing distance, they did not get up or dare to take the chance that their figures might be silhouetted against the sky. Ben was breathing hard. "Those other two—the buffalo hunters. What in God's name is Oliver doing with them?"

Badness has its own reasons. Kitty said nothing, her lips tightly compressed and her eyes hard as she stared into the darkness.

"We've got to get out of here." Ben pulled at her arm again. "Those men are killers, and who knows what Oliver will do. Let's go."

"No." Kitty's voice was low, and her body went rigid against Ben's efforts to urge her away. She stared forward at the halo of the distant fire. "They've got three horses. Three horses would get our people out of here alive, Ben. We're taking them."

At first he appeared not to have heard her. His

voice was incredulous when he spoke. "Do you mean—steal them?"

She nodded grimly. "That's just what I mean. And don't you start quoting the Bible at me, Ben Adamson. The Lord helps those who help themselves."

His whisper was an angry hiss in the darkness. "I don't need a Bible to tell me when you've lost your mind! We wouldn't get within ten feet of that camp before somebody started shooting—and they wouldn't be firing warning shots, either. Use your common sense, girl! Boothe didn't send us out here to get killed!"

Kitty rolled over to look at him. Her face was grave. "Boothe didn't expect us to make it to the mission, either," she said quietly. "At least not in time to help the others. You know that as well as I do, Ben. All he was hoping for was that, with a horse, *we'd* have a chance of getting through alive. The only chance the others have is if we can bring back horses and guns—and quick. Those men out there . . ." She nodded briefly toward the fire. "They've got both."

Ben was silent for a time. Kitty could feel his inner struggle as though it were a physical thing.

"We'll never get close enough," he said at last.

"Oliver did. We'll wait till they're sleeping, near dawn. They don't know anybody else is out here; they won't think to post a guard."

Ben's voice was heavy with defeat when he spoke again. "If I could think of one good reason why you're wrong, I'd tie you up and drag you out of here, Kitty Kincaid. But I can't."

She squeezed his hand, and they backed off to wait for moonset.

*   *   *

Oliver had given up trying to tell himself he'd done the right thing; stopped repeating to himself the credo he'd lived by for years—that a man has only one duty in this life, to himself. He'd counted on it being easy to hate Boothe, and for a time it had been. Boothe Carlyle, a legend among men, the hero of his childhood, should have stayed quietly buried in Cairo, pushing a plow and singing hymns for the rest of his life. He should have known that if he came out here again, there would be debts to pay. He should have quit while he was ahead, and since he hadn't, he deserved what he got.

Oliver hadn't counted on Ben and Kitty, or the memories they had brought back. He hadn't counted on Miss Katherine's face haunting him every step of the way. Once, he had called them family, but he had been a child then. Too much had happened for him to ever call anyone family again.

What he had done had been no worse than what Boothe had done when he'd left Judith and all those others to die in the mountains. At least he wasn't a woman-killer. At least those he'd left behind had food and water, and they would make it to the mission . . . Boothe would see to that. And that was the irony of it. Because all along, deep inside, he had been counting on the strength and ingenuity of the man he was attempting to destroy. While he plotted to bring down the legend, he was secretly praying that Boothe Carlyle would emerge the hero.

Ben and Kitty did not deserve to die. Poor, mad Lucy did not deserve what had happened to her.

Effie Creller and her baby; Martin Creller, who had been crippled trying to save them all . . . It had never been his intention to kill them. They would have made it to the mission, bruised, beaten, and stumbling but alive. Except for this . . .

He had not counted on a massacre. He had not counted on being forced to lead the killers straight into a defenseless camp. He hadn't counted on the way his conscience kept gnawing at him when he thought of Miss Katherine, holding baby Kitty in her arms, or of Ben, five years old and clinging to his hand as they trudged through the wilderness. And he came to realize that whatever else he might have become over the years, he wasn't cut out for cold-blooded murder. He couldn't escape the past any more than Boothe Carlyle could.

He knew that neither one of the men with whom he had thrown in his lot trusted him, and one false move would earn him a bullet through the head. If he hadn't volunteered to lead them to the camp he would be dead already, because all they wanted was the rifles. They might kill him anyway before another day was out. He had thought about killing them in their sleep, but neither one of them was as stupid as he looked. Oliver might get off one shot, but not two.

The best he could do was to keep riding, keep watching for a chance. But they were moving closer to the camp, and time was running out.

He slept lightly, if at all, his hand wrapped around the pistol in his belt. The first whinny of a horse in the predawn stillness brought him to his feet, the pistol drawn, but he wasn't as fast as Hammock. A rifle shot cracked through the darkness and Hammock shouted, "Son of a *bitch!*"

"The horses!" Cob cried, and another shot rang out.

One of the horses had been loosened from its tether, and Oliver could see the silhouette of a man trying to mount it. With another shot the man stumbled and the horse trotted away; Oliver started to fire, but it was hard to get a clean shot between the rearing horses, and just then another horse raced up—a white pony. Oliver lowered his gun.

Cob and Hammock were stumbling through the dark, shouting obscenities and firing blindly. Oliver saw that their confusion gave Ben a chance to turn back and try to loosen the tethers of the other horses. One of them broke free and raced across the prairie; a woman's frantic shouts clamored against the echo of gunfire and Ben left the third horse, climbing on the back of the white pony as it galloped away.

"Stop shooting!" Oliver shouted. "The horses, goddammit, the horses!"

Hammock, whom Oliver had discovered was marginally brighter than his partner, finally realized that the gunfire was only frightening the two horses into further flight. Before Oliver could do it himself, Hammock jumped on the back of the remaining horse and took off across the prairie.

Oliver ran on foot after his own horse, which was too weighted down by the saddle and guns—only four of which Cob and Hammock had not already appropriated for their own use—to go very far on its own. None of the men unsaddled at night; it was hard on the horses but, at moments like this, worth the disadvantage.

"Hey! Catch my horse!" Cob shouted.

Oliver kicked his horse into a fast gallop and ducked low as a bullet whizzed past his head.

Ben's arms were around Kitty's waist and his chest pressed into her back as they raced across the prairie. She could feel a warm wetness soaking into the back of her shirt and she prayed it wasn't what she knew it was. A rifle shot cracked and they both ducked, but it was too far away to harm them.

"The guns!" Ben gasped into her ear. "I had my hands on them! I should have—"

His words were cut off by a sharp breath of pain as Snow stumbled on a rock, and for one horrifying moment his arms loosened on her waist. "Hold on!" she shouted. "For God's sake, Ben, hold on!"

His arms tightened, but he did not speak again.

Snow was a strong pony, but he was no match for a horse with only one rider, and he was beginning to tire. Ben couldn't hold on much longer either, and even the darkness worked against them: The white pony made a perfect silhouette against the night. They had to find shelter, and quickly, while the uneven lay of the land still offered them moments of invisibility from the pursuer who was closing fast.

There were no rocks or trees to hide behind, no gullies or creeks within riding distance. But there was a buffalo wallow they had ridden through that afternoon, a wide depression in the earth about four feet deep that was mostly screened with prairie grass. Kitty made for it at a wide angle, cutting around and approaching it from behind so that, if she was lucky and God was good, it would look to anyone following at a distance as though the pony had simply disappeared into the night.

She rode Snow down the slight incline, and as soon as she drew him to a stop Ben slid to the ground. Her heart lurched with a stab of fear, but she refrained from running to him. She had to cover the pony's white hide, which would shine like a beacon as soon as the rider—or riders—drew close enough.

She knelt down and grabbed the pony's right foreleg and left rear leg, jerking hard and jumping quickly out of the way as the startled animal went down with a snort and a surprised whinny. Before he could right himself again, Kitty threw her arms around his neck, leaning her weight against him and murmuring soothing syllables into his ear until he calmed. Then, with one hand still pressed against his neck, she jerked off the blanket that served as a saddle and spread it full-length over him, covering the animal from ears to rump.

Snow seemed to understand what was expected of him, as Kitty had no doubt he would, and he stayed down. Still resting her hand on his neck for reassurance, she reached for Ben. He was crawling up next to her, and she could hear the sound of his uneven breathing. Her hand brushed his shirt and came away wet and sticky.

"I'm—all right," he whispered. But he didn't sound all right. He sounded as though every word was cutting him in two. "Just stay still. Keep the horse quiet. We're going to be—all right."

And so Kitty waited, pressed between Ben on one side and Snow on the other, straining to hear the sound of approaching hoofbeats over the pounding of her own heart, trying not to breathe too loudly, praying Snow would not whinny, and that Ben wasn't hurt too badly. *Please don't let Ben be hurt too badly* . . .

The hoofbeats were growing closer; the rider was heading straight toward them. Then there was a shout in the distance. The hoofbeats slowed and another shout, closer, replied, "Over here! They went this way!"

Kitty squeezed her eyes tightly shut and prayed wordlessly.

There were two riders now, one set of hooves fainter but growing closer. Maybe they should try to run. Snow was rested; maybe he could outdistance the riders. If they stayed here they were sure to be seen. Maybe they should run . . .

"Ben," she whispered desperately.

There was no answer. Ben had passed out.

Closer now. So close she could hear their coarse voices, practically smell their fetid breath.

"Goddamm it all to hell! Had to chase my own horse!"

"Where's Sherrod?"

"Took off. Thought he was with you!"

"Shit! What'd you let him get away fer? He had the goddamn guns! I knowed we shoulda took 'em all when we had the chance!"

"We'll find him, Ham."

"We ain't findin' nothin' in the dark. Forgit 'im; he wadn't worth shit anyway."

"What about them two horse thieves?"

"You see any goddamn tracks?" It was practically a roar. "You're so shit-assed stupid it's a wonder your ma didn't drown you when you popped out! You can't track nothing in the goddamn dark!"

"We can't just let them get away!"

"We got bigger game in our sights. We don't need them. We don't need nothin'!"

The hoofbeats turned away.

Thank you God, oh God thank you . . .

Kitty lay there with her eyes tightly closed and every muscle in her body trembling, until she could no longer hear the hoofbeats at all.

The bright yellow shafts of dawn pierced Kitty's eyes and she awoke with a start. She had dozed sitting up with her back against the bank, Ben's head in her lap. Snow was munching grass a few feet away, his flanks still splattered with blood— not the animal's, but Ben's.

The bullet had gone clean through Ben's right side, shaving off flesh and cracking a rib and leaving an exit hole the size of a small fist. Kitty had packed the wounds with grass as best she could, but he had lost an awful lot of blood. Her skirt was still damp with it, her hands stained with it.

Ben's skin was hot and dry and his color gray, but he opened his eyes when Kitty touched his face. The eyes were bright with fever, but still lucid. Kitty offered him a drink from their improvised canteen. Most of it spilled, but he drank enough to wet his throat.

"Sorry," he said huskily, and tried to smile. "I guess I'm not much of a horse thief."

"It was a stupid idea." Kitty's voice was roughened by the ache in her throat. Despair, regret, and hoplessness threatened to choke her. "You never should have listened to me. Mama—Mama sent me here to take care of you, you and Boothe . . . and look what I've done. Oh, Ben, I'm so sorry!"

The shadow of a smile flickered and grew deeper for a moment. "Sent you to take care of me, did she? Funny. All I wanted to do . . . was take care of you."

But the effort to talk had exhausted him, and he closed his eyes, the smile fading.

"We've got to get you back to camp," Kitty said urgently.

He moved his head to the side. "No. I'd never make it."

"It's not so far away, a couple of days—"

"No." He opened his eyes. "There's no help for me back there."

She opened her mouth to protest, desperation tearing through her, but he generated enormous energy to make his voice firm.

"Kitty, listen to me. This is important. Yesterday—when we were tracking those men—they're heading straight back the way we came. If we turn back to camp, we're going to ride right into them and we're in no shape to outrun them this time."

He stopped, breathing hard, and Kitty couldn't see any flaw in his logic, as frantically as she tried.

"There's something else." He drew a shaky breath. "I—think they're circling back toward the camp. Oliver . . . they know our people are unarmed now. You've got to go on, Kitty. You've got to get some help. Ride on to the mission."

Everything within her rebelled wildly. "No! I can't leave you! It'll take me days to reach the mission, and then—"

"I can't go with you," he said. His tone was flat, exhausted, and matter-of-fact. "The ride would kill me, and I'd only slow you down. Here—I can rest, and heal. You've got to go alone."

A sob burst inside her throat, but she clamped her lips together and wouldn't let it out. She couldn't leave Ben. She couldn't leave him to die out here alone on the prairie. *God, please not Ben, too. Don't take Ben, too . . .*

"You promised Boothe," he said weakly, "that one of us would get through. We're all—counting on you to keep that promise."

And she knew she had no choice.

She wouldn't cry. She forced the tears back until they seared her chest, until her stomach cramped with the effort, until her eyes blurred and it hurt even to breathe. But she wouldn't let Ben see her cry; he needed all the strength he could get now.

She stretched the saddle blanket between two sticks to give Ben some shelter from the sun, and she left him the canteen, though he protested. "I can find water," she said shortly. "You can't."

She kept two strips of the beef for herself and left the rest to Ben, making sure he didn't see how she divided it. She could survive; her mother had raised her to survive. But Ben . . . nothing but the hand of God could keep him alive until she returned. She knew that in her deepest heart, but refused to let her mind acknowledge it. To admit it even to herself would be as good as saying Ben was dead already.

Then there was nothing left to do but go. She knelt beside him and looked into his face for a long time. *I can't leave you, I can't . . .*

She had to.

She reached into her pocket and felt the heavy weight of the gold coin. Slowly she drew it out and placed it in Ben's hand. "Hold on to this for me, all right?" she said huskily. "I'll be back for it."

His fingers were hot as they closed around the coin. "I'll be here," he said.

She leaned forward and kissed his lips. "I'm going to marry you, Ben Adamson," she said.

And then quickly, while she still could, she got up and mounted Snow. Tears were streaming down her face as she rode away, and she did not look back.

Chapter Sixteen

Kitty had been riding forever. She was six years old and Byrd was leading the reins of a small squat pony; she was twelve and holding her little sister in front of her on the back of a square-shouldered mare while Katherine called her to be careful. She was fourteen and clutching the neck of Ben Adamson's stallion as it leaped over fence boards. She was climbing the rocky slopes of the Flint Hills with the wind buffeting her. She was an old woman with liver spots on her hands and gray tangled in her hair, and she was still riding.

The sun was brutal; the dry, stubbly ground gave back waves of shimmering heat. The world was painted in shades of yellow and brown, on and on, as far as she could see. She could die out here, and no one would ever find her bones. She would be swallowed up by the infinite sameness of the plains, and no one would ever know a girl named Kitty Kincaid had ever existed.

She wanted to go home. She had to turn the pony around, right now, and go home. Her pa was waiting for her; Mama would be worried. She'd been gone too long, and Miss Caroline was always scolding her for riding in the sun. But she couldn't remember where home was, and she'd never find her way back in the dark.

Except it wasn't dark. The sun was as bright as polished copper and it burned her eyes. Her pa was dead, and she had promised her mama . . . something . . .

She couldn't go home. She'd never see her mother again. Boothe was depending on her, Ben was lying back there on the plains with the lifeblood slowly seeping out of him, and she had to go on. She had to do something, but she was lost and exhausted and she didn't know what to do.

I'm sorry, Mama . . . She wanted to cry, but she had no tears. Her lips were cracked and swollen, and her eyes felt as tight as drumheads from staring into the sun. Even her sweat glands had dried up, and it was hard to blink. Everything kept blurring in and out. She pushed a hand across her eyes to clear them, and when she looked again there was something in the distance, something green, something unbelievable.

It was the cool, quiet curve of a riverbank. A cottonwood tree grew crookedly toward the sun, spreading its roots to drink from the river, and oaks lined the opposite bank. Beyond those oaks she could see the roofs of neat wooden houses, and people strolled along the shore. The Solomon River, it had to be, and those houses belonged to the mission. She had made it, she never thought she would but she had; she had made it and everything was going to be all right . . .

She gave a little cry that came out as a croak, and urged Snow to greater speed. The pony was exhausted and he stumbled, but she climbed off and pulled him along on foot. There was water, there was food, there were people with wagons and oxen and medical supplies, there was *life* and it all was no more than half a mile ahead . . . She could make it that far. She could make it!

Except suddenly it wasn't there anymore. She didn't know what happened. She was staring at the riverbank, and the people were so close she could almost see their faces, and then she glanced around to get a firmer grip on Snow's rope and when she looked back there was nothing but dry yellow grass and blazing sky as far as she could see.

Frantically she turned to the east, and the south, and the north. She stumbled a few more steps forward, searching the western horizon, and her heart was pounding desperately, wildly, but it wasn't there. The river was gone, the houses were gone, the people . . .

None of it had ever been there at all.

"No," she whispered.

And then she screamed, *"No!"* It was a hoarse sound that tore her throat and made it bleed, and it shattered the stillness of the plains like a rent in the sky. But no one answered.

She fell to her knees and wept with dry, tearless sobs.

Ben felt the shadow fall over him and prepared to die. His water was almost gone, and though he had tried to eat the smoked meat, he couldn't keep any of it down. Time had blurred into a meaningless conglomeration of blazing sun and feverish dreams. Sometimes Kitty was with him, placing a cool hand across his brow; sometimes it was his mother. Sometimes he was perfectly lucid and strong enough to sit up and drink, and once he had made himself crawl to the edge of the buffalo wallow and look around, scouting for signs of discovery or rescue. He did not know how long ago that had been.

Now they had found him, and in a moment there would be a bullet through his head that would end it all. His fingers tightened around the coin in his hand. *Kitty, I'm sorry . . .*

Oliver knelt beside him and, slipping a hand beneath Ben's head, lifted him and pressed a canteen to his lips. Ben drank.

"You left a trail like a stuck buffalo," Oliver said. "If those bastards had stayed around till sunrise, they would've had you for sure."

"How long?" Ben croaked.

"A day and a half. I back-tracked you."

Ben wanted to ask about Kitty, and perhaps he did, but he never heard the answer. The darkness closed in.

When Ben opened his eyes again, the darkness was night, and a small fire crackled a few feet away. He watched Oliver stirring something in a pot, and he did not question his presence; he didn't question anything. When Oliver felt his eyes on him, he came over and helped Ben sit up. He pressed a cup of broth into his hand.

"It's got some gopher meat in it," he said, "and plenty of blood. That hole in your side doesn't look too bad; Kitty did a good job. You'll live."

When Ben's head stopped spinning, he took a sip of the broth. The taste was foul, but it was hot and he forced his rebellious stomach to keep it down. He sipped again, and his head felt a little clearer. His hands began to steady.

After a time he said, "Why?" He wasn't sure whether he meant to ask why Oliver had left them, or why he had come back. He was pretty sure he wouldn't get an answer to either question.

"The reasons don't matter anymore," Oliver said. "I don't guess they ever did. What happened?"

Ben made himself drink more of the broth. "Cyclone. The wagons—gone. Food, water, everything."

Oliver swore softly.

Ben looked at him. "You missed Boothe's gun."

"I didn't miss it," Oliver muttered.

Ben was silent for a time thinking about that but not very hard. He said, "Kitty went on—to try to make it to the mission."

Oliver looked at him sharply. "She hasn't got a chance."

Ben rubbed his thumb over the coin in his hand and said nothing.

"Those killers are headed straight for the camp," Oliver said abruptly. "We're not going to make it in time to warn them."

"You shouldn't have come back for me."

Oliver just looked at him. "Better finish that broth. We ride at first light."

Ben shook his head. "You go. It'll be faster."

There was a peculiar expression on Oliver's face, something almost like a smile in the flickering firelight. "You trust me to do that?"

"Yes."

Oliver shook his head. "We both go." His voice was a little gruff. "I'm not as good as I thought I'd be at leaving folks to die. Besides . . ." He glanced at Ben. "I need you along to keep me honest."

The two men's eyes met in agreement.

The first shot came at dawn, when Effie Creller was returning from the creek with a saucepan full of water. The rifle shot cracked like a whip, and Effie stumbled forward and sprawled on the ground; Rachel screamed and ran toward her, but another bullet split the earth a few inches in front of her feet. Boothe appeared from behind the canvas shelter and fired blindly at a movement to his left; the figure was running and he fired again, but the man disappeared down the slope of the creek bank a hundred yards away.

Martin stumbled forward, shouting hoarsely for Effie. Boothe thrust the rifle into his hands. "Cover me!" He could hear Effie sobbing and he knew she was alive; Syms was trying to pull his wife back as she struggled for Effie. Boothe ran, keeping low, but another bullet streaked past his shoulder before he reached her. Martin fired back.

"I'm all right!" Effie cried. Her face was streaked with dirt and tears, but Boothe could see she was more scared than hurt. "My leg—I can walk—"

He took no chances. He scooped her up in his arms and started running with her. As soon as he did Martin fired again. This time when the gunfire was returned it was too far away to do any harm.

"Save your ammunition!" Boothe cried. "Behind the canvas—everybody!"

He reached the shelter of the canvas at the same

time everyone else did and laid Effie on the ground as gently as he could. Martin fell beside her and raised her head and shoulders to his chest, gasping and holding her tight. "I'm all right, I'm all right . . ." she kept sobbing, but no one believed it until Rachel lifted the hem of her bloodstained skirt and saw that the bullet had only grazed her calf.

"The buffalo hunters?" Syms said hoarsely.

Boothe nodded. For a moment his face was grim, then he said crisply, "Start bringing as much of that lumber up here as you can. Barricade this side of the canvas. They could start shooting again any minute."

"But there're only two of them!" Rachel cried.

"And we've got only one gun." Boothe was already dragging forward the lumber they had scavenged for firewood, trying to wedge the biggest pieces together to form some sort of rough protection. Martin reluctantly left his wife to help as Rachel tore off strips of petticoat for bandages, and Syms said fearfully, "How long can we hold them off?"

Boothe met his eyes. "I think you'd better start praying, Reverend."

"Goddamn lying son of a bitch!" Hammock flung himself facedown on the ground behind the pile of rocks on the opposite creek bank. "Said they didn't have no guns! Nearly got my goddamn head blowed off!"

"Lying son of a bitch!" echoed Cob violently. "I don't see no goddamn wagons!"

"Forget the wagons! We didn't come all this way for no goddamn wagons!" He turned on Cob.

"What the hell you mean, shootin' at women? We got better things to do with women, goddamn you!"

"I didn't mean to hit her, just scare her a little. Anyways, she's alive, ain't she?" Cob's eyes narrowed. "I say we rush 'em."

"Yeah, you just go right ahead and rush 'em. I'll sit back and watch the buzzards pick your bones."

"Goddammit, Ham, what're we going to do?"

Hammock lay on his belly, squinting through the grass at the camp. "I didn't see but one gun. Can't hold out forever on one gun. And we got the water. Sooner or later, they got to make a break for it." He grinned. "That's when we just sit back and pick 'em off, one by one."

Kitty saw figures forming on the horizon. Her eyes were blurred and wouldn't focus, but they looked like riders, six or maybe more, shimmering and wavering in the haze of bright sunlight as they moved toward her. She knew they weren't real, she didn't believe in them, but she moved toward them anyway because the vision gave her something to concentrate on in the vast open prairie.

She tried to lead Snow at least half the day; he was as dehydrated as she was and his strength was failing. But her own legs had given out shortly after noon and now she was riding, letting the little pony carry her with inexorable plodding steps toward the illusion of riders.

But this mirage kicked up dust as it moved and carried the sound of thundering horses. She could see the faces—fierce and copper-colored with bold black eyes. Their heads were covered with dusty turbans of various colors, and they carried rifles and wore belts of ammunition around their necks. Where had she seen such men before?

Shawnee.

This was no vision born of heat and exhaustion. The riders were real. Their battle-torn clothes and hard, disdainful eyes were real, and so were the weapons they carried in their hands.

Shawnee.

She knew them by their turbans and their white man's clothes. But there were no Shawnee this far west. Except for something Boothe had told her, something she couldn't remember.

Even if she had wanted to run, she couldn't have done so. She was in the midst of them before she knew to be afraid, and they spread out around her, encircling her on all sides. They did not aim their rifles; they didn't have to. She had no defense against them; they knew she was theirs for the taking.

She had thought it was impossible to feel terror again. She thought her poor brain was too dulled even to register the emotion, her body too drained to tense for fight. But her heart was pounding so that it shook her limbs and throbbed in her parched throat. Her mind was suddenly sharp and clear with the imprint of danger; she saw every detail, she knew every possibility. And everything she saw, everything she felt combined to form sheer, paralyzing fear with no hope of escape.

Their horses shifted restlessly around her. She could feel eyes boring into her back, arms, legs. She was pinned by the force of their stares. The brave directly in front of her, the tallest, the proudest, the angriest, was the most frightening of all.

He was staring at her breasts. Her blood flowed

icy cold, then feverishly, with dizzying rapidity. Her hands tightened on the rope around Snow's neck. But she couldn't move.

Then he looked at her face, and he said in English, "You come from the Firebird."

He wasn't looking at her breasts, but at the cross! The Celtic cross that Boothe had given her.

"I am White Feather," the brave said.

Kitty lifted her chin, steeling her muscles, forcing energy into her limbs. She raised her hand and ripped her blouse at the shoulder, revealing the scar for all to see.

"My name is Warrior Woman," she said.

The brave's eyes went to her shoulder. Some of the others moved closer, their horses snorting and tossing their heads at the scent of the strange pony. There were murmurings in a language Kitty didn't understand, but the brave in front of her said nothing.

"The Firebird is in trouble," she said.

The brave looked at the cross, and Kitty's pounding heart counted off the minutes. Then he met her eyes.

"We go," he said.

The siege was two days old. Every hour or so the assailants would fire a spate of bullets toward the shelter, but they were too far out of range to hit anything. It was at night, when they often got bold enough to cross the creek and take an accurate shot, that Boothe sat in wait for them and returned fire. That these attempts were more an effort to make him waste his ammunition than to do any physical damage was obvious, but Boothe knew if he ever quit firing, the two of them would descend with all guns blasting. They had proven themselves wily and wouldn't make easy targets; Boothe knew he wouldn't have much of a chance if they attacked. But neither could he go to them. Their position gave them a clear view of the camp at all times, while the rough bank of the creek made their own movements easy to hide. He would be dead before he got half a dozen yards from the shelter.

Two men. How could two men hold down a party of six? Boothe had been in some tight situations before, but there had always been a solution, a plan, a strategy that needed nothing but time to be brought into action. Now, think as he might, he could not see a way out.

They had stored their meat in a makeshift rock shelter some distance from the camp to protect it from scavengers, but the lack of food was not the worst of their problems. They were completely cut off from the creek. The saucepan that Effie had dropped was their only means of transporting water, and the last time Boothe had tried to retrieve it the gunmen had blasted it full of holes. The days were brutal, the nights hot and dry. They would all slowly die of dehydration.

At first the baby had cried continually, and Boothe was glad to hear it. As long as the boy cried, he was all right. But now all he could manage was a few dry hiccoughs, and an occasional hoarse, squeaky wail that was cut off too soon. Effie had no more milk, and the beef broth she had been feeding him by soaking it in a strip of cloth was all gone. The child wouldn't last much longer.

Lucy Syms had retreated so far inside herself that she no longer moved, or sobbed, or closed her eyes. For over a day now she had sat like a statue at the far end of the barricade, to all appearances already dead.

There had been no gunfire for over an hour. Everyone's nerves were growing taut with expectation, their thirst and hunger slicing their senses to a ragged edge. The sun had just set, and everyone feared what the dusk concealed.

"Maybe they're planning something," Martin suggested uneasily.

Boothe shook his head. "They're just playing with us. They want us to worry." His voice was tired. "They got time on their side, they know that. They can wait as long as it takes for us to break."

"How much ammunition have you got left?"

Boothe had been hoping no one would ask that. But all eyes were on him, and they had a right to know. "Three shots."

"We can't outwait them," Effie said thinly. She was cradling the baby, still and limp, in her arms. "We can't last through another day of this heat. We can't wait for them to walk right up and let them shoot us . . ."

"No, ma'am, we can't," Boothe said quietly. And he knew that as soon as it was dark, he was going to have to try to rush them.

John Syms began to pull off his boots. Everyone watched him as though he had taken leave of his senses, and when he spoke in a quiet, matter-of-fact voice their suspicions were all but confirmed. "Don't know why we didn't think of it before. We can carry water in our boots. Simplest thing in the world."

"We can't get to the creek," Martin protested.

Boothe grabbed Syms's arm. "Don't be a fool, man! That's just what they're waiting for, for one of us to lose our heads and do something stupid. They'll cut you down like a lantern-froze deer!"

"Maybe," Syms replied calmly. "But it will draw their fire long enough for you to get up close. With only three shots left, Mr. Carlyle, two of them have got to count."

"John, no!" Rachel cried.

Syms ignored her, smiling at Boothe. "You're surprised I knew what you were planning. You have a military mind, sir, and it may also surprise you to know that I'm something of a scholar of military men. David was a warrior, as was Joshua . . . and Moses, in his way. I don't think any of them, finding themselves in this situation, would have come to a much different solution."

Boothe did not release his arm. "You're out of your mind," he said quietly. "You'll be killed."

"So will you, if you try it alone. And these people need your protection a lot more than they do mine."

The vision of a black wolf flashed through Boothe's head, and he said, "No." He was not meant to die this way, in this place. "Stay here. I can do it on my own."

Syms was silent for a moment, gazing at the boots in his hand, then he looked at Boothe. "We've all learned a lot about one another on this journey," he said. "One of the things everyone has learned about me—including myself, to my dismay—is that I'm a coward, hiding behind the shield of God's word but without the strength of conviction to do what His word demands. Let me serve my God, Mr. Carlyle. Let me protect my own."

"A brave man doesn't have to prove his courage," Boothe said hoarsely.

"No," agreed Syms. "He doesn't."

And before Boothe could stop him, he broke away and out of the shelter.

Immediately Boothe swung in the opposite direction, running parallel to Syms toward the creek bank. The first shot went wild. The second split the ground six inches before Syms's feet. Syms didn't falter. Boothe wasted one shot to draw their fire away from Syms, and the returned bullet snagged Boothe's coat sleeve and he swung to the left, staying low, refusing to fire blindly even though it might buy Syms an extra moment of life. Too many people were depending on him. Too many . . .

Syms went down, though Boothe couldn't tell whether he was hit or had simply thrown himself out of the line of fire. Boothe saw a shadow move behind the pile of rocks and fired. The bullet tore off a chunk of rock with a screeching sound and a flash of fire. Syms was on his feet again, running. A man appeared behind the rock, boldly taking aim at Syms. Boothe had a clear shot. He dropped, swung the rifle up, and squeezed the trigger.

Nothing happened. His last shot was worthless; the rifle was jammed. He watched in helpless rage as the gunman prepared to assassinate John Syms.

And then there was another shot, from far off and behind the shelter to the west; too far off to do anything but distract the gunman, but it was enough to make his shot go wild. He swung to the west as he reloaded. The second man returned fire wildly.

Boothe flung himself to his belly and began to crawl toward Syms.

*   *   *

Ben slid off the horse as soon as they heard the gunfire. He grabbed a rifle from the back of Oliver's saddle and fired blindly, though the recoil sent bolts of pain through him and almost knocked him off his feet. "Go!" he shouted to Oliver. "Get their guns to them! I'll cover you as best I can!"

Oliver charged across the plains, brandishing his pistol and firing at random.

Ben ran forward as far as he could, every breath searing pain through his lungs, then dropped to one knee and drew a shaky arm across his eyes to clear them of sweat before he fired again. The jolt shot dizziness through his brain and made him break out in a cold sweat. He could feel his wound leaking again. But he still wasn't close enough to do any good. He could see the canvas shelter jerk as it was peppered with gunfire and he started running again. Oliver was halfway to them now, and his wild yelling and pistol fire drew the gunmen's attention away from Boothe and Syms, who were on the ground and defenseless. Ben could see the gunmen behind the rocks; he stopped, reloaded, and fired again, but he *couldn't get close enough* . . .

Oliver's horse screamed and went down hard. The rifles scattered, too far away for anyone to reach them. Oliver was motionless.

Ben started running, but he knew he wouldn't make it in time. The two gunmen had already stepped boldly from behind the rocks and were moving toward the creek.

A wild cackle drifted across the creek bank, echoing in Boothe's ear. "I got you now, you son of a bitch! I damn sure got you!"

Boothe reached Syms. The other man was white-faced and sweating, but he stayed on the ground, stayed still as Boothe had commanded him to. But it didn't matter anymore. There was no place to hide now.

"I got you in my sights, Red! Ain't no use crawling. I got you!"

There was the sound of water splashing as two men entered the creek.

"I ain't gonna kill you right off, you know. First I'm gonna shoot out your kneecaps. Then I'm gonna put a bullet through the soft part of that fella right next to you. Then I'm gonna drag me out a woman—"

Boothe reached for Syms's hand and clasped it. "I'm sorry," he said. *God, all I ever asked of You was that You let me get these people through alive . . .* "We'll put up a fight. I'll protect the women as long as I can."

Syms nodded. "No man could ask more—than what you've already done. But there's always time for one more miracle."

"I think I've used up my quota, Reverend." *All I ever asked, God, was to—*

There was thunder on the horizon.

"Holy Christ, Ham! Look!"

Boothe twisted around. Silhouetted against the orange sky was a band of Indians, riding hard and fast and headed straight for them. At the forefront, riding a white pony, with her hair and her skirts flying out behind her, was Kitty Kincaid.

Epilogue

The wedding took place in the chapel of the Mission for the Education of Pawnee Children, a small, unpretentious building made of chinked logs and oilcloth windows. The bride wore a freshly pressed butternut skirt and an oft-mended calico blouse, with a spray of wildflowers in her hair. Exactly one month after the travelers had arrived at the mission on the Solomon River under their Shawnee escort, Reverend John Syms pronounced Kitty Kincaid and Benjamin Adamson husband and wife.

The congregation was composed of strangers: the resident missionaries and their wives, many brown-faced children, a few Pawnee women with their newly civilized trapper husbands. And the congregation was filled with friends: Martin Creller, who was now walking with the aid of only a short cane; Effie and a very vociferous Adam; Rachel Syms, who beamed as proudly as if she were the mother of the bride; and Lucy,

who had that morning brushed her hair by herself
and tied it back with a bright pink ribbon. Oliver
Sherrod had been up half the night soaking his hat
and brushing his boots, and Boothe Carlyle gave
the bride away.

The Presbyterian settlement on the Solomon
River was much different from the Shawnee mission they had visited. There the missionaries had
striven to fit the Shawnee into the white man's way
of life, to civilize the Shawnee and make them into
Christian gentlemen. But here on the plains life
was harder and survival was more important than
white fences and a newspaper.

The teachers and missionaries lived in soddies,
houses of earth cut from the prairie floor which
huddled low to the ground to provide warmth in
the winter and coolness in the summer. There were
trees along the riverbank, and some of these had
been felled to build the church and the schoolhouse. Fields had been cultivated, too; corn and
beans and fodder for the animals were the main
crops. Most of the Indians lived outside the settlement, but their children did attend the school with
enough consistency to make the missionaries feel
they had a reason for staying in this lonely land so
far from civilization.

After the ceremony there was a wedding breakfast of honey cakes and fresh berries, roast par-
tridge and trout. Tables were set up in the yard
outside the chapel, children ran back and forth
in squealing laughter, and one of the trappers
brought out a fiddle and began to play. Kitty
wrapped her hands around Ben's arm and pressed
her head against his shoulder, so happy she could
have shouted it into the wind.

"I wish you'd change your mind and stay," Martin said. "There's a lot that needs doing here, and a man could spend a lifetime just learning what this land"—he smiled, gesturing to include the Indian children who played around them—"and these people have to teach him."

"It's good land," John Syms added, taking in with a practiced eye the fertile riverbank, the flat, easily cultivated plains, and even the rock-strewn mountain foothills in the distance. "A good place to build a home. It won't be long before those folks up on the Platte start drifting down this way, and then they'll start coming out from the East. All the good land will be gone."

Ben smiled. "And I figure those folks'll need some help getting out here. That's why we're going back."

As soon as they could provision themselves, the newlyweds were returning to the Flint Hills, where they intended to set up a breeding ranch of horses. From there they would be able to trade both with easterners and with those westward-bound who were eager to seed their farms with hearty, western-bred livestock.

"I don't know how you can bear the thought of making that trip again," Rachel said, worried.

"And once you get there," Effie put in, "you'll be all alone, and that's hard country. It won't be an easy life."

"It gets in your blood, I guess." Kitty looked up at Ben. "This feeling of being—I don't know. Alive. I don't think we'd ever be satisfied with having an easy life again."

She glanced at the others, a little embarrassed. "Sounds crazy, I guess."

But she was met with smiles, and no one thought that it was crazy at all. For Kitty and Ben, hardship would take the form of another journey, but for the others getting here had been only half the battle. They had paid for this land with their blood, but no one expected an easy life now. Nor did they want it.

The newlyweds were not the only ones for whom the mission was just an interim stop. Oliver paused beside her. "Do you have a message for your mother, Mrs. Adamson?"

The others tensed, for despite the sack of gold coins he had donated to the mission, no one had quite forgiven Oliver for what he had done, nor had they been able to resign themselves to his presence . . . No one but Ben, and for Ben's sake, Kitty forgave Oliver, too.

Oliver's arm was still in a sling from the wound he had sustained during the battle, and his face was that of a quieter, more mature man than the one Kitty had first met when they had begun this journey together. Some of the hardness was gone from his eyes, and his smile was warm, and sincere. Kitty couldn't help returning that smile as she looked up at him. "Are you really going back to Cairo?"

He nodded. "For a while. I left some things unfinished there." His smile faded for a moment as the past shadowed his eyes. "Some things I want to explain to your ma." The twinkle came back. "After that, I just might mosey on over to see my sister Amy. Who knows, she might have use for an experienced storekeeper, with that family of hers to raise and all. I think I could be right satisfied, toting up bills in my old age."

Kitty smiled and laid a hand on his arm. "Tell Mama that I'm happy and . . ." She glanced at Ben. "That I've found my place."

Oliver nodded and glanced up as Boothe approached.

Boothe rested his hand on Kitty's shoulder. "Give me a kiss, Kitten. The sun's getting up in the sky, and I'd best be moving on."

Kitty turned and felt her heart clench as she looked into her uncle's face. "I wish you wouldn't go."

He smiled as he looked around, the smile of a man who knows final contentment and can ask no more of life. "I did what I set out to do. There's nothing to keep me here." And then he turned his smile back to her. "You know me, Kitten. Itchy feet. Some folks just aren't made to put down roots."

"Will I—" She wanted to ask if she would ever see him again, but something stopped her. Instead she swallowed back the words and reached inside her pocket. She drew out the Celtic cross and stood on tiptoe to place it around his neck. Gently, she kissed his bearded cheek. "Go in God's grace, Uncle Boothe."

His smile was tender as he brushed his hand across her hair and looked down at her. "That I will, little girl."

There was much fuss over Boothe's leave-taking, as everyone had something to say to him, some thanks to be made or good wish to be presented that they felt they had not adequately expressed before. Kitty stood back and fought bittersweet tears as she watched him mount his horse and ride out of the mission with Oliver. Once he paused and turned back and lifted his hand to her.

Kitty raised her own hand in salute and held it up until she could no longer see him. Then the tears spilled over.

"I hate to cry," she muttered irritably to herself and scrubbed at her wet lashes.

"Kitty." The voice was small and unfamiliar, and Kitty turned in surprise.

It was Lucy.

The other girl smiled at her. "It's going to be all right," she said.

A gasp of wonder and surprise tore at her throat and vanquished the last of the tears. "Lucy! You spoke!" Kitty caught the girl to her, hugging her hard, laughing and crying. "Miss Rachel—Reverend Syms! Come quick! It's Lucy! She can talk! She can talk!"

She held on to Lucy and Lucy held on to her, and this time the tears were tears of joy.

Boothe and Oliver traveled south together for a couple of miles before they stopped. "Well, I reckon this is where we part company," Boothe said.

Oliver nodded and seemed to hesitate before he spoke. "Boothe . . . there's something you ought to know. A fella back in St. Louis by the name of Gerrard—he's gunning for you. And he's a mighty determined man."

Boothe just smiled. "Well now. That answers a lot of questions, don't it?" He sobered. "I'm glad you told me, Oliver. I would've wondered."

Oliver looked away.

"Do me a favor, will you?"

When Oliver looked at him, Boothe was removing the Celtic cross from around his neck. He handed it to Oliver. "Give this to my sister. Tell her I don't need it anymore. She'll understand."

As Oliver held the heavy cross in his hand, he felt a chill. He thought he understood, too.

He placed the cross carefully in his pocket. "I'll give it to her." Then he had to ask. "Where're you headed?"

Boothe turned in the saddle and gazed west for a long time. "Where I belong."

Then he nudged his horse around and rode toward the distant western mountains, where a black wolf waited and the future belonged only to him.

**The Following is a Selection from
BOOK THREE:
MOUNTAIN FURY
Taylor Brady's
Next Book in THE KINCAIDS Series
Coming Soon
from Avon Books**

*The Rocky Mountains
1843*

Boothe Carlyle looked up from the stream and the wolf was there, watching him from the opposite bank. Its eyes were keen and observant, and its coat was as black as ink.

Instinctively, Boothe's fingers slid toward his rifle. But they never closed on it.

There wasn't much in this world Boothe Carlyle had not done or seen. He had never seen a black wolf before, but he had dreamed of it many, many times.

He had spent the past six years of his life waiting for this wolf to appear.

He always dreamed true. And he had come into the mountains to die as he had lived, a free man in the last of this untamed country, close to the heart of God. His time had been rich and full, and he was ready.

Yet a man will cling to survival, and instinctively Boothe dropped his eyes to his rifle for an instant, measuring the time it would take to lift and fire. When he glanced up again the wolf was gone, having melted into the shadows from whence it came.

After a time Boothe stood and shouldered his rifle and continued on his way, moving from the stream to make his camp for the night. But his sleep was troubled, and he felt as though something fundamental inside him had been shaken.

The Indians would say it was a sign. Boothe had no doubt they would be right. But a sign of what?

He did not rest easy that night, or for many nights to come.

Kitty Kincaid Adamson stood for a moment, her eyes narrowed in the sun, searching the landscape. As far as she could see was emptiness—rocky hills, trees just beginning to come into spring bloom, multi-colored grasses stirred only by the passage of some small animal or an errant breeze. Once the emptiness of this place, the vastness of it, had threatened to overwhelm her and she had felt lost within it. But over the years the rugged, undulating landscape had become familiar, and the emptiness a friend. Still, she wondered how many more years it would take before she learned to look over the landscape without expecting, or even hoping, to see another human being somewhere upon it.

Abruptly, her frown sharpened into one of pure irritation, and she resumed the saddle again, jerking the reins. This was more than ordinary foolishness. No one was there, no one was coming. She was a grown woman and far too busy to listen to the fantasies of her little sister. She gave the pony a light kick and headed back toward the farm. Snow picked her way confidently out of the tall grass, across a carpet of bright wildflowers, and along a stream.

Near the source of the stream, a spring that bubbled out of the limestone, stood the Adamson farm. It topped a small rise above the valley and the meadow, sheltered in a stand of cottonwood that kept the house and outbuildings cool in the summer but admitted the sun's warming rays in the winter.

The homestead was not grand or even very big, but already Kitty had more than her mother had had at her age, and her needs were simple. As long as her children and her animals were sheltered and well fed, Kitty rarely took time to wish for more.

Kitty swung down from Snow and in a few deft movements divested her of saddle and bridle and turned her out into the corral. She returned her tack to the barn then crossed the yard to her husband, who was loading the wagon for their trip tomorrow.

In the morning the family would depart for their semi-annual trading rendezvous with the Cheyenne. Usually Kitty's spirits were high before such an expedition, her anticipation strong. The uneasiness she felt now annoyed her because it was totally unfounded and because it threatened to spoil one of the highlights of her year.

Ben looked up from his work as she approached, and smiled sympathetically when she came close enough for him to see her expression.

"Nothing, huh?"

Kitty gave an impatient shake of her head and pulled off the grass hat. Her blond hair spilled untidily from beneath it, a tangled braid that gleamed golden in the afternoon sun. "Of course not. That Sarah, what an imagination. Why do I listen to her, anyway?"

Ben carefully wedged white blankets, which the Cheyenne coveted, around jugs of New Orleans molasses. Kitty hoisted herself onto a spoke of the wagon wheel, and leaned over the side to help him.

"That's what I've been wondering," Ben said. "That letter from your ma is over three weeks old. What makes you womenfolk think young Jim will come riding up just as soon as we leave the house is beyond me. It could be months before he gets here, and probably will be." He shot her a grin. "You know how those Kincaid men are, wandering feet, every last one of the them. Jim's liable to see something that strikes his fancy and take off in another direction altogether. Myself, I'm not going to start looking for him 'til the snow flies, earliest."

But Kitty was not coaxed by his grin, and her eyes were still shadowed as she looked toward the horizon. "I know," she admitted. "It is foolish. But Sarah is so sure, and . . . there's something between them, Ben, that's hard to explain. I love my brother but there's a bond between Sarah and Jim that's different from anything the rest of us have. Sarah's always been able to—well, *know* things, and if she's worried about Jim, I reckon it's with good cause."

"Or," suggested Ben gently, "it could be she's just lonesome for her brother and wishing him here."

Kitty's eyes returned to Ben's, and after a moment she smiled. "You're probably right. It hasn't been easy for her since she came out here, and she does have a mighty big imagination." She shrugged. "Besides, if Jim does show up while we're gone, I wager he'll have sense enough to sit and wait a spell for us to get back, after riding all this way."

Slowly she allowed the tension to leave her shoulders and the familiar anticipation for the adventure ahead to warm her with its glow. She had missed the autumn expedition because Carrie, her last born, had been too young to travel.

Reading her thoughts, Ben squeezed her hand briefly. "You're glad to be on the move again, aren't you?"

Kitty smiled. "Even though I'm only an adopted Kincaid, I've got the wanderlust too, and there's nothing I like better than to be going somewhere."

"Well, I can't complain about that." Ben turned to pick up a stack of buffalo hides, and Kitty helped him spread them over the trade goods in the wagon. "If you hadn't been so all-fired set on traipsing after me and Boothe when we set out for the Platte, I might not have ever found myself a wife."

"You might not have *made* it to the Platte if it hadn't been for me," Kitty retorted, and just in time she saw the twinkle in her husband's eyes.

"Are you ever sorry, Ben Adamson?" she inquired softly.

And Ben replied without hesitation, "Never, Mrs. Adamson."

They shared a smile and a quiet moment at the end of the day. Then Kitty sprang down from the wagon wheel and together they started toward the house for supper.

But she couldn't resist one last look over her shoulder, toward the empty horizon.

Jim Kincaid hadn't eaten anything but corn pone and hard jerky since he'd left Cairo, Illinois—or at least that was how it seemed to him. His diet had been supplemented on occasion by rabbit, muskrat, or prairie hen, sometimes accompanied by a handful of wild onions or Indian potatoes, but such feasts were few and far between. The truth was, a man who spent all his time hunting didn't have much left over for traveling, and as far as Jim was concerned there was far too much to see in this world to waste any time at all.

But his supplies were running low, and so was his taste for jerked beef. The buck he had pinned in his sites made his mouth water.

It was twilight, and the big buck—an eight-pointer— had come to the stream to drink. Jim was upwind of it ten or twenty yards, but his line of vision was partially obscured by the wooded landscape that separated him from his quarry. He dared not move for fear of alerting the buck. He waited patiently for the animal to shift its position—a fraction was all it would take—and give him a clear shot.

The buck looked up, seeming to sniff something on the wind. The movement gave Jim the clearing he needed and he squeezed the trigger. Jim Kincaid was the best shot in the county where he came from. The buck fell.

Jim didn't even wait for the smoke to clear. He let out a yell of self-congratulatory triumph and started down the hill toward the stream.

He took the stream in one bounding step and dropped down on one knee beside the carcass, pulling his knife out of the scabbard on his thigh. He felt the shadow fall across him in the same moment he noticed the feather-tipped arrow protruding from the buck's neck. The whole world went still around him.

His rifle was on the ground near his foot, not even an arm's length away. But it didn't matter. He hadn't reloaded after he'd fired; a foolish mistake that no man with real wilderness experience would have made. Now it was starting to look as though that mistake might be his last.

He lifted his eyes slowly. The Indian wore moccasins and buckskin leggings. His breechcloth was made of deerskin too, and his torso, naked and hairless, was streaked with blue and red paint and draped with a multitude of feathered charms and amulets, metal chains and stone decorations. His face was brightly painted too, and his head was shaved except for one sharp distinctive tuft at the very top, the greased distinctive scalp lock.

He was a Pawnee. And he had his bow drawn back, arrow aimed for Jim's throat.

Pawnee. The fiercest of the fighting tribes, more apt to wage war on each other than the white man but possessing no scruples about flaying a man alive just for the sport of it if the mood struck them, or so Jim had heard. But there shouldn't be any Pawnee this far east. How deep was he into Indian territory anyway? Jesus God, why hadn't he paid attention at that last trading post, why hadn't he been more careful . . . Because if this Indian wasn't part of a tribe, he was a renegade and Jim was now living out his last few minutes on this earth.

And then the Indian said something in harsh, rapid Pawnee. The sound was startling, unexpected, and it frightened Jim so badly that he froze in place, not flinching a muscle or changing his expression. Three other braves appeared from the underbrush, all of them with bows. They moved toward Jim.

But only the scowling brave who stood over him had his bow drawn, and suddenly Jim understood. It was a hunting party. The three Indians approaching were less interested in him than in the deer, and the drawn bow was only meant to guard the kill.

Two of the braves grasped the deer and swung it between them. The third swept up Jim's rifle, and shared a grin with his comrades over the prize. And then they were all grinning, even the big one with the drawn bow, laughing at the boy on the ground. Jim felt a cry of outrage rising in his throat as they moved away, still grinning, his supper swinging between them. But the bow was still drawn and the big one kept his aim true, walking backward to the cover of the woods. Then he turned and disappeared.

Even then it was a moment before Jim could lurch to his feet, his heart pounding so hard it felt like it was shaking his whole body, and shout, "Hey!" But even indignation was swallowed by the thundering of his heart and what should have been an angry cry instead sounded hoarse and querulous.

He stood there for a time, breathing hard, letting the sweat of fear dry in his shirt and hair. In the distance he heard the sound of retreating hoof beats. *Indians*, he thought, and the word seemed to echo through his soul with a kind of awe-struck wonder, tinged more than a little with the residue of fear. He had survived an encounter with Indians.

It was then that he looked down and saw the knife still gripped in his hand, and a wave of incredulity and self-disgust swept over him. It had been there all the time. All the time he'd sat there with a weapon in his hand and hadn't once thought to defend what was his. No wonder they'd laughed.

With a grimace of contempt he threw the knife, hard, piercing the ground ten feet away. He wanted to swear, he wanted to cuss up a blue streak, but his ma had never allowed cussing in the house and he didn't know any words suitable for the occasion. So he dragged at his hair in frustration, kicked the ground, spat, and at last strode over to pick up the knife and started back up the hill toward his horse.

Here he was, miles from he knew-not-where, hungry, cold, and alone. Tomorrow would see the last of his coffee and the bottom of his provisions sack didn't hold anything but a few dried jerky strips and half a handful of meal. He didn't have a gun. A man couldn't hunt without a gun. And if the Pawnee came back he'd be easy pickings.

He wondered how far he was from Fort Leavenworth. He wondered how many hunting parties, scouting parties, or war parties he might expect to run into before he reached it, and how far off course he'd have to wander before he was in the heart of Indian territory.

His sister Kitty's homestead was only a couple of days away from the Fort. Surely he couldn't be more than a week away. He'd make do till then somehow. It would be good to see family again though.

The sky had never seemed so big, the dark had never seemed so thick. Jim Kincaid leaned back against a tree and tried to get comfortable, but it was a long time before he slept.

More than anything in her life, Meg Kincaid O'Hare wished she could go home. She stood over the body of her husband with the carving knife weighing heavy in her hand, and she knew that she had to get out of this place, tonight. And that she would never see home again.

The sounds and smells of the riverfront drifted in through the broken window of their room, and with them the raucous noises from the saloon below. Thick and humid and fetid, something slowly rotting in the fog—that was what St. Louis smelled like to Meg. And it sounded even worse.

Caleb O'Hare was not dead, just drunk. But as Meg stood over him feeling the heft of the knife, watching with a kind of fascinated detachment the glint of moonlight on steel, she knew that if she lingered much longer, she would kill him. And that was why she had to leave.

She crossed the room silently on bare feet and, using the point of the knife, pried out the loose wallboard behind the bed. It made a slight squeaking sound, and though she knew Caleb, passed out in the chair across the room, couldn't possibly hear, her muscles froze instinctively.

She reached behind the wallboard and drew out a silk reticule. It was empty except for a single gold coin. And it could mean the difference between life and death for her.

She went back to her husband and this time didn't hesitate. While her courage was high, and still holding the knife ready in one hand, she dipped the other hand into his pockets. He had for once quit while he was ahead and tonight those pockets contained something beside lint. She dropped the money into her reticule, and he didn't stir.

The reticule was large enough to hold the knife, though the handle protruded. She slipped it inside and tied the bag around her waist by the drawstring. Then she picked up her shoes—a pair of battered cloth slippers twice turned and lined with newspaper at the soles—and left the room. After five years of imprisonment, it was that easy. She just walked out. The simplicity of it, the relief, the overwhelming power of it, struck her all at once and left her so weak she almost stumbled; she had to brace her hand against the wall before she could go on. But she recovered quickly, for recovery was something she had a great deal of practice with. She slipped her shoes on her feet and hurried down the back stairs without looking back.

In 1843 St. Louis was fast becoming the queen of cities; no city in the United States was growing faster. Her location was strategic, at the mouth of the Missouri River, the Big Muddy, where it met the Mississippi. For years the city had been well known to beaver and other fur traders whose pelts were sold in St. Louis to be shipped to the eastern seaboard and then on to Europe. But the coming of the steamboat into St. Louis in 1817 dramatically affected the growth of the city. It was still a center for trade, but it also became an important jumping off place for westward migration.

As in any large bustling city, not all the citizenry was upstanding. There were con men and thieves, prostitutes and villains who hung around the taverns and the seedy hostelries near the waterfront. Meg feared none of them. She walked down the mist-shrouded pier and heard the occasional catcall or drunken shout from the taverns behind her, felt the lascivious gaze of narrowed eyes following her. She walked with her head up, her steps purposeful. She was free, and she feared no man.

Staying close to the water, she moved as silently as a wisp of the fog that shrouded her toward the shadowed end of the pier.

It would leave before dawn. Meg didn't know where the steamboat was bound, and it didn't matter. All that mattered was that it would be away from here.

There was a short, fat man standing by the gangplank, checking his pocketwatch and looking official. Meg hurried up to him. "I'd like to book passage," she said.

"Where to?"

"Upriver?" she asked hesitantly.

"How far?" He was exasperated. "I only got a few minutes, miss. We're pulling out soon."

Meg thrust a handful of money at him. "How far will this take me?"

He counted it quickly. "If you share a cabin, and that's the only space we got left, this should take you to Bellevue."

Bellevue. Beautiful view. "It sounds nice," she said.

"Names can be deceiving. Make up your mind."

"Yes, I want to go."

"Then tell the first mate to put you in a cabin with a lady traveling up to Fort Pierre. Her husband's a trapper with American Fur Company. You don't mind sharing with children, do you?"

"I don't mind anything," Meg answered.

"Luggage?"

"I don't have any." Meg looked him in the eye, daring him to ask questions. The captain's face was lined and wrinkled, his eyes tired.

He looked back at her. "I don't care as long as your money's good. Step aboard."

Thousands of people were heading west. It would be easy for one woman to get lost in the crowd. If she could get to the trail, join in a train and then . . . vanish . . .

She'd spent all the money she'd stolen from her husband on passage, but she still had the gold coin her mother had given her. Perhaps that coin would buy her a new life in a new land.